AN ILL WIND

SECURITY SPECIALISTS INTERNATIONAL, BOOK 5

MONETTE MICHAELS

D1059524

An Ill Wind, Security Specialists International, Book 5

ISBN: 978-0-9973565-1-9

Copyright, 2017, Monette Michaels.

E-Book version: January, 2017.

Cover art: Copyright, 2015, April Martinez.

All rights reserved. No part of this publication may be reproduced, stored in a retrieval system, or transmitted in any form or by any means, electronic, mechanical, recording or otherwise, without the prior written permission of the author.

Manufactured in the United States of America.

This is a work of fiction. The characters, incidents and dialogues in this book are of the author's imagination and are not to be construed as real. Any resemblance to actual events or persons, living or dead, is completely coincidental.

A damaged woman fleeing her past.

After being stalked then attacked by a colleague, Dr. Fiona Teague flees to a New Mexico border town. Working in a clinic, Fee endeavors to overcome the horror of that night. To her dismay, Trey Maddox, her brother's friend, refuses to be deterred from pursuing a relationship with her. If only she weren't so broken … Trey's everything a woman could want—honorable, strong, heroic, but he deserves better than a damaged woman.

A strong, capable protector determined to lure her into the shelter of his arms.

During an Idaho blizzard, SSI operative Trey Maddox met Fee over the barrel of a rifle as she protected his pregnant sister-in-law. The gutsy little doc then ignored her own physical injuries to deliver his nephew. How could Trey not fall for her? Before he could persuade her to stay in Idaho, she'd cut and run to New Mexico. Undeterred by the distance, he pursues her, eroding her resistance with patience and tenacious good humor. And, finally, she agrees to an actual "date."

But the ill wind that had destroyed her once before now sweeps through Fee's life again. She's kidnapped by a drug cartel. Trey arrives to find her house a bloody crime scene. The cartel has no idea of the ruthless hunter they've unleashed. Trey will storm hell itself in order to rescue Fee and make her his, once and for all.

ACKNOWLEDGMENTS

Thanks to Elizabeth Neal for sharing her ideas for a perfect hero — Sheriff Levi Gray Wolf is the result.

Thanks to my beta-readers: Debbie Kline, Valerie Samouillan, Teresa Wilson, and Gail Northman. Some of them even read it more than once as I fine-tuned the plot. Love these gals.

Thanks to my critique partner Cherise Sinclair for always being there with constructive comments and for listening to me whine when I get to the "hate my book" stage.

Thanks to my long-time final line editor Ezra Solomon for taking the time from being a busy grad student to take a pass at this book. His objective set of eyes is always welcome.

Thanks to my wonderful cover artist April Martinez for making my heroes and heroines come to life in living color.

Finally, thanks to my fans. I wouldn't be doing this without you.

But it's an ill wind blaws naebody gude.
—Sir Walter Scott, *Rob Roy*

PROLOGUE

February 20th, 11 p.m.
Stanley Parker Health Center
Columbus, New Mexico

D r. Fiona Teague's stomach growled. Six-year-old Maria Cortez giggled, the first sound from her that wasn't a whimper or a mewl of pain since the child's arrival at the emergency room. Fee swept a lock of black silky hair off Maria's face. The girl had an ugly bruise on her forehead. Maria's brother had shoved the little girl and she'd fallen off her front porch and—head met sidewalk.

"Are you feeling better, *chica?*"

The x-rays hadn't shown any fracture, thank goodness. Fee had cleaned the bloody scrape, administered a prescription-strength dose of Tylenol, and applied ice to get the swelling down. There really wasn't anything else she could do.

Maria shrugged, her big brown eyes still moist from earlier tears.

Fee looked at Maria's mother. "Señora, just keep an eye on Maria. Wake her up every hour just to make sure she can. If you can't rouse her, or if she throws up or complains of severe headaches, bring her back in right away. I'm going to have Nurse Pia schedule a follow-up visit for Maria at the clinic on Monday."

"*Gracias*, Dr. Teague." Señora Cortez picked up Maria who clung like a monkey to her mother. The woman left the exam area. The now-chastised older brother fell into step with his mother. The father was missing in action. Pia Lopez had told her the man was a drug runner for the Sinaloa cartel.

It was don't ask, don't tell—business as usual in this ER in a U.S.-Mexico border community.

Pia walked up to Fee. "Well, that was different." The petite nurse was a Mexican-American who'd lived in Columbus, New Mexico, her whole life except for the time she'd left to attend nursing school in Austin, Texas. She was one of the best nurses Fee had ever worked with anywhere.

"Well, it definitely was a break from treating addicts who've decided to mix heroin and crystal meth." Drug overdoses or, in the case of speedballing, drug stupidity was a lot of what Fee dealt with during her shifts, day or night. The rest of her cases tended to be knifings and gunshot wounds that arose out of the running and selling of drugs.

Fee's stomach growled again. "I need to eat. Want to grab a bite with me? I brought a couple of sandwiches and am happy to share."

Pia shook her head, a sly smile on her face. "I've eaten, thanks. Besides, someone is here and has brought you some of my *mamá's* chicken enchiladas you like so well."

Carmela Lopez owned and was the chief cook for a local diner called *Mamacitas*. Fee ate or carried out a lot of her meals from there.

Fee smiled. "Your mother is so sweet to think of me. What did she bring you?"

"Not my *mamá*." Pia shoved her in the direction of the small break room. "Go see."

Her surprise meal guest had to be Price. Her brother had mentioned something about visiting this week. It would be just like him to get Pia's mother to make Fee's favorite Mexican meal.

Would Trey Maddox be with him? Fee's pulse raced and a tingle of excitement traveled over her skin. She would never admit it out loud, but when Trey hadn't come the last time Price visited, she'd missed him. Missed him a lot—more than a lot—and that had shocked her. She still wasn't sure she was ready for the type of relationship Trey wanted with her. A relationship he'd patiently pursued for months, making the trip from Idaho frequently, most often in the company of her brother.

Fee entered the break room and stopped just inside the door.

Her heart stuttered as she took in all that was Trey Maddox. The man was six-foot, four inches of alpha-male with thick, dark hair and green eyes. Those eyes now gleamed as he approached her in a panther-like glide. "Hey, little doc."

Only Trey called her that. She'd grown to like his pet name for her, mostly because of the affectionate tone in his voice when he said it. No one before him had ever cared enough to use an endearment when speaking to her.

"You look beautiful." His languid perusal burned over every inch of her. His expression grew more sensual.

Trey needed his eyes examined. She had on no make-up and a set of green scrubs that had blood and other bodily fluids that would put most people off their food. But the look in his eyes had her believing his words. To him, she was beautiful and that fact both confused her and made her grateful.

"Trey…" Flustered at his all-encompassing gaze, Fee looked around. "…um, where's my brother?"

"He's on an op…" he said.

Trey stopped less than a foot away from her. His gaze seemed fixed on her mouth. Her breath caught in her throat and she wondered if he'd kiss her.

Kiss him. You know you want to.

No, she couldn't. She was a woman who'd had really bad luck with the men in her past.

Trey's not those other guys, and, for sure, he isn't the stalker-rapist Adam-fucking-Stall.

Definitely not. She shuddered at the thought of the former colleague who'd stalked her, denied he'd done it, then raped her and got away with it. He was the reason she'd run from Detroit to this middle of effin' nowhere border town.

"...so I came in his place and brought you a meal." Trey held out his hand. "Come and sit down. Let me serve you. The smell has had me salivating ever since I picked up the food from Señora Lopez's house."

Fee placed her cold hand in his large, warm one. The innocent touch thrilled her, more so than kisses from any other man. "You didn't have to come."

"Yes, I did." Trey lifted her hand to his lips and kissed the tips of her fingers. "I missed seeing you last month." He looked into her eyes. "I wasn't missing this month, too."

"Okay." She swallowed hard. His expression ... his voice ... his words overwhelmed her. He looked at her as if she were as essential to him as oxygen.

Looking away, she focused on the table. *Oh my.* Happy tears threatened to choke her.

He'd set the cheap plastic table with a bouquet of flowers, candles, china, silver, and cloth napkins.

No one, not even her beloved brother Price, had ever done anything so nice, so special for her. "Y-y-you put my Diet Pepsi in a wine glass."

Past bad experiences with and insecurities about men were swept away in a groundswell of joy. Fee pulled her hand loose, stood on her tip toes, and brushed a kiss over his lips. "Th-that's so sweet. Th-thank you."

"You're welcome ... and you're the sweet one." Leaning down, he cupped her face and gave her kiss back to her and then took it up another notch.

Holy hell. The man could kiss.

Trey took his time as he nibbled and licked her lips. There was no aggression in his touch; if there had been, she'd have recoiled. Instead, he was gently insistent, and she opened to his lips and tongue and shyly returned the kiss.

"Fee," he murmured as he continued to press light kisses on her mouth. "You taste good, and I'd love nothing more than to kiss you for hours, but this probably isn't the best time or place."

Damn, one kiss, and a fairly innocent one at that, and Fee's brain took a short vacation, losing all sense of time and space. No man's kisses or intimate touch had ever taken her out of herself before.

Shaking off the sensual haze, she nodded. "Yeah. The ER's quiet right now, but—" Her stomach rumbled loudly.

Trey chuckled. Tucking some of her curls behind her ear, he kissed the tip of her nose. "But it could get busy, and you need fuel so you can handle the rest of your shift. Sit, let me serve you supper."

He took her arm and led her to the table and then held the wobbly plastic and metal chair for her. She sat and scooted closer to the table and placed the napkin on her lap. Taking a sip of the Diet Pepsi, she watched as he pulled out the food and served her two chicken enchiladas along with some beans and rice.

Fee inhaled the aroma and her mouth watered. "Smells divine. What did Carmela make you?"

"I have the pork enchiladas, but with the same tomatillo sauce she put on yours." Trey sat and took a long pull from the dewy bottle of Dos Equis by his place setting. "Eat. Catch me up on what's happened since I was here last."

Fee took a bite of her food and found it was easy to talk to Trey about her patients—in general terms, of course, she'd never violate their privacy—and about life in the small border town. She even told him how Pia was ignoring Sheriff Levi Gray Wolf's romantic overtures and how worried both

Carmela and Pia were about Pia's brother Ernesto who ran drugs for the cartel.

Trey's expression grew darker the more Fee revealed about Pia's brother. He held up a hand, halting her words. "Are you using the security system Price and I installed at your place?"

"Yes." She let out an exasperated sigh at the autocratic note in his tone. Both men had lectured her on safety rules several times since she'd moved to New Mexico. "I set the system every night."

"Fee..." A stern look on his face, Trey reached across the small table and tipped up her chin. "You're very precious to your brother, to my sister-in-law and her family—and to me. Use the system whenever you're home, day or night. Cartel asshats can attack during the day just as easily as the night. Okay?"

She captured his hand and squeezed it. "Okay. You know you're as bossy as my brother."

Trey pulled his hand from hers and traced her lips with the tip of a finger. "I ain't your brother, sweetheart."

God, and didn't she know it. Her feelings for Trey were intense—had always been strong from the day she met him—but the feelings had grown over the months. He'd burrowed under her skin, slowly but surely.

All too soon, they finished their meal. Drawing out her time with him, she helped him clean up the table and then walked him to the ER exit. "Thanks again for visiting and bringing me a meal."

"You're very welcome, little doc." Trey took her in his arms and kissed her deeply, then let her go. "See you in a month. Maybe I can take you out for a real date next time?"

"Maybe. I'll think on it."

"You do that." He gave her a panty-melting smile, then turned and left.

Fee watched until he got in his rental car and drove away. She already missed him.

CHAPTER 1

March 20th

Death wasn't a stranger to Fee, but the death of Trina Sevilla's fetus was an abomination. The unborn child hadn't even had a fighting chance. Hell, neither had Trina, the victim of an abusive boyfriend who may or may not have been the baby's father. Rubbing her forehead, Fee hit the Enter key to sign off on the update to Trina's medical chart.

You did all you could. The law was stacked against you—and Trina refused to get help.

Yeah, well, screw the law. It sucked. The restrictions on reporting "suspected" domestic abuse had resulted in a savagely murdered mother and her unborn baby.

Wearily, Fee glanced at the clock. 11:00 p.m. *Damn.* She was only four hours into her twelve-hour-shift at the two-bed emergency room located in the Stanley Parker Health Center. Time had raced by as she'd tried to save Trina from bleeding out. The baby'd had no chance at all.

At the moment, all Fee wanted to do was crawl into a hole, pull it in after her, and cry for the unnecessary loss of life. But that would have to wait; she needed to be there for the next injured person who required care.

Arching her neck, she sighed. On nights like these, she thought maybe she should've gone into dermatology as her family had urged.

That's the depression talking. You love the adrenaline ride and the challenge of emergency medicine.

Yeah, she did. While battling injury and death in the ER, she felt strong, capable, and more fully alive in a way she could never manage to achieve in her personal life.

That's not true. Trey Maddox makes you feel alive.

Yes, he did and does … but not in control, and Fee had always been a person who needed a sense of control.

Trey was so masculine—and very dominant. When she first met him, she'd been in shock and pain after being stalked and raped by Dr. Adam-fucking-Stall and hadn't been ready to trust another male, especially a large one. She'd also learned how ephemeral control could be and that knowledge had scared her. So, she'd run from her instant attraction to Trey.

Running had done no good. She'd finally acknowledged that fact last month when Trey had surprised her with a candlelight dinner in the ER break room during her shift. Her heart still fluttered when she recalled how he'd gently and thoroughly returned her kiss of thanks.

After that last visit, she'd missed Trey terribly. So she finally decided to take the next step in their relationship and go out on a date with him. The decision had been hers and hers alone; Trey had made that very clear from the beginning of his long-distance pursuit. She also knew there'd be no back-pedaling after she finally moved off the dime.

Nine months ago she wouldn't have been okay with this next step. But somehow Trey Maddox had evolved into a man she trusted completely. Where this new path might lead, she wasn't a hundred percent sure, but knew she wanted to explore it.

As Trina's death proved, life could be stolen away in an instant; so Fee needed to begin to live each day as if it were her last.

"Here," a can of Diet Pepsi was thrust in front of her, "you look like you need some caffeine."

"Thanks." Fee turned and attempted to smile at Pia.

"You okay?" Pia leaned a small but shapely hip against the computer station. Her pretty face was couched in lines of concern. Her dark eyes looked as tired as Fee felt.

"Nope," Fee said. "How about you?"

"Been better." Pia looked down the short hallway toward the cubicle where Trina lay, covered by a sheet.

Fee swivelled her chair so her back was to the computer monitor and the horrific story of violence and sudden death now detailed in black and white on Trina's chart. "It never gets any easier … especially when we *knew* she was in danger. We should've—"

"*¡Basta!* Don't even go there." Pia reached over to rub Fee's arm. "We did everything we *legally* could. We counseled her, gave her referrals to the shelter…"

None of which had done a shit load of good and had been like putting a band aid on an arterial bleed. The State of New Mexico had basically tied the medical staff's hands.

"…and without Trina's cooperation…" Pia trailed off and sighed. "When will someone come to take our statements and transport her to the coroner?"

Fee's lips thinned. "Any time. Sheriff Gray Wolf is taking control of this death investigation personally."

Eyes flashing dark fire, Pia hissed and muttered, "*Maldición,* Levi! *Cielo sálvame.*" Which Fee who'd picked up a lot of Spanish in her months in New Mexico loosely translated as "Damn, Levi! Heaven save me."

Fee narrowed her eyes. "What *is* your problem with the sheriff?"

"*Nada.*" Pia's response came out sounding like the snarl of the bobcat Fee frequently caught rooting through her garbage can.

"I call bullshit." Fee took a sip of her soda and allowed Pia's issues with the sheriff to push the two deaths out of her mind for the moment. "That man has the hots for you, and you don't give him the time of day." She pointed her can at Pia. "Levi Gray Wolf is one fine male specimen. Unlike most of the single male population in the area, he has a job. He's also a decent human being who doesn't abuse women, children, or animals, which is also a rarity around here. You should be all over that. And shall I mention again lest you've failed to notice?—he is f-i-i-ne."

Pia bristled. Fee could almost see the hairs standing up on the nurse's body.

"Look who's talking," Pia shot back. "You have sex-on-a-stick, tall-dark-and-handsome visiting you from up north almost every month—and you won't even eat a meal—in public—with him."

"Not true," Fee said. "I've had meals in public with him."

"But only when your brother's with you," Pia pointed out with a smirk. "Or when Trey brings food into the clinic as he did on his last visit."

"I know you had a hand in that, getting your mama to fix the meals for Trey outside of her diner's hours," Fee said. Pia smirked, but remained silent. "Anyway, after Trey's last visit, I missed him. A lot. So, I've decided to go out on a real date with him—just the two of us and in public—the next time he visits."

"Really?" Pia straightened and shot her such a look of disbelief that Fee laughed.

"Really." Missing Trey had made her heart hurt, and if that wasn't telling, then nothing was. She'd also had very hot dreams of him kissing her all over. "I'm manning up ... so what are you gonna do about Levi?"

"*Nada*." Pia looked away. "My father was killed while running drugs for the Sinaloa cartel. Now my brother's doing the same damn thing. The sheriff can do much better than dating the sister of criminals."

"So that's why you ignore me as if I had rabies or something?" Levi Gray Wolf came around the corner of the counter and entered the small computer area situated to the side of the ER triage desk.

While Fee was attracted to Trey's particular brand of tall, dark, and ruggedly handsome, she wasn't completely immune to the picture Levi made. He was six-foot-four-inches of muscular alpha-male with distinct teddy bear tendencies when it came to women. She'd once seen him carefully carry a laboring woman into the emergency room, crooning to her in his deep, soothing voice and then remaining by her side until her husband had arrived.

Right now, with his long, straight, dark hair tied back and his dark amber eyes flashing with sparks, he looked fierce, ready to take on whatever demons plagued Pia.

A muscle in Levi's sculpted jaw twitched as he ground out, "I could fucking care less about your father and Ernesto's cartel connections. I'd be dating *you* ... not your family."

"But your job ... what would the county commissioners say?" Pia stared at him. Emotions chased across her face—fear, wariness, and longing.

Damn, her friend had it bad, almost as bad as Levi from the expression on the warrior's face.

"They could fire you—" Pia faltered. "After what happened in Columbus ... with the mayor and the police department..."

Pia had a valid point. Right before Fee had arrived in town, the Columbus police chief, the majority of his staff, and the mayor had been convicted of running guns across the border for the cartel. The county commissioners had cleaned house and dissolved the police department altogether and appointed a temporary mayor. The Luna County Sheriff's office had taken over policing the town. Levi had to keep his office clean and above reproach after the scandal and its aftermath, which had brought intense scrutiny to the area from the state and the Federal government.

"Pia," Levi crooned, his tone that of a man trying to lure a frightened animal to come to him … to trust him. "I don't care about this job. There are other jobs. I want you."

Pia shook her head, either in denial or disbelief.

It was a toss up in Fee's mind which emotion her friend felt. Fee wasn't even certain Pia knew, either.

"Um, I need to ch-check on some-something," Pia stammered, tears welled in her eyes, her gaze fixed on Fee and nowhere near Levi.

Then the nurse hurried off, brushing by Levi who'd refused to move out of her way. He growled under his breath. "Goddammit, Pia."

"Levi—" Fee drew his attention when it looked as if he'd chase after Pia. She wanted to give her friend a chance to regain her composure. "Have you arrested the murdering dickhead?"

After one last, longing look at Pia's retreating figure, Levi turned. His face was dark with his repressed feelings for Pia … and anger.

Fee's gut clenched. She didn't do well with angry males.

But when Levi spoke, his tone was cool and all business. "Benito Rivera is on the run. I put out a BOLO on him. We'll find him. He's a stupid motherfucker." He moved toward her. She stiffened, but didn't retreat. Levi's emotions were under control—he was like Trey in that respect.

Levi's gaze traveled over her face. "You okay?"

Fee appreciated his concern. She'd dealt with Levi a lot since she'd started work at the clinic, because of the local drug and cartel violence that had been frequent and bloody. She considered him a friend.

"Yes … no." Her lips twisted into a wry smile. "You'd think with all the blood and gore I've seen in my time here and back in Detroit, I'd get used to the horrors man can perpetrate on his fellow human beings, but … but what happened to Trina—" She shrugged. "It hit me—and Pia—hard."

Harder than she'd admit to Levi. Abuse toward women hit far too close to home.

No matter her emotional status, she'd deal. She still had duties toward Trina and her unborn child.

Levi's face grew even darker. "What *specifically* caused the deaths? You were light on the details over the phone."

"It's all here." Fee put the can of soda down, picked up the report she'd typed and printed out, then added it to a copy of Trina's medical file she'd made for Levi.

"The fetus died from a lack of oxygen as a result of Trina's loss of blood from multiple stab wounds. The bastard severed Trina's splenic artery"—more like hacked it up—"and the internal bleeding was catastrophic. Trina had no blood pressure by the time she was brought to the clinic. I … I did everything I could, but…"

Fee choked on the anger and grief lodged in her throat. She coughed, then continued, "She had no fricking chance. Not even getting her to a major trauma unit would've saved her."

She shoved the medical file at him. "My official report of fetal abuse and death is in the file. It is also my personal and medical opinion that the murdering asshole was the reason for Trina's previous emergency visits … every blessed one of them. His repeated abuse led to Trina's death. I've given you all my medical notes and observations. At this point, Trina's medical privacy is moot and my hands are no longer tied."

While New Mexico law required Fee to report the death of a fetus brought about by abuse, it fucking well hadn't allowed her to report the ongoing domestic abuse toward Trina since such a report violated Trina's privacy.

Levi frowned at the thick file in his hands and then flipped through it. "Jesus Christ, there's almost a hundred pages here. How many times had she been seen?" He reached the back of the file and inhaled sharply. When he looked up, his expression was that of inchoate rage. He'd obviously reached the part of the file where Fee had photographically documented Trina's damage from her boyfriend's fists.

"Twice a month since I've been here, so eighteen times, not counting this evening." Fee glared at Levi, even though none of what had happened was his fault. "Your law sucks. In Michigan, I could've reported the abusive asshole the first time Trina came in with a black eye and a broken wrist. His finger marks were on the wrist to prove he'd done it. Fell down the stairs, my ass."

"Did you photograph her at every ER visit?" Levi's face was now blank of all emotion, his voice almost preternaturally calm. But his body language, the flames in his dark gold eyes, indicated he was boiling underneath.

"As many times as I could without Trina catching on." Fee smiled, a cynical twist to her lips. "I over-charted the injuries, because I knew he'd do something I could eventually report."

Fee'd had a premonition the abuse would get worse. With each subsequent emergency visit, there was evidence the abuse escalated. But Trina had always made excuses for Rivera, refused to say a bad word against the asshole. So, no one could do a thing until Trina filed a complaint.

Guilt tasted bitter in her mouth. "I want the fucker to pay for it. All of it. No man should be allowed to terrorize and abuse a woman." She swallowed hard as anger and remembered terror constricted her throat.

Dr. Adam-fucking-Stall had beaten and raped her—had taken her confidence and sense of self away from her. But no longer. The passage of time and the patient pursuit by Trey had reinforced that there were good men in the world.

Trina, however, had never gotten the chance to learn that fact.

Levi would make sure Trina's death was avenged, because he was another one of those good guys.

Yeah, Pia was due to have a come-to-Jesus moment. Fee would point out that time was a-wasting and her friend shouldn't let a decent man like Levi get away because of some family baggage out of her control.

"Rivera will pay for it. I'll see to it." Levi looked in the direction Pia had gone. "I'll just go take a look at Trina before the coroner's people take her—"

"Levi…" Fee shook her head and sighed. "Give Pia some time. I'll talk to her. She's trying to protect you."

"I can protect me," he said, "and her."

"I know that." Fee lips twisted. "But she's ashamed."

"She needs to get the fuck over it." Levi stared at the floor and rubbed the back of his neck. When he looked up, Fee's heart ached at the love and the pain on his face. "I'm serious about that little gal."

"I suspected." Fee touched his arm. His muscles were tense, hard as the bedrock in the area. "She is more than attracted to you, too."

"Really?" He looked up. Hope shone on his face.

"Really." She smiled. "Now, go and get the asshole who killed Trina. Pia needs some time to realize her family's criminal background doesn't matter to you."

"Thanks, Fee." Levi gently squeezed her shoulder. "You need to stop feeling so guilty about Trina. Hell, I suspected something was going on with her, but when I asked her, she'd smile and say everything was okay. Until she asked for help, or I saw the bastard hitting her, my hands were tied as much as yours."

"But not now," Pia stated.

"Now Rivera's ass is mine." Levi looked at her, his eyes glowing with an unholy light. "I will lean on the prosecutor to go for murder—in both cases. Your file will demonstrate the history of abuse, showing intent. Manslaughter is off the table, if I have anything to say about it."

"Good," Fee said. "I'll be happy to testify."

"I figured." His smile was feral. "We've got the bastard this time." He turned to leave, then stopped. "Thanks for talking to me about Pia." His expression lightened. "How about you? I know something bad happened to you in the past, because why in the hell would a city girl with your medical qualifications move to this backwater? 'Course that's none of my business, unless you want me to know. But that Maddox fellow who comes to visit with your brother, he's got it bad for you. And from what I just overheard, you like him, too." She shrugged and he chuckled. "So, are you really gonna cut the guy some slack and go out with him?"

"Nosy much?" Fee asked with an indignant whine.

"Yeah, it's a small town. The county's sparsely populated. Everyone knows everyone's business or tries to. You and him have been the topic of a lot of speculation, especially since good-looking professional women are as rare as hen's teeth in these parts. You kept giving him the cold shoulder. Got me worrying. So, I ran Maddox through the system—you know, just in case he was stalking you."

"Really?" Her breath caught at the thought of Levi watching over her just as her brother would've done.

"Yep." His expression was blank, but his eyes crinkled at the corners. "So, you gonna give Maddox a break?"

"Yeah. Trey's like water on stone. It might take longer for water to wear the stone down, but it gets the job done eventually."

"Good. From what I found out, Maddox is a good man," Levi said.

"He is." Fee nodded.

"Maybe we can double-date when he comes down the next time."

Fee snorted. "Good luck getting Pia on board with that. Seriously, Levi, she's not ready."

"We'll see." Levi touched two fingers to his forehead in a mock salute and then walked out of the computer area.

With dating on her mind, she pulled out her cell to text Trey and found a voice mail from an unknown number.

She played it and heard nothing followed by the click of a disconnect. She deleted the message and blocked the number.

Fee'd gotten a lot of these types of calls right after she'd moved to New Mexico. The phone company said the calls had come from a pre-paid phone. So she'd had her number changed and that had stopped the calls. Now, it looked as if they'd started again.

A vague unease settled in her gut.

As much as she wanted to rationalize these hang-ups as wrong numbers or nuisance calls by bored teenagers, Fee had to accept that Stall was stalking her ... yet again.

But why would he? He'd won. No one had believed her when she'd reported Stall's stalking and harassment of her to the hospital. He'd then raped her, and she'd run, believing him when he'd said no one would take her word over his. People liked to blame the victim. She'd seen it often enough in her ER and on the news.

She sighed. Time to change her number again.

Eventually Stall would give up. He'd find a new victim; hopefully, one who could make a case against him and have it stick.

Maybe you should tell Trey and Price?

No. Price and Trey had gone to Detroit last June. According to Keely, they'd delivered a forceful message to Stall. A physical message. They hadn't gotten in any trouble, but they could've. If she told them about the calls, they might decide to deliver a second, even more forceful message, and she didn't want either of them to get in trouble over a bunch of phone calls.

The calls were just an irritating pain in the ass. Stall was nowhere near New Mexico.

Ostrich, much?

Shoving the edgy feeling and her past aside, she took a step toward a potential future and sent Trey a text: *I'm ready for that date. Let's start with dinner in Deming next time you visit. OK?*

She imagined the look of shock on Trey's face when he received the message, and a warm feeling replaced the disquiet the hang-up had caused. Just thinking about Trey made her feel safe.

"Doctor Teague, we need you in Exam Two," came blaring over the intercom.

Fee got up and headed back to work. The living still needed her skills.

Same night, Sanctuary, Idaho

THE PUSH NOTIFICATION ON HIS cell drew Trey's attention from his shitty hand. Using the distraction as an excuse to keep Price and Vanko guessing as to what his cards might be, he pulled the phone out and checked the text.

Trey smiled and looked at Price. "Your baby sis wants me to take her to dinner in Deming the next time I visit. She says she's ready to date."

"Well, halle-fucking-lujah, it's about time." Price slammed his hand on the table, a big grin on his face. "Did she indicate what changed her mind?"

Trey shook his head. "Nope—and I'm not going to ask. I'm just fucking happy she has. Not gonna give her time to change her mind. I'll take her up on her offer … this Saturday evening." He hesitated. "You don't mind if this trip is another solo…"

"No. Go. This tells me she's finally over what Doctor Douchebag did to her. Maybe now we can convince her to leave that dangerous dust pile." Price frowned. "Her risk of getting shot by a cartel wannabe is higher than getting taken out by a gang-banger at the inner city Detroit hospital she left."

"Columbus is Sinaloa territory, yes?" Vanko asked.

"Yeah. Vicious fucking bastards." Trey growled and squeezed the phone. "The cartel owns Colombus, no matter what law enforcement did to clean up that gun-running mess. No one in that place is safe. Hell, the cartel runs loose all over the damn border."

And a fucking wall still wouldn't keep the drug cartels from conducting their violent, dirty business, no matter what some politicians thought. The only place his little doc would be safe was in his home—in his arms and bed each night.

Vanko looked from Trey to Price. "Your sister has three more months in order to satisfy her year so the government will forgive a year of medical student loans, yes?"

Fee also had another whole year after that to work off, but—"I'll buy it out...." Trey said.

Trey had made that decision a while ago, right after he'd visited her the first time in the dangerous New Mexico border town. But Fee hadn't been ready to let him into her life nine months ago. Hell, she'd refused to let her own brother pay her medical student loans.

"...or suggest she transfer to Idaho and take the deal Keely's worked out for Fee to do the rest of her loan repayment here."

Trey would have to tread carefully with Fee. His woman had a great deal of pride and a stubborn streak a mile wide.

"Wonder what happened to make her agree to dinner? It wasn't all that long ago she was using me as a buffer." Price stared at his cards, then looked at Trey. "Should I call her and find out if she's okay?"

"Why wouldn't she be okay?" Trey growled. "Maybe she's finally realized I'd cut off my dick before hurting her?"

While the three men had discussed Fee's about-face, Trey's sister-in-law Keely had sidled closer to the card table and was listening intently to their conversation. He shook his head and grinned. The nosy little sprite would report the whole conversation word-for-word to her hubby and everyone else on Sanctuary. His long-distance pursuit of Fee was a hot topic of discussion, and bets had been placed on how long Fee would hold out against him.

"Maybe," mused Price. "But she's my sister and I know her better than you. Something happened."

"Or…" Vanko drawled. "Trey is correct, and his patience and faithfulness wore her down and won her over."

Price threw popcorn at Vanko who caught some of the kernels and ate them. "Shut it, Vanko. That's pussy-type thinking."

"Pussy-type thinking?" Vanko laughed and shook his head. "Fuck you, Price."

Keely narrowed her gaze at the back of Price's head.

"She's my sister, and I say something happened."

"Want to bet on it?" Trey took offense at the insult to his carefully thought-out plan to win Fee's trust. Unlike Price, Trey had seen her face when she'd first noticed the flowers and candles when he'd brought her a meal last month. She'd kissed him in thanks. He replayed her shy brushing of lips—and his return of the kiss—every night in his dreams since then.

"Sure." Price grinned. "If I'm right and Fee decided to have dinner with you because something specific happened to get her to change her mind, then you'll do my next three months of climbing duty with Tweeter to check on the security arrays."

Trey winced. *Fuck, Price.* Trey hated climbing, hanging in mid-air on ropes, and crawling like a freaking spider over cold and often icy rock walls to do the seemingly unending maintenance to Sanctuary's early warning system. He heaved out a breath. "Fine, you bastard, but if I'm right and she decided to date me because of my patience and persistence all these months, then you have to take the wild land firefighting training and join me and the others on the Grangeville hot shot crew."

Keely crept closer, her focus now on her ever-present computer tablet as she tap-typed furiously.

Price glowered. "Fine. Was gonna do it anyway…" At Vanko's hoot of derisive laughter, Price turned his hot gaze on the other man. "…sooner or later."

Every man on Sanctuary, but Price, had taken the training to become a hot shot in order to fight fires in the densely wooded mountains which surrounded their acreage. Wild land fires could happen at any time and did more frequently with climate change and the increasingly hotter and drier conditions they experienced in the panhandle of Idaho.

"It's a deal." Trey held out his hand. "Shake on it."

Price grabbed Trey's hand and squeezed the shit out of it, but Trey just smiled.

"How will you judge who wins?" Vanko looked at each man in turn. "Neither of you can ask her—and if you did, she might not tell you."

Trey looked at Keely and then at Price. "Fee would admit it to Keely, right?"

"Yeah, she would," Price smiled. "Having three sisters, I can tell you women stick together and share all sorts of personal shit."

Keely whacked Price on the back of the head with the flat of her hand. "Women are more evolved than you knuckle-dragging alpha-males. Want to know what Fee said?"

"You already asked?" Price rubbed the back of his head. "You were eavesdropping on our conversation?"

"Yep and yep." The smart, feisty blonde leaned over Price's shoulder and rubbed her cheek over his. "The next wild land firefighting class in Grangeville starts the end of April. I'll have Ren sign you up."

Trey laughed and threw his losing cards in. He didn't feel the need to bluff his way through the hand to win the poker pot, because he'd just won the lottery—Fee trusted him and that was the first step to making her his forever.

CHAPTER 2

Fee frowned as she listened to yet another silent voice mail and a hang-up from yet another unknown number. Changing her phone number two days ago hadn't stopped the calls.

Anger, frustration, and, yes, fear fluttered in her stomach.

"Fee, how'd it go last night?" Dr. Stanley Parker, the health center's namesake, braced his lean, runner-fit body against the intake counter, a warm smile on his face.

Fee jerked, having not heard his approach. Yeah, she was spooked all right. She shoved her cell into the pocket of her scrubs, then turned to fully face her boss.

Damn, for a sixty-eight-year-old, he looked full of vim and vigor. Had to be a result of all the healthy living he did at Sun City, the intentional community that shared borders with Columbus.

Ten years ago, Stan had made a financial killing on a couple of patents for medical treatments for traumatic wounds. Most doctors in his shoes would've retired, but he'd chosen to come home. He'd used his wealth and political connections to open the health center—and then kept his hand in by alternating twelve-hour shifts with her in the small ER.

She wanted to be Stan when she grew up.

"Typical Friday night stuff. Domestic abuse. Drug overdoses. Knife wounds when words might have been a better choice." Her lips twisted into a mockery of a smile. "The life of an ER doc."

But no more innocent deaths, for which she counted her blessings. The staff still hadn't recovered from Trina and her unborn's deaths three nights ago. At least, Levi had arrested the abusive, murdering bastard.

"Get out of here and enjoy your weekend off." Stan patted her hand where it rested on the counter. "I twisted the arm of one of the residents at the county hospital to cover your call this weekend. I don't expect to see you back here until seven o'clock, Monday evening. Got that?"

Two whole days to spend with Trey?

Her mood lightened. The disturbing phone calls were shoved to the back of her mind since nothing could hurt her if Trey were near. He wouldn't allow it.

This weekend could be the beginning of a future with the hunky former Marine.

"You're the best." She walked around the triage desk and gave him a hug. "If your wife wasn't such a nice lady, I'd give her a run for her money."

Stan grinned. "I think that fella making all those trips from up north might have something to say about that." He winked. "Pia told me you're finally gonna give the guy a break. About damn time. As much as I love having you here, you should think about moving closer to him so he doesn't have to fly down here so often. Save the environment in the process."

Fee shook her head and laughed. Stan was all about saving the environment and his harangues on fossil fuels, air pollution, and climate change were legendary.

"I'm finishing my year contract for sure." She looked him in the eye. "I'm not a quitter."

Um, yeah, you are. You let Dr. Adam-effin'-Stall run you out of Detroit.

That had been a totally different situation.

Pia joined them. "Hey, Dr. Parker." She gave the older man her thousand-watt smile, then turned to Fee. "Want to catch some breakfast at my *mamá's* restaurant? Then you can get your beauty rest on a full stomach and be relaxed and ready to eat when that man of yours arrives to take you to dinner."

"Sure." Fee's phone vibrated. Distress set her stomach to churning. She gave Pia a forced smile. "Give me a sec to take this call and then I'll meet you at the exit." She pulled the phone from her pocket and waved Pia off.

"Whoever it is tell them you're busy!" Pia jabbed a finger toward Fee. "No doing anyone favors on your weekend off."

"Got it, mom." As Fee swept the screen, she snorted as Pia gave her a middle finger. "Dr. Teague here."

Silence.

"Hello?" She looked at the screen. Another unknown number. The call was still connected. "Is anyone there?"

Then came the sound of breathing. Masculine-sounding breathing. Her blood turned cold and dread settled like a lead weight in her stomach. It was Stall. He'd breathed in just that way as he held her down and brutally took her body.

The call disconnected.

Blankly, she stared at the phone and tried not to vomit. She swallowed a whimper, then firmed her jaw and blocked the phone number. Then she turned the phone off. Stall wasn't here. He couldn't intimidate her with cowardly, anonymous phone calls.

He just did.

God, why wouldn't he leave her alone?

Because he's a sociopathic raping bastard?

"Fee?" Stan touched her arm. "What's wrong? You turned green there for a second. Who was on the phone?"

She shook off the lingering sickness the call had caused. "Um … a heavy breather."

The older doctor's gaze narrowed. His lips turned down. "Have you had other calls like that?"

"Yeah…" Fee looked into Stan's eyes and hoped hers didn't show her fear that the hell that was Adam-fucking-Stall was starting all over again. "Right after I got here. I reported them to the phone company, and they said the calls came from pre-paid phones and couldn't trace them. So, I changed my number and the calls stopped for a while."

"And now they've started again." It was a statement, not a question.

She nodded.

"Do you have any idea who's on the other end?" Stan asked.

"Yes." She pulled her frazzled emotions together. There was no use in burdening this kind man with her problems. "I'll handle it. Don't worry about me."

Stan covered her hand with his. "You don't have to deal with this alone, you know. You have friends that can help."

Such as Trey. Your brother who's so not like your stick-up-his-butt father. The folks at SSI. Maybe it's time to stop being so stubbornly self-sufficient and let people who care about you help.

"Yeah, I know. Thanks." She pasted on a bright smile. "Pia's waiting. I'm starved, and she has to be also. We didn't stop moving all night. No time for a meal break."

And she was babbling.

Stan eyed her closely, opened his mouth, probably to quiz her further, then shook his head. "Run along. Have a great weekend. See you Monday evening."

Fee headed for the exit to the emergency clinic wing of the health center. Since it was Saturday morning and the regular clinic wasn't open, the emergency waiting area was full of mothers with sick children and people with injuries that wouldn't normally be considered an emergency.

Stan's philosophy was patients should be seen no matter the time of day or night or the severity of their condition. So on weekends, the ER docs covered all illnesses and injuries. Come Monday morning, it was all about triage; the less sick people would be seen in the general clinic and the real emergencies would be seen by Stan from 7:00 a.m. to 7:00 p.m. and by Fee from 7:00 p.m. to 7:00 a.m., 24/7. That was the schedule— two doctors with only the odd substitution, now and then, of a resident from the county hospital to give them a break.

Yeah, it was hectic and exhausting being on twelve and off twelve, but she'd finish out her year so as to give Stan time to find a replacement or replacements for her. She'd already made the decision to move to Idaho at the end of her contracted year. Several months after arriving in New Mexico, she realized she was ready to move on from what had happened in Detroit. Missing Trey after his last visit had merely cemented her decision.

Pia sat in a chair by the exit and scanned her cell phone. The nurse looked up as Fee approached, then frowned. "What's wrong? Did Dr. Parker cancel your weekend off?"

"No?" Fee stared at the best friend she had in Columbus. In fact, her best friend ever. "Why?"

"You look … freaked. What happened?"

Pia had a mulish look on her face. Fee knew from past experience the nurse wouldn't budge an inch until she told Pia what was wrong.

"That call I took?" Pia nodded. "No one was on the other end. Just breathing."

"You got a heavy breathing call? Is this the first?"

"Uh, yes … and no. There've been other calls, but no breathing, just silence." Fee hesitated, not used to sharing her burdens, but Pia was one of those friends Stan had alluded to.

Go on tell, her what you suspect.

"I told you about the doctor who'd raped me?"

Pia nodded, a look of grave concern on her face.

"I'm sure the calls are from him." Fee rubbed a hand over her diaphragm to release the tension so she could catch a full breath.

"That bottom-feeding, scum-sucking *culo* is now stalking you long-distance?" Pia surged to her feet, her hands fisted. "You need to tell Levi."

Fee wasn't going to bother Levi. He had enough local criminals to deal with.

"I can change my number again." She and Pia exited the building. "He'll eventually get tired of calling and stop."

You don't really believe that, do you?

No.

"Not good enough. If you don't tell Levi, I will." Pia was furious on her behalf, and maybe a little bit of that fury was aimed Fee's way. "Fee, you have to see, this is the sign of a seriously disturbed man."

"He's in Detroit." Fee opened the door of her Jeep Cherokee, but remained outside. The heat buildup in the vehicle was already unbearable, and it was only half past seven in the morning. The temperatures were already in the low eighties and it was only March. "Stall won't come here."

Head in the sand ... again?

Pia opened the passenger side door and leaned in, but also stayed outside until the interior cooled a bit. "There are these miraculous contraptions called airplanes. He could be here even now."

Fee opened her mouth—

"Anh," Pia held up a hand, "I don't want to hear one more rationalization. Tell Levi or tell that hunk Trey—or both. You don't have to handle this alone."

What she said.

Fee climbed into the Jeep and slammed the door. "I don't want to be one of those weak women who relies on a man to solve her problems."

"Fee—" Pia's tone was full of exasperation. "Everyone needs help at one time or another."

Not according to her father who'd preached self-sufficiency, stiff upper lip, and gut it up at every turn.

Pia climbed in and slammed her door. "Ignore me, if you must. But I'm deliriously happy you've decided to date Trey. His presence means your burdens will be history. I don't see that man—one who adores you—allowing anyone or anything harm you."

Fee couldn't deny the truth of what Pia said. Trey, like her brother Price, was a protector. But—

Stop with the buts. Just let Trey handle it. Tell him about the calls tonight.

Fine, she would, and just like that, the fear roiling in her gut melted away. Trey would handle it, and he wouldn't think less of her. He wasn't like her father. He wasn't like Stall. He was a paladin.

The short drive to *Mamacitas Restaurante* took less than three minutes. They could've easily walked it from the clinic, but afterwards they'd head to Fee's two-room-plus-a-full-bath adobe on the outskirts of Columbus, located in a sparsely built-out subdivision. Pia had left her car there the evening before and had ridden into work with Fee. The plan had been for Pia to vet Fee's outfit for her first date with Trey.

Entering the restaurant, the spicy-fatty smells of Tex-Mex breakfasts hit Fee in the face and had her mouth watering. She placed a hand on her stomach which growled loudly at the scent of food.

They sat at the counter and then Fee turned to Pia. "When did we eat last?"

"We only took one break, and it was a short one," Pia responded. "I think we both had a diet Pepsi and a granola bar … and dammit, one of the techs had brought in homemade lasagna and I wanted some, but never got around to it."

"Patients rank before eating." Fee shrugged. It was the life she'd chosen and so a growling stomach was a small price to pay. "We're here now, so let's eat."

Fee practically bounced on the stool at the thought of the tasty treats coming her way. She smiled at Pia's mother. *"Hola,* Carmela. Chilequiles and a Diet Pepsi, please."

"Hola, Fee. You will have fresh squeezed orange juice also," the older woman informed her then turned to her daughter. *"Hola, hija preciosa.* What do you want to eat?"

"Huevos rancheros, *mamá."* Pia got up and hugged her mother, then sat back down. *"Mamá,* what's this?" She traced an ugly, dark bruise around her mother's wrist.

"Nothing, *mi hija.* Let me get your order." Pia's mother scurried off.

"Not nothing," a man with a raspy voice uttered.

Fee and Pia turned as one. An attractive older man with the deportment of a former soldier, someone Fee had seen frequently in the restaurant, had spoken. His light eyes held a glint of anger.

"Who hurt Carmela…" What was the guy's name? Matty? Macky? "…Manny?" Fee asked in a low voice so it wouldn't carry back to the kitchen where Pia's mother was cooking.

"Ernesto." Manny spat the name as if it left a bad taste in his mouth. "He was in earlier. Argued with Carmela. Didn't catch all of it, because they were arguing in Spanish … but I did hear her mention the cartel. She was angry—and scared. That's when Ernesto grabbed her and shook her. I shouted at the worthless piece of shit to stop and headed over to make him. But—"

Manny clenched his hands at his sides. "The little bastard cursed me, then flung Carmela aside and ran out of here." He fixed his worried gaze on Fee. "Dr. Teague, please check Carmela over. She hit the edge of the counter and then the floor really hard."

"I will." Fee stood and headed for the kitchen area.

Pia muttered "thanks, Manny" and followed her.

"Carmela—" Fee walked behind the counter and entered the small galley kitchen. She then gently pulled the older woman away from the stove. "Leave the food for now. Let me check your hip and side." She yelled over her shoulder to where Manny now stood at the end of the counter and had a view of them. "Which side, Manny?"

"Same side as her wrist. The little bastard jerked her toward him then whipped her to the side and let her go." Manny's face was red with anger. He blew out a harsh breath. "I couldn't get to her in time to keep her from being hurt."

Manny's guilt at failing Carmela radiated in every line and angle of his body. He obviously had strong, deep feelings for Pia's mother.

Carmela protested, "Manny, why did you…"

"Hush, *mamá*. Ernesto is a pig. Let Fee check you over." Pia's tone was filled with a simmering anger that would certainly boil over once she found her brother. "Manny, please make sure we aren't interrupted."

"You got it, Pia." The older man turned his back and stood guard.

Fee gently pulled Carmela's blouse from the waistband of her jeans and then lowered her pants to expose her upper hip. Pia's sharp inhale said it all.

"Some really nice bruising going on here." Fee lightly traced the ugly blue-red markings while watching Carmela's reactions. "Did you hit anything else on the way down? Your ribs? Your stomach?"

"No, no." Carmela shoved gently at Fee. "I am fine. It was nothing."

"Check her ribs," Manny put in loudly. "She wouldn't let me take her to the emergency clinic. She grimaces when she takes a deep breath and fucking limps when she doesn't think anyone's looking."

"Manny!" Carmela yelled.

And the man was correct—Carmela was wincing and gasping.

"Dammit, woman. I'm worried about you," he yelled back.

Even though the situation with Ernesto and his mother wasn't even a little bit amusing, Fee had to bite her lip to keep from laughing at the byplay between Pia's mother and Manny. "Carmela, let's go to the clinic and get an X-ray just to make sure your hip and ribs aren't fractured."

"Fee…" Carmela began to refuse.

"You're going, *mamá*." Pia had a mulish look on her face. "I'll cook. Manny can help me by taking orders."

"Damn straight, she's going." Manny came to stand by them. His worried glance zeroing in on the bruising. Sparks flashed in his eyes and he muttered, "I'll fucking gut that little bastard."

"Manny," Carmela whispered, tears in her eyes. "He is *mi hijo*."

"He sure doesn't act like a good son should." Manny turned to Fee. "Me and Pia can cover the diner until the other servers come in for the lunch crowd. Don't let Carmela give you any crap. Better to be safe than sorry, I always say."

"I won't." Fee helped rearrange the older woman's clothing and placed an arm around her shoulders. "Let's go. I'll take the X-rays myself. If there's only bruising, we'll be back before you know it." If there was a hip fracture, and depending on the severity, Carmela would be in an ambulance to the county hospital in Deming, the Luna County seat.

Pia brought Fee a foil-wrapped bundle that smelled heavenly. "Take this. It's a breakfast burrito. It'll tide you over until you return." Her friend turned toward her mother and hugged her gently. "Behave, *mamá*. Do what Fee says. Manny and I can handle the *restaurante*."

"*Gracias, mi hija*." Carmela stroked her daughter's face. "Do not confront Ernesto. He was not himself."

Fee took that to mean the idiot had been jacked up on some drug. She hoped it wasn't the meth and heroin combo.

The locals had taken to speedballing, and she'd seen a lot of overdoses in the ER and more than a few deaths. The next time, Ernesto's violent behavior could easily escalate and result in a more serious injury or even death, maybe even his own.

If Pia's mother refused to file a complaint with the Sheriff's Office, Fee would call Levi and suggest he talk to Manny about the altercation in *Mamacitas*.

As Fee walked Carmela toward the exit, Pia's words to Manny followed them out the door, "Just what are you doing with *mi mamá*? And what exactly did Ernesto say to her? And don't tell me you didn't understand, old man, because I know you speak fluent border Spanglish."

9:30 am, Fee's place

"PIA, YOU DON'T NEED TO stick around. I can pick out a date night outfit." As soon as they entered the cozy adobe, Fee turned on the chiller unit. The ceiling fan had lost the battle against the morning heat. "You need to go and ride herd on your mother. Even with cracked ribs and a severely bruised hip, we both know she won't rest when she has a business to run even with your Aunt Ingreta there to help her."

"*Tía* Ingreta is the meaner older sister," Pia said. "*Mamá* will listen to her. Plus Manny is there. He has promised to care for *mi mamá*." Her friend giggled. "He's courting her and she's letting him. This is good. Ernesto always takes advantage of *mamá*. Manny will stop that."

Fee frowned and turned to look at Pia. "Ernesto has already shown he can be violent. What's to keep him from going in there and using a gun next time?"

Pia's lips thinned. "Nothing. This is why Manny will begin to wear his gun on his hip. *Mi mamá's* new man is retired Army and still a virile man. He will do what is needed to protect his woman."

Hell, this sounded like the wild west circa the 21st century. Someone could get killed if the situation wasn't nipped in the bud. So she was glad she'd—"I called Levi."

"Why did you do that? My family and Manny can handle Ernesto. Did *mi mamá* hear you?" Pia looked worried—and scared. But for whom—her mother or her brother?

"Your mother asked me to." Fee hugged her friend. "Your brother threatened your mother if she didn't stop insulting his friends by asking them to leave the restaurant. Pia, your brother and his home boys had previously shot up drugs when there were families present with small children." Pia gasped. "Levi will have a word with your brother."

More than a word. The normally taciturn sheriff had exploded when he'd heard what Ernesto had done to Carmela. Levi had come to the emergency room and taken a statement from Pia's mother, who'd cried, but had done the right thing. Carmela had admitted she was afraid her son would die doing favors with his friends for the cartel—just as her husband had. Ernesto's blatant disrespect had been ongoing for a long time, but when he'd turned violent with her … that had been the last straw. She wanted her only son scared straight.

"*Santo infierno,*" Pia muttered. She wiped away a tear that had leaked from her eye. "Ernesto is in deeper with the cartel than my father had been. This is very bad."

"I'm so sorry." Fee rubbed Pia's back. "Let Levi handle it. Let Manny protect your mother. Ernesto has chosen the wrong path and the law will have to handle it now."

Pia nodded and sniffled, then straightened her shoulders. "*Mamá* is fine for now. I want … no, I need, to help you pick out your outfit. If I leave the choice up to you, you will wear something boring." Her friend entered Fee's bedroom and walked into the one feature which had sold Fee on the tiny house—the master bathroom with a large walk-in closet off to the side. "You need to show some skin so your man will see your glowing New Mexico tan."

Fee laughed and followed her friend. "He'll see my freckles. I don't burn. I don't tan. I get spots."

Pia glanced at Fee as she stripped to her lacy peach-colored bra and panties, her one concession to femininity under her work clothes. "He'll adore your spots since you'll be exposing lots of skin along with them. Try this." Pia shoved an aqua chiffon sleeveless dress with a built-in, silky slip underneath. "It matches your eyes. Do you have any silver and turquoise jewelry?"

Fee took the dress and pulled it on over her head, then shimmied until it settled over her hips. "Damn, I can't wear a bra with this." She unclipped the bra, slipped it off one arm, then the other, and pulled it out through the armhole. "Yes, in the top drawer of the chest. Pia, this dress is far too fancy for any of the restaurants in Deming."

The nicest sit-down restaurant in the county seat was a chain steak restaurant in a strip mall. The last time she'd worn this particular dress it had been to a three-star Michelin restaurant in New York where she'd attended an AMA meeting.

"It'll be fine." Pia eyed Fee's hips. "Lose the undies. The fabric clings. You have a pronounced panty line."

"I refuse to go without undies." Fee's face flushed at the thought of sitting across from Trey with no underwear. The man would definitely notice, since he scanned her body with an intense, laser-like regard each and every time he'd seen her.

"You must have a pair of thong panties. Wear those."

"I don't." Fee had tossed out all her thongs after Adam-fucking-Stall had raped her. She'd worn a pair of lacy thong panties that night. She could still hear Stall leeringly comment on them as he'd ripped them off her nearly unconscious body.

"Then lose the panties," Pia ordered and then smiled as Fee slipped the undies off and tugged the dress back into place. "Much better. Trey will be much envied since he'll be the one dining with you."

"I agree with the lady ... no panties is much better." The words uttered in an accented, harsh male growl came from behind her.

CHAPTER 3

Fee and Pia gasped and turned.

A man dressed in designer jeans and what looked to be a silk golf shirt stood in Fee's bedroom, just outside the master bath doorway. He was dark-haired and swarthy-skinned, and definitely of Hispanic lineage with maybe a bit of Spanish European blood mixed in, but his accent was pure Mexican.

What might have normally been an attractive package was spoiled by the fact his pale yellow gaze was feral, he had a big, ugly gun pointed at them, and he had lots of blood on his shirt.

After a swift examination, she determined it wasn't his blood, and his eyes showed no pain, merely the promise of giving it. His expression was all too familiar. It was the same rapacious look Stall had worn each time he'd approached her … had stalked her like an animal.

Icy dread raised goose bumps over Fee's skin. Her heart pounded as adrenaline poured into her bloodstream and every primitive instinct told her to run or hide.

Evil stood in her bedroom, and there was no escaping him.

She clenched her jaw and forced herself to breathe slowly. The mere threat of him had thrust her back into the dark place she'd recently begun to emerge from.

Focus.

A loud, pained groan sounded from behind the man blocking the bathroom doorway. The noise startled Fee out of her momentary paralysis and helped her find the control of the ER physician she'd trained to be.

She shot a sharp glance at the gunman. "Who's hurt? Did you shoot someone? And why in the hell did you bring him here?"

Before she'd finished speaking, the man had crossed the few feet between them and back-handed her across the face with his free hand. "Silence, *puta*."

Eyes watering from the vicious hit, Fee stumbled back a few steps and covered the side of her face with a shaky hand.

"Fee..." Pia's voice was thready with shock. "That's Raimundo Chavez." Utter fear colored her friend's tone. "He's Jaime Aznar's *segundo*."

The acting head of the Sinaloa cartel, Jaime Aznar a.k.a. *El Hacha*—the Ax—had gotten his nickname as a result of how he dealt with those who crossed him—he dismembered them with an ax.

Fee swallowed hard as dread slithered down her spine. She'd also heard of Chavez. *El Halcón.* The Hawk. Rumors along the border had painted him as even more deadly than his boss. Eyeing Chavez, it was easy to believe the stories. The cold yellow gleam of his eyes resembled that of the predatory bird he was named after.

Just look at him. He's eyeballing you as if you were a tasty mouse he wanted to gut.

Fee froze in place just as prey did when being hunted and not wanting to draw the hungry hunter's attention. She wanted to pull her gaze from his—to back away, to escape—

but couldn't. She was afraid he'd swoop in and attack once more. Her throbbing cheek was evidence of his short fuse.

"*Mi jefe* has been shot." His relentless stare fixed on her, Chavez stepped aside to reveal through the doorway a short, swarthy-skinned, and very bloody male lying on her ivory linen bedspread. A hulking brute leaned over the body, applying pressure in two places on the victim's torso. The hulk's hands and forearms were covered in blood.

"We are here, because I have been told you are an emergency doctor. So, Dr. Fiona Teague, you will do what is needed to help *El Hacha* ... now."

It scared the ever-loving shit out of her that this man knew even that much about her.

Fee somehow found the strength to tear her gaze away from Chavez's calculating look and to focus on the critically wounded man. She winced and swore silently. Even this far away, she could tell the man needed to be in a surgical suite in Deming, at the main hospital, and not lying on her bed. The victim's dark skin was gray-tinged. There was too much fresh blood.

Taking a deep breath, she forced herself to confront Chavez. "He'll die if you don't get him to a hospital." She used her best don't-mess-with-me-I'm-a-doctor voice even as her knees shook like jelly.

When Chavez raised his arm, his eyes lit with rage, she held up her hand and moved back a few steps. "I'm giving you my honest medical opinion here. Even without examining him, I can see he needs a trauma surgeon and blood."

"Lopez said you have much experience."

Damn, Ernesto. If she survived this, she'd happily skewer the bastard.

"Señor Chavez," she held her hands out in a placating manner, "no matter what my emergency experience is, treating this man under these conditions is consigning him to die. The room, the bedding ... nothing is sterile. I don't have X-rays to see how much internal damage there is and where any bullet fragments might be lodged. I can't type and match his blood ... never mind I don't have any blood..."

Chavez grabbed her arm hard enough that she'd have bruises to match the one on her face. He pulled her into his body and lowered his voice. "Stop telling me what you can't do, *puta*, and take care of *mi jefe* or..."

"Or what?" Fee whispered as she tried to shrink away from Chavez's cruel touch and coldly menacing voice.

Chavez leaned into her and said, "Or Ernesto's lovely sister will die a horrible death in front of you." Then he dragged Fee toward the doorway and shoved her toward the bedroom. She stumbled, but managed to latch onto the door frame to keep from falling to her knees.

Fee glanced over her shoulder at Pia whose face was whiter than the lace curtains covering the bedroom window. Another thug had stepped past Fee and entered the bathroom. He now held her friend against him, a gun pointed at the side of Pia's forehead.

"I don't have any surgical tools. No pain medication. No IV solution. Nothing." Fee looked back at Chavez who'd followed her so closely he could've have been her shadow.

"We have two field medical kits," he said. "One is similar to what the U.S. Special Forces use. I think you will find one or both will have all you need to stabilize him. After you do, I will take him to his personal surgeon in Mexico."

"Fee—" Pia's voice hitched as the man holding her forced her into the bedroom. The thug traced the barrel of his gun down the side of her friend's face then back up again. "You can do it ... please..."

Fee had no choice. If she did nothing, she and Pia would surely die. If she stabilized the cartel leader, Chavez might let them live.

All she could do was her best. Besides, it wouldn't be the first time she'd operated on a criminal under less than ideal conditions. Her previous hospital in Detroit had often seemed like a battlefield MASH unit during the all-too-frequent inner city gang violence.

"Where are these kits?" Fee walked to the dresser and pulled a clean scrub top out of a drawer and tugged it over her head to cover most of her dress. Then she moved to go by Chavez and back into the bathroom to wash her hands. He didn't step aside. Instead, he forced her to slide past him in the narrow space he'd left. His lips curved upward in a cruelly taunting smile as she tried to touch as little of him as possible.

"You are so tiny," he murmured and stopped her forward movement by grabbing her chin and forcing her face toward his. "A beauty with spirit." His eyes gleamed with twisted interest. "I wonder how long it would take for me to break you?"

Fee swallowed the bile threatening to come up her throat and refused to rise to his taunts. "Your boss is dying. I need to wash up. You're wasting precious seconds. I can't save him if you don't get out of my way. Or do you *want* your boss to die?"

Was bringing Aznar here, instead of taking him to a hospital in Mexico, Chavez's way of taking over? Was she part of a power play where she'd be the patsy blamed for the cartel leader's death?

Chavez surrounded her throat with his large hand and then squeezed. Fee couldn't breathe. Her heart raced out of control. Her vision blurred. She tugged at his hand, but his grip was too powerful. There was no way she could stop him from choking her.

He won't kill you.

"If *mi jefe* did not need your aid, I'd kill you now." He tightened his grip even more.

She closed her eyes and waited for the incipient darkness to take her. Then he released her. She took in huge, gulping breaths of air.

"Prepare yourself. See that he does not die." Chavez moved, and she scuttled past him into the bathroom. "The medical kits will be here when you are ready." He turned and spoke rapid Mexican Spanish in a dialect she couldn't quite follow. The man who'd held the gun on Pia ran out of the room.

Weak, shaking, Fee turned to the vanity and braced herself for a second before she began to wash up. She glanced in the mirror. The woman staring back at her was pale, a bruise already blooming on her face, and dark red marks showed on her throat. God, would she even survive this?

You can. You will.

She'd damn sure try.

"I need Pia to assist," she called out, her voice hoarse from being almost strangled to death. "I also need someone to help…"

Heavy feet sounded on her wood floors. She looked in the mirror and saw the guy who'd held the gun on Pia had returned with two large medical kits. Ernesto had also entered the bedroom. The hulking brute still applied pressure to Aznar's wounds; she realized he was someone she'd seen in her emergency clinic for a drug overdose. She also processed, for the first time, that Chavez and his men were armed to the teeth with rifles slung across their chests, handguns holstered around their waists, and knives strapped to their thighs.

She prayed to any deity listening that she and Pia would live through this somehow.

"…strip Señor Aznar's clothing off. Try to keep pressure on the wounds while doing so. There are clean sheets in the hall closet, get several. Place one under him and then use any sterile drapes in the kit to create a field for me to work in."

"*Sí*, Doctor." Pia's voice was strained, but at least her friend no longer had a gun aimed at her head.

Fee turned to leave the bathroom, and Chavez blocked her way once again. "I will be watching you closely."

His tone was a dark promise.

Jaime Aznar might be a piece of crud, but he was now her patient. Being the ruthless thug he was, Chavez wouldn't understand her moral code—she'd do her best to keep the bloody butcher alive, no matter the dire circumstances, because she'd sworn an oath to preserve life.

Fee swallowed painfully and forced herself not to gulp in each blessed breath. Mining every bit of stubborn Teague pride in her body, she met Chavez's gaze. While working in the inner city, she'd learned never to let the animals see you blink—they'd use that split-second to tear out your throat. "I'm sure you will."

Chavez's lips twisted savagely, and he moved just enough that she was forced to rub up against him yet again. She inhaled sharply. Fucking typical male dominance bullshit, but it was effective. He scared the bejesus out of her, because if she fought him, she'd lose. He was bigger and stronger—and a stone-cold killer.

Fee approached the bed and nodded at Pia who was preparing to start an IV. Her nurse had the one cartel thug she'd recognized from the ER still applying pressure on the wounds. The bastard who'd held a gun on Pia was now absent, probably outside standing guard.

Pia's brother Ernesto stood away from the bed, leaning against the wall beside the room's only window. He held a hand gun in a very shaky hand.

Narrowing her eyes, she examined his face. His eyes were wild and dilated. His body jittered. He was on something and looked to be in the early stages of withdrawal.

"Chavez," Fee said as she pulled out what she needed from one of the medical kits, "should Ernesto be holding a loaded gun near my patient? He isn't competent at the moment."

Chavez moved to stand next to her and stared across the bed, then swore under his breath. He pulled his hand gun and pointed it at Ernesto and then shot him. The bullet caught the edge of Ernesto's sleeve and grazed his upper arm.

Ernesto cried out in pain. Blood bloomed on the olive drab cloth.

Pia whimpered and Fee muttered, "Sweet Jesus."

"*Segundo*?" Ernesto's voice was slurred, but his attention was on the here and now and not on his next fix, for sure.

"Get out of here, *pendejo*. Guard the outside. Send Garcia back in. You know better than to take drugs while on duty."

Ernesto's lips thinned, but didn't argue. He left after shooting a nasty glare at Fee and then another at his sister. Pia tracked her brother's exit with sadness in her eyes and posture.

"Pia?" Fee murmured. Her heart ached for her friend. It wasn't as if Pia hadn't known her brother abused drugs; Manny had said as much earlier today. But to see it confirmed under the current circumstances had to make the knowledge even worse. "You with me?"

Nodding, Pia inhaled on a slight sob, started the IV drip, hanging the bag from the canopy on Fee's bed, and began to clean the patient's sweaty, bloody torso with antiseptic wipes from the field medical kits. Moving the hulking brute aside, Pia applied pressure bandages to stave off the bleeding until Fee could work on each of the wounds. The nurse's hands trembled only slightly. Like Fee, Pia was holding it together … for now.

Once the blood, sweat, and dirt were removed, Fee's earlier determination of the critical nature of her patient's injury was reconfirmed. There were three bullet wounds—two in the mid-torso, one near the lower lobe of the lung and one in the stomach, and the third bullet had gouged the edge of the patient's right hip. All the shots had come from the front and from mid-to-long distance range since there were only minor abrasion rings around the holes in the soft tissue.

"Vitals, Pia," Fee requested in a soft voice.

"BP is 85 over 50. Pulse is 100 and thready," Pia replied.

Fee eyed the two men who stood by the bed. "I need you two to roll the patient gently onto his side and hold him in place."

The men didn't move and stared at her, insolence in their gazes.

"Do as she says," Chavez snapped out. "Now."

The men moved swiftly and turned Aznar as she'd instructed. She walked around to the other side of the bed to view her patient's back. Of the two torso wounds, there was only one exit wound, the one where the bullet had entered through the stomach. The exit wound was massive and was located just above the upper buttock. The shot had come from above and the wound track would go down through the intestines. A dirty gut wound.

All she could do was flush the wound as best as possible and pray Chavez got his boss to a good surgeon before peritonitis set in.

The other bullet was still inside, near the man's lung.

Fee turned and looked at Chavez who raised a brow and said, "Well?"

"I can't remove the bullet near the lung." As he opened his mouth, she hurried on, "I could puncture his lung and cause even more damage. The best I can do is flush both wounds, pack them, and get fluid in him to replace blood volume lost."

Chavez snorted. "I agree. It is good you did not lie to me. Do these things and then we will leave."

Fee let out the breath she hadn't realized she'd been holding. She turned to Pia who already had a syringe ready to administer a pain medication. "I also can't guarantee to get all the debris cleansed from any of the internal wound tracks. Infection is a given."

"Woman," Chavez growled, "he will die for certain if nothing is done." He moved to her side as she prepared to inject the pain meds into the IV. He stopped her hand and peered suspiciously at the medication label on the pre-prepared syringe, then nodded. "Go ahead."

She raised a brow at him and then injected the meds. Then she proceeded to work on the gut wound.

"Pia, what's in the kit to pack the wounds once I finish flushing them?"

Chavez answered before Pia could open her mouth, "There is wound sealant. It is sterile and will do the job."

"Yes, that'll work." Fee turned to see him pluck a packet of wound sealant out of one of two field medical kits and place it on the bed within her reach. "I'll need help to hold him still. Even with the pain meds, the saline solution I use to flush will cause him pain."

His face grim, he nodded and spoke to the others in rapid Spanish.

"Turn him onto his back … gently now," she instructed.

Aznar moaned piteously at the movement.

The men did their best to hold the arching patient in place. To the background noise of Aznar alternately screaming and moaning piteously, she flushed both wounds until she was sure she'd gotten as much detritus out of the wounds as possible. Anything left in the wound tracks would have to have to stay there until the man reached Mexico.

After what seemed like hours, she straightened from her position bent over the patient. She then began to apply the wound sealant to the entrance wounds.

With a roaring shout, Aznar surged upward, managed to tear one of his arms loose from the man holding it, and swung out blindly. He hit Fee across the face in the exact same spot Chavez had struck her earlier.

She saw stars as she fell backward and would've landed on her butt, but Chavez caught her and steadied her against his body.

"*Puta torpe*," he ground out, then took advantage of the position and grabbed one of her breasts and squeezed it hard. "Very nice."

"Let me go, you bastard." She shrugged away from his loathsome touch. Taking several deep breaths, she got the nausea his touch evoked under control. "Vitals, Pia."

"Um, pulse is 180 and thready. Blood pressure is 70 over 45." Pia rattled off the numbers. Her friend's frightened gaze caught hers.

Shit. Aznar was bleeding internally.

"What's his blood type? He needs blood stat."

Chavez's nostrils flared at her tone. She imagined she'd pay for her tone and for moving away from his touch later, but right now, he still needed her to save his boss.

"He's O-positive." Chavez rolled up his sleeve. "I'm a universal donor. He will have my blood." He snapped out an order at the other two men who pulled their weapons and stood guard, their gazes fixed on her and Pia.

"I can't use your blood." Fee stared at Chavez. "Even if I trust that you are a universal donor, it still needs to be tested for disease."

Chavez stared back, his anger reflected by a pulsing muscle in his jaw, and stated defiantly, "I do not use drugs. When I fuck," he raked her body slowly with a leering glance, "I always use a condom."

Fee felt herself going pale, but nodded. "Fine. It's his life."

Beggars and loathsome drug cartel butchers couldn't be choosy.

Fee pulled off her bloody gloves and tossed them onto the pile of used gauze, towels, and sheets. She allowed Pia to help her pull on clean gloves and began to prep Chavez's arm as he sat on the side of the bed. "After we give him some blood, he'll be as stable as I can make him. So what happens then?"

As Fee prepared to insert a second IV into Aznar, Pia covered the packed wounds with gauze.

Chavez wrapped the rubber tubing around his upper arm, pulling it tightly with his teeth, then picked up a needle and found his own vein. He then allowed Fee to hook the tubing from his arm to Aznar's IV. "After we're through here, my men and I will drive to a ranch where a Mexican Army helicopter will pick us up and take us across the border. We have a trauma surgeon and medical equipment back in Madera awaiting our arrival."

"You'll need to monitor him carefully during the transport," Fee said. "You can easily switch out the bags of saline. I'll show you how before you leave. I'll also write down the pain med dosages you should inject into the drip by volume. I'll give him a loading dose of antibiotics now. Do you know if he's allergic to any meds?"

Fee stripped off her gloves and then rummaged through the pharmacy tray of one of the field kits and found it was stocked with every wide-spectrum antibiotic known to man.

"Yes, I *could* handle all that." Chavez sat on the edge of the bed, his arm elevated as blood flowed from him into Aznar. His sly tone raised the hairs on the back of her neck. "But since you and Señorita Lopez will be coming with us, you will handle his care during the journey to our base."

"What?" Fee's head shot up. Her pulse thrummed loudly in her ears. She couldn't catch her breath. Her vision dimmed and she was afraid she might faint. "No."

"No." Pia echoed and backed away from the bed only to be stopped by Garcia who grabbed her arm and held her in place.

Chavez lifted his hand as if to strike Fee for her refusal. She backed further away. "You will not die as long as *mi jefe* lives. If he dies, you'll feed the wolves after I and my men are through with you."

Fee caught Pia's gaze. Her friend looked as frightened as Fee felt. Chavez held their lives in his hands.

As Chavez's blood steadily flowed into her patient's vein, Fee considered and rejected their options and came to realize they had none for now. If she and Pia tried to escape, they'd die, but only after Chavez made them pay in ways Fee didn't want to think about.

Fee really wanted to live.

"You are thinking of escaping, *sí*? Do not try. It will only make things worse for you." Chavez sneered at her as he calmly pulled the needle from his vein. "We must be going."

Fee automatically covered the injection site with sterile gauze and then wound an elastic wrap around it.

"Now go change." Chavez stood and pushed Fee toward the bathroom and dressing area. He followed her inside and closed the door behind them.

Pia's strangled "Fee!" was cut off and the sounds of a scuffle could be heard through the thin wood.

"Pia!" Fee headed for the door.

Chavez yanked her against him before she could reach for the door knob. His hard-on jutted against her abdomen. His grip on her arms was punishing. She could smell the lust oozing from his pores as his breathing escalated.

Hard-learned lessons took over. She went still. Moving away got you beaten. However she couldn't stop the whimper that escaped her throat.

"Do what I say. Give me everything I want, and you and your friend will not suffer." He rubbed the patchy stubble on his jaw over the bruise he'd given her. She inhaled at the burning pain. He chuckled. "Keep these thoughts in your mind. We will talk of what I want from you later. For now, Garcia is merely taking your friend to her brother. She will be in the truck when we get there. Now, you need some better fucking clothes. These are bloody."

He turned her around and shoved her toward the dressing room. She entered it, and the once spacious dressing area closed in on her with his added presence. The air seemed to grow thicker and she fought to breathe.

Holding her in place with one large hand, he jerked a long-sleeved cotton T-shirt and a shearling jacket off the rods and a pair of jeans from a shelf. "These will do."

She clutched the clothing he thrust at her and held them to her chest as he rummaged through her lingerie drawers. Her stomach revolted at the thought of wearing anything he'd touched.

A leering smile on his lips, he handed her a sheer, sky-blue-colored lacy bra and matching boy short panties. "Wear these. I like them." Then he leaned against the wall. "Change. Now."

She was so scared, so cold inside, that she couldn't control the shivers that took over her body. "I can't. P-p-please…"

Chavez glowered and moved a step closer. Frozen in place, Fee waited, eyes closed, resigned to her fate.

He grabbed her by her upper arms, his grip merciless. "Since you begged so nicely, I will give you privacy … for now." He pulled her roughly against his body, then took her mouth, biting at her lips until she gasped with pain. Her mouth open, he thrust his thick, fat tongue inside.

Gagging, Fee fell into the memories from another time … of another cruel mouth and hands. And just as she had when Stall had raped her mouth, her body … her mind, Fee endured, holding onto her sanity with everything in her.

Just when she thought she might faint from sheer terror, Chavez pushed her away. "You will get used to me, Fiona Teague." He cupped the bulge in his pants. "I can be very generous to a woman who seeks to please me."

Fee bit her lip and managed not to gag or scream. With a last painful tweak of her nipple, he left the room and shut the bathroom door with a definitive thud that rang in her ears like the sound of doom.

She changed clothes quickly, not trusting him to stay away.

Tears streamed down her cheeks. The only hope she had in her heart and mind was the knowledge that Trey would arrive for their date later. He'd see the bloody mess in her bedroom. He would try to find her … but how?

Use your brain, Fee. He'll need clues … a place to start looking.

She turned on the water to cover the noise of her actions. Opening her vanity drawer, she pulled out an eyeliner pencil and wrote what she knew of the cartel base's location and the name *El Hacha* on the back of her medicine cabinet door. Carefully, she closed the door, the *snick* it made sounding like a boom of thunder to her scared-shitless ears. Then she proceeded to wash her face and apply the moisturizer she'd removed from the cabinet, just in case Chavez had heard the door closing.

Chavez suddenly entered the bathroom. "Ready?"

Fee nodded, unable to utter a word and held her breath as he looked around the room with the piercing glance of a predatory animal. He looked at the bottle she had in her hand and then at the medicine cabinet.

Please … please … please don't look inside the cabinet.

Finally, Chavez grunted and held out his hand. "Come." The unyielding look on his face dared her to refuse him.

Since Fee was sure she wouldn't like any retribution he'd take, she took his hand. As he dragged her out of the house, she prayed Trey was as thorough of a hunter as she thought he was.

Chapter 4

The cul-de-sac Fee's adobe was located on was filled to the max with emergency vehicles and a small crowd of gawkers. A sense of dread and urgency propelled Trey out of his rental and past the twenty or so people standing behind the yellow police tape. They might be stopped by a thin strip of plastic, but he wouldn't be.

He ducked under the tape and headed for Fee's house at a ground-eating pace.

"Sir, you need to move back behind the tape. This is a crime scene." A man wearing the tan shirt of a Luna County Deputy moved to stand in front of Trey.

Trey cast the much shorter and younger man a stone-cold glance. "That's my woman's house. You'll have to shoot me to stop me, and, son, you don't wanna do that."

"Sir..." The deputy had his hand over his weapon. "You can't..."

Trey growled and circumvented the cop who trotted after him, sputtering. The kid wouldn't shoot him in the back, but it might be a good idea to de-escalate the situation. "Gray Wolf! It's Trey Maddox and I'm coming in. Call off your boy."

Levi Gray Wolf exited the house. The man he'd come to know and trust with the safety of his little doc during the time Fee had lived in Luna County looked tired, grim, mad as hell, and almost panicked.

Trey's dread level soared to DEFCON 1.

"Where's Fee? Is she okay?" Trey moved to pass Levi, but the man snagged Trey's arm and held him in an iron grip, keeping him on the porch. A porch where a trail of blood led into the house.

"Trey—"

"I'll put you down, man. Move out of the way." Trey broke the hold Levi had on him and entered the tiny house which had suited the petite Fee perfectly.

Crime scene techs were dusting everything. The trail of blood led to the only bedroom. Pain, fear, and grief stole his breath and threatened to drive him to his knees.

Trey stopped, throttled back the howl of rage that fought to escape his throat, and took several, deep, gulping breaths. "Fee? Is she hurt? Is she on the way to the hospital?"

She couldn't be dead. He refused to consider that possibility.

"Fee's not here. We don't think the blood is hers." Levi was at his side. "We're fairly certain she … and Pia … were taken away after whatever went down in here."

Pia's involvement explained the expression of panic on the normally contained Levi's face.

"Who took them? And what do you think happened in there that involved all that blood?" The blood trail was from more than a flesh wound. Someone had bled severely—life-and-death levels of severe.

"We think it was cartel." Levi's voice held a deep snarl of rage. "There were rumors *El Hacha* was ambushed on this side of the border—"

Jaime "*El Hacha*" Aznar. Just the name chilled Trey to his marrow. And The Ax's men could have taken Fee and Pia?

"Rumors? Don't you fucking know?" Trey barreled past a tech and entered the bedroom. The room looked like a charnel house. There was blood all over the bed and the surrounding area. "And why in the fuck are you standing around here, Levi? You should be out searching for Fee and Pia."

"I have no idea where to start looking." Levi stormed in after him. "It's a big fucking empty desert out there."

Trey stopped and forced himself to calm the fuck down. None of this was Levi's fault. The sheriff had a job to do, and he was doing it. Plus, even if Levi were one hundred percent sure it was *El Hacha's* doing, he couldn't cut corners and go chasing across an international border after cartel fuckers.

However, Trey could and would. But before he called in Price and some SSI backup, he needed to know exactly what had gone down and the time line. "Start from the beginning. What the fuck is going on with the cartel and *El Hacha*?"

Levi ran agitated fingers over his head and blew out a breath. "Got an anonymous phone call a little after ten this morning."

Trey snorted with disgust.

Levi grimaced. "Yeah, I hate fucking anonymous calls, but I have to follow up shit. This call directed us to an area north of Columbus where a rumored ambush on *El Hacha* was supposed to have occurred. There was blood. Lots of blood. There were tracks and tread marks from dozens of vehicles. There were hundreds of shell casings. But no bodies. This crime scene team," he gestured to the white, jump-suited techs collecting evidence in Fee's bedroom, "and me and several deputies spent hours at that scene collecting evidence."

Levi paced Fee's small bedroom and reminded Trey of a cougar he'd seen at a zoo, prowling the confines of his caged-in environment. The man like the cat would much rather have been on the hunt than where he was. "Hours later when I finally got back to my office, there were several messages from Pia's mother. When I called her, she was frantic. Pia and Fee had left *Mamacitas* around 9:25 this morning and had come here."

"Why was Pia coming home with Fee?" Trey asked. "They'd both worked all night. Wouldn't Pia go home and go to bed?"

Levi eyed Trey. "I wondered that also. Seems Pia'd ridden into the clinic last night with Fee so she could come home with Fee and help her pick an outfit for your date this evening. Señora Lopez was worried when Pia hadn't come back to the restaurant as she'd promised. The Señora couldn't reach either of them by phone."

"Why didn't Pia's mom come and check on the girls?" Trey cast Levi a glance.

"The Señora was injured earlier today." Levi growled under his breath. "Her son Ernesto had gone to the restaurant, argued with his mother, and threw her to the floor. Ernesto, like his father before him, runs drugs and guns across the border for the cartel. The Señora told me he'd asked her to close her restaurant so his cartel buddies could use it today for a *meeting*."

Trey's head jerked around, drawing his gaze away from all the bloody detritus that indicated that Fee had probably treated *El Hacha's* wounds. "Fuck me. That can't be coincidental."

"I agree. Seems the meeting was moved elsewhere. Lucky for the Señora." Levi added, "Pia and Fee came in just after the confrontation had happened with Ernesto. Fee took the Señora to the emergency clinic and then convinced her to call me. I came to Columbus and took her statement."

Levi ran his fingers through his hair, dislodging the tie that kept the Native American's long black hair away from his face. "I already had put a BOLO out on Ernesto for attacking his mother when I received the anonymous call about the ambush on *El Hacha*."

"Fuck. Fuck. Fuck." Trey scanned the area. "That fucking cowardly bastard Ernesto led them to Fee's place. The phone call got you away from Columbus and eliminated the chance of you stumbling over them at Fee's. Have you found *any* clues as to where they took our women?"

Even though Fee might've just recognized she wanted to date him, she was his. Pia might not have accepted that she belonged to the sheriff, but Levi had claimed her. The normally tight-lipped sheriff had confided his intentions, and posted a no trespassing sign, one evening over tequila shots with Trey and Price. It was that same evening Trey and Price had entrusted Fee's care to Levi since they couldn't be here to watch over her.

"Nothing yet." Levi ran his fingers over his head once again. "The Sinaloa cartel has lots of places on both sides of the border in which to hide."

Trey moved out of the way as a crime scene tech removed the bloody bedding. "You know they'll cross the border as soon as they can." He moved into the bathroom where the blood seemed to be relegated to the sink area and a bloody scrub top and a dress left on the floor. "If *El Hacha* was the patient and was bleeding out, Fee would have to stabilize him for travel."

"Yeah," Levi said. "The medical packaging we found were wound sealants, gauze dressings, and IV set ups. The items looked to have come from a well-supplied field medical kit like we used in Spec Ops."

Trey looked at Levi. "*El Hacha* could still need blood and a hospital, so they'd move him out quickly. That means a chopper or small plane. I'm betting a helicopter since it could fly low, stay under the radar. It would have to be marked so as not to raise border patrol suspicions if it were seen."

"A Mexican Army helicopter, maybe?" Levi suggested. "The cartel has contacts in both the upper levels of the Mexican government and Army. They could send out false intel about joint maneuvers or some fucking crap."

"I can get a handle on that." Trey pulled his satphone from its leather holster on his belt and hit a stored number. "Keely? It's Trey. Got a situation."

"Hey, Trey. What's wrong? Fee stand you up?" Keely's voice was warm, loving, and slightly amused.

"She's been kidnapped."

"What? Who?" Keely's tone shifted to cool and all-business in a split second.

"We think Sinaloa cartel." Her gasp told him she understood how dangerous the situation was.

"What do you need?"

"I need backup and a Black Hawk, but first I need you to find"—translated as hack into—"any satellites which would've been over Columbus, New Mexico and the surrounding area over the last twelve hours or so. Need you to look for a helicopter, possibly with Mexican Army markings, crossing the international border during that time—both ways. I'll need images, and I'll need to know what direction the transport headed when it crossed back over into Mexico and the exact time it crossed the border."

"On it." The sound of typing in the background reassured Trey. When Keely was "on it," results were guaranteed. "Who do you want besides Price to back you up? And where will you want them?"

"Whoever is available. As for where, not sure yet. But we'll be crossing illegally into Mexico, so you and Ren need to be prepared to chill out the right parties on our side of the border. Because of the Sinaloa cartel's long reach, I'd like to keep this off the Mexican government's radar until after we bring Fee and her friend Pia home."

Levi's grunt of approval was loud.

"Gotcha. I'll get back to you as soon as I have anything. Expect a call from Price and my hubby. By the way, Tweeter and DJ got home yesterday. They're up for an assignment and that gives you tech support and two extra pilots."

"Be glad to have them. Thanks, Keely."

"No thanks needed. You just get Fee and her friend back. Then bring Fee home to Sanctuary where she belongs. Enough with her living in frick-fracking New Mexico and being all independent and closed-off. The woman needs family and friends around her."

"I'll do my best. Out." Trey swiped off his phone and shoved it in its holster.

Trey rubbed a hand over his face and concentrated on controlling the side effects of all the adrenaline coursing through his bloodstream. Keely and the resources of SSI were on the job now. It was only a matter of time before he had a general trail to follow, but even with a solid lead, Mexico was a big damn country.

His gut burned as he watched the crime scene techs collect blood samples from the bedroom wood floor. What the fuck were those butchers doing to his woman? Fucking hell, his little doc had to be scared. But he had faith she'd hold it together, just as she had when she'd helped deliver Keely's baby in a cave after running from mercs during a blizzard. His woman was stronger than she thought. Plus, she'd have to know he and Price would come after her.

A thought struck him. His Fee was not only gutsy, she was also incredibly smart.

"Levi … Fee would've left me a clue or a message about where she was being taken."

"She might not have known where they were taking her and Pia." Levi looked around the decent-sized bathroom for such a small house. "She changed out of her bloody clothes. Hell, they probably had someone standing guard while she did. I would've."

Every muscle in Trey's body tightened in protest at the thought of some cartel fucker in the room with Fee, watching her dress. "But in case she was alone…"

Yeah, that thought lessened his need to punch something.

"…and did know where she was being taken, she would've left a message. So let's look for it. She stood right where I'm standing and washed blood off her hands."

Trey opened cabinet doors under the sink and found it organized to an inch and no obvious clues. He then looked at the vanity top. It wasn't cluttered like his sister's vanity often had been. All that was out were a comb, hand soap, moisturizer … eyeliner. There was no other makeup out.

"Levi, when a woman's getting ready to go out, she'd have a lot more makeup shit out, right?"

"How the fuck would I know?" Levi blew out a disgusted breath as he pulled open the glass shower door. "Nothing here, dammit. Didn't have sisters. My mom doesn't wear makeup. And the only woman I want to live with in order to find out about that kind of girly shit is keeping me at arm's length."

"If my sister was any example, she'd have shit all over the damn place. But Fee is also extremely neat … yet there's this eyeliner pencil." Trey pulled open the single vanity drawer and smiled at being proven correct. His very A-type little doc had all her makeup organized by type in the drawer with only one empty space. "So, why is one eyeliner pencil lying on this very uncluttered counter top?"

Light dawned in Levi's eyes. "She used it to write a message."

"Yeah." Trey looked at the mirror and then felt around the edges to find hinges. "Fuck me, it's a medicine cabinet." He opened the cabinet door and read the words written on the back. "*El Hacha* and Madera … that's in the Sierra Madre Occidentals."

Trey considered what he knew about the Sinaloa cartel and froze. "Fuck. He's taking her to the cartel's main drug distribution center. From the intel I've read, the place is a fucking fortress. Plus, the cartel is the biggest landowner and provides most of the good-paying jobs in the area. Money buys loyalty. We'll play hell finding local help."

"Fuck help. You have the resource you just spoke with on the phone," Levi said. "I know all about SSI. I also know your skill set, because I have a similar one—and I know you fucking know that since you'd never have trusted me to watch over your woman all these months if you hadn't read my file. So, we go the fuck in, surveil, eliminate any fucker who gets in our way, get our women, and get them the fuck out."

"That's the plan." Trey turned to face Levi. "You going in as the sitting sheriff of Luna County?"

"No," Levi answered. "I'll be taking a leave of absence, because, brother, I don't care what we have to do to get Pia and Fee back."

"Good." Trey moved past Levi. "Then we're done here. Time to make plans and get ready to go dark."

CHAPTER 5

March 23rd, 9 p.m.
En route to Madera, Mexico

Through the small windows of the helicopter's cabin, the night sky was pitch black but for the stars scattered over the darkness like diamond dust over black velvet. The headphones Fee wore suppressed most of the cabin noise and allowed communication among the passengers. But they couldn't block out the animal-like howl of pain from Aznar strapped on the gurney positioned next to her jump seat. On her other side sat Chavez who'd monitored her every movement like a hawk. She'd already had several run-ins with him when she'd left her seat without seeking his permission to care for her boss. Her face throbbed from being slapped. Absently, she rubbed at the bruises on her wrist where he'd grabbed her.

Across from her, Pia was sandwiched between her brother and Garcia. Her friend's face was white with shock. Her gaze, blank. Pia hadn't even looked at her when Fee had bandaged Ernesto's gunshot wound.

A vicious bump of turbulence had Aznar once again crying out with pain. When the helicopter steadied, his cries died down to low, animal-like moans.

Fee checked her watch. She could give him another dose of pain meds. It was also time to take vitals. A half hour ago his temperature had officially gone from a low-grade temperature to 102 degrees. Low-grade was okay; it was his body working to fight infection. Anything above that meant she was working on a tightrope without a net. So, she'd give him another dose of Keflex and cross her fingers it would help enough to keep him alive to get him to the surgeon Chavez said was waiting on their arrival.

Hell, at this point, she'd take a first-year surgery resident as long as he came with a lab, an X-ray machine, and a surgical suite. She didn't like losing patients.

She unstrapped herself. Chavez stirred instantly. "*La zorra...*"—which literally translated as fox, but his tone indicated he used it as slang for bitch. It definitely wasn't an endearment.

Chavez's growled admonishment pissed her the hell off. She turned in her seat and glared at the man who'd made it clear with every word, touch, and look since they'd started this nightmarish trip that she only had two uses: keeping Aznar alive and as Chavez's next sex toy.

"Listen, I can't ask permission each time I determine my patient, your boss, needs help. So let me do my fucking job."

The backhand to her face was quick and vicious, knocking her sideways. She broke her fall by grabbing onto the edge of the gurney. Chavez pulled her up with a casual strength that scared the hell out of her and turned her around to face him. He gripped her shoulders so hard she swore the bones crunched.

Fee inhaled sharply. Chavez's expression was livid. His acid yellow eyes had turned dark with his rage. "Watch your tongue, *puta*. You will treat me with respect." He shook her. "Do not ever forget I hold your life in my hands."

Fee took two full breaths and worked her jaw. Just bruised,

but she wasn't sure that side of her face could take the brunt of his anger again without something breaking.

Oddly enough, she was more pissed than scared at his latest aggression. But respect? Never. But she would have to be careful … be smarter than Chavez in order to survive.

Trey and Price could even now be on their way to rescue them. She wanted to be alive when they arrived.

Aznar moaned.

Chavez thrust her from him and began to unstrap. "See to your patient."

Fee mentally prepared herself to be braced against Chavez's body as she cared for Aznar. Unfortunately, it was a necessity. The first time she'd unstrapped to work on her patient, she'd bounced off the cabin wall when the chopper hit rough air. Chavez had used his body to buffer her from the worst of the bumps. When she'd cringed away from him, he'd threatened to have Garcia slice Pia's face if Fee didn't allow him to touch her. It was that first time he'd made it clear she was to tell him each time before she moved about the cabin.

She'd do what she felt necessary to treat her patient. Besides, why should Chavez care if her body was black and blue from bouncing around the helicopter cabin? The bastard would rape her with or without accompanying contusions. Maybe if she was one big bruise from top to bottom, he wouldn't desire her any longer.

Fat chance. The beast's got your scent now. He'll harry you until he gets what he wants.

Just like Adam-fucking-Stall.

Fee grabbed the handle on the cabin wall to steady herself, then shuffled the two steps to the gurney and dropped to her knees beside the unconscious cartel leader. She touched his forehead with the back of her hand and swore under her breath. If anything, he was hotter than the last time she'd taken his temperature.

"What is wrong?" Chavez knelt behind her, fencing her in with his loathsome bulk. "He is very red. Sweating. Is it the pain or is—"

"Hush up and give me a second," Fee snapped. Chavez's body stiffened behind her and she prepared to be hit again, but he didn't do or say anything. Letting out a shaky breath, she took her patient's pulse. "Shit, shit, shit. Way too fast."

She then took Aznar's temp using the ear thermometer from the kit. Her stomach pitched at the number. It was 104. It had gone up two more degrees.

Chavez took the thermometer from her and grunted. "Talk to me. What do you need?"

"What do I need? I need a fucking hospital with a surgeon and an infection disease specialist—now. An hour ago would've been better." She angled her head and looked at him. "The gut wound is infected."

The helicopter took that moment to bounce around like The Beast roller coaster at King's Island Amusement Park.

Fee inhaled and swallowed the bile that threatened to rise up as she was bounced back and forth between the gurney and Chavez's body, then her stomach hit the edge of the gurney extremely hard and at a bad angle. She cried out in pain and tried to keep from continuing forward to fall on top of Aznar who screamed from pain and a fever-induced delirium.

"*Mierda.*" Chavez grabbed her and angled his body to keep her from being tossed onto his boss.

Finally, the helicopter pilot found calmer air and the chopper stopped its rabid jumping bean imitation.

"Thanks." Fee panted through the pain in her upper abdomen just under her ribs. When she could take a full breath without wanting to bawl, she shoved out of Chavez's hold and turned her attention back to Aznar. "Since I have *none* of what I need, get me all the gel ice packs from the two kits, two more doses of the Keflex…"

So what if she killed his kidneys with an overdose of antibiotics. If she didn't get his fever down, the infection would finish him off. "… and try to keep me from flying around the damn cabin."

Chavez grunted, then muttered, "Just keep him alive. We have what is needed at the *castelo* in Madera."

The castle in Madera?

God, how would Trey and her brother find them? The clues she'd left had been so general.

Have faith in SSI. Keely will figure it out. Trey and Price will come.

Yeah, Keely Walsh-Maddox was a genius. Chavez and his cartel home boys had to have left a trail of clues for Trey's sister-in-law to follow. It was just a matter of time.

"Then you'd better get us there in a hurry. He's out of time," Fee said.

Time also wasn't on her and Pia's side. Chavez had made it clear in gut-turning detail how he'd bed her. Fee didn't want to think what might happen to Pia, a woman Chavez seemed to have no interest in other than using her as a hostage against Fee's cooperation.

So, once Fee was on the ground and had gotten a lay of the land, she and Pia would do what all good prisoners are obligated to do—try to escape.

"What can I do, Fee?" Pia's soft voice came out of the darkness. Those were the first words friend had uttered since they'd left New Mexico.

"Just stay strapped in, Pia. Chavez has enough medic training to assist and seems to know how to ride with the air currents. No need for both of us to be black-and-blue."

"To hell with that, Fee. You need me. I'm there." Pia sounded mad and that was much better than frightened, shocked silence.

"*Mi hermana*, do as the doctor says." Ernesto's words were not quite as slurred as they'd been earlier that evening. He was finally coming down off whatever drug he'd taken. She'd given him nothing for his wound on Chavez's orders.

Pia looked at her brother and hissed, "Shut up, Ernesto. You have no rights over me any longer. You hit *nuestra madre*. You brought your cartel business buddies to my friend's house." She turned away from him. "You are no longer *mi familia*."

"Pia…" Ernesto pleaded.

"Shut up, Lopez," Chavez ordered. "He hit his mother?"

Fee almost laughed at the look of disgusted shock on the face of a ruthless cartel enforcer. Guess, it was true—even bad men could love their mothers.

Since Pia didn't answer, Fee did. "Yes, she has two cracked ribs and a severely bruised hip."

Ernesto moaned and closed his eyes. Now, he felt bad. *Asshole*.

"*Mierda*." Chavez handed her the two doses of the antibiotics she asked for and then he began activating the gel packs and packing Aznar's body with them.

After injecting the meds into the IV, she pumped up the blood pressure cuff. "Shit." She took the pressure again. "Fuck. I thought we had him stabilized, but the pressure is dropping again." With all the jostling, she shouldn't be all that surprised that the bleeding was worse.

"What can we do?" Chavez asked.

"What we're doing. Keep pushing fluids and antibiotics. Only a surgeon can help him now—if he doesn't bleed to death first," she mumbled under her breath. "How far are we from this surgeon you promised?"

"Fifteen minutes or so," Chavez replied, a grim look on his face.

Aznar choked, gasped, stiffened, and then went limp.

"Shit, fuck, shit. He doesn't have fifteen minutes." She pushed Chavez away from her and then climbed over Aznar and began chest compressions. "Someone needs to bag him."

"I'll do it." Chavez grabbed the bag from the kit and picked up her rhythm, giving Aznar air as Fee fought for the life of a murdering drug dealer.

CHAPTER 6

Trey stood next to Levi and stared at a body who'd been in the wrong place at the wrong time. He and Levi had arranged to meet Price and the rest of the SSI backup team at this remote ranch from which the cartel had taken off a little over two hours ago for the approximately two-hour chopper flight to Madera.

Keely's appropriation of intel from two different spy satellites, neither of them belonging to the United States, had given them highly accurate intel. Photos of the landing at the ranch by what looked to be a Mexican Army Black Hawk helicopter had occurred right around the time Trey had arrived at Fee's house. The U.S. Border Patrol and Homeland Security had no fucking clue what was going on in this no-man's land blind spot along the border. If the Mexican government had a clue on their side, Trey would be very much surprised.

When he and Levi had arrived to await the SSI team, they'd found five agitated horses hovering around the man's body as if guarding it. They'd urged the horses into the corral to the side of the barn and shut the gate.

Levi spoke into his walkie-talkie. "Get the crime scene crew and the coroner out to Joe Blanca's ranch. Yes, now, Charlene. The buzzards have already been at him." Levi looked to the star-filled, moonless, night sky and mouthed, "Why me, Lord?"

Trey bit back a totally inappropriate under the circumstances chuckle. But he'd met Charlene when he'd first stopped by the Luna County Sheriff's office not long after Fee had moved to New Mexico. Charlene looked to be about twenty years old and had purple hair with blue streaks and more piercings than a heavy metal band. Her accent was all New Jersey as was her attitude. Why the girl had moved to the middle of fricking nowhere New Mexico, he hadn't asked, but she had a lot to learn about dead bodies and wilderness conditions.

"Charlene, you also need to figure out where Joe's wife is and get someone to her to break the news." He turned to look at Trey. "Yes, Duke's in charge while I'm in the field. Then learn to get along with him for my sake, okay? Roger that and out."

"*In the field?*" Trey walked toward the corral. The horses needed fed. "When are you going to break it to them that 'in the field' translates going AWOL for a while?"

Levi paced him. "Called Duke while you were coordinating shit with your people. He knows what's going on and will cover for me as long as he can." He opened the gate and let Trey precede him, then closed it. The horses eagerly nudged the two men. "I wanted to be ready to go when our transport and backup got here."

They petted the horses who were still upset from the smell of recent death on top of being hungry. "Joe was probably getting ready to feed the stock when the helicopter landed. They shot him down like a dog."

Trey followed Levi into the barn. "You know what that means, right?"

"We go in hard and don't take names."

"Roger that," Trey said.

Levi's expression was fierce as he put his foot on the first rung of the ladder to the loft where the alfalfa was stored. "I'll toss out enough hay so Joe's wife won't have to worry about it for a while."

"It's the least we can do." Trey climbed up after Levi. His satphone buzzed with a text push. After he stood in the hay loft, he pulled his phone off his belt and read the message with grim satisfaction. "Price and the gang just landed in Deming. They're checking out the Black Hawk Ren arranged and loading the gear they brought from Sanctuary. They'll be here soon."

Trey texted in his acknowledgment, added the info about the ranch being a crime scene and that they should land farther away from the outbuildings, and sent it. "With the holes in the radar in this area and the moonless night, we can leave from here without too much notice."

After all, the cartel fucks had done so.

Trey was already mentally composing a terse report to Homeland and the Border patrol about their shitty defense of United States' borders. From information extrapolated from the satellite photos, the cartel chopper pilot hadn't even bothered to fly under the radar, but DJ would.

They could easily, and legally, cross the border and drive to Madera, which was a fairly straight, five-plus hour drive on Mexico Highway 10. However, the area closer to Madera was rugged with mountain roads that were death traps, being narrow with a lot of switchbacks.

Getting in and out of Madera quickly and safely was the goal. A chopper was the most efficient mode of transportation, plus it gave them an offensive advantage, if needed.

"I know a Black Hawk has a 320 nautical mile range and Madera is just over 181 nautical miles away. We'll need to refuel eventually. How are we going to find quality fuel?"

Levi's question was a logical one, but he didn't look all that concerned about it.

"The Black Hawk is fitted with extra tanks. That said, we want that extra fuel for emergencies. That's why after we get there, Tweeter and DJ will be in charge of appropriating fuel and standing by to extract us. Keely has already noted several potential fuel sources."

Levi's mouth widened into an unholy smile. "Shit, just like in Afghanistan. Me and my unit liberated a lot of things while doing recon."

The sheriff's classified Army file had been interesting reading. Levi had been a Ranger and a damn good one with enough privately awarded medals and commendations to bling up his dress uniform if he'd been allowed to wear them openly. He'd participated in some black ops for SOCOM just as Trey had during his time with Force Recon. Trey bet Ren was already figuring a way to recruit the talented Native American for SSI.

"I know Price." Levi used a pulley system and hooked a large bale of alfalfa and swung it out the double-doors and released it into the corral. The bale burst apart as it hit the hard ground and the horses eagerly began to eat. "But who are Tweeter and DJ?"

"DJ Poe, now DJ Walsh, is a former Army helicopter pilot. I'd trust her flying me into a war zone with shit exploding all around. Several of her military missions are classified, just like some of yours and mine are. She did several tours in the 'Stan and also worked in Central and South America flying support in the joint missions to halt drug trafficking from the South American cartels into the U.S."

Levi's grunt was approving. He hooked another bale with Trey's help and sent it out the hay mow door as he had the previous one.

"And this Tweeter?" Levi sat at the edge of the open hay mow and stared at the sky. "And what the fuck kind of name is that?"

"Tweeter's a tech genius. His real name is Stuart Walsh, but DJ usually calls him Ace." Trey chuckled. "He might be the youngest of Keely's brothers and may not have gone into the military like his four older brothers and his dad, but he's had as much training as a Force Recon Marine. His dad is Lt. Colonel Kennard Walsh who has kicked more than a few Marine trainee butts in his day. Tweeter's also a pilot, both rotor and fixed wing, plus a damn good mountaineer and rock climber. He married DJ several weeks ago, and they just returned to the States from their honeymoon. I'd trust both of them with my life and, more importantly, with Fee's."

Levi turned to look at him. "That's good enough for me." He pointed toward the northeast. "Your people are coming. Let's get down there and meet them."

CHAPTER 7

March 23rd, 9:30 p.m.
El Hacha's Compound, Madera, Mexico

As soon as the helicopter landed, the gurney was off-loaded and Fee resumed doing chest compressions straddling Aznar's body as Chavez ran alongside. After the gurney was shoved into a small brightly lit building and then into what looked to be a fully equipped surgical suite, Chavez lifted her off Aznar, and several people clothed in scrubs moved in to take over her patient.

This was *her* patient. These people knew nothing of what had or hadn't been done. Her job wasn't complete until she made her report and officially turned over Aznar's welfare to another qualified medical professional. She hadn't worked to the point of exhaustion to keep him alive to fall down on her professional responsibilities at this point.

With no sleep in over twenty-four hours and no food since the half-eaten breakfast burrito she'd had that morning, Fee was operating on sheer pigheadedness and a dyed-in-the-wool sense of duty.

"Let go." She shrugged off Chavez's hold. "I have to give the medical personnel a report on the patient."

"I say your job is done now." Chavez placed an arm around her waist, pulled her more tightly against his body, and then fondled her ass. "I have other uses for you."

The world faded in and out as the heat of nausea swept over her, but she'd be damned if she let this bastard tell her what to do. Plus, she'd rather collapse in a dead faint than allow him to touch her.

"Fuck you. Let … me … go." She jerked away from him and stumbled three short steps toward the man who looked to be in charge of her patient.

Chavez swore viciously as he followed closely on her heels. "Report to Dr. Vasilov, quickly."

And she did so.

While Fee turned her patient over to Dr. Vasilov, Chavez came to stand next to her, his body touching her, shoulder to hip. She inched away.

Chavez growled. "Do not move away from me."

His barely leashed rage felt like a fire storm licking over her skin.

Dr. Vasilov winced and shook his head at her. Was he warning her?

Fuck, Fee. Cool your jets. Even this guy knows not to tempt a raging lunatic. You need to be in condition to run if help arrives.

When help arrived. Trey would come. She knew it with every molecule of her being.

"Doctor, thank you for your report. I have this." Dr. Vasilov's English was excellent and spoken with an Eastern European or Russian accent. "Go, rest … eat … or you will be my next patient."

Fee acknowledged his advice and the unspoken warning with a slight tip of her head, then turned to walk away. She wobbled as her knees gave way and dizziness overwhelmed her. The reserve energy upon which she'd been operating since well before they'd left the States had finally run out. The world fell away in a kaleidoscope of colors and flashes of light and finally into darkness. She hit the ground hard.

———

March 24ᵗʰ, just before dawn

FEE AWOKE SLOWLY. HER BRUISED body twinged and throbbed as she shifted position. She was lying on a comfortable mattress and was covered by a thick comforter. Smooth linen sheets were soft against her skin—all her skin.

She was naked. Vulnerable. Just as she'd been ten months ago and thousands of miles away. She was at the mercy of yet another ruthless male, and there was no one to help her—

No. This time help is coming. Hold on.

Fighting to halt the panic fluttering along every nerve ending, she forced herself to breathe slowly. With her eyes closed and her pulse pounding not quite as loudly in her ears, she reached out with her other senses to determine if she was alone.

She wasn't. There was someone there—watching her. She heard his breaths as he patiently waited for his prey to move. Scented his lust in the sweat and sexual pheromones his body put off. He was too fucking close. If she moved, he'd be on her in a split-second.

"I know you are awake." The ugly sound of his voice scraped over nerves already raw from hours of his company and from her fear and exhaustion.

Rescue coming or not, Fee was terrified to the marrow of her bones. Chavez would rape her now. There was no one to stop him. She wasn't sure she could survive this time.

Stop it. Use your head. Stay calm.

Using her head hadn't saved her the last time.

Different bastard then. Different Fee now. You've been forged in the crucible of violence and came out stronger. You're a survivor.

Fee opened her eyes slightly. There was natural light coming through a set of balcony doors. From the nature of the light she guessed it was just before dawn.

The room was decorated in multiple shades of dark. Heavy wooden furniture. Black drapes. The decor seemed to absorb the light, casting the room in a funereal murkiness. She was in Chavez's room ... in his bed.

A whimper escaped her throat. She closed her eyes. Every muscle in her body was rigid; her hands fisted at her sides. She counted herself lucky he wasn't into raping unconscious women.

"Where's Pia?" Her voice was a croak from lack of use. She sounded weak ... sick. An idea formed of how she might escape his lust ... for a while, maybe even long enough to be rescued ... or to escape.

"She is not your concern. For now, I am your only concern. You will stay in this room until I tire of you."

Asshole. Bastard. Son-of-a-bitch.

"Where's Pia?" Fee opened her eyes wider and turned her head to the right. Chavez sat in a chair next to the bed. Within arm's reach. Far too close.

Chavez was bare to the waist, exposing a scarred torso which documented his violent life. The loose, drawstring pants did nothing to hide his erection. His feral-yellow eyes gleamed with a blatantly foul lust.

Fee tugged the covers farther up her body as if they could shield her from his repellant gaze and touch.

"Where's Pia?" Her voice was even more of a croak.

Her repeated question irritated him.

Stupid to taunt a wild animal.

Chavez's face darkened. His body went unnaturally still, just like a cat right before it leapt and clamped its teeth around its prey's neck. "She is safe—assisting Dr. Vasilov with *mi jefe's* care."

A small sense of satisfaction warmed her chilled bones. She'd forced him to answer her question. She was still scared spitless of what he might do to her, but refused to go down without some sort of fight.

Chavez hadn't realized it yet, but she'd figured out how to play him and would continue to do so for all she was worth.

Fee coughed … and coughed until she choked. An easily triggered cough reflex had been the bane of her existence growing up. A sign of weakness, her father had called it. Now, it just might be a factor in saving her sanity … her life.

Chavez frowned, then rose and moved closer. "What is wrong with you?"

Still coughing and choking—soon to be followed by gagging—and her eyes watering, she weakly flapped a hand.

"*Mierda.*" He stripped the covers away from her, then climbed onto the bed and covered her body with his.

Trapped. She was trapped. Her body froze even as she struggled to breathe between coughing fits.

"Stop it, *puta.* I will have you. Now."

Don't just lie there, dummy.

Fee tried to shove him off. He was too heavy, too strong. She was weak, always too weak to save herself.

Moaning in the back of her throat, she tried to say "no," but nothing came out.

Chavez caught her flailing hands and trapped them above her head with one of his. He used his other hand to grab and maul her breasts until she managed a weak scream at the pain. Her scream quickly dissolved into gagging on the bile his touch had roused.

It could've been seconds or minutes, but it seemed like hours as he pinched and pawed her skin from her breasts to her mound.

When he untied the string on his pants and released his erection to slide along her labia, she heaved. Finally. She turned her head and threw up over the side of the bed.

"*Hijo de puta.*" Chavez leapt off her as if she had leprosy.

She'd never been so thankful for her sensitive gag reflex in her life. Curling on her side, she hugged herself and rocked—and tried not to hack up a lung. Her body, covered in a cold sweat, shook with uncontrollable tremors.

Chavez yanked her head back by her hair and touched her forehead with the back of his hand. "You have a fever. Your skin is breaking out in red splotches." A curse of pale Celtic skin, but he didn't need to know that. "You are sick."

Anh, wrong answer, you freaking bastard. But keep right on thinking that way.

"*Pinche caborron.*" He let go of her hair and moved away as if she were a plague carrier. "I will call the doctor. If you are faking, *puta*, my men will have you after I am done with you. All of them."

Never. Fee would run into the wilds of Mexico, naked, before she let any of that happen.

"Doctor Vasilov," Chavez snapped into the phone. "The doctor *puta* has a fever. You must check her over again." He ended the call and shoved the phone into a pocket.

Again? She shook her head in denial. "No—"

The doctor would know she wasn't sick.

Chavez stood near the bed, a foreboding expression on his face. Far too quickly, a sharp knock sounded. Her doom was near.

"Enter," Chavez shouted as he kept a sharp and wary eye on her.

The doctor who'd taken over Aznar's care entered the room with an old-fashioned doctor's bag in his hand. His concern was evident in his expression. "Doctor Teague, I understand you are still not well."

Still? What had he told Chavez about her earlier fainting spell? Could the doctor be her savior and not her destroyer?

"I…" She coughed until she curled on her side again and hugged her aching abdomen.

"She has coughed like that since she woke up," Chavez told the doctor. "Fix her."

Doctor Vasilov hummed under his breath and opened his bag. "I would like to examine my patient in private, please."

Chavez grunted. "Very well. I will be in my office," he eyed Fee and added, "next door. Make it fast." He strode out of the room, his anger and frustration evident in his rigid posture.

"Bastard," she muttered under her breath, then inhaled sharply as she glanced at the doctor to see his reaction.

Vasilov held a finger to his lips and then subtly pointed to his ears, then circled his hand to encompass the room.

The room was bugged. No wonder Chavez had acquiesced to leaving her alone so easily with the doctor. The bastard was listening.

The doctor had warned her because ... because why?

Good question. She had to be cautious. Dr. Vasilov might be willing to help her and Pia escape, or he could lure her into a trap set by Chavez. Only time would tell.

Warily, she touched her eye, asking if it was visual also. He nodded, one small movement of his head.

"He kidnapped me and Pia, you know."

"Yes. This is not my business." Vasilov pulled out a blood pressure cuff and then put his stethoscope around his neck. "But, Doctor, I must advise you not to push back at Chavez. He has no patience with women who refuse him."

"I understand." And she did, because she'd experienced Chavez's impatience first hand. "I have a man back in the States," she said for the benefit of Chavez or whoever was listening. "He'll raise holy hell, as will my brother, to get me back."

"I have no doubt," Vasilov murmured as he wrapped the cuff around her arm and then pumped it up. "Chavez is no—how you Americans say—slouch. He guards closely what he considers his. And, my dear, you are currently in his keeping, yes? Do not give him cause him to throw you away. I may not be able to fix what he breaks. Now, be silent and let me take your vitals so we can figure out what is wrong with you."

Vasilov's warning was delivered with a solemn expression and flat tone that said he was serious. Shocked by his words, she shushed and wondered how many of Chavez's victims the doctor had not been able to fix.

"90 over 65. Is that normal for you?" he asked.

"Yes."

He nodded and then took her pulse.

"Is Aznar still alive?" she asked to make conversation. Just two doctors talking shop.

"Yes." Vasilov looked up, anger glittered in his eyes and his lips twisted into a grimace. A muscle along his jaw pulsed rapidly. She could almost hear him gritting his teeth.

Body language did not lie. This man wasn't a fan of Aznar or Chavez. Hope took root in her heart.

"And it was all due to you," the doctor continued. "Chavez told me you treated the wounds under primitive conditions with only the contents of some field medical kits. You did a good job. I worked on him for several hours. He is still critical and has a fever."

"Infection in the gut wound," she stated.

"Yes, as it usually is, eh?" A slight smile of shared knowledge crossed his face before turning serious once again. "You kept him alive and that was *all* that should be required of you."

Vasilov's expression revealed he wished she'd let the bastard die. His tone indicated he didn't approve of the situation she now found herself in.

He patted her hand where she had a deadly grip on the comforter. "Now, release the blanket and let me listen to your chest so Chavez doesn't get any angrier with either of us." He stared her in the eye. "You do not want to make him any angrier."

Fee nodded, acknowledging his message. She wouldn't test Chavez's patience. For now. She didn't want what little freedom of movement she might have restricted. If she pissed off Chavez too much, the Mexican would do more than confine her to his bedroom. She tensed at the memories of Stall's fists and the resulting pain, then flashed forward to how Chavez had so casually back-handed her when she'd defied his orders, and—

Stop thinking about the past. Gut it up, cupcake, You need to be totally in the now.

Okay, with the good doctor's help, she would play the role of a sick female until she could escape. But placation could only go so far. She refused to lie back and allow Chavez to rape her.

Fee really needed to talk to Vasilov away from the hidden cameras.

She loosened her hold on the blanket and let Vasilov place the cold stethoscope on her chest. "Have you checked over Pia also?"

"No," he arched a dark brow, "why would I? Chavez has no interest in Señorita Lopez."

Fee mouthed the word "bastard," and Vasilov nodded.

"I'm chilled. I need some clothes. I also want to see my friend to make sure she is okay," Fee said.

"I am sorry, Doctor. You will need to take those issues up with Chavez. Sit forward, so I can listen to your lungs and do percussions on your back."

She gave him her back and he tapped. His concerned "hmm" was loud and confirmed her hope that Vasilov would be proactive in helping her fool Chavez.

"What *hmm*?" She angled her head to look at him. His gaze was reassuring.

"In a second, Doctor." He held up a digital oral thermometer. "Say ahh." She opened her mouth and he placed it under her tongue.

The thermometer beeped and he pulled it out. "Temp is 101."

She widened her eyes—and he shook his head and a slight, twisted smile crossed his lips.

"I didn't like the sound of your lungs." Vasilov winked. He wouldn't have chanced that gesture unless he knew his back was to the cameras. "They are congested."

They weren't. She could breathe just fine, but coughed to play into the diagnosis Vasilov was constructing.

It looks like we have an ally!

Fee touched his hand in gratitude.

Loudly, he said, "I do not like these symptoms, Doctor." He stepped away and replaced his stethoscope and thermometer in his bag. "You may cover yourself and lie back. I will want to take an X-ray and run some blood work. This means a trip across the compound to my clinic. Now, it will be my duty to inform Chavez that you need warm clothing. We can't have you make the trip outside in only your skin, eh?"

Without knocking, Chavez re-entered the room and moved swiftly toward them. "What is your diagnosis, Vasilov?"

Asshole *had* been watching and listening, but he acted as if he hadn't, which made him a Grade-A asshole.

Yeah, Fee planned to milk her "illness" and play Chavez for all she was worth. While she wasn't physically strong enough to take him down—and while his lust scared her to death—she had weapons to use against him now—her brain, her extreme desire to get as far away from him as possible, and an ally.

"Her temperature is elevated. Her lung sounds are suppressed. I need to get some X-rays," Vasilov said.

"Why X-rays?" asked Chavez.

Even to Fee's distrusting eyes, the man looked worried.

He thinks you're Typhoid Fee. He could care less for you.

"Señor Chavez, she could have pneumonia," explained Vasilov. "I need either to confirm or rule that out. If she has pneumonia, I will require further tests to see if it is bacterial and she might need drugs to keep the situation from worsening."

Fee admired how Vasilov qualified every word he uttered. He wasn't lying, exactly, but did paint a picture of her condition as dire as possible.

"Bacteria?" Chavez stepped farther away from the bed. "Take her to the clinic. Run the tests," he ordered. "But she will recover here, in my bed." Where he could keep an eye on her, was left unsaid.

"Understood. Before we do this, she needs clothes and food. She must keep up her strength to recover from the fever," Vasilov said in a humble tone that had Fee coughing into her hand to cover the smile on her lips.

"I will send in warm clothing." He turned to leave and already was issuing orders into his phone.

"She will also need warm boots, Señor. The courtyard stones are cold and slippery this morning from frost. It is well below freezing," Vasilov added, laying it on a bit thick.

"Yes, of course. Some food will be here soon," Chavez added. "See that she eats."

"Yes, I will have a care for her." Vasilov, his back to Chavez, grinned at Fee, a full grin that made him look a lot younger than she'd guessed. He mouthed "cough," and she did so until her eyes watered.

Chavez cursed as he stared at her. "See that you do. She is to get well … quickly." He left the room and slammed the door behind him. He'd definitely shown his hand—he wanted to rape her, but not badly enough to expose himself to any germs she might give him.

For the time being, this meant Fee had the upper hand solely due to the cards Vasilov had slipped her. She planned to bluff the shit out of Chavez to win the game.

"Thank you for *all* your care of me, Dr. Vasilov," she whispered.

"Call me, Anton." He patted her hand where it gripped the covers. "Remember to cough now and then," he muttered in a barely there whisper.

She nodded. "I'm Fee," she offered with the first smile she'd had since before this all started.

"Fee." Anton bowed his head in acknowledgment. "I could do nothing less for a fellow physician." As he finished packing his bag, he leaned over and said in a low monotone, carrying no farther than the two of them, "We'll talk more. Later. Do not worry."

Fee reached for his hand and squeezed it.

Anton pulled away when a knock sounded. The door opened. A maid entered, pushing a cart filled with food—an armed guard on her heels. "Looks as if Chavez thinks you have a large stomach."

Fee's jaw dropped open at the sight of all the food. "I can't eat all that." Then the smells reached her and her stomach growled loudly.

Anton chuckled. "Maybe you can do justice to at least a small portion. I was serious about building up your strength. If I may say, you look as if you haven't been taking very good care of yourself for quite a while."

She frowned, but didn't deny his words. Her appetite had suffered after Stall's attack. The move to New Mexico and a new work situation hadn't helped. In fact, it had only been recently, after the last time Trey had visited, when she'd truly felt hungry for the first time in a long time. "Join me since you *are* supposed to see that I eat. We can talk medicine."

"I could eat." Anton took the cart from the maid and pushed it toward the bed. He stopped and frowned at the floor. He turned to the maid. "Senorita, Doctor Teague has been ill. Please clean the floor and then you may leave us."

The maid nodded. After cleaning the floor, she left. The guard followed the servant out and shut the door, with him on the outside.

"Shall I prepare you a plate?" Anton gestured at the food.

"Um, eggs with chili verde would be nice. And some corn tortillas. I never got to eat the breakfast I'd ordered … God, was it only yesterday morning?"

"It was," Anton nodded. "Get comfortable. I will bring the food to you."

Fee propped herself up in bed, tucking the sheet up around her chest. Her mouth watered and the empty spot in her stomach once again demanded loudly to be fed.

Chuckling, Anton handed her a plate, then went back to the cart and prepared his.

With a good hand of cards in the game to beat Chavez, Fee dug into her food with relish. She didn't fool herself that getting away would be easy, even with Anton's help, so she'd refuel and rest, building the strength she needed to slant the odds even more in her favor.

CHAPTER 8

March 24th, dawn
A valley in the Sierra Madre Occidentals

"Shit, are those what I think they are?" Price leaned over Tweeter's shoulder and pointed at the satellite images of *El Hacha's* place just outside of Madera.

"If you think they're SAM installations," said Tweeter, "then you'd be correct."

"He's got fucking surface-to-air missiles protecting his property?" Levi sounded incredulous.

"And a nifty radar setup also." Tweeter pointed to a building with a large satellite dish. "Not as comprehensive as my 3-D coverage of Sanctuary, but still effective."

Shit. Damn. Fuck.

Trey clenched his jaw until pain shot through his head. Taking a deep breath and forcing his jaw to relax, he scanned the relief map he'd already scanned three times in the last five minutes. Nothing had changed.

To rescue Fee and Pia, they could *not* fly in close to *El Hacha's* compound, hike over fairly level ground, take out a few bad asses, and then scram out of there.—What would've been a piece of cake op in their business.

Instead, they had to remain in this valley outside of the range of the cartel's radar, then hike, climb, and rappel extremely rugged mountain terrain to infiltrate the cartel fortress.

Fuck, just fuck. He hated mountains—had learned to detest them after several tours of duty in the dangerous, desolate mountain war zones of Afghanistan and Pakistan. In fact, this whole operation to save Fee and Pia was beginning to resemble scenes from his worst nightmares of his time in Force Recon. Fuck.

"The air security also means no flyovers to get a closer look," Trey said. "They'd shoot down an unidentified chopper."

Hell, they'd been lucky to find this fallow poppy field in a valley merely two miles away from their destination, well, two miles as a crow flies. There was no telling exactly how many miles or how long it would take to reach the valley in which *El Hacha's* compound was located. Tweeter probably could calculate how far they'd have to travel, but Trey didn't give a flying fuck since the territory had to be crossed no matter how far it was in order to get to Fee.

"Why do we need a closer look?" Levi asked. "Looks pretty damn obvious to me we've got the makings of a clusterfuck no matter how we go in to get our women."

"SSI is all about accurate, up-to-date intel. Saves lives of the operatives and any assets we're hired to retrieve." DJ looked up from field-stripping her assault rifle. "We'll be going in at night, and we sure as hell don't want to have to check every frigging building for the gals." She looked over at her husband. "What is it, Ace ... almost twenty buildings?"

"Twenty-two," Tweeter replied. "And you aren't going. So stop messing with your weapons. You'll be staying with the chopper."

"I'm pregnant, not disabled," she gritted out. "Remember? We talked about this."

Trey figured this would be a regular argument whenever DJ had to go in the field. At least he could end the argument before it grew more heated. "Both of you'll be staying with the chopper. We'll call for extraction once we have the women well away from the compound. DJ, you'll be flying, and Tweeter will cover us from the air."

DJ snorted. "Fine."

"Roger that." Tweeter patted his wife's hand. "And, Trey, we don't need to fly the chopper over the compound to obtain close-in, live surveillance. I'll send in my drone."

"Hate to tell you, buddy, but they'll shoot that sucker down as soon as they see it," Price said.

"Not if they think it's a hawk," Tweeter replied. "I camouflaged it for just such a situation. As long as they don't know their predatory birds and can't distinguish bird species, we're good."

The smartest thing his brother Ren had ever done was marry Keely Walsh, because with Keely came Tweeter. Trey knew of no other private security firm that had two tech geniuses who could translate their innovative ideas into practice.

"Do it," Trey said. "I want eyes on that compound ASAP. It's gonna take us hours to get there. Once we are, as DJ so rightly pointed out, I don't want to be checking out twenty-two buildings in the dark with God knows how many unfriendlies wandering about."

Tweeter nodded and moved to the large duffle he'd brought with him.

As the tech genius began to assemble his drone, Trey turned to Levi. "If you have any issues with slicing throats and breaking necks, speak now, because this will be a silent infiltration and extraction. We don't want to get in a gun battle, if we can avoid it."

Levi patted the knife in a thigh sheath. "No problem at all. How will we get the women to a place of safety? One where the helicopter can land to extract us all? I don't see Fee and Pia climbing and hiking that kind of terrain." He angled his head at the relief map Trey had spread out next to Tweeter's computer tablet. "Hell, we'll have enough trouble making it ourselves."

DJ snorted. "Speaking on behalf of my fellow sisters ... bullshit."

"He has a point, DJ," Trey said.

"You know better, Trey." DJ glared at him. "Keely told me all about Fee and how—despite altitude sickness, lingering injuries from her stalker-rapist, and being scared out of her mind—the city gal did just fine helping a laboring Keely escape and hide in rugged terrain in a freaking snowstorm, and then delivered Riley in a fricking cave. I don't know this Pia, but the gal lives in one of the most violent border towns in the States and most likely has the same kind of grit that Fee does. I'm putting my money on those two gals to do what is needed to escape."

Levi bowed his head. "You have good points, but we have no idea what condition they might be in. By the time we get there, they'll have been held for almost twenty-four hours." He added softly, "Emotional trauma is a very real issue, DJ. Whatever has happened to them will still be immediate with no time for them to process and come to terms with what has happened. They could freeze at the wrong moment."

"I know all about emotional trauma." Her face a blank, it was DJ's eyes that told the story of lingering pain from violence in her past. "I think you're wrong. The instinct to survive trumps everything." She slapped the magazine into her rifle and picked up Tweeter's weapon and began to strip it. "I say Fee and Pia will handle it. Plus, who said they'll hang around and wait on rescue? I wouldn't be surprised if they aren't already plotting to get away on their own. I would be. Y'all had better factor that in and be thinking about where they might run."

"Shit," Price said. "DJ's right. That's exactly what Fee would do." He laughed, a slightly bitter sound. "After all, my stubborn-as-a-mule sister dealt with the douchebag Stall on her own. Pissed me off big time. But, hell, it showed my baby sister had guts and inner strength no one in the family even suspected she had. How about Pia?" He turned to Levi.

The frown on Levi's face said it all. "Yes, Pia has the same kind of stubborn strength. That woman has kept me at arm's length for months, even though I've offered time and again to shoulder her and her mother's burdens. Pia's survived living with her drug-trafficking father and her no-good, cartel-wanna-be brother. She's seen violence and its aftermath first-hand every day. Yeah, she'd be planning an escape."

The consensus that the women would try to escape struck fear into Trey's heart. He didn't want to think about Fee fleeing into the treacherous wilderness surrounding Madera.

Dammit, Fee, you have to know I'd come get you. Stay put, little doc. And if you can't stay put, stay safe. I'll find you no matter where you are.

"Fuck. Just fuck." Trey looked at Tweeter, who had a halfway realistic-looking hawk drone ready to go. "Get me eyes on that compound. I'll want reports hourly, more often if you see any activity that might indicate they're moving the women or that the women might've escaped."

Tweeter nodded.

"Price, Levi ... load up." Trey eyed the other men. "Check your coms." Each man clicked their headsets. "Right. Let's go get our women."

Levi emitted an ululating war cry that echoed off the steep mountain walls surrounding the isolated field. He shrugged at the startled glances he received. "Apache war cry."

Yeah, it was war.

"Hoo-rah," Trey shouted. Price added the SEALs battle cry, and they were off. Each man carried eighty pounds of gear and weapons. While they might now be civilians, they'd been trained by the best armed forces in the world and had reached the elite status of Spec Ops. They were warriors honed in battle.

El Hacha's people wouldn't know what hit them.

After breakfast, El Hacha's compound

ANTON HELD ONTO FEE'S ARM and put on a good show of assisting her to his clinic. An armed guard was about three yards behind them.

"Lean on me and don't forget to cough now and then," Anton muttered. "We can talk now. The guard does not speak English well, plus as long as we keep our voices down, he won't hear anything to memorize and repeat to Chavez."

"Are you going to help me and Pia?" she asked, matching his tone and volume. Then she coughed, her breath frosty in the cold mountain air.

"Yes."

Fee's knees went weak with relief and she stumbled. Anton swore and shifted his arm around her waist, but kept them moving toward the small building where Aznar had been taken last night before.

"Your friend is in more danger than you," he muttered close to her ear. "Chavez is giving her to his men. Tonight, they will fight to win their position in line to rape her."

"No-o-o," Fee moaned and latched onto the arm Anton had around her waist. Just as she thought her fake illness had bought them both some time, the rug was pulled out from under her. "Has she…?"

She couldn't finish the sentence. And where in the hell was Pia's worthless brother while all this was happening?

"She is fine … for now. She is under guard in the clinic and being forced to nurse *El Hacha*. Our patient is not doing well. He will be air-lifted to Mexico City soon."

"Pia—"

"Shh. I will have her moved to the main house to nurse you through your illness," Anton said. "It should buy her some safety until the fights tonight. Chavez will never back off his promise to his men. He often buys their continued loyalty in such a way."

"Thank you." Fee couldn't help the quiver in her voice. He was putting himself on the line for them. "How can I ever repay you?"

"No, thanks are needed." Anton lowered his voice even more. "And I will be calling in repayment immediately. I will help you escape this evening *before* Pia is endangered. All I ask is that you take my pregnant fiancee Lucia with you. No one here knows about us. I must get her away before anyone learns of our love."

She looked up at him. "Of course she can come with us. But what about you?"

"Do not worry about me. You three are more important. Lucia and I have prepared a hiding place for just such a day. I will remain in the compound until your men come to rescue you." He added darkly, "If they come."

"They'll come." Fee took in his frowning countenance. This man didn't have much faith in his fellow man. There was a story there, but it would have to wait for another time. "I expect they're already on their way."

"How would they know where to look?" Anton inquired.

Her lips twisted into a slight smile. "I left them clues. They know in general where we are and who has us. The company my…"

What was Trey? Boyfriend seemed too tame.

"…man owns with his brother has intelligent community resources. He'll probably know within a half mile or less where I am."

Anton's expression was questioning and more than a bit skeptical. "Then as soon as they arrive, I will lead them to you and Lucia … and we'll all escape Mexico together." He stiffened and Fee realized the guard was closer than before. "Fall down," he hissed.

Fee pretended to trip over her feet, and Anton scooped her into his arms. Over his shoulder, he ordered in perfect Spanish, "Fool, she has fainted. Run ahead and open the door."

The man hurried to do Anton's bidding.

Anton followed the man at a steady pace. He whispered against her ear. "See the small building to our left? Closer to the trees?" She found it and nodded. "At eight o'clock this evening, you and your friend will knock out your door guard then inject him with a light anesthetic I will provide you. Then you will escape out of the back of the house. The security lights will be out. Lucia and I will meet you at that building. She will lead you to some ancient cliff dwellers ruins about a mile from here. You will be safe until I lead your men there."

"Won't Chavez suspect your involvement once he discovers Pia and I are gone?" Fee whispered.

"No. There will be an outside distraction." Anton stopped speaking as they approached the guard holding the door open. He instructed the man, "Stay here and keep everyone out."

The guard nodded and closed the door behind them.

Anton walked to the end of a small hallway and placed her on an exam table in a room set up as a small lab. He shut the door and locked it. "I sweep for bugs every day. We can speak here."

"The distraction … what is it?" she asked.

He pulled the portable X-ray over to the side of the exam table. "After you join up with Lucia, you will wait at the meeting spot until Chavez and his men pursue a vehicle that will tear out of the compound around eight o'clock also." He lips thinned. "Pia's brother will lead Chavez and his men out of the valley while you hike to the cliff houses."

"But that's … that's a suicide mission," Fee stuttered, a sick feeling in her stomach. She didn't like Ernesto, but she didn't want him dead. She didn't want anyone dead. "Will Ernesto have any chance of getting away alive?"

"First, Ernesto came to me. This was his plan." Anton shrugged. "He is aware of the risks and will take every precaution to remain alive. He is cunning, that one. He has plans to cover his escape by faking his death. He has money and weapons. He knows how to live off the land. Eventually, he will head for an obscure border crossing and re-enter the U.S."

"You believed him? Trusted him?" she asked. "You don't think he's setting a trap?"

"Yes, I believed him. He was sober for a change. His voice rang with truth when he admitted he was ashamed of his actions. Said he'd never have led Chavez to you if he had known Chavez would bring you both here and hand his sister over for a gang raping."

"He should've thought of that before," Fee snarled. "Before he endangered both of us."

"You are correct, but I take it he was high on drugs at the time."

Fee nodded.

"His brain was not processing." Anton shrugged. "As soon as Ernesto came down and realized what was actually happening, he knew he had to get both of you away tonight." His face darkened. "I've treated the women who've managed to survive being used by these animals. Several committed suicide. Others have tried to escape and were killed. Others are imprisoned here and still being treated as sex slaves."

Fee shuddered and couldn't help recall the first moments after Stall had beaten and raped her; she'd considered ending it all. The pain and degradation had thrown her into a deep, dark pit of despair. But the will to survive and sheer Teague stubbornness had her fighting back.—Yes, she'd run clear across the country and had abandoned her home and job, but it was what she had to do to come through the darkness and out the other side. The process of rebirth had taken her months, aided by the patient, long-distance wooing of a real man, a good man … of Trey.

Silently, she vowed to find a way to help the women being kept here against their will. But she could only do that after she escaped.

Anton patted the table. "Lie back. Let me take an image. Your lungs did sound a bit congested, maybe due to the change in altitude. Since this is digital, I can enhance the image to cloud your lung in case Chavez asks to see."

Fee lay back on the table. Remembering the delivery of Keely's baby in a cave, she wondered if history would repeat itself this evening with Lucia, but this time without any of the equipment and modern conveniences SSI considered essential for a cave on their property. "How far along is your Lucia?"

"Three months. Do not worry. She is very healthy. We need to leave Madera before she begins to show." Anton positioned the unit for a PA chest view and retreated behind the windowed-lead panel and took the image, which immediately showed up on a computer monitor on the counter. "She is *El Hacha*'s niece."

Fee inhaled sharply. "Well, hell. That complicates things."

"Yes. He doesn't know we are in love. He thinks she is still a virgin." Anton's love for Lucia was evident on his face, in his voice.

He walked to the computer, tapped some keys, and moved the mouse around a bit as he continued with his story. "I met her in Mexico City where I did my residency. She came into the ER while I was covering for a friend. She had a nasty cut. She's a chef and had sliced her thumb instead of a tomato. We dated, fell in love, and had planned to get married when her uncle called her home for a family emergency."

Anton's face turned dark with anger. "Her uncle had arranged her marriage to one of his men. Thankfully, the man was stupid and got himself killed by an irate father of a young girl he'd raped. But Lucia was stuck here. Her uncle saw her as a bargaining piece to buy loyalty among his lieutenants. We couldn't chance him finding another marriage candidate, so I came to Madera and started a clinic. I made sure I came to *El Hacha*'s attention. He sees himself as a feudal lord and was easily convinced he needed a personal physician. So here I am."

Fascinated, Fee stared at him. "Did you even have an exit plan before she became pregnant?"

He nodded. "She was due to visit relatives in the States next year for Cinco de Mayo. I'd planned to take an overlapping vacation to see my mother in the States. But the pregnancy was an accident—and so I began preparing a safe place to hide and plotted our eventual escape route."

"What if Aznar had discovered your romance before now?"

Anton made a chopping motion across his throat.

Fee's stomach turned. So the stories she'd read about how Aznar had gotten his nickname were true. "I should've let him die."

"No, you couldn't have." Anton's voice was gentle and filled with understanding. "You, like me, believe in the oath we swore as doctors. We let others take care of justice, eh?"

"Yes, we do." Fee thought of men like her brother and Trey—like Levi Gray Wolf—men who fought everyday to protect innocents from filth such as Aznar, Chavez, and men who used young women as objects of their base desires.

A hammering knock on the door had them both jumping.

"Coming," Anton shouted. "My patient isn't decent." He helped her into the sweater she'd worn for the trip to the clinic and then pulled the sheet up. "Just lie still. Cough, act frail." He pointed to the doctored image on the monitor. "Remember, you are very ill."

Fee turned her laugh of surprised delight into a cough. He'd occluded three-quarters of her left lung. "Pneumonia?"

He nodded. "We'll call it bacterial pneumonia. Can you play this role for the next few hours?"

"I'll handle it." She'd deliver an Oscar-worthy performance and play the invalid to the hilt while resting up for the night ahead. "Send Pia to me?" she whispered.

"Yes. I will." Anton then moved to unlock and open the door to a pissed-off Chavez. "Ahh, Señor, just in time. Doctor Teague has bacterial pneumonia."

"This is contagious?" Chavez asked and backed away as Fee coughed, spewing moisture into the air. A talent she'd used growing up to freak out her older, germ-phobic sister.

"Yes. She needs to be watched closely while I perform my clinic duties." Anton looked at Chavez. "I would ask that Señorita Lopez care for the patient."

"*Sí*, it will be done." Chavez turned to the man who'd stood guard. "Escort Señorita Lopez here to assist Doctor Vasilov."

"*Sí, El Halcón.*" The guard headed toward another portion of the clinic.

Chavez eyed Fee from across the room. "She will get well?"

"Yes. I have started her on some antibiotics for the infection and administered acetaminophen for the fever," Anton lied with a straight face. "Her left lung is filled with fluid and air." He pointed to the image on the monitor. "It will resorb, but for now, she needs to take it easy and not stress her body, or her lung might collapse. I would rather not have to drain her lung."

"How long?" Chavez's rapacious stare never left her.

Fee didn't have to pretend to be weak or frail since the man's single-minded focus scared the bejesus out of her.

Anton shrugged. "It is hard to tell, maybe four weeks."

"Make it happen in less time, Doctor, or…" Chavez's growled threat trailed off as he turned to leave. "She will recover in my suite."

"I will escort her there myself." Anton bundled Fee into some blankets and scooped her off the table, then carried her out of the clinic. The armed guard arrived with Pia and accompanied them to the main house.

This evening's escape plan was a temporary fix.

True escape would be when Fee and the others were far away from Aznar's compound and then out of Mexico. The more quickly that was achieved, the better. While Anton was proving to be a godsend, she wasn't sure about his ability to get three women out of the rugged mountainous area. They definitely needed more help.

Hurry, Trey. I really need a hero right about now.

CHAPTER 9

March 24th, dusk
In the mountains

After a hellacious day of hiking rugged mountain terrain that only a mountain goat would love, then climbing and rappelling mountain walls like human spiders, Trey lay on his stomach at the edge of a steep escarpment. Every muscle in his body screamed with strain and fatigue, but he pushed the feelings away.

Gut it up, asshole.

Hoo-rah.

Trey aimed a pair of powerful computerized binoculars at *El Hacha's* compound in a valley over a mile away and one thousand feet below him. He didn't even want to think about the hiking and rappelling yet to come. Of course, the cartel asshole would find the most remote valley in Mexico surrounded by sheer mountain walls.

Quit your bellyaching. Fee is down there, and there is where you're gonna have to go.

Tense, he spoke into the microphone aligned along his jaw. "Sit rep, Tweeter."

"No more visuals on Fee since the video I sent this morning. Keely identified the man who carried Fee from the building as Dr. Anton Vasilov. He is reputed to be *El Hacha's* personal physician. The man who stormed out before Fee and Pia exited was Raimundo Chavez a.k.a. *El Halcón*, second-in-command over this facility. We've had several visuals of Pia opening and closing drapes on a second-floor room, northeast corner of the main house."

"The main house is our target then." Trey moved the binoculars and located the building and found the window and balcony doors Tweeter had described. The drapes were pulled at the moment.

"It is if they're still there," Price said. "Are they, Tweeter?"

"As far as we can tell," Tweeter said. "I have the drone resting on a shorter building straight across from that set of windows and French doors. There's a light on and I can see movement through the sheer drapes."

"What's our best way into the house?" Trey asked.

"No good one, buddy," Tweeter replied. "There are three extremely alert guards patrolling the house's perimeter." He paused. "DJ has been timing the guards from the live video we have streaming."

"Hey, Trey." DJ's slightly accented voice was filled with concern. "The house perimeter guards are good and motivated…"

Trey thought about *El Hacha's* predilection of chopping off body parts of those who failed him, so the guards being motivated was understandable.

"…no slacking off. No playing with cell phones or taking a break to smoke. Just regular, like clockwork, overlapping patrols. So, when breaching the house, you're gonna have to take them all out at once and then pray no one notices until you've got the gals out."

"Shit. Think we could get on the roof between guards and rappel onto the balcony?" Trey asked.

"Might be an option," DJ said. "From the last time Ace had the drone circle the house, the back was all dark. Unlike the front and sides which are lit up like Christmas. So the back looks to be your better choice."

"We'll keep both options on the table." Trey stiffened as he swept the binoculars over the compound and his gaze froze on one area. "There seems to be a lot of activity centered around the building on the far northwest side of the compound."

Men were laughing and slapping each other's backs as they entered what might be a gym or training facility.

Tweeter coughed. "Uh, yeah, about that ... wanted to wait until you were closer and in position for the last haul, because there's really nothing y'all could do until—"

"Fuck, Tweeter, just spit it out," Price snarled.

Tweeter grunted. "The drone's microphones picked up a conversation earlier this afternoon between two of *El Hacha*'s soldiers. Seems the fucker Chavez is staging a fight club type contest. The last man left standing gets first dibs at Pia, then any still-able participants will follow in descending order. Fucking raping assholes."

Roaring an outcry, Levi surged to his feet. If it hadn't been certain death to descend the mountain without a climbing buddy, the man would've been on his way to the valley.

Trey knew exactly how Levi felt, but hot blood and going off half-cocked would just get them all killed, including the women. What they needed now was ice in their veins and to stick to the plan.

"No mention of Fee?" Trey asked, burying his rage in layers of ice.

"No. The men joked that Chavez was keeping *la pequeña llama*"—the little flame—"for himself." DJ added, "Y'all better get those gals out of there tonight. From what audio we've managed to record, right now, they're safe as houses, but that won't last much longer."

"Then we'd better get to it." Trey moved away from the cliff and then stood up. He looked back at the way they'd come. The trek had taken them from just after dawn until about fifteen minutes ago. He turned and stared at their destination. They still had a dangerous descent and even more rugged and potentially guarded terrain to cross. "Keep that bird warmed up, DJ. If we can't get down in time to avoid Pia being attacked, you'll have to chance an emergency evac."

"Roger that, Trey. We're ready," DJ responded. "We'll have a fighting chance. My brilliant husband has hacked into their radar array and can shut it down at will. He's working on their other security and weapons systems now. Even if they have portable surface-to-air missiles, the chopper has a missile avoidance system. It's a good one since Keely and my husband designed it for the Army. Also, Ace and I brought a few sidewinders with us from Sanctuary and loaded them on the Hawk in Deming, just in case we needed them."

Trey would have absolutely no problem blowing up *El Hacha's* compound and starting a small war if either of the women had been physically harmed.

"Roger that." Trey was extremely grateful the honeymooning couple had returned home early and had been eager to jump into the fray to save Fee.

"We'll keep a close eye on things in the compound," Tweeter said. "Just take care, brother. The drone's doing its job and has hours of more battery life, but—"

Trey hated it when Tweeter hesitated. "But what, Tweeter?"

"The weather's gonna turn bad over this entire region, sooner rather than later. If you don't get the gals out by nine or so, the chopper could be grounded until it blows through. Just sent you the weather report and the current weather radar. High winds. Torrential rain on the level of one to two inches an hour. The river valley you're heading into has a history of flooding. The compound becomes an island according to local reports. Once you get the gals out of the compound, you might have to head to higher ground and hole up in the mountains for the night. Copy?"

"Shit. Copy that. Out." Trey turned to face his team. "We need to get the fuck down there before the weather hits."

The main objective was still the same—to get Fee and Pia under their control. He'd worry about getting the hell out of Madera and Mexico after he made that happen. If the last step didn't happen tonight, so be it. They'd brought survival gear; they'd make do.

"The storm will hit soon. I can smell the moisture," Levi commented as he looked to the sky, a frown on his face. "The winds will be vicious and unpredictable at this altitude. Climbing in this weather will be risky."

"We'll make it," Price said, checking his climbing harness. "Because we have to.""Hell, yeah, we'll make it," Trey said. "Now, let's get off this rock before the sun sets fully and the rain starts. We can reassess our options on how to get the gals out of *El Hacha*'s house once we're in the valley." He also checked over his climbing harness and rope, then checked Levi's. "Keep your eyes open for a good place to shelter, if we need to."

"Roger that," Price and Levi said in unison.

———

Shortly before 8 p.m.
El Hacha's mansion

FEE SAT ON THE BED dressed in warm layers. Pia sat in the chair next to the bed, also dressed in some of the clothing Chavez had provided for Fee at Anton's urging. Both of them had their gazes fixed on the clock.

Maintaining silence due to the listening devices in the room, Fee gave Pia a hand signal out of the sight of the camera.

They stood, then moved as one to the exit. Once there, they were out of the camera's range.

From a table just inside the bedroom door, Pia picked up a heavy lamp as the main weapon to knock out the guard. Fee stood ready with the pressure syringe filled with enough ketamine to keep the man down and from alerting the compound long after they made their escape.

Her hand on the door lever, Fee nodded at Pia, who nodded back. Her friend's eyes were filled with apprehension along with determination.

After Fee opened the door, which was blessedly soundless, Pia didn't hesitate and whacked the guard over the head as he started to turn toward the open door. Her first hit stunned the man who grunted as he went to his knees. Pia's next hit knocked him out. Fee injected the ketamine in his upper arm.

They paused and waited to see if anyone responded to the noise the guard's body had made when falling. After several, breathless seconds, no one had come.

Fee nudged Pia who led the way swiftly down the upper hall and toward the servants' stairs at the back of the house as instructed by Anton. He'd told them the servants hated both Aznar and Chavez and wouldn't interfere.

Fee hoped the doctor was correct, but she had several more ketamine pressure syringes to use if she had to.

Pia held up a hand to signal a halt as they reached the bottom of the stairwell.

Fee came to her side and peeked around the corner and then to the right. There was light and motion in what had to be the kitchen. To the left was a darkened hallway which led to the back entrance of the house. She pointed to the left and they moved out on tip-toes as quietly as possible toward what she hoped would be their freedom.

Fee's rapid pulse pounded loudly in her ears. Her breaths were shallow and emitted as harsh gasps as tension and the fear of the unknown took her over. If they didn't get out soon, she'd faint from the stress.

When Fee reached the exterior door, she rested her head against the cool wood and attempted to control her breathing.

Get your head in the game. You can't give in to fear now.

"Fee?" Pia's strained murmur brought it all home.

If she didn't regain control, it wouldn't only be her that suffered, it would also be Pia at the hands of Chavez's men.

Fee turned and attempted a smile, then mouthed, "I'm okay."

Pia laid her forehead on Fee's shoulder and stifled a sniffle.

Fee opened the back door a crack. The rear of the house was dark just as Anton promised. She saw no one, heard nothing, so she exited, keeping a syringe at ready. Pia slid out behind her. The door closed with a quiet *snick*.

Motioning with her hand, Fee headed for the small outbuilding Anton had shown her earlier today. A flash of lightning lit up the area. A guard stood about ten feet in front of her, his back to them.

Fee stopped like a deer in headlights and held her breath. She prayed he wouldn't turn around. For several long seconds, neither she nor Pia moved; they stood there, paralyzed.

Thunder boomed, startling her, still Fee couldn't make her feet move. Thank the gods, Pia grabbed her arm and tugged her into the shadows of a small building and behind some shrubbery just as another guard came around the corner of the main house. He approached the other man.

The two conversed in the Spanish of the Mexican-United States border. Fee translated in her head as they spoke.

"The fight is beginning. My money is on Arturo to get first chance at the woman."

"Ernesto is not happy."

"Ernesto is a fucking wimp."

"You are right about that, my friend. Are we the only guards on the house tonight?"

"For the time being. I'd better move or *El Halcón* will strip the skin off my back."

"Or worse—cut off your balls."

The guard muttered a foul prayer then resumed his patrol with a quickened step.

Her legs shaking at the close call, Fee allowed the side of the building to hold her up for a few precious seconds until the other guard also resumed his patrol, following the sidewalk around the other corner of the house.

It was now or never. She turned toward Pia and whispered, "Let's go."

Pia nodded and followed Fee as she headed for the outbuilding illuminated by frequent flashes of lightning as the storm rumbled toward the valley.

"Fee!" Anton's voice came from the dark shadows surrounding the small building. "Over here."

She and Pia ran toward the sound of his voice.

Anton stepped out. At his side, he held a short, beautiful woman who had to be Lucia. "You had no trouble?" he asked Fee.

"Not much."

"Good." Anton turned to look toward the front of the compound. "Ernesto leaves now. It is my cue to interrupt the fight and announce Ernesto has stolen you away. This diversion should give you time to make your way safely across open ground and then up the path to the cliff houses without pursuit."

"Anton?" Lucia's uneasiness was obvious in her strained voice.

"I will be safe, *dushenka*. You lead the women. Be brave for me." Anton kissed her on the lips and rubbed a gentle hand over his fiancee's stomach. "I'll be with you soon. I have too much to live for. Be sure to wait for the mass pursuit of Ernesto and then move out. *Da?*"

"*Sí*," Lucia whispered. "*Te quiero mucho.*"

"And I love you." Anton waved as he melted into the darkness.

CHAPTER 10

Trey signaled for a halt and hunkered down in a stand of trees. Price and Levi moved closer and knelt next to him. They were about forty-six meters away from what Tweeter had determined, after studying hours of footage from the drone, was the outside edge of the patrolled perimeter.

"We're in position. Sit rep, Tweeter," Trey spoke into his headset.

"Most of the men are in the building on the far northwest side of the compound. There are now only two guards patrolling the outside of the main house. There is one guard at the gate, probably more inside the gatehouse we can't see. A vehicle just left the compound and is heading toward Madera. Other than that, the compound seems quiet. Can't tell you who's monitoring any electronic perimeter security they might have or where, but I've managed to hack into their systems and can blind them at any time. I also determined the building Fee was carried out of is their medical clinic."

"Shit," Price said. "Fee could be hurt."

"We'll cross that bridge when we come to it." Trey clenched his jaw and deep-sixed his anger and fears into a dark corner of his mind. Fee—and Pia—needed him at his best. Going off half-cocked as he and the others were about to enter the danger zone wouldn't help either of the women. He sensed Price and Levi locking down their emotions, readying themselves for whatever lay ahead.

"DJ and I can risk the weather and any ground fire if you have injured," Tweeter said. "Chopper is warmed up and fully fueled courtesy of a little breaking and entering at a vacant lumber operation. DJ and I loaded the sidewinders, so we can come in blazing fire."

"Heck, Trey," DJ said. "With Ace shutting down their radar and most of *El Hacha's* men congregated in one place, we could come in, take out the SAM sites, blast some outbuildings, and create a little chaos before they even realize what's going on. Chaos is always a good cover for an extraction."

"My wife speaks the truth. So if you need us, don't hesitate. Just holler." Tweeter's voice was calm and confident. "We can be there in less than fifteen minutes. Fuck the lousy weather."

Fifteen fucking minutes? It had taken them all day to get to this point from the field where the chopper sat, but Trey hadn't seen any other way to get the gals out without getting everyone killed or starting a war with the Sinaloa cartel.

"Heck, yeah," DJ said, sounding almost chipper. "Can't be any worse than the Hindu Kush during a blizzard."

Fuck, wasn't that the truth.

But still … blowing shit up was a last resort. While certain U.S. alphabet agencies and the Mexican president knew they were here, this was still considered a black op. Both governments would deny all knowledge of them and their rescue mission if they were caught by the cartel. If DJ and Tweeter swooped in and began firing upon the compound, the mostly collegial relationship between the U.S. and Mexico could suffer a serious setback.

Tweeter's drone surveillance video had verified the intelligence Keely had gotten from her CIA sources that *El*

Hacha was highly paranoid and had fortified his home and center of operations better than most small countries.

"Roger that." Trey snorted. "We'll holler if we need you."

"Copy that. Good luck. Out," Tweeter said.

Trey looked at the other two. "We all know what we're gonna do?"

Price nodded, "We're going in to get my baby sister and her friend back."

Levi grunted, and Trey took the noise as one of assent.

The sheriff shifted his dark amber gaze between the compound and the skies to the northwest. "We need to do this soon. The weather will worsen quickly."

Trey scanned the skies and grimaced at the cloud-to-cloud lightning over the tops of the mountains. He looked at his watch. "It's 2010 hours." The other men checked their watches. "We'll grab the gals. Hoof it to the safety point Levi pointed out earlier and set up camp. We can then reassess our options for immediate extraction or not." He looked each man in the eye. "We aren't leaving this valley without Fee and Pia."

"Damn straight, we aren't," Price said.

Levi nodded, his thumb stroking the hilt of his sheathed knife.

"Subdue any unfriendlies. If you can't subdue, wipe, don't wound," Trey said, his focus on Levi. Knife work and broken necks could always be chalked up to a rival cartel.

Levi grimaced, but nodded.

Trey understood the lawman's dilemma. But while this might not be a war zone in Iraq or Afghanistan, they were still executing a stealth mission on a smaller scale. None of them wanted an escalation to a bloody battle. But they all recognized *El Hacha's* drug-war-hardened men wouldn't hesitate to kill intruders.

The wind suddenly picked up and buffeted the men in ever-stronger gusts. An ill wind? He prayed not.

Multiple sky-to-ground lightning strikes presaged the storm heading their way. The thunder rumbling ever closer. At least they weren't dangling off cliffs and being battered against basalt mountain walls any longer.

Trey stood. "Head out."

They turned as one and made their way across mostly open meadow, using what few boulders and the occasional tree for cover. They'd reached the protection of a small outbuilding which looked to be used for storage when—

"Trey." Tweeter's voice sounded tense. "All hell just broke loose. The men are evacuating the building on the northwest side and scrambling for vehicles. They're tearing out of the compound and hitting the road to Madera like the devil's on their asses. Not sure what's going on since the drone's audio is being drowned out by all the white noise. But this could be your window of opportunity to waltz in there and get the gals."

"Are you sure Fee and Pia aren't in any of those vehicles?" Levi asked.

"No one has come out of the front of the house. Can't see the back of the house, but they would've had to load them within the view of the drone's camera. The house guards are still patrolling," Tweeter said, "so my guess—the gals are still in the house."

"Copy that," Trey said. "Keep us updated on the situation. Out."

"Roger that. Out."

Trey turned to Price and Levi as the rain began to fall in sheets. "Shit, it's a frigging monsoon. The clock just got shorter. All egresses will flood quickly in this kind of downpour. Let's move out."

He left the cover of the storage unit. Price and Levi followed on his heels. They zig-zagged their way toward the main house.

Shortly after 8:05 p.m.

AFTER THE MASS EXODUS OF vehicles, Fee followed Pia and Lucia as they picked their way across the uneven ground of a rock-strewn meadow. They were heading out of the valley toward a darkly shadowed gap between two steep mountain walls. The light show which preceded the oncoming storm provided more than enough light for them to see their way, but Lucia had given them tactical flashlights that could be shielded to help light their path if the lightning died down.

When they reached the gap, Fee could see that it was a slot canyon carved by wind and water over the millennia. What was on most days a shallow creek wound its way down the center of the canyon. It was now threatening to flow outside its banks as rainwater from farther up the mountains reached the canyon floor. When the rain was directly over them, the area would flood.

"Watch your step," Lucia called out. "Very slippery."

The three of them crossed the swiftly rushing waters, using large flat rocks obviously placed for just such a purpose.

Once they reached the other side, Fee spotted the path that led upward. The track was one-person wide and like the canyon had been sculpted by wind and water and then worn down further by human feet over time.

Lucia stopped at the base of the path which looked more suited for a mountain goat than a human and pointed upward. "We're going there."

A flash of lightning illuminated the cliff dwellings which clung precariously, high above the canyon floor. The ancients who'd chosen this area to build their homes had chosen well. The only access to their cliff homes could easily be defended from above.

Unfortunately, what made the cliff houses safe and defensible, also made them difficult to get to in bad weather and at night. Even with Mother Nature lighting the area like a used car parking lot, the steeply inclined path was treacherous. The now-falling rain added slippery to the already rugged track, which was liberally littered with loose stones and scrub plants growing from between cracks in the rocks.

A wet and chilled Fee followed the others, tripping over unseen depressions and sliding on areas where the rock was like a polished floor. She only managed to stay upright because she could brace herself on the rock that formed a wall on one side. The other side of the track was a drop-off to the roiling waters of the rock-strewn creek below. The increasingly deeper creek.

A particularly large lightning flash immediately followed by a deafening crack of thunder shook the very ground they trod. A fierce wind roared through the narrow canyon on its way to the valley below. The rainfall changed from an irritating mist to large drops that bounced off the rock walls and hurt any exposed skin.

The storm's leading wind threatened to blow Fee right off the path. She stopped in her tracks and clung like a leech to a jagged abutment on the sheer rock wall next to her.

"Shit. Lucia, the storm is right above us," Fee yelled to be heard over the storm's fury.

Lucia waved them forward. "Keep moving. We are close." Her words carried to Fee on the wind. "Just around this next set of boulders and then up a ladder. Hurry."

With the promise of safety looming, Fee increased her speed as much as she dared. She caught up with Pia, who followed close behind Lucia.

Then the rain fell in sheets. What had been merely a miserable wetting before had become a potentially life-threatening deluge. The creek was far out of its banks and filling the canyon floor. It had already covered the bottom of the path they'd just climbed.

"Up. Quickly." Lucia put her foot on the rain-slickened bottom rung of a handmade wooden ladder that looked to be fifteen feet or so high. "Even more dangerous waters will come."

"Shit," Fee breathed out. She could make out the marks on the rock walls that previous gully-washers had made.

Pia began climbing. Fee waited, giving the other two some space. She didn't want to put too much weight on the rickety ladder. When the two were about halfway up, she placed her foot on the bottom rung and began to climb.

Fee's fingers had gone numb and trembled from cold—and, hell yeah, she'd admit it, from gut-wrenching fear. She wasn't fond of heights and ladders on a normal day, and today was so far beyond normal it didn't register on any scale she could claim to have familiarity with. The climb was made worse by the water rolling in rivulets down the ladder. Each step up was one step away from slipping and falling to certain death.

The gushing sound of fast-moving water pouring over rocks turned into a roar in less than a split-second.

"Oh, shit." Fee climbed faster.

From above her, Pia screamed, "Fee, come on. Lucia said we have to pull up the ladder or—"

The shrieking wind and the noise of the raging flood waters swept away what her friend said next.

Fee didn't need to hear what the "or" was; she could guess—the rising, fast-moving water would sweep the ladder away. She forced herself into overdrive and scrambled up the ladder like a monkey. She was within three rungs of the top and safety when the first surge of water hit the bottom of the ladder and shifted it to her left with a jerky hop-like movement. "Oh shit, oh shit, oh shit."

The next wave of water hit and the ladder wobbled wildly. She clung to the wood and hemp creation like a lover.

Now the water was a constant driving force as it sought its way through the narrow canyon to the valley below. The ladder was battered, but still holding. She wasn't even sure why it hadn't been swept away yet and her with it.

"Fee, move your ass!" Pia yelled.

The horrified panic in her friend's voice cut through Fee's stupor. She needed to get up and off the damn ladder, or she'd end up clinging to the rock wall like a barnacle.

"Dammit, Fee, hurry," Pia cried out. "We can't hold it much longer."

Rain streaming down her face, Fee looked up through the downpour. "Shit."

The two small women strained to hold the ladder in place. She could've told them it was a lesson in futility. The laws of physics were against them.

The angry water shoved the ladder to the left yet again. A loud crack indicated physics had won and damaged the ladder.

Pia and Lucia cried out in pain as the ladder was ripped out of their hands. Somehow, the ladder held together as it moved yet again. And Fee still clung to it.

Pia screamed, "Fee … grab onto the ledge … to your right. Now!"

Fee turned her head and looked to the right. Ledge? Was Pia nuts?

Lightning revealed what appeared to be a tiny gouge in the rock. But it was Fee's only hope. She reached with her right hand and foot just as the ladder was torn out from under her. She kicked the remnants away with her left foot and found another small rock jutting out to grab with her left hand.

"Fee," Pia yelled.

"What!" Fee didn't look up. She was too busy trying to keep the toehold her right foot had found and to hold onto the small protrusions her hands had found. Her left leg dangled wildly with no anchor.

Turning her face to the rock wall, she leaned her forehead on the smooth, wet rock. "Oh God, oh God," she chanted under her breath as she held on and tried to slow her breathing down before she hyperventilated. She didn't dare get any more light-headed than she already was or they'd find her broken body in the valley meadow after the flood waters receded.

"Fee," Pia yelled yet again.

"Dammit, Pia, I'm sort of busy here," she shouted, "hanging on."

"Climb," Pia ordered.

"Um, would love to. Any suggestions how?" Fee was afraid to look up since it could throw her off-balance.

"Use the rope ladder," Lucia shouted above the sound of the wind, rain, and the gulley-washer still moving swiftly below.

"What effin' rope ladder?" Fee gritted out.

"To your right." Pia sounded pissed and scared. Exactly how Fee felt at the moment. "It's anchored to a huge rock up here and isn't going anywhere."

Okay then, that was what Fee had needed to know, but still, she was scared shitless to move too much.

"Fee," Pia shouted down, "reach out with your right hand. Pull it to you. There's enough slack."

"God, Pia, you get awfully damn bossy when you're scared." Fee gingerly turned her head to the right. She let out a huge sobbing sigh. The ladder was there. All rough, knotted rope and beautiful.

Taking a deep breath, she let go of her right hand-hold and grabbed the left side of the rope ladder. She pulled it to her until she could get her right foot on it. She then got her left foot onto it, shifted her right hand to the right side of the rope, and then let go of the rock wall with her left hand.

With her full weight and all appendages safely on the rope ladder, it swung slightly. She bounced off the wall for a few seconds, then the ladder steadied under her more balanced weight. Yep, she'd have bruises, cuts, and rope burns, but she was alive. She rested for a second and murmured, "Thank you, Jesus." Then she looked up at the two worried faces and smiled. "I'm okay. Coming up."

When she finally pulled herself onto the ledge, she kissed the rock. Yeah, it was wet and dirty, but it was solid and flat. She loved that damn ledge at that moment.

"Come on, Fee." Pia held out her hand. "Let's get inside where Lucia says we can have a fire and something hot to drink. She even has dry clothes in there that should fit us."

Fee took her friend's hand and sent Lucia a look of heartfelt gratitude. "Sounds great."

"I will pull up the rope ladder," Lucia said. "You may tell Anton that I told him so when I said the wooden ladder wasn't practical. He humored me with the backup ladder."

Fee laughed, the sound a bit hysterical. "I'll be happy to rub it in. Bless you, Lucia. I don't think I could've made it up the wall without it."

Pia nudged Fee's arm. "You'd have done it."

Maybe, but she was damn glad she hadn't had to find her inner spider.

8:15 p.m.
El Hacha's compound

"WHERE THE FUCK ARE THEY?" A scowl on his face, Trey looked around the bedroom suite which corresponded with the French doors Tweeter had indicated from his surveillance. There were signs Fee and Pia had been here at one time. Empty plates. Scattered items of female clothing, size small.

Dread festered in Trey's gut.

The entry into the house had been far easier than they'd anticipated. With one less roving guard, Trey and the others quickly subdued and tied up the two guards. They'd then entered through the back of the house and found four servants whom they locked in the pantry. The servants hadn't seemed willing to cause any trouble.

With Price guarding their exit point, Trey and Levi had searched the house, bottom to top, and found no one but an unconscious guard lying outside the now-empty bedroom.

Levi opened a drawer in one of the heavy wooden chests and held up some men's boxer briefs. "This is a man's room." He growled and tore the briefs into shreds.

Trey would rather shred the suite's owner.

Levi turned a murderous look Trey's way. "What now?"

Since Tweeter hadn't given them a heads-up, that meant the drone hadn't been in the right place when the women left the house. So—

"We search and clear the other buildings until we find our women ... or, better yet, we find someone who can tell us where they are." Trey headed for the entrance to the suite. "We'll start with the medical clinic Tweeter mentioned."

Levi followed him. When they reached the lower-level back hallway, Price looked at them. The hope in his eyes fizzled out like a spent firecracker. "Where the fuck are they?"

"Not here." Trey opened the back door and checked the area. "It's clear. Let's go."

"Where are we going," Price muttered into his headset so as not to alert anyone who might be close by.

Other than the house guards, the servants, and the two guards at the gate house, the compound was deserted. Tweeter had shut down all the electronic surveillance, and there had been no response to that maneuver. Maybe the systems often got glitchy in bad weather and Tweeter's sabotage just presented as an act of Mother Nature. Whatever the reason, no offensive response to their infiltration was all good in his book.

"The clinic," Trey responded.

The three of them used the shadows and the heavy rainfall to obscure their presence as they made their way to the clinic building, which was closer to their original point of entry.

Once outside their destination, Trey held up his hand and listened. Hearing nothing but the storm, he opened the door and entered a dimly lit and empty hall. The others followed and closed the door.

A man moved out of a doorway farther down the hall. He was dressed for the weather in a heavy anorak and boots and carried a black backpack. His hands were in the air, showing he had no weapon.

"Did you come for Fee and Pia?" the man asked in Russian-accented English.

"Yeah." Trey aimed his weapon at the man's center of mass. "Where are they?"

The man stepped further into the light. "Your women are at the cliff dwellings at the north end of the valley. With my pregnant fiancee. We are leaving with you. We are not safe here any longer."

"Who are you?" Price asked.

"Dr. Anton Vasilov. Call me Anton. My Lucia is *El Hacha*'s niece and we must leave before he realizes she carries my child. Fee and Pia's kidnapping moved our timetable up." The tall, well-formed male moved toward them. He lowered his hands and gestured toward the door. "Hurry. Ernesto's distraction will not last much longer I am afraid. Plus, the flood waters will soon be worse than they are now."

"Pia's brother helped you?" Levi asked as they moved toward the clinic's front door.

"Yes. He did not like what Chavez planned for Pia," Vasilov said. "So he is leading them away. Chavez thinks Ernesto has taken the women with him."

"And why does Chavez think that?" Price said as Trey checked outside to make sure no one had sneaked up on the clinic while they were inside.

"I told him, of course," Vasilov said. "We needed a diversion so the women could cross the open meadow to get to the cliff dwellings' path."

"It's clear." Trey looked at Vasilov. "Where are we headed … exactly?"

"Follow me." Vasilov shoved past them and began jogging toward the northern part of the compound. "We'll need a boat to cross the meadow. It is under water by now. I have one. Hurry."

Trey exchanged looks with Levi and Price who both shrugged and followed the Russian. While Vasilov forged ahead, Trey and the others kept a lookout for signs of danger.

Tapping his headset, Trey muttered, "Tweeter, we're heading out of the compound. The women escaped earlier and are hiding in the cliffs at the north end of the valley. Keep an eye on our six, if you can."

Trey wasn't sure Tweeter could see anything on the video feed with as heavy as the rain was.

"Copy that," Tweeter said. "The drone's still on the building across from the house. Still getting a good feed of most of the facility. Nice takedown of the guards by the way. The guards at the gatehouse are still in place. When the rain lightens and the winds die down, I'll reposition the drone to the northernmost building and keep an eye on your back trail from there. Stay safe, buddy. Out."

"Copy that. Out." The men had reached a small outbuilding. Trey looked at the boat being inflated and cracked a smile. "Just like the Marines." It was a six-man inflatable boat with a powerful outboard motor.

Vasilov smiled. "I appropriated it from *El Hacha*'s supply shed and hid it in this building for just such a situation. During heavy rains or after a snow melt-off, the stream flowing from the canyon combines with the river to flood the meadow before it all drains to the lowlands." He waved a hand. "Gentlemen, I have a feeling you know how to handle this boat better than I. My military service usually didn't place me on the water."

Trey nodded. "Price, handle the motor. Levi and Anton climb in."

After they were all on board, Price started the motor and headed a northerly direction. The storm raged all around them. Lightning flashed and turned the dark night skies to day. The thunder boomed so loudly Trey felt it in his bones.

"Where exactly am I aiming for?" Price asked.

When the next flash of lightning lit up the flooded meadow, Vasilov pointed to a place where it looked as if two sheer mountain walls met in a thick seam of darkness. "Head for the mountains. Once we're closer, you'll see the canyon entrance and the cliff dwellings. If we're lucky, the water will not have reached the path leading to the ladder to the cliff."

"Gotcha," Price kept his hand on the tiller. "Levi, aim a tac-light ahead of us. Shout out if you see anything I need to avoid in the water. Would hate to have to swim the rest of the way."

Trey laughed when Levi grunted and muttered, "Easy for you to say since you were a SEAL. I'm not a damn trout."

Chapter 11

Bruised and dripping wet, Fee followed Pia and Lucia toward a cliff house in the middle of the row of dwellings.

"Please wait," Lucia said, a flashlight in her hand. "I will go first and light the lanterns."

What Lucia hadn't mentioned was rooting out all the snakes, scorpions, rodents and other assorted wildlife which might've taken up residence to escape the rainy night—ugh. Fee was so not a rough-it-in-the-wild gal.

Better roughing it in the wild than being Chavez's sex toy.

Yep.

Fee and Pia huddled closer to the building under what little overhang that remained after hundreds of years of erosion. The storm raged and howled overhead like an angry beast, adding to their misery. A lightning crack nearby had both of them jumping.

"Th-that was too c-c-close." Fee's teeth chattered.

Spring in the mountains was usually cold in the evenings, but adding in the wind and rain brought the ambient temperature down to below freezing. She couldn't ever remember being this cold, not even in Detroit in January. Her three layers of clothing were soaked, leeching away any warmth her shivering body could produce.

"Way to-o-o close," Pia agreed. "Lucia? Is it safe?"

The dark hole that was the doorway suddenly lit up as Lucia appeared, having shoved aside whatever covered the entrance from the inside. "Come in. It is clear."

Entering the dwelling, the first thing Fee spotted was a fireplace off to the side. She moved toward it. A fire was just what they needed, but she didn't know the first thing about starting a fire. Her Girl Scout badges had been in First Aid, CPR, and Crafts. She was such a loser.

"F-f-fire?" Fee stuttered and looked around the rest of the room that made up the entire living area of their shelter. There were several stacks of supplies, obviously placed there by Anton and Lucia for their eventual escape. Spaced around the room were four LED lanterns.

The room was very well-lit. Too well. Her breath hitched with fright and she glanced at the two small window openings. She was relieved to see thick animal skins covering them, just like the one covering the doorway.

"Will Chavez's people see the light?" Fee asked.

"No. Anton and I checked this many times. We would sneak out here to be together." Lucia blushed prettily. "I will build the fire now."

Lucia pulled out a firelighter from a pack that had already been in the room and began assembling paper and kindling in the rugged hearth. "The room will warm up quickly due to the rock reflecting the heat. Then we will get our wet clothing off. I keep several changes of clothing here. We are all about the same size. I will then make us something warm to drink, yes?"

"Y-y-es," Fee said, then coughed. Her throat was raw, irritated. She clenched her jaw and managed to speak without stuttering or coughing. "Sounds wonderful, Lucia. Thank you."

"Are you well, Fee?" Lucia's eyes reflected concern.

"I'm fine. Just chilled. Dry clothes and a hot drink will fix me right up." She couldn't be sick. She refused.

Blind as a bat.

Fee ignored the snarky little voice in her head just as she ignored her sore throat, earache, and the devils playing a heavy metal concert on her skull. Instead, she concentrated on rubbing her hands up and down her arms in an attempt to warm up enough so she'd stop shivering.

Pia frowned at Fee, but remained silent. Her friend didn't have to say a word. Pia had that "don't mess with me, I'm a nurse" look in her eye." If this had been the clinic, Pia would already be taking Fee's vitals.

"I'll help you, Lucia." Pia knelt by the fireplace and began shredding up the paper while Lucia placed the kindling.

After the fire caught, Fee sat by Pia on some boxes stacked to each side of the hearth.

Pia's eyes welled with tears. "I'm worried about Ernesto. Do you think he got away?" She sniffled.

Fee touched Pia's shoulder and squeezed. "I know you are, sweetie. Your brother knew what he was doing. Anton gave him a good head start. I have to figure the storm will give him an advantage also. He could've already ditched the vehicle and hid before Chavez and his men pursued. He has a good chance."

Pia nodded, but didn't looked convinced. Fee didn't really blame her, because Chavez was ruthless and wouldn't take betrayal well—and had sent a lot of vehicles filled with hardened cartel soldiers after Ernesto.

The wind had died down a bit. The thunder sounded farther away, more toward where the compound lay, now cut off from them by a meadow full of water. The relative silence was welcome.

Fee stiffened as a rhythmic, rumbling-buzz reached her ears. "Listen. Do you hear that?"

Pia and Lucia stopped a conversation about Lucia's pregnancy. Barely breathing, the three of them listened.

The sound grew louder. It was coming closer. It sounded like a—

"It's a boat motor." Fee looked at the others. "Do you think Chavez—"

Her face ashen, Lucia hunched her shoulders and whispered, "No, why would he?"

"Maybe someone saw us while we climbed up the path from the canyon floor." Pia got off her box and moved toward the packs. "Are there any weapons?"

Lucia opened her mouth to reply, but Fee held up a hand. "Shh … listen, the boat is even closer."

Then the motor cut-off. Fee's heart leapt into her throat and she swallowed hard. The three of them huddled together.

Fee forced her breathing to slow down so she could hear over the pulse pounding loudly in her ears. Men's voices. Their words indistinct.

Pia reached over and picked up one of the larger pieces of firewood. It was a pathetic weapon, but it was all they had.

Long minutes later, the voices became clearer.

One man's voice sounded familiar. Exasperation colored every syllable as he said, "Thought you said there was a ladder."

Fee let out a shuddering breath of relief—of joy. He'd come for her. "It's Trey. He's here." She turned to Lucia. "Time to let the rope ladder down again."

"Anton will be with him." Lucia grinned, then rushed to the door covering and shoved it aside.

Pia and Fee followed, making sure the skin covered the door when they left so no light escaped to reveal their presence to anyone looking toward the mountains.

While Lucia and Pia unrolled the rope ladder, Fee leaned over the side to hear her brother and Trey make the decision to set pitons and climb the sheer, slippery rock wall.

"NEITHER OF YOU HAVE TO do that. Use this." The amused, slightly raspy, feminine voice floated down from above, followed by a rope ladder that practically hit Trey on the head.

Fee's dirty, grinning face peeked over the edge. *Thank you, God.* He returned her smile. "You okay, little doc?"

"All things considered…" Her lips twisted. "…yeah. Now, get up here. We started a fire and were getting ready to fix something hot to drink. All the comforts of home on a wet, chilly night."

Fee sounded hoarse. Her lips in the light of his flashlight were tinged blue. She shivered like a bedraggled kitten left out in the rain. All of this renewed his anger at the circumstances that had placed her in the situation and prompted an emerging concern over her health.

"Get inside where its warm and dry, Fee. We'll be right up." Trey tugged on the rope ladder to assure himself it could handle his weight plus his pack. He slung his pack over his shoulder and quickly ascended the handmade ladder.

As soon as he reached the wide ledge that fronted the row of cliff dwellings, he sought and found Fee leaning against the outer wall of a house in the middle. He grumbled under his breath. Why in the fuck hadn't she gone inside? She was soaked, visibly trembling, and looked exhausted, but still … so … so beautiful to him that his heart hurt.

"Fee, I told you to go inside." He walked toward her. As he got closer, he noted what he'd thought was dirt on her face was, in reality, bruises. "Fee … what the fuck? Who hit you?"

He'd kill the fucker.

Trey reached for her and she shrank away.

Way to go, asshole. She's scared of you.

"Trey…" Price's tone warned him to proceed with caution. Both men knew exactly what had happened to Fee in Detroit all those months ago, because they'd beaten the truth out of the mother-fucking douchebag Stall. Neither of them were one hundred percent sure whether or not Fee had totally processed through her trauma yet. Her willingness to date Trey had been seen as a huge step forward. But that progress had occurred right before this traumatic turn of events ... and now she'd been beaten again. It appeared she was as scared as she'd been when he'd first met her.

Fuck ... had she been ... raped, too?

Trey lowered his arm and stepped back—afraid to take Fee in his arms as he wanted, no, needed to.

Seconds turned into a minute. A light rain fell, but no one moved from the ledge. Even Price, bristling with big-brother-concern, waited to see what would happen next. The others seemed to be as aware as Trey that this was a make-it-or-break-it moment for him and Fee.

"Fee?" He crooned as he might to coax an injured animal to trust him and then opened his arms. "Sweetheart ... are you...?"

With a sob, Fee shot into his arms like a bullet from a sniper rifle and buried her face against his chest.

"Thank you, baby. Thank you for your trust." Trey wrapped his arms around her much smaller, fragile, and quivering body. He surrounded her with as much of himself as he could ... sheltering her as if he could protect her from all future danger.

When Fee let out a shuddering sob, he rubbed his cheek against her unbruised one. "Fee ... sweetheart ... shh ... I'm here." His words had her shaking even harder. Her weeping threatened to drive him to his knees.

Movement had Trey turning his head to find Price hovering close by, a look of extreme helplessness on his friend's face. "What the fuck?" Price mouthed.

Trey shrugged. But he'd damn well find out and fix whatever was making Fee cry so hard.

"Baby, where are you hurt? Does the doctor need to look you over?" He scanned the area and found Vasilov holding his woman closely against his side. The couple looked concerned. "You didn't tell me Fee'd been hurt."

Vasilov frowned and looked Fee over. "Other than the bruise on her face, she was not hurt—not in the way you're thinking. We tricked Chavez with a made-up illness so he would leave her alone. However, she does seem to be moving more stiffly than before." He looked down. "Lucia, what happened? Fee has injuries she did not have earlier."

Sniffling and rubbing her wet cheek against Trey's chest, Fee lifted her head. "I can speak for myself." She looked between him and Price who'd moved in even closer. "It was pouring rain. The water was rising. I was on the wooden ladder, climbing, when—"

"Fuck," Trey muttered, picturing a wall of water sweeping the ladder down the valley with Fee clinging. "You let go?"

"Uh-huh." She looked indignant which added a flush of red to the pale purple-blue-green bruises on her white face. "I wasn't planning on swimming or dying, Trey."

Her indignant and challenging tone was more like the spunky doctor who'd held an assault rifle on him, a total stranger at the time, while protecting Keely in the wilds of Idaho.

"Fuck, baby." He placed a kiss on the tip of her nose. "You have more lives than a cat."

She nodded and croaked out, "Yeah … go figure."

"Jesus, sis, don't joke. You could've been—" Price stroked a hand down her back.

"I wasn't." Fee clutched at Trey's arm. Her hands had cuts, scrapes, and torn nails from what had to have been a life-and-death struggle. "I found my inner barnacle pretty damn fast and clung to the rock walls until I realized Lucia and Pia had thrown me a rope."

She chuckled and then coughed a couple of times. Taking a rasping breath, she sighed and rubbed a cheek over Trey's chest. "I hate heights."

Trey might never let her out of his sight again. He kissed her forehead. "Right there with ya, sweetheart."

"Stop hogging my sister," Price said. "I need a hug."

"Let's do the hugging inside," Levi suggested. "Another thunderstorm is sweeping down the canyon. Our women are wet and cold and don't need to get any wetter."

Levi had his arm around Pia's shoulders. The nurse whom Trey had met several times during his visits to New Mexico stared at Levi with a look in her eyes that should've warned the sheriff to tone down the possessiveness a bit.

However, Trey knew exactly how Levi felt. It was hard to meet the right woman and find she had issues which kept her from trusting any man. It had almost killed Trey to keep his distance from Fee and not claim her immediately after he'd met her. But he'd managed and given her the time she'd needed to heal. She was in his arms now and he planned to keep her there—but only if she wished to be.

Pia addressed Levi in a sharp tone, "I'm not your woman." But something in her eyes hinted at vulnerability.

Yep, Levi had a ways to go before he could fully claim Pia.

After climbing and hiking alongside the sheriff over some of the worst terrain since Trey's Force Recon days, Trey'd put his money on Levi winning the day … eventually.

Pia poked Levi in the chest. "And we were getting warm and dry when we heard your arrival. We don't need macho, know-it-all men to tell us to get out of the rain."

Levi pulled Pia under his arm to shelter her as a blast of wind came roaring through the canyon ahead of the storm. "Make no mistake. You are my woman, and this know-it-all man will take care of you and your mother."

The sheriff tipped up Pia's chin and took her lips in a kiss that looked about as hungry and needy as the one Trey wanted to give Fee—but was afraid to in case he scared her again.

"Well, I'd say that was pretty damn blatant," muttered Fee as Trey gently moved her toward the opening through which Vasilov had already taken Lucia. "About damn time, too. Pia's crazy about that man. Thinks she isn't good enough for him. Levi has been more than patient."

"Some men can be patient hunters when we find the one perfect woman," he teased as he angled his body to bear the brunt of the gusting winds. He could tease now since Fee was safely in his arms.

Fee sniffed and looked at him from between her thick lashes. Trey winked at her and ushered her inside the cliff house. The one room dwelling was warm and cozy due to the fire the women had started. He led Fee to the far side of the room and held up a blanket he found on a pile of what looked to be bedding. He held it up high enough to give her privacy.

"You need to get dry," Trey said. When he didn't hear any movement from her, he lowered the blanket and found her staring into space.

"Get those wet clothes off," he ordered. His voice came out rougher than he'd intended.

Her body shaking, his little doc still managed to glare at him, her eyebrow arched imperiously. He could picture her looking just that way at an intern or nurse who'd dared to tell her what to do.

Trey would give her a few seconds to see the reason in his command, then he'd strip her himself.

Fee's eyebrow relaxed. Her face went blank and she shook her head.

Fuck me. Had he put his foot in it? Lost all the ground his patient pursuit had won him?

When she began to unbutton her shirt, Trey let out a relieved breath.

Fee smiled, a slight upward twist to her lips, and her dark blue-green gaze never left his. "The magic word is *please*," she said in a low tone just for his ears. "But you get a pass this time, since I know you're extremely worried about me and risked your life to come after me."

Dodged that bullet, asshole.

Fee tossed each piece of wet clothing aside as she removed a total of three layers. Each of them soaking wet, dammit.

When she was down to a very sexy, sheer bra that did nothing to hide her beaded nipples—

She's cold, fuckhead.

—and matching panties which clearly revealed a neat vee of red curls, he groaned low in his throat. He raised the blanket up higher until he blocked out the alluring sight.

Blanket or not, he couldn't unsee what he'd seen. His little doc was perfection—and, dammit, had just been through hell. Before he could scare her with his lust, he'd go outside and let the cold rain dampen his totally untimely, but natural reaction to her curvy little body. A body he dreamed of making love to and cherishing every night for the last nine months.

Cold. Traumatized. Control your lust.

"You can look now."

Trey lowered the blanket and hugged it close to his chest so he wouldn't make a bone-headed move and grab her.

Her cheeks flushed, Fee's lips twisted into a shy smile. She was now covered head to toe in some thermal leggings and a woven sweater Pia had quietly shoved under the blanket for her. The sweater reached her mid-thigh and was far too large for her, so it must've been one of Vasilov's. Thank fuck, it hid all her curvy bits he didn't want Levi and Vasilov to see.

"Better?" Fee asked.

He didn't trust himself to talk, afraid he'd say something that would embarrass or frighten her, so he nodded.

"Okay." She pulled her hair out from the sweater's neckline so it hung down her back in damp, red-gold curls. He wanted to bury his face in them and inhale her scent. "Trey?"

"What?" He drew his gaze away from one particularly long curl that reached the part of the sweater where he knew her breasts were.

"Your turn." She looked him up and down. "Strip ... please. See? Magic word." She grinned cheekily. "Can't have my rescuer get sick. I can't get us out of here." Her voice was husky and fierce.

His cock got hard at the protectiveness in her feminine ferocity.

Down, boy.

Trey also got off on the fact that Fee relied on him to get her to safety despite the fact that Price and Levi could do so equally as well.

"Yes, ma'am." Trey dropped the blanket he'd used to keep the other men from seeing her change. He began shucking off his clothes, adding them to the soggy pile she'd made.

Some day, their clothes would be a mixed pile on the floor of what would be their bedroom in his Sanctuary home, the one he built with her in mind. He'd take her to their bed and make love to her and then shield her with his body as they slept.

"Trey! Geez Louise. Wait—" Fee coughed as she picked up the blanket he'd dropped and tried to hold it in front of him. When she realized she couldn't block the view of his whole body as easily as he had hers, she covered the lower half and snarled over her shoulder, "Don't anyone look over here."

Price, who stood off to the side of the fireplace with a cup of what smelled like coffee in his hand, laughed. "Jesus, sis, no one wants to see Trey's naked junk."

Trey shot Price a fulminating look that shut his buddy up, then turned back to Fee, who stood less than a foot away. He extended a now-bare arm and swept that taunting strand of red-gold hair back over her shoulder.

"Sweetheart," he murmured. "They aren't looking. Other than Price, the rest are dealing with their own clothing." He lowered his arm and finished stripping down to his military-style boxer briefs. He found the room warm enough, so he merely pulled on a pair of sweat pants from his pack. "Gimme the blanket. We'll sit on it."

Fee handed him the heavily woven blanket.

Trey spread it on the ground a bit closer to the fire. He placed his back to the mountain wall that made up the rear of the dwelling and then pulled Fee onto his lap. He needed to hold her, plus he didn't want her sitting on a hard floor.

His heart rejoiced when she sighed and snuggled against his bare chest. Her warm breath touched the underside of his jaw. One of her hands rested over his heart.

"You're so warm," she said, "and surprisingly comfortable, even with all those muscles." She patted his pecs. It was all he could do to stifle the groan her touch evoked. His cock was fully erect and pushing against the back of her thighs.

If they'd been alone and their relationship was further along, he'd turn her to face him. She'd straddle his thighs. He'd release his erection and make love to her.

But now was neither the time nor place.

Plus, the next steps in their fledgling relationship were all under her control. He'd make sure to stress that point again once he got her the fuck out of Mexico and safely back to the States—that being in Idaho and not fucking New Mexico.

Price, Keely, and the whole of SSI had his back on Fee moving to Idaho. He prayed she'd agree to make the move to the small satellite clinic located between Elk City and Sanctuary. SSI had made a generous donation to the medical center in Grangeville so the rural clinic could be reopened.

Pushing aside images of how Fee would look, her long golden-red curls framing her naked breasts, as she rode him, he focused on checking her arms and legs for sprains or breaks. "Does this hurt?" he asked as he cradled one particularly bruised and scraped wrist in one hand.

"Trey…" She placed her free hand on his cheek and stroked him. "I'm fine. No breaks. No sprains. Am I sore? Yes"—he inhaled sharply at her admission— "but nothing time and rest won't help."

He nodded and finally checked out their shelter. He hummed his approval. Vasilov had picked and prepared for the escape well.

Price caught Trey's eye and his friend's next words proved they thought a lot alike. "This seems to be a good place to hide out until we can get the chopper in to pick up the gals."

"The gals? Why not pick up all of us?" Fee straightened on Trey's lap and looked from her brother to Trey. "You're not staying here. When we go, we all go."

Pia and Lucia nodded, but kept silent.

"Sis…" Price began, his tone so condescending that Trey wanted to punch him.

Before Trey could shut down what was an unnecessary line of discussion since no final decision had been made on how they'd all get out of Madera—Fee beat him to it.

"Shut it, Price," she snarled. "I'm not six-years-old any longer. Don't talk to me like that."

"You tell him, sweetheart." Trey brushed a kiss over her cheek. "But before you and Price have a sibling brawl, let me say, we'll make the decision on how to get the fuck out of here and who will go tomorrow. The decision will be based on the weather conditions and where all the bad actors are and what they're doing."

Fee looked at Price who wasn't happy, but was smart enough to keep his opinions and any anger he felt at Trey's statement to himself. "That makes sense." She then turned her blue-green gaze on him. "And, of course, all of us get to weigh in on the final course of action, right?"

Trey would remember to tell DJ she'd been correct; the women hadn't wanted to be seen as helpless victims, but as partners in their escape.

"Trey…" Price's growl drew a pissed-off look from Fee.

Trey had all he could do not to laugh when his little doc stuck her tongue out at her brother who stiffened and snarled, "Pest."

"Fee, look at me." Trey waited until Fee turned away from the stare-down the two siblings engaged in. "We've basically invaded a foreign country with an armed military helicopter and other weapons, without obtaining permission in advance. That could be considered an act of war. Ren and I will have to deal with the diplomatic heat if we end up killing Mexican citizens to get you out of here." And so far, they'd managed to avoid any deaths.

"I understand, but—"

"Sweetheart, I realize you feel out of control right now and want some say in what happens next. But consider how I'd feel if after all this effort, I failed to keep you safe?" He cupped her face and gently rubbed his thumb over her bruised cheek. "My main objective, my fucking only objective, was to get you and Pia—and now Vasilov and Lucia—to safety. Me, Price, and Levi can go to ground, evade, and find our own way out, because we have that training. So, if I make the call to evacuate you women and Vasilov, that's my call and no one else's. Understood?"

Fee worried her lower lip with her teeth, then let it go and nodded. "Yes, it's your call. I trust you, Trey. I didn't even think about how you got into Mexico. I'm sorry for all the trouble."

"Baby, you did nothing wrong," Trey placed a light kiss on the lip she'd abused.

"Fee, your man is correct." Vasilov rubbed his fiancee's stomach almost absentmindedly. "The fault is with men like *El Hacha* and Chavez. They are animals." He looked at Trey, then Price, and finally Levi. "If the helicopter comes in under fire and can only get the women out, then that is what will happen."

"Anton, no," Lucia cried.

"Shh, *dushenka*. You know my training. I can also evade the enemy and live off the land." He stared Trey in the eye. "I have Russian special forces training. I did not mislead you earlier about the boat. I am more familiar with land operations. But that is for later discussion. Now, it is my medical opinion, we should eat, drink warm fluids, and rest. Tomorrow will bring new challenges. Fee, do I need to examine your injuries?"

"No, I'm fine," she said.

Trey growled. "Your hands aren't. They need to be cleaned and bandaged. I'll check her over, Anton." He didn't want any other man to touch her. "If I think she needs a doctor, I'll shout out."

Fee slapped a hand on his chest. "I said I'm fine."

A wracking cough gave lie to her assertion.

"You sound like you're catching a cold. So you're not fine." Trey picked up her hand and kissed the tips of her dirty and scraped fingers. "Plus your hands need care. So, you'll sit there and let me."

"Bossy much?" Fee had a mulish look on her face.

She was cute when she was feisty. Trey liked feisty. He leaned in and took her lips in a much-tamer kiss than he'd like. "Yep. After I'm done treating your wounds, you'll get something warm in your belly and take some ibuprofen for all the aches and pains. Then we'll take Anton's advice and lie down—and you'll sleep in my arms."

Tension tightened Trey's throat until he thought he'd choke as Fee stared at him. He could almost see her mind consider and reject several responses to his dictates. She was quiet for so long, her expression, so blank, he worried he'd moved too far too fast again.

Trey was ready to retract the sleeping-in-his-arms bit when Fee took one deep breath, then another, and finally nodded. She pulled her hand from his and traced his beard-shadowed jaw with a dirty, abraded finger. "I trust you, Trey, even when you're being all high-and-mighty. I wouldn't have made the dinner date if I didn't. So I'll let you take care of me."

His tension evaporated with her words, her touch. "Thank you, Fee." He covered her hand with his and held it to his face. "I won't abuse your trust in me ... ever."

"I know." She touched her forehead to his chin. "I know."

CHAPTER 12

March 25th, just before dawn

Fee woke slowly. Warmth surrounded her. Memories of the previous day's ordeal flooded her first waking thoughts, but the one thought hovering above all others was—she was safe. Trey was here. He'd come for her, fought the terrain ... the elements, and would've fought every single cartel soldier to free her.

He was a hero—her hero.

Smiling sleepily, she coughed several times. Her throat hurt ... burned. She sniffled. Damn congestion and the drainage it caused.

Crap, her pretend cold was now real. She couldn't afford to be sick right now, but was too tired to worry about it. And when it came right down to it, there wasn't really anything she could do about it anyway.

So, instead, she snuggled into the living, breathing warmth which had sheltered her throughout the long night from the chilly, damp air. Her eyes flew open as she registered she was no longer being cuddled, spoon-fashion against Trey, but was now lying on top of him. Her head, on his chest. One arm rested on his shoulder and the other curved at his lean waist. Her legs lay on top of his. His arms encircled her body, one hand on her back and the other cupping her ass.

Fee wiggled to see if she could move off him, but his arms tightened even as he slept. She didn't want to wake him. Plus, she really didn't want to move. She was still chilled and Trey was better than a furnace. Amazingly, his hard, muscular body was also a very comfortable bed. She could get used to sleeping on top of this man.

Thata girl.

Fee nuzzled his chest, now covered in the dry T-shirt he'd donned before they'd gone to sleep. Distracted, and maybe even a bit delirious, she wondered what it would feel like to lie on top of him, naked skin to naked skin. A frisson of sexual excitement swept through her and had her clenching her thighs together and her pussy dampening at the image in her mind. Taking a deep, calming breath, she let her body relax onto his and allowed his unique male scent, all mountain fresh and male musk with a hint of some citrus, to soothe her back into a drowse.

A few or maybe it was many seconds later—Trey's nearness tended to blur all sense of time—his morning wood prodded her stomach, then jerked between them.

Startled, she struggled to get off him. Not because she was afraid, she wasn't—well, not much. Her prior sexual experience had been either disappointing with big-egoed men with small dicks or brutally violent courtesy of Adam-fucking-Stall.

While Trey had more than enough self-confidence, he wasn't conceited or violent or small-dicked. In fact, from what she'd seen outlined by his much-washed sweats the previous evening and felt against her now, his cock was larger than most men's penises she'd seen while training to be a doctor. And she'd seen a lot of penises … from flaccid to chemically induced erect. Emergency rooms had a lot of penis emergencies primarily due to adolescent male stupidity and violence.

Mostly, she wanted to move, because she didn't want him to be uncomfortable when he couldn't do anything to relieve the pressure.

"Stay." Trey's voice was deeper than normal and really rough, more like the purr of a contented lion than anything.

"I have to be hurting ... you." There was no way she was going to say "your cock" out loud. The others were even now stirring awake and might overhear.

"You're not." His voice was a rumbling vibration felt along every inch of her skin and down to her bones.

Fee clenched her thighs again against the throbbing from her clit into her vagina. So far lying on top of Trey was the most sexually exciting experience of her life. Yeah, that said a lot about her former sexual partners. Pathetic.

"But..." she croaked, her voice breaking into a hacking cough that made her chest hurt.

Shit, shit, shit. She couldn't be sick, not now. She buried her face in the crook of Trey's neck, not allowing the tears gathering in her eyes to fall.

"Just stay put, little doc." Trey stroked her back in soothing circles. "The rest of the day is coming far too soon. In a bit, we'll have to make some tough decisions. So rest while you can." He pressed a kiss to the top of her head.

She stayed put, because she was exactly where she wanted to be at that moment. But his cock remained hard and prodding and difficult to ignore.

But you can ignore your health? Tell him. Tell Anton.

"Trey..." She started to confess that her condition was more serious than a common cold when he patted her butt. Damn, his touch felt good ... right ... almost sweet. She wallowed in the sensation for a second, then tried again. "Trey..."

"Shh, baby. I'll survive," he murmured against her ear as he soothed away the tension between her shoulder blades with what seemed to be magical fingers. "Relax. When we get back to the States, we'll talk about how our relationship will progress. We are starting a relationship, right?"

The uncertainty in his voice destroyed her and drove every other thought out of her head. The tension in every muscle of his body awed her. He was vulnerable when it came to her. She held power over him—and hadn't done a damn thing to earn his care and affection.

Love is a gift. There's no tit for tat. Give the man what he needs to hear right now, then let him know you're sick, stupid.

Fee pressed a kiss to the underside of his jaw. "We are. Trey…"

His arm tightened convulsively around her. "Thank you for your trust in me. I swear on all I hold dear, we'll take this at your pace. I might grumble, but I'll never do anything to make you afraid of me."

"I'm not afraid of you." She stroked his chest, soothing him. "Trey…"

"Stop worrying about what ifs…"

She wasn't worrying about "what ifs" whatever they were, she was trying to tell him she thought her lungs were congested and she most likely had strep throat.

"…we'll take it slow. I haven't waited for you this long to rush my fences and scare you away now."

Before Fee could get a word in edgewise, Trey shifted her so he could tilt her head back against his shoulder. He kissed her then, a teasing nibbling and licking at the seam of her mouth until she opened for him. He groaned and took it deeper, claiming her with his tongue in a slow journey that touched every square inch of her mouth.

Hell, he was a good kisser. She let all her thoughts and worries go, melted into his hold, and let him make love to her with his lips and tongue.

"Hey, you two."

Price's voice intruded into the best kiss Trey had ever

experienced. Ren had been right when he told Trey that kissing the woman you loved was far better than kissing any other woman. He might just have to kill Price for ruining his first real kiss with Fee. The ones they'd shared previously had paled in comparison.

"Bad weather. Crap location. Bad guys. Escape. Any of that sound familiar?" Price said.

Trey broke off the kiss and glared at Fee's brother who stood over them, his hands on his hips and a smirk on his face. "Timing could've been better, assclown."

"Um, same could be said for you playing tonsil hockey with my baby sis, jerkwad." There was no anger in Price's voice, just amusement.

"It was kissing, not tonsil hockey, big brother." Fee nuzzled the base of Trey's throat. "And it was wonderful, but…"

Trey shuddered. Just the smallest touch or look from Fee and his cock got hard enough to set pitons into granite mountain walls. They had chemistry, always had from the first time they met. But Fee hadn't acknowledged it fully—yet. Their sex life would be off the charts hot, but he wouldn't move any faster than his little doc could handle.

"But what, baby?" Trey rubbed his beard-roughened cheek over the top of her head.

Fee snuggled against his chest. "We need to get the heck out of here. Chavez will eventually realize Ernesto didn't take me and Pia with him. He'll realize Anton and Lucia are missing. He'll add it up and start looking for us, bad weather or not—oh, and I'm sick."

"Isn't that what I said?" Price asked, looking around for confirmation from the others.

"Yours was more sarcastic," Levi said. "Fee's statement was more conclusive. So, what do we do? The canyon's stream is still in full spate. The currents, as we found last night, are twisty and treacherous. Plus, even if the current was manageable, the inflatable boat is gone, torn away during the storms last night. But—"

"You're sick?" roared Trey, cutting Levi off.

Trey lifted Fee off him just as he might lift a bar bell and lay her gently on the blanket next to him. He knelt beside her and cupped her hot face between his hands. "Sick … why didn't you say something before now?"

"I tried." She looked up at him. Her eyes were glassy. Tears leaked down her pale face, pale but for the red flushing her cheeks. "But you kept distracting me."

Trey frowned and gently swiped away the tears with his thumb. "Where do you hurt, sweetheart?"

"My throat. My chest. My ears. Every muscle and joint in my body." She smiled wryly. "You kissed me, so I'm thinking you're gonna get sick, too."

He could care less about what might happen to him. Fee was sick *now*, in the middle of cartel lands in fucking Mexico.

"Anton?" Trey looked at Vasilov who stood over them, his black backpack in hand. "She's burning up."

Damn, he could kick his own horny ass. He'd played opossum while she'd awakened and wiggled on top of him. He'd enjoyed every single wiggle while she kept trying to tell him she was sick. He'd assumed she was nervous about his hard-on poking her stomach and wanted to tell him she wasn't ready for that part of their relationship yet.

Assumption is the mother of all fuck ups and misunderstandings, bozo.

Vasilov frowned at Fee. "You had a *real* low-grade temp yesterday, not the higher one I made up for Chavez's sake." He turned to look at Trey. "At the time, I wasn't all that concerned since Fee was tired, stressed, and dehydrated." He turned his focus back on Fee. "So, let's see where we're at, yes?"

"Yes," Fee croaked out.

His little doc looked so frail. So wan. Exhaustion dimmed the light in her blue-green eyes.

Trey needed to hold her, to soothe her. Hell, who was he kidding? He just needed *her*. "Come on, sweetheart. Let's get you off the floor. You can sit on my lap while the doctor examines you."

"Yes, please."

Trey opened his arms. Fee crawled onto his lap and then rested her head on his shoulder as Vasilov took her temperature.

The thermometer beeped. The doctor's forehead creased with concern. "102." Vasilov rummaged in his backpack. He pulled out a tongue depressor and a penlight, then knelt next to them. "Let's see this sore throat. Say 'ahh'."

Fee turned her head and opened her mouth. "Ahhhhh."

After a few seconds, Vasilov sat back on his heels. "Her throat is definitely inflamed. It appears to be strep throat." He felt her neck and then looked into her ears with another device he pulled from the bag. "Hmm. Fluid behind the ear drums. Her glands are swollen."

"Great," she muttered and turned her face into Trey's neck. "We don't need a lab test. I know it's strep throat, dammit."

"Yep. She got that a lot as a kid," Price put in, worry on his face. "She'd miss a week or so of school every year."

Vasilov patted her arm. "I can't test a throat swab to be sure, but treating for strep would be my choice even if I did have lab facilities. I have several kinds of antibiotics in my pack. I'll give her a shot with a loading dose and then she can take tablets." He looked at her. "Fee, you allergic to any medicines?"

Fee's muttered "no" was barely audible. She'd buried her face against him once again. Her hair caught in his heavy morning beard scruff as she snuggled in as close as she could. He hugged her and kissed her hot forehead. Her body stiffened when Vasilov gave her a shot in her upper arm.

Trey looked at the others. "Between the continued nasty weather and Fee's illness, there's no way any of us are going to walk out of here."

"Well, I agree even though you didn't let me finish my report earlier which confirms your conclusion," Levi said. "Fee's illness took precedence."

Hell yes, it did.

"Report?" Trey asked. "What do you have to report?"

"I went down the ladder an hour or so before dawn," Levi said. "Yes, it was—and is—raining. The creek remains out of its banks and the current's strong, but not as much as it was last night. I hiked, or waded was more like it, to the meadow which is still underwater. It's doable, even for the height-challenged among us."

Pia punched him in the arm. Levi snorted with what sounded like amusement before continuing. "Once you're past the creek bed and its banks, the current isn't as bad. We all could make it to the meadow for extraction. It's far enough from the compound that with the proper distraction to keep the cartel clowns chasing their tails, the chopper could swoop in from the northeast and hover long enough to load everyone."

Levi paused and stared at Trey, then Price. "You did say DJ was Army-trained and had flown in battle in Afghanistan."

Price answered, "I've ridden with her. She's damn good."

"So, she should be used to swooping in, hovering, and picking up troops under fire," Levi concluded.

"Hell, yeah," Trey said. "And Tweeter's just as good as DJ. So we're covered on the extraction end. Just what kind of distraction do you have in mind?"

A grin of unholy glee crossed Levi's face. "A couple of us could head down to the compound. Blow some shit up. Cause some fear and chaos. Then high-tail it to the meadow and meet the rest of the group for extraction."

"There are explosives in the building where we picked up the boat," Anton said.

Levi's grin was almost evil. "Yeah, I saw them. More than enough to do some serious damage."

"I wanted to avoid a small war." Trey cuddled Fee's suddenly stiff body closer to him. "But we really don't have a lot of other options."

"They peddle heroin. They're cooking meth," Levi stated. "Those drugs are destined for the States. A lot of that shit is coming through *my* county. I have no problem blowing up their drug operations. Plus, they have no fucking clue who we are. We could be from one of their rivals."

Trey couldn't disagree with Levi's feelings and reasoning. Hell, Ren and Keely were already working on justifying their incursion to rescue U.S. citizens, how much more harm were a few explosions in a drug cartel compound? Especially as Levi pointed out, *El Hacha's* men would have no clue who'd done the damage.

"Sounds good to me." Price put on his headset. "Explosive distraction it is. I'll touch base with Tweeter and see what's going on at the compound. He pulled in the drone last night to recharge it, but had planned to send it back this morning. I'll also ask if he's managed to fuck up anymore of their defense systems."

"Yeah, we want that radar and their SAMs installations dead as the dodos." Trey blew out a breath, "I'll contact Ren and let him know that he and Keely need to lay the groundwork for an upset Mexican government, just in case."

Trey looked at Vasilov. "You and Price will stay with the women."

The fact Price didn't argue said his buddy knew he was needed to get the women safely to the meadow. He was the strongest swimmer and was even more lethal in water than on land.

"You should take Price with you," Vasilov suggested. "You will need him. I can take care of the women by myself. I would just need a weapon and the boat, if it can be found."

"I have an idea where the boat went," Levi said. "I'll go hunt for it while we still have cloud cover."

Trey nodded. "Thanks, Levi. Anton, we'll fix you up with one of our extra rifles."

The doctor nodded, then moved to his fiancee who stirred something over the fire.

Trey looked down at Fee. "How you doing, sweetheart?"

"I hate being sick," Fee mumbled into his neck.

"Me, too." Trey caressed the back of her head. The curls felt like silk against his rough skin. As he sought to soothe her, he reviewed the plan. It should work. Then he thought about all that could go wrong. If FUBAR happened, then, fuck, they still might have to hike and climb out of here.

"You stiffened up just then." Fee angled her head to look at him. "What's wrong?"

"If shit happens and DJ can't get the helicopter in to airlift you out…" He trailed off. He figured she was smart enough to fill in the blanks.

"Then I'll do what needs to be done to get to a place where it's safe for her and Tweeter to pick us up." Fee stroked his neck with her fingers. "I don't want anyone taking extraordinary chances because of me."

"I want you safe." He squeezed her more tightly against him as if he could absorb her and protect her from what might be coming.

"I know." She coughed, the sound echoing harshly off the rock walls. "I'll be fine."

Hell yeah, she'd be fine. He'd carry her out on his back, if necessary.

CHAPTER 13

Later in the morning

"Let's go." Anton stood in the open doorway of the cliff dwelling. He tapped the headset Trey had given him. "Trey just signaled they made it to the compound without incident and are setting the explosives. We need to get to the meadow. The helicopter is on its way."

Fee's nagging worry for Trey's—and the others'—safety eased somewhat at the news. She stifled a moan as she shoved up from the box she sat upon. Her joints were stiff and sore. She'd be better once she got to moving … she hoped.

She stood and stumbled as the room spun around her. She braced a hand on the rock wall.

"Fee?" Pia whispered as she placed an arm around Fee's waist. "You okay?"

"Been better." She aimed a wry grin at her friend. "But I'll make it." She refused to let the team down. She looked at Anton and Lucia. "So, no boat?"

"No, Levi had the right direction, though." Anton grimaced. "He found it, but the rocks had shredded it."

"So we walk or wade as the case may be." Fee moved away from Pia's hold and headed toward the doorway. "How's the path down to the creek bed?"

"It is slick." Anton moved out of the doorway and let Fee and Pia exit. "You will need to remain close to the rock wall. I will lead. Lucia will walk behind you two."

Fee looked at the gray sky. No sun peeked through the thick-cloud cover. The rain was a miserably cold drizzle, but thunder from the north indicated things could get worse at anytime.

As she waited for Anton to go down the rope ladder so he could anchor it for the rest of them, she muttered, "Damn, couldn't Mother Nature cut us a break?"

"Nope. At least Chavez has to deal with this crap, too," Pia said. "Levi said the lousy conditions would also make it easier for our guys to get in and out of the compound since Chavez's men are staying inside for the most part."

Tweeter's report on the compound had been a mixture of good news/bad news. The good had been what Pia had already mentioned—the cartel soldiers were mostly inside—plus Ernesto, from what Tweeter could tell from visual and audio feeds, had gotten away. The bad news was Chavez and all of his men had returned to the compound. If discovered, Trey and the others would be out-numbered by a huge amount.

He'll be fine.

Fee sure as hell hoped so. If something happened to Trey because of her, she'd never forgive herself for wasting the last nine months and the possibility of a life with him.

"Fee," Anton called. "You can come down now."

Pia patted her on the shoulder. "Go. Don't think about the height. Just stare at the rocks."

Fee nodded. She turned and got down on her knees at the edge of the ledge, then felt to place her foot on the first rung of the rope ladder. Pia and Lucia hovered over her as if she were a two-year-old learning to go down the stairs for the first time. God, she only wished she could go down the ladder on her butt.

No, you don't, then you'd see where you're going. Just do it, pansy ass.

Taking a deep calming breath led to a bout of coughing. She waited until she'd stopped trying to hack up a lung, then scooched until she had both feet on the ladder and had a grip on both sides.

"I've got you, Fee." Anton's voice was closer.

She chanced a look over her shoulder and found he'd come halfway up the ladder. "I'm fine. You can go down."

He smiled and shook his head. "I will remain here. The ladder won't sway as much with my weight on it."

But would it hold their combined weight?

Something on her face must've clued him into her thoughts, since he added with a chuckle, "And, yes, it will hold both of us."

She nodded, turned her head to stare at the rock wall again, then forced herself to move. Finally she reached the bottom where Anton helped her off and then moved her to the side. "Hold onto this rock—and breathe, Fee."

Good suggestion, since the world was lurching from side to side—oh, that was her. She concentrated on her breathing and gripped the jutting stone until she found her balance.

When Pia and Lucia reached the path, Anton turned, his gaze finding each woman in turn. "Remember, hug the wall. Take small steps. Put your weight on the back of your feet since we're going down the incline."

"How deep is the water once we get down the path?" Pia asked.

"To my shins, so maybe to your knees," he replied. "The current is swift in spots, so that is why we'll be using this rope." He held up a long length of rope. "To link us to each other."

What he didn't say was—"to link the three midgets to him so he could keep them from being swept downstream and dashed against the rocks like the inflatable boat."

Fee helped Anton tie the rope around her waist, then waited as he helped each of the other women with their safety lines.

"Okay, slow and steady," Anton said. "Trey just signaled they are wiring the last building and will be on their way to meet us in the meadow soon. So far no one has seen them."

Fee prayed that their good luck would continue.

After the explosions began, DJ would sweep in and pick them all up. As long as Chavez was occupied with burning buildings, they should be able to get away scot-free. Or that was the theory.

Please, God, let that happen.

Anton led the way down the path with Fee right behind him, then Pia, and Lucia anchoring the rear. The path wasn't as bad as she'd anticipated, but then she remembered how much worse it had been the night before with the wind and heavier rain threatening to shove them off the narrow, slippery trail.

When they reached bottom and stood on a small triangular area of soggy ground, Anton turned to them. "Okay, Levi and I went over the safest route to approach the area where the helicopter has the best chance of picking us up and still be out of range of weapons from the compound."

Everything relied on the cartel assholes staying in or near the compound and not rushing the meadow weapons blazing.

Glass half-empty, much?

Fee wouldn't hold her breath about Chavez being distracted by the chaos in the compound. Helicopters were big and noisy. There was no way the soldiers in the compound wouldn't notice a chopper hovering in the meadow and picking up people.

Pessimistic bitch when you're sick, aren't you?

No, realistic bitch when kidnapped and taken to a foreign country.

"Watch your step," Anton warned. "It's a short drop from this level and then I'll lead you to the stepping stone path across the creek."

The submerged stepping stone path, but it was better to walk on than the sucking mud and rocks of an uneven creek bed.

Fee stepped down and immediately tripped on a rock that she hit off-center with her right foot.

Anton caught her arm and steadied her. "Okay, Fee?"

She nodded and then looked over her shoulder at Pia. "Watch that first step. It's really rocky here."

Pia nodded. "Yeah, and I imagine the gully-washer brought even more loose stones down with it."

Fee turned and followed Anton as he led them a few more feet along what had used to be the banks of the creek and waited for Lucia. Once his fiancee had stepped down, she sent him a slight smile. "Go ahead, Anton. I am fine."

Anton led them to the flat rocks which made up a natural bridge across the wide creek. The water was about ankle deep once they stepped up onto the first stepping stone. But the next few minutes proved to be dicey. The rocks were slippery and the current was strong enough to hamper a straight-forward walk across the stones. Several times one or another of their party found bad footing, slid off a stepping stone, and then got wet up to their thighs or higher.

Fee shivered constantly now as the wet and cold got to her. She recognized the early stages of hypothermia. Her reaction time had slowed immeasurably, and she had to focus on each and every movement she made. And she wasn't the only one. Even Anton's large body trembled and his movements were much less graceful than just minutes ago.

When they finally reached the edge of the stepping-stone bridge and climbed up onto what had been the night before a grassy and flower-filled meadow, but was now a water-filled one, Fee could sense the relief from the others as if the rope tying them together transmitted their shudders down the line. But they still weren't out of the woods—they were wet and cold and needed dry clothes and a warm, dry place sooner rather than later.

Anton pointed to a single tree sitting off to the side of a larger copse of trees and bushes. "The helicopter will hover to the east of that tree. We'll keep the safety lines on until we get there. The meadow is uneven and who knows what might have washed into it from the raging creek waters."

"Snakes?" Pia muttered.

Anton looked at her. "It is cold and wet so I would think most of the snakes in this region do not tolerate such conditions. If there are any, they will be by the tree where we will shelter. Ignore them."

"Easy for you to say." Fee's body quaked and then she coughed. Her skin itched like a bitch at the thought of a snake sliding around her legs, looking for a warm place.

They'd just begun the arduous trek toward the rendezvous point when the sound of a large explosion thundered across the meadow. It was quickly followed by a series of smaller explosions. The noise echoed off the sheer mountain walls surrounding the valley.

Looking toward the compound, Fee saw billowing clouds of flames, smoke, and debris. "Sweet Jesus." She inhaled sharply and stopped in place.

Pia screeched, "*Madre de Dios.*"

Anton grinned over his shoulder. "That must have been the building they were cooking meth in. There were lots of flammable chemicals in it. I also made sure Trey and the others knew which buildings held all the stored drugs. They will be blowing up millions and millions of dollars of drugs, in street value. This will be a devastating loss to the Sinaloa cartel."

"Good," Fee said.

The next explosion startled her, but this time she kept moving, following Anton toward the pickup point. The sound of small weapons' fire sent a cold chill over her already freezing body.

"Trey…" Fee whimpered. *Please let him be safe.*

"They are fine." Anton halted by the tree, then shrugged the weapon off his shoulder and checked it over just as she'd seen her brother and Trey do. Her Russian doctor friend knew his way around an assault rifle, it seemed. "Lucia, come."

Lucia took the rope off her waist and handed her end of the rope to Pia. "Get the rope off and be ready." She moved to her man and took the handgun he gave her and then checked the weapon. Okay, so Lucia also knew her way around a gun.

Fee wanted a gun. Yeah, Keely had only shown her the basics that one time, and Pia had dragged her to a gun range once. But how hard could it be? Safety off, point, and shoot. At this moment in time, she was totally in the mindset she could kill a cartel bastard if one shot at her friends.

The *whup-whup* sound of a helicopter echoed loudly in the meadow.

Fee turned and found the speck coming from the northeast, but it could've been any helicopter.

"Is that our ride?" she screamed to be heard above another explosion reverberating over the meadow.

"Yes," Anton shouted back, his gaze fixed on the direction their men would come from the compound. "When the helicopter hovers, keep your head down and move to it quickly. A man will help you into it."

"What about Levi and the others?" Pia yelled.

"They are coming now. Just get on the helicopter." Anton moved to cover them with his weapon.

The chopper came in fast and low.

Tweeter stood in the open cabin door, a rifle in his hands. God, she hoped he was anchored in. When the pilot, DJ, placed the helicopter into a hover, Fee ran toward it, pulling Pia with her who, in turn, tugged at Lucia. "Let's go."

Fee wasn't sure how the men would make it in time, but one thing Fee knew, they weren't leaving without Trey, Price, and Levi.

"Hey, Fee." Tweeter set his weapon down and lifted her up and then swung her into the cabin as if she weighed nothing. When the other two women were inside, he handed them headsets and indicated the jump seats. "Strap-in," he shouted.

Fee sat in a seat facing the front of the helicopter and pulled the shoulder harness over her chest and snapped it into the buckle. Pia and Lucia sat across from her. Once she figured out how to operate the headset, she could hear the chatter among DJ, Tweeter, and the others on the ground.

"Ace, everybody secure? We gotta go," DJ's calm voice cut through all the chatter. "Visual shows Chavez's men aren't as disorganized as we'd hoped."

"Shit. Give it a few more seconds, DJ." Tweeter's voice was tense. "Vasilov, get in here. Trey, you guys find a place to hunker down. DJ is going to do her thing."

"Roger that," Trey's calm voice came across the headset. "Anton, get on board. We'll be fine."

Some of the tension went out of Fee's shoulders, but not all. DJ having to "do her thing" didn't sound good. But there had been no fear in Trey's voice. She would've heard it. She knew him well enough for that. Would she have a chance to get to know all the rest of his moods?

He's got this. Chill.

Her snarky inner voice shouldn't have reminded her of how cold and wet she was. Fee shuddered, her teeth chattering so hard, she clenched her jaw to stop them.

From her view out the open door, she watched Anton back up toward the helicopter, then turn and leap into the cabin. In the distance, *El Hacha's* compound had become a hell on Earth of fire, smoke, and even more explosions. Somewhere between the middle of the field where they were located and the chaos in the compound, Trey and the others were trapped.

Tweeter yelled, "Go, go, go!" He turned toward them. "Make sure you're strapped in tight, ladies. It's gonna get rough in a bit. Vasilov, you comfortable riding on the edge with the cabin door open? I could use some help in taking out some bogies."

Anton nodded. "*Da.*" He moved about the helicopter with ease, showing his former Russian military training had never quite gone away. He hooked himself onto the cabin wall by the doorway and then sat, his legs dangling over the edge. The weapon in his hands seemed almost like an extension of his body.

As DJ took the helicopter up and swung around and away from the meadow, away from the compound, Fee could see Chavez's men spreading out from the conflagration, searching the outbuildings that were still intact for Trey, Price, and Levi and shooting at—

"God, who are they shooting at?" Fee whispered. "Trey…"

"Button it, sis."

Fee recognized her brother's stop-being-a-pest voice. Price was irritated, but not in danger.

Trey's voice came over the headset. "Just sit tight, little doc. Once DJ clears the way, we'll be right there." He sounded steady, fearless. Not in pain.

"Heads up on the ground. We're coming in," DJ said. "I'm going to take out a group of bad asses on the north side of the compound."

"Roger that," Trey said. "We're ready."

Ready to do what? Were they going to run across half the meadow with the hounds of hell on their asses? What?

Fee gripped the harness and leaned forward, straining to see out the door. But Tweeter and Anton now filled it, their weapons aimed at the ground.

"Go, go, go. Light them up, sugar," Tweeter said.

DJ let out a rebel yell. Fee was thrown back as the helicopter suddenly went faster and began to weave. Then came a roar and the chopper jerked. What looked like a rocket left the underside of the chopper. The missile hit the ground among a group of men who approached the outermost building of the compound. The one where Anton had met Fee and Pia. The one that had held the boat—and the explosives that Anton had mentioned.

Beyond that same building, she could make out three men as they ran toward the thicket of trees near where DJ had picked her and the others up just minutes ago.

The cartel soldiers zeroed in on Trey, Price, and Levi and gave chase, shooting at them.

Tweeter and Anton fired at the enemy, giving Trey and the men cover.

"We're away. Take out the building, DJ," Trey ordered.

"Roger that." DJ swooped away from the compound and some ground fire. Then she put the helicopter into a wide turn and began the approach toward her target.

"Sugar, this one is for all the money," Tweeter said. "Shit. Evasive…"

"Shut it, Ace," DJ snarled, "I got this."

And she did. She swerved and the rocket launched from a shoulder-held weapon held by a cartel soldier missed.

"Shoot at me, will ya?" DJ swooped over the landscape like a giant dragonfly and lined up for her next fly-by. She held steady, shots streaming from the belly of the helicopter. The bullets ate at the ground and took out anything in their path including the man with the rocket-launcher. His last shot went wild and took out some of the cartel men.

"Good shooting, DJ," Trey said.

"Thanks." DJ swooped over the stand of trees where their men hid. "Be back in a few to pick you up, guys."

DJ maneuvered the chopper until she hovered in a direct line with the last building on the north side of the compound.

Cartel soldiers ran from the compound and headed for the trees where her man and the others hid.

"Okay, sugar, keep the cartel jack-offs pinned down," Tweeter said. "Then blow that sucker."

"You got it, Ace." DJ sent a fusillade of bullets at the cartel soldiers. Those who weren't hit, dropped down. Still others shot at the chopper.

Then a roar came from under the helicopter and the cabin vibrated as another rocket was launched. It hit the building and the percussion from the resulting huge explosion rocked the chopper.

DJ moved away from the blast and then circled around and behind the copse where Trey, Price, and Levi hid. "Ride's here. Get the lead out," DJ said.

"Roger that." Trey led the way as Anton and Tweeter lay down cover fire. He jumped up and inside, then came straight to Fee. "You okay, sweetheart?" He stroked her face with a grimy hand that smelled of smoke and gunshot residue.

Fee checked him over with hands and eyes. He was covered in dirt and sweat. No blood. She let out a heartfelt sigh. "I am now." Tears streamed down her cheeks as Trey sat next to her and put his arm around her. "I am now."

CHAPTER 14

Fee locked the door behind her last patient of a very long day. The small rural clinic was a bare bones satellite operation of the medical group that staffed the Grangeville Medical Center. Serving a sparsely populated area of Idaho, the clinic was only open three days a week— Monday, Wednesday, and Friday. It boasted a staff of three—Fee, Pia, and a receptionist who doubled as bookkeeper, plus a cleaning crew that did the heavy duty cleaning after clinic hours ended. Prior to her arrival, the Elk City clinic had been closed for over a year due to the lack of a doctor willing to live in the middle of nowhere. For that year, the population in the area had driven the two hours to Grangeville for their medical needs.

Her arrival had been celebrated by the locals, and her clinic days had been full ever since.

"Thank God, it's Friday," she muttered to the empty reception area that looked as if a mini-cyclone had hit it. Actually, one had—in the form of two-year-old twin boys who'd been brought in by their much-harried mother for some routine shots and a check-up.

Chuckling at the memory of the toddlers' non-stop jabbering and antics, Fee began picking up toys and tossing them into a much-abused toy box. Cute little buggers. With their dark-hair and light green eyes, they could've been Trey's sons.

At the errant thought, Fee froze in mid-toss. An onslaught of biological urges swamped her and had her heart melting. She shook off the hormonal storm and threw the last toy into the box, then slammed the lid on the cleanup and wayward thoughts. Thoughts which had begun to pop up more often since her time in Mexico and Trey's rescue of her. Thoughts that ruled her lonely nights as she tossed and turned on the lumpy bed in the barely adequate living space situated over the clinic.

Premature thoughts, because her relationship hadn't moved past first base with Trey. There were sixteen-year-old girls who came to her clinic who had a more active sex life than she did.

To be honest, things had been hectic. First, there'd been the precipitous move from New Mexico to Idaho and all that entailed, with her in New Mexico tying up loose ends and Trey working on SSI ops out of the country.

Upon arrival in Idaho, she'd moved into the provided apartment over the clinic and then immediately jumped into her job's first gargantuan task—reopening the long-shuttered clinic. There had been a lot of work to do to bring the clinic up to her standards.

After opening the clinic and establishing routine office hours, she'd then taken up the reins of her other medical staff duties by working an ER night shift every other Friday at the main hospital in Grangeville.

Her work schedule and Trey being away for most of the last three weeks had precluded building on the connection that had been cemented during the ordeal in Mexico.

With a free weekend looming ahead, she and Trey were finally getting together for their first real date—dinner and a movie.

Since it was almost an hour drive from Elk City to Sanctuary, Fee had also been invited by Ren and Keely to spend the weekend at the Main Lodge on Sanctuary. That way, Trey wouldn't have to make a two-hour round trip to take her home after their date. She'd been looking forward to the stay at the Lodge since her studio apartment was a poorly finished attic space with a half-assed stall shower, a sink, and a toilet in what looked to be a cardboard closet.

Now that her work day was done, her mind turned to the issue which had lurked in her subconscious since the night she'd slept in Trey's arms in the cliff house above Madera. Was she ready to "sleep" with Trey?

He hasn't asked you yet. But if he does? My vote is—go for it.

Yeah, that was the problem.

Trey hadn't even tried anything sexual during the few times they'd connected for a quick meal between his SSI missions and her work schedule. In fact, he'd never gone past kissing her—and even Trey's kisses had ranked above the best sex Fee had ever had.

Fee was fairly certain she was ready to skip a few bases and round home with Trey, but...

But?

Trey had been very vocal about her taking the lead in the going-to-bed decision. He wouldn't make the next move. Dammit.

"But I want him to lead," Fee muttered. Mostly because she was an insecure wuss.

"What did you say?" Pia came around the corner of the check-in desk with a bag of dirty linen to be set outside for pickup by the laundry service the main hospital had all its satellite clinics use.

Pia moving to Idaho had been an unexpected blessing. With the Sinaloa cartel on the warpath after the destruction of its Madera facilities, the border had no longer been safe for Pia or her mother. The two women had accepted SSI's generous offer of a place to live. The same offer Fee had refused and now regretted, because—crap apartment—but she hadn't known that at the time.

Pia and Carmela made the move to Idaho. Levi hadn't been thrilled about that, but Fee suspected he was making plans to move to Sanctuary and work for SSI, or at least, Trey had hinted at such during one of their few times together.

The Lopez women shared a two-bedroom suite in Sanctuary's Main Lodge. The medical center had hired Pia to work in the Elk City clinic. And soon Pia's mother would reopen a shuttered diner located on the road between Sanctuary and Grangeville. Ren Maddox would be Señora Lopez's silent partner.

"Nothing." Fee forced a smile to her lips. "So, what are *your* plans for our first truly free weekend?"

Her friend raised a brow and shook her head at Fee's obvious deflection. "This evening, *mamá* and I are going to visit the diner to take an inventory of plates, glasses, and other kitchen items the previous owners left behind." Pia straightened some magazines. "Tomorrow, Keely will take us to the outlet mall to do some serious shopping."

"Does Ren really think the restaurant will draw enough business?" Fee asked, visualizing the building which sat in the middle of fricking nowhere.

Everything is in the middle of nowhere out here.

Too true.

"He said SSI and forestry service personnel alone will flock to it. Not to mention all the hunters, hikers, and climbers that come here year-round." Pia shoved a chair back against the wall, then turned her focus on Fee. "So, what're—"

"Did Ren say what happened to the last owner?" She wanted to keep Pia on the diner topic so Fee's personal life wouldn't come into the discussion. She wasn't sure she had answers for any of the questions Pia might bring up.

"Uh huh." Pia shot Fee a "you still aren't fooling me" look, but answered the question, "The previous owner died. His kids didn't want to run a restaurant. Ren bought the property since it abutted his land and would give him frontage access to the highway. He eventually plans to build more cabins and condos in that direction for SSI support personnel."

"I can see that," Fee said. "There's not a lot of homes for sale in the area because of the national forest. Keely told me many of their employees made the drive in from Grangeville and from even farther every day. Also, they can't attract new employees, especially those with a family, if they can't house them."

The clinic reopening would also be a lure for future SSI hires.

"Yeah, winter travel must suck around here. I'm really not looking forward to that hour drive each way to the clinic once the snow flies." Pia moved to lean her hip against the check-in desk. "So, what are *you* doing this weekend?"

Busted.

Fee had known better than to think she could keep Pia from circling back around to Fee's private life.

"Trey is taking me to dinner and a movie tonight and…" She hesitated.

"And?" Pia gestured with a hurry up motion.

"And I'm staying at the Lodge at Ren and Keely's invitation…"

"And…" Pia wiggled her fingers in a give-me-more gesture.

Fee wrinkled her nose. "And I'm trying to figure out whether Trey will want sex or not."

"Ahh." Pia smiled. "So Trey's the one you want to take the lead."

Fee jabbed her finger at Pia. "You did hear what I'd said."

"Yep. So what's the problem?"

"The problem is he insists that *I* have to take the lead with the next step into intimacy." Fee bit her lip. "And I don't know how … to lead."

"It's simple, *chica*. Just start shedding clothes as you walk into his bedroom. His male hormones will force him to take over."

"It's not that simple … I, uh, hell…" Fee scraped her fingers through her tangled curls. "If he takes the hint…"

"Oh, he will," Pia said with a wicked grin.

"If…" Fee repeated. "Then we'll get in bed, and he'll be kissing and touching me, but…"

"But what, Fee? What are you worried about?" Pia prodded.

"I'm afraid I'll balk … at the last minute … no matter who leads. Then Trey will get frustrated and…" Fee choked as tears streamed down her face. "God, I'm a mess."

Pia came over and hugged Fee. "*Chica*, Trey's not that *cabrón* who hurt you. He's the man who patiently pursued you over many months with a long-distance commute that would've driven away any man just wanting to get his *cojones* off."

"I know that." Fee sniffled, then mumbled, "I'm scared he'll be disappointed … find out I'm not worth all that effort. God knows, even the guys I had sex with prior to Adam-fucking-Stall attacking me were disappointed after having sex with me."

Pia rolled her eyes. "Did you ever think the problem was them and not you?"

Fee shrugged, not wanting to go into full detail on her sad, former sex life, but she knew Pia wouldn't leave the topic alone. So, she offered the Cliff's Notes version. "Most of the guys I dated were fellow doctors I met during training. They were safe, more like buddies I could share a meal or a movie with. The ones that weren't safe were selfish and wanted to go bed to get their rocks off and could care less if I got any pleasure."

Plus, none of them were macho former Marines like Trey. Just inhaling Trey's scent made her horny.

"I take it Stall fell into the latter bunch," Pia said.

"No. I never dated him. I sensed he was *off* from the moment I met him. He didn't like me turning him down, so he stalked me. He's a sociopath and fooled everyone." Fee sighed, suddenly tired to the bone.

"*Maldito* Stall aside, it sounds like your former sex partners and you had a total lack of chemistry," Pia said with the bluntness Fee had come to expect from her friend. "As for Trey? I predict there'd be no disappointment on either side. Sparks fly when you two are together."

Fee shook her head.

"Truth." Pia patted Fee's arm. "Back in New Mexico, when he visited the emergency clinic that first time, I said to myself 'he wants her, and she wants him, but is denying it.'"

"Okay, I admit I've wanted him from the day I met him. I wasn't ready back then." Fee ran her fingers through her curls and kneaded the tense muscles at the base of her skull. "I'm not sure I'm ready even now."

Especially if she had to lead in the bedroom.

"Trust Trey. That man is in a class all by himself, and he cares about you … more than a lot," Pia said. "So, do what I said—shed clothes and let him take over." She tugged on Fee's hand. "Come on, let's get the heck out of here. You have a date to get ready for, and I need to get back to Sanctuary and pick up *mi madre.*"

Fee allowed Pia to lead her out the clinic's front door, then her friend locked up after them. The entrance to Fee's studio apartment from hell was accessible only from an exterior staircase.

"I want to come," Fee said. "Tomorrow. Shopping. To the outlet mall."

"But what about spending the weekend doing things with Trey?" Pia frowned. "Even if you don't have sex tonight, this will be the first quality couple time you two have had."

She's right. Grow a pair.

Trey would have the only balls in their relationship. Fee just wanted to scrape up enough courage to get her hands on them.

"Okay, I'll amend my request … may I come if the date turns out to be a bust?" Fee said.

"It's not going to be a bust." Pia turned, took Fee by the upper arms, and shook her. "Lose the negative attitude, *chica*. Now, repeat after me—my date with Trey will be wonderful, and I'll spend my weekend off doing fun things with him."

Fee laughed. "My date with Trey will be wonderful, and I'll spend my weekend off doing fun—and sexy—things with him."

Pia released her arms and high-fived her. "Now that's the kind of positive attitude that'll get results."

Later that evening, Sanctuary, Trey's house

TREY STOOD JUST INSIDE HIS front door and smiled with an overwhelming amount of satisfaction. Finally, Fee was here, where he'd envisioned her for too many long and lonely months.

"Wow." Fee turned in a circle as she took in his home's open concept great room and kitchen.

Was that a good wow? Or a who-in-the-hell-decorated-this-dump wow?

If she didn't like the masculine decor with its leather and wood Arts & Crafts furniture and the Native American artifacts and rugs, he'd change it all. He wanted her to want to move in with him—sooner rather than later. He'd already marshaled his arguments.

First and foremost, the place she lived in wasn't secure. A four-year-old with a hair pin could pick her apartment entry door lock, and a hundred-pound weakling could kick in the flimsy wood door.

Second, the area around the spot-in-the-road called Elk City was rough, wild, and isolated. More than its fair share of dropouts from society lived in the mountains and forests surrounding the area. Some of those dropouts could be highly dangerous to a single woman living alone in a shitty apartment with zilch security.

Third, pushing aside the lack of security—which Trey couldn't—the studio apartment itself was inherently dangerous. The electrical was antiquated knob-and-tube, a fire waiting to happen. The water pipes had burst over the last winter when the place was empty and the repair job done by the landlord had been half-assed. If there wasn't mold growing in the less than adequate insulation, he was a one-eyed jackass. There were raccoons living above the drop-ceiling, and packs of wolves in the surrounding forest. Plus, he'd seen bear scat behind the clinic. He didn't even want to think about her taking out the trash and running into a hungry bear or wolves.

Keely had checked out the apartment before Fee arrived and told him and Ren the place wasn't fit for human habitation. Probably why the two previous doctors, both male, hadn't even lived in it.

But no amount of persuasion, and even an invitation to stay in the Lodge, had budged his stubborn little doc from taking up residence in the ratty-assed apartment. She'd pled the need to be close by while getting the clinic up and running.

Well, the clinic was now open. No more excuses. If she wasn't ready to move in with him, then he'd convince her to move into the Lodge for her safety and comfort. He wanted her free from all dangers and living on Sanctuary.

And close at hand for a more intense courtship.

Yeah, that, too.

Trey tracked Fee as she moved about the great room and into the kitchen. His gaze grew warmer as she trailed fingers lightly over the dark granite counter tops in the kitchen and peeked in the reclaimed wood cupboards. A light smile played about her full lips. Her blue-green eyes gleamed with delight.

She liked his kitchen.

Trey, being a Neanderthal, liked seeing her in his kitchen. He could care less if she cooked. Instead, he pictured her there each morning, sharing his space, puttering around making coffee, and talking about the coming day.

Did it make him a sick fuck that he'd also envisioned beginning each day laying her out on the kitchen island and eating her for breakfast? Probably. Of course, that would only occur after he'd awakened her first in their bed by making love to her.

Getting ahead of yourself, Maddox. First you have to convince her to move in.

"What do you think of the place?" He walked to where she stood at the folding glass doors leading to the double-level deck which wrapped this side of the house and overlooked the river gorge.

She turned her head from the view and smiled. "Gorgeous house. Fabulous view. And I love the outdoor kitchen on the deck—is that a hot tub I see down one level?"

"Yep. You want to sit in the hot tub, drink a little wine, and enjoy the stars?" he murmured as he swept a hand down her back and then settled his arm around her waist.

Shit, her body had gone rigid. He lightened his hold, but didn't remove his arm. If she needed to pull away, she easily could.

Trey was relieved when she didn't.

Actually, Fee had been tense since he picked her up for their date. Although she'd said all the right things at dinner and laughed at the romantic comedy she'd chosen, her stress had been evident in the tautness of her neck and facial muscles.

Now, he felt it in her whole body as she held herself immobile within the circle of his arm. Her reactions were those of a small animal freezing in place so as not to attract the further notice of a predator.

Was she afraid he'd attack her as soon as he had her in his house? Hadn't she processed anything he'd said over the months he'd visited her and more recently in Madera?

Fee was in control of whatever happened next. And as much as he wanted to make love to her—to make her completely his—he'd die before he went back on his word. Her trust in him would lay the foundation for their future.

"Fee, relax," he whispered against her hair. "I'm not gonna attack you."

"I know." She sighed and let her body go lax.

Some of his own tension released. Thank fuck, she wasn't retreating as she'd done so often in the early months of their acquaintance.

"I'm sorry," she muttered as she stared at her feet.

"Nothing to be sorry about." He brushed a kiss over the top of her head. Her hair was so soft and smelled like peaches and vanilla. Her scent alone had his cock hard and pushing against the placket of his jeans. If she brushed against him intimately, he'd shoot his wad before he'd even kissed her. No other woman had ever gotten him so hot so fast with just her scent before.

If he were more sure of her, he'd strip off her clothes, lift her off her feet, and make love to her against the glass as the sun set behind the mountains. Then he'd take her on the couch. And finally he'd make love to her in his bed where neither of them would get any sleep for the rest of the night.

God, if she knew what he was thinking … what he was imagining, she'd run.

Don't fuck it up now, asshole. Stay the course.

That would be the course he'd set for himself when he'd first met her across the barrel of an assault rifle as she'd protected a pregnant and in labor Keely. Fee's fire and courage had impressed him and captured his previously fickle heart. He'd fallen head over heels in love with her at first sight—and she'd run from him. He'd managed a patient pursuit since that time, and he'd stick to that path until Fee trusted him, unconditionally, to care for her body, heart, and soul.

Momentary pleasure wasn't worth losing what ground he'd gained. He had a right hand, if he needed relief.

Fee angled her head. Her silky curls caught in his five o'clock shadow as he leaned over her. Her gaze was quizzical and a bit wary. "What would we wear in the hot tub?"

"Skin?" Shit, his mouth had gotten ahead of his brain.

Trying to cover for the lame-ass mistake worthy of a horny teenage boy, he chuckled and winked. "Just kidding. I have some gym shorts with a draw-string waist and a T-shirt you can wear. I'll keep my boxers on."

Fee stared at him quizzically. Her fair skin flushed dark pink.

After several tense seconds in which he wasn't even sure he'd taken a breath, she bit her lip, then muttered, "Yeah, this'll work."

Her phrasing puzzled him, but he wouldn't look a gift horse in the mouth. He blew out a relieved breath. After rubbing her waist, he released her. "I'll just go—"

Before he could finish the sentence, she moved away, turned her back to him, and stripped her loose peasant top over her head and dropped it over the back of his leather sectional. Then she shimmied out of the long, gauzy skirt she'd worn and laid it on top of the blouse. She was now clad in only an emerald green bra and lace-edged panties which hugged her sweet ass cheeks. Her skin glowed almost pearlescent in one overall pale pink blush.

Trey almost swallowed his tongue. Her near nakedness had his cock ready for some action. Only his iron will kept him from embarrassing himself.

Shit, Fee just did it for him. The smell of her … the look of her bare skin, and he was ready to blow.

When she turned around, all the moisture in his mouth dried up instantly. With her petite stature and subtle curves, she looked like a fairy or pixie from some fantasy tale. Make that an erotic fairy or pixie. Her sheer bra and panties did nothing to hide her feminine attributes. Her nipples were dark and beaded. Her pussy was framed by red-gold curls. The only jarring notes to the titillating picture she made were the scuffed motorcycle boots she wore with some sort of frilly socks sticking out of the top of them.

"Trey—" Fee's eyes widened as she skimmed his body, from top to bottom. Her gaze lingered over the bulge in his jeans. "Um, are you gonna get naked, too?"

"Yep." He pulled off his thermal T-shirt. With his gaze fixed on her, he unbuckled his belt, toed off his boots, and then stripped off his jeans.

The dying light from the setting sun glinted off something on Fee's abdomen. His dry mouth suddenly watered and a blast of lust hit him so hard, he fought with every bit of his strength to rein it in. She had a naval piercing, a gold ring with a green jewel centered in her cute little belly button.

"Fuck me. You are the sexiest thing I've ever seen in my life." He moved slowly toward her, afraid if he moved too fast she'd fly away like the fairy she resembled. A punk fairy in motorcycle boots … with a piercing.

His punk fairy.

When he was within arm's length, he swept some of her curls back over her shoulders, then traced her collar bones with the tip of one finger. "Freckles. I plan on kissing every single one. Does that scare you?"

Breathing slightly faster than a few seconds ago, Fee's eyes were so dilated that only a thin blue-green band surrounded the pupil. She licked her lips, took a deep breath, and then let out a shaky sigh. She didn't move away—but didn't move closer, either. She'd frozen in place.

Fee was either scared shitless or highly aroused. Then he scented the female musk of her arousal. Noted that her nipples had tightened even more than a few seconds ago. She quivered under his light touch. Her skin flushed a darker pink in response.

She was definitely aroused, but still she held back. Her higher brain must've made the decision to strip off her clothes and indicate an interest in further intimacy. But her more primitive brain, it seemed, hadn't gotten on board yet. She was still poised for flight, the instinctive reaction of a smaller, weaker female to a larger, aroused male looming over her.

The trust bond had yet to be fully formed between them, and until it had, Fee would likely face this same struggle the first few times intimacy arose between them.

Trey wished he'd killed the pecker-headed douchebag Stall when he'd had the chance.

Slow and steady. Earn that deeper trust bond, dumb shit.

Using a light stroke, Trey moved his finger from her collar bone, up the column of her throat, then to her chin where he tipped up her face.

Fee's breath hitched, and a tiny whimper caught in her throat.

"Shh, little doc. You're safe with me." He placed a gentle, reverent kiss on her lips, a mere brushing of their mouths.

When she sighed against his mouth and brushed her lips over his in return, he smiled. Emboldened by her response, he licked along the seam of her mouth and placed tiny nibbling kisses along her upper and lower lip. Twining her arms around his neck, Fee leaned into his body and opened to him.

Trey groaned his satisfaction and swept his tongue inside the silken heat of her mouth. She tasted like the wine they had at dinner and something sweet and uniquely Fee. He forced himself to tighten the reins on the urge to take her mouth in a deep, tongue-thrusting kiss. Instead, he continued to lick and kiss her slightly parted lips, giving her small touches of his tongue, until she responded by chasing his tongue with hers.

As she tasted him, shyly explored his mouth, his libido howled to be let loose, but he managed to throttle back his lustful urges.

Slow. Steady.

Trey continued to follow Fee's lead and kept his kisses sweet and non-threatening. Still, her kisses had the power to drive him to his knees, begging. He reveled in her slight weight braced against him. Craved the touch of her nipples, even through the sexy bra, against his naked chest. Trembled at the way her fingers played with his ear lobe and the nape of his neck.

Then Fee sucked his lower lip into her mouth and lightly bit it.

He growled. She swallowed the sound and leaned even more heavily against him. He groaned and gathered her even closer, until his hard-on probed her bare stomach through his boxer briefs. He fisted his other hand at his side so he wouldn't scoop her up, one-armed, and hold her still so he could align his cock with her pussy.

Slow. Steady. Don't fuck it up now.

Time passed, slowly, fast—hell, he didn't know, didn't fucking care—as they engaged in a duel of tongues and ever-deeper kisses.

When Fee moaned and rubbed her body against him like a cat begging to be petted and dug her fingers into his shoulders as if she never wanted to let him go, he almost roared in triumph.

Don't. Fuck. Up. Now.

Carefully, he enfolded her with both arms and then lifted her. Still kissing him, she wrapped her legs around his waist and held on. As their kisses turned even more fevered and seeking, he held her trembling body as close to his as he could.

CHAPTER 15

Pia's suggestion about shedding clothes had been right on the mark. It hadn't taken Trey long to follow Fee's lead.

Fee moaned at the sheer pleasure of being held by Trey. His strength awed her, and his body gave off so much heat that even being almost nude she wasn't cold. His kisses had grown hungrier and held the promise of even more intimacies.

Smart move on using the hot tub as an excuse to get naked.

Yeah, she'd been inspired, but the well of inspiration had run dry. What did she do now? Neither she nor Trey were totally naked yet. And while Trey's kisses were smoking hot, he still held her as if she were a fine piece of porcelain he was afraid to drop. His long, thick cock was a mere pair of sheer silk panties and his boxers away from her pussy, but he hadn't even rubbed his cock against her very wet slit.

Fee was more aroused than she could ever remember being. The only other time she'd even come close to being this turned on had been with Trey in the cliff dwelling, and that had been bad timing all around.

She moaned as Trey sucked on her tongue. In response, she tilted her hips and undulated against his erection in an attempt to lure him to rip away her panties and take her right where they stood. While his foreplay was nice—the naughty kind of nice—she was so close to coming and wanted him inside her when she fell over the edge into climax.

Trey's response was to break their kiss and to begin kissing and nibbling along her jaw line to her ear where he sweetly tortured the lobe with his teeth and lips.

The man had too much damn control.

Then make him lose it.

How? She was no femme fatale. Being a late bloomer, she'd lost her virginity in college, a totally lackluster experience. During med school, she'd been too tired to play the dating game. The sexual fiascos during her residency were, well … fiascos. And every blessed one of her past sex partners had made all the initial moves to get her into bed.

Speak up, maybe? Tell him what you want.

Moving one of her hands from clutching at his shoulders, she cupped his face and halted his sensual attack on her neck and ears. "Trey…"

Then … nothing. She'd meant to suggest they move to the next stage, but nada. Not a whimper. Not a moan. Not a sigh. Not a single fucking word. Zilch.

Chicken.

His sharp cheek bones flushed with arousal, Trey looked into her eyes. The longer she didn't speak, the more worried he looked. Finally, he whispered, "Fee?"

Shit. She didn't want him concerned. She wanted him horny … needed him to take control and fuck her senseless.

Fee looked him in the eye and tried again. "Um…" She licked her kiss-swollen lips and tried to swallow past what seemed to be a huge boulder lodged in her throat. "Hot tub?" finally came out on a croak.

Her inner self head-desked.

Trey moved one of his supporting hands and let her slide down his front.

He was letting her go?

For the first time since Fee had taken off her outer clothing, she felt horribly exposed. She struggled not to cry.

"Sweetheart." Trey held her face with both hands and swiped away a tear she hadn't even realized had slid out. He stared at her for several agonizingly long seconds as if she were a puzzle he was trying to solve.

Fee sure as hell hoped he'd figure her out, because damned if she could.

Finally, he nodded. "Get in the hot tub, little doc. You want a glass of wine or something else?"

She breathed a sigh of relief. He wasn't giving up on her. There was still a chance she'd finally realize what real passion was all about. Her past sexual encounters had been more about her curiosity and her partners wanting to scratch an itch. All she'd gotten was disillusioned.

There'd be no disappointment if Trey made love to her. God knew, she was more attracted to him than any man she'd ever seen or fantasized about, and that included the Hemsworth brothers and Chris Pratt post-*Parks and Recreation*.

"Wine. White, if you have it. Thank you."

When Trey moved away, she shivered at the loss of heat radiating off his big body. The early spring night air was colder at this elevation and latitude than even in the New Mexico high desert.

Fee moved quickly out of the great room, across the deck, and down the steps to the hot tub. She folded back the top and hit the button to start the jets.

Stripping off her bra and panties, she dropped them on a nearby lounge chair and then eased into the hot, bubbling water.

"God, that feels good." She rested her head against the smooth lip of the tub and closed her eyes. Maybe now that she was totally nude, Trey would make all the future moves.

It's called communication. Just ask him for what you want.

No, she couldn't. Just couldn't. She'd used up all the audaciousness she possessed in her when she'd first stripped to her undies.

Besides, asking a man for anything sexual hadn't worked that well in the past. The first time she'd asked a man for more clitoral stimulation, her bed partner, a fellow medical resident, had lost his erection and called her a ball-breaking bitch. He'd left her naked and humiliated in her bed.

Thinking the situation might've been more about his issues, she'd attempted to be more subtle with her next lover, also a fellow medical resident. He'd ignored her hints and had taken what he wanted, leaving her in pain. Then the selfish asshole had talked about her behind her back at the hospital where they both worked, said sex with her had been like fucking a cadaver. She soon acquired the reputation of a frigid bitch.

Needless to say, she'd stopped dating guys on the medical staff. Hell, she'd stopped dating period.

So, no … opening her mouth and asking for what she wanted sexually hadn't worked for her.

Trey is not those metrosexual, narcissistic douchebags.

Fee knew that. Trey was … an alpha-male. From what she'd gleaned listening to her female friends who associated with that particular subset of the male species, dominant males liked to take control. Even Pia had said Fee getting naked would send a clear message she was ready, because Trey was more masculine than most.

Fee was naked. Message sent.

Picture me shaking my head.

"Fee?" Trey's deep rumbling voice was close. He hadn't made a sound on his approach. The man moved like a huge, stealthy cat. "Here's your wine."

She opened her eyes. She'd been so lost in her depressing sexual past that he'd also managed to enter the hot tub without alerting her. He now sat across from her.

Leaning forward, she reached for the glass. She frowned when she noticed Trey still had on his boxers.

Fee looked up and found his glittering gaze fixed on her breasts as they gently bobbed on the waves caused by the water jets.

"Th-thank you." Feeling very alone and self-conscious in her nakedness, she took the glass, sat back, and slouched further down on the seat until her breasts were submerged.

"Don't be shy now, little doc." The corners of his eyes creased as an affectionate smile settled on his lips. "You're beautiful. Perfect. Your sexy undies really didn't hide a thing from me." He winked. "By the way, I like your choice of lingerie."

Fee wasn't sure how to respond to his gentle, sexual teasing. So she took a sip of her wine and concentrated on watching the hot tub lights flicker with the movement of the water.

God, she was a loser. First, she sucked at sex. Second, she couldn't ask for what she needed. Now, even light sexual repartee was outside her skill set. Strike three, she was out, right?

"Fee..." Trey's warm breath whispered across her left ear. While she'd been worrying about how to respond, he'd moved next to her.

"Relax, Fee. We have all night. It's not a race, sweetheart." He placed his arm around her shoulders and eased her even closer to his body. "Lean on me. Drink your wine—and just be."

Letting out a tremulous sigh, Fee did as he suggested. It was so much easier when he just told her what he wanted her to do. She could make life-and-death decisions, but when it came to sexual decisions, she needed some damn direction.

Fee sipped the potent wine and let the warm, bubbling water and Trey's scent and touch lull her into a drowsing dream-state. Time had no meaning. She moved from floating on warm damp waves to drifting in a world filled with a cool mist. Shivering slightly, she whimpered, "Cold."

"Shh, sweetheart." A deep male voice—Trey's voice—soothed her. "You'll be warm soon, I promise."

Trey would warm her up. He'd cover her with his hot body and—

The next sensation was her body sinking into a pillowy cloud that smelled of lemons and musk and something she'd scented before but in her lethargy couldn't quite name now.

Warm and feeling safer than she'd ever felt in her life, she succumbed to the lure of the night and dreamt of a mountain god with a panty-melting baritone who enfolded her within his muscled strength.

April 16th, early morning

FEE WOKE SLOWLY. SHE ARCHED and stretched like a contented cat. Yawning widely, she turned onto her side and snuggled her face into the downy pillow which smelled like musk, citrus, and—Trey.

Trey!

She sat up and looked around. This wasn't her assigned guest room in the Lodge. This wasn't even a room she'd seen before. The bedroom's colors were all grays and golds, with two stone walls and two gold-plastered ones. The floor was stamped concrete and covered with animal hide area rugs. A masculine room.

For a terrifying split-second, she thought she was back in Madera. But no, she'd been rescued. She was in Idaho, and this must be Trey's bedroom.

Last night was a myriad of disjointed images floating in a pea-soup fog in her head. Dinner. Two glasses of wine. Movie. Trey's house. First saw hot tub. She got naked. Hot, hungry kissing. Entered hot tub. More wine. Trey hugging her. Then—nada.

Well, not exactly nothing, because here she was. Her dreams of floating and a mountain god had obviously been Trey carrying her to bed and tucking her in like a child.

Rubbing fingers over her aching-from-too-much-wine forehead, she moaned. "I'm such a dweeb." She scraped her hair off her face and tugged it. "He slept next to me. All night. Nothing happened."

Her face flushed hotly as she recalled how difficult it had been to strip off her clothing in front of Trey. But for a few precious seconds, Pia's advice had seemed to work. There'd been sexual interest in his eyes. So much so, he'd taken off some of his clothes, too. God, she prayed her jaw hadn't dropped at the sight of his long, muscled body. Even though he'd still worn his boxers, she'd seen the outline of the very impressive erection she'd previously caught glimpses of in the cliff dwelling.

Kissing had definitely happened, and it had been superb. But then she'd fallen asleep like a cheap drunk. He'd put her to bed to sleep it off … where she'd woken up alone.

How could she ever face him again?

By staying put … naked in his bed.

Fee bitch-slapped her inner self. She couldn't stay here. Hell, she'd been sketchy on how she might've handled the morning-after even if they'd had a night before.

One thing she was sure of—she damn well couldn't handle this particular morning-after. Trey was probably disgusted, maybe even mad. After all, she'd led him on and then left him hanging. She'd also learned from her previous disappointing sexual encounters that men didn't like to be left high-and-dry when it came to sex.

Fee swung her legs over the edge of the bed and sat as the world swirled around her aching head. Her shoulders slumped as dejection settled on them. She had to get out of here.

Listening carefully, she heard no evidence of anyone in the house. She winced. He hadn't even stuck around. Something akin to grief stabbed her in the heart and churned her stomach.

Chalk up another epic fail in the intimacy arena. This time, she'd managed to disappoint her sexual partner even before they'd gotten to the sex part of the program.

Moving off the bed, she spied her clothing neatly folded on a chair. Well, all of it but her undies. Where in the hell had they gone? Then she vaguely recalled dropping her outer clothes in the great room and her bra and panties on the chair by the hot tub. No, she couldn't revisit the site of her failure to lure Trey into having sex. Plus, what if he returned while she was hunting down her underwear?

Fee couldn't face him this soon after the debacle of the previous night. She'd go commando until she reached her guest suite in the Lodge.

That's the coward's way out.

She'd rather think of it as a strategic retreat until she could regroup—and talk to Pia about where she'd gone wrong.

Yellow belly.

Whatever.

It was half past seven. Pia and the others had planned to leave Sanctuary at eight to go outlet mall shopping—a perfect way to avoid Trey for the rest of the day.

Fee dressed, breaking her own personal best record for speed, and left Trey's house by the side door off the laundry area. She saw no one as she sneaked into the Lodge through the kitchen door. She grabbed a bagel and a can of Diet Pepsi to settle her stomach and went up the back stairs to the third floor where her assigned room was located.

Less than twenty minutes after waking in Trey's bed, she was in the back seat of the Hummer that Keely had pulled around for the shopping trip. Fee hadn't seen Trey anywhere, and she wasn't going to ask if anyone knew where he was. No use tempting Fate. Someone might call and tell him where she was.

Pia climbed into the back seat with her. "What happened?"

"Nothing." Which was the complete truth. No wild hot tub sex. No night of any kind of sex. No morning nookie. Nothing. Fee blinked the tears away.

"Fee?" Pia said. "Look at me. What the fuck happened? Do I need to kick some Maddox ass?"

Fee noticed the other women walking toward the Hummer. "Nothing happened. I'll explain later. Please ... I can't talk about it now. Can we just enjoy the outing with the gals?"

Pia's lips thinned. "*Sí*, but later I want details."

"Later." Fee turned and managed a smile for Pia's mother. "Carmela, are you excited about shopping for your new diner?"

The change of topic worked, and when Keely, DJ, and Elana joined them, a lively discussion ensued of color schemes and how many plates, glasses, and flatware would be needed.

8:30 a.m., Trey's house

TREY RETURNED TO HIS HOUSE much later than he'd planned. He hadn't wanted to leave Fee at all, but Ren had called him to help check out a perimeter breech along their eastern border with the national forest. He'd hoped to be gone for no more than an hour, but they'd found evidence of illegal bear hunting on their land. Following the intruders' trail onto the national forest lands, they found an empty squatters' camp and evidence of drugs. They'd called in the park rangers and turned the case over to them.

Now that he was back, he needed to shower off the sweat and stink of investigating a disembowled bear and hiking up hills, through creeks and the woods. Only after he was clean would he crawl back into bed with Fee. He'd be there to wake her up and ease her into the wonders of morning sex.

There'd be no more waiting to make her his. When she'd stripped down to some of the sexiest lingerie he'd ever seen, he understood that salient fact. When Fee had gotten into his hot tub, naked, he took her actions as a silent invitation for sex.

They would've had sex if his little doc hadn't fallen asleep.

Poor little doc. Too much stress plus too much wine at this altitude and she'd drifted off as soon as the hot water added to the alcohol's effects.

Sleeping with her in his arms had felt right—and as frustrating as hell.

Ren had been lucky the intrusion alert had uncovered a real problem, or Trey would've kicked his brother's ass clear into Canada.

Trey toed off his boots and left them in the mud room off the laundry. He moved into the kitchen, started the coffee maker, and snagged a bottle of water to hydrate after all the hiking and climbing he and Ren had done. He stood at the kitchen island and drank the bottle of water. Other than the noises of his refrigerator and the gurgling of the coffee maker, the house was quiet. Too quiet.

Every muscle in his body stiffened. His sixth sense went on alert. The place was empty. Rage and fear roiled in his gut. Had someone managed to get into his house and snatch Fee without triggering Keely and Tweeter's security system?

It would be difficult, but it could be done.

"Fee!" he shouted.

No answer.

He ran to the bedroom and found it empty. There was no sign of a struggle. She'd left on her own.

Relief calmed his rage, but fear still swam in his gut.

Fee was out there, unprotected and ignorant of the lingering danger from her kidnapping by the cartel. Yet another reason he wanted her living on Sanctuary, preferably in his house.

Chavez had escaped Madera immediately after he, Price, and Levi had blown up *El Hacha's* drug operations. Chavez and a recovering *El Hacha* then had gone into hiding. The cartel had placed a bounty on Fee's and the Lopez's heads plus on any others who'd had a part in blowing up the Madera drug operation.

Drug money bought a lot of cooperation on both sides of the border.

Several times since Fee's rescue, Trey and an SSI team had gone back into Mexico on joint drug enforcement missions to track the bastards down and eliminate the danger. But the cartel fuckwits were well-hidden ... for now.

Eventually, they'd crawl out of their lair, and Trey would lead the SSI team that would take both Chavez and his boss down for threatening Fee.

What twisted his gut into a guilty knot was he and Price had agreed not to tell her about the reward for her capture. They'd thought they could protect her.

Trey cursed, then stalked to the bed and touched the sheet. Her sweet musk still lingered on the air, but the sheet was cool. She'd been gone for a while.

Fuming, he pulled his satphone phone from his pocket and hit number three on his speed dial.

"Yo," Tweeter answered. "What do you need, Trey?"

"Where's Fee's tracker?" The tracker had been injected under Fee's skin when she'd gotten a flu shot upon arriving in Idaho. Lacey Jones, a nurse and the wife of Quinn, SSI's third in command, hadn't liked doing it without Fee's permission, but Trey and Price with Keely chiming in had convinced the nurse. He'd figured on telling Fee about it after she lived with him for three or four years.

"You lost your woman already?"

Trey heard the amusement in his friend's voice. He didn't appreciate it … at all. He took one breath, than another, until he could respond without swearing. "Just tell me where she is, Tweeter," he snarled.

"She's with Keely and the others. They're on the way to the outlet mall." Tweeter's voice held no amusement now. "DJ is with them. So between her and my sis, Fee is safe."

Tweeter had zeroed in on Trey's concern.

Trey blew out a frustrated breath. "Okay, thanks, buddy. Did DJ say how long they'd be gone?"

Tweeter snorted. "Her response was when they were done. Can't come between a woman and her outlet mall shopping. Even my kick-ass Army helicopter pilot loves the outlet mall. Hey, maybe they'll hit the lingerie outlet, and we'll both get lucky."

Trey muttered under his breath, "I could only be so lucky."

Tweeter inhaled sharply. "You mean you haven't bedded her yet? What's wrong with you, man?"

"She wasn't ready, asshat." Trey gritted his teeth and throttled back his anger. This wasn't Tweeter's fault, nor was it Fee's. Fuck, it wasn't even his fault. It was bad timing yet again.

Good news was, Fee was ready to take the next step with him—naked hot tub time had clinched that. When she returned to Sanctuary later today, he'd make it clear that tonight she'd be in his arms, in his bed, and he'd make love to her until she fell asleep. Then he'd wake her up tomorrow morning and treat her to Sunday morning marathon sex until it was time for one of Sanctuary Chef Scotty's famous brunches.

After he'd ticked off those boxes, he'd explain her safety and well-being were his top priorities and the only way they could be guaranteed would be if she slept in his arms every night until the day they died.

CHAPTER 16

Later that day
Ma's Bar and Grill, Grangeville

"Fee," Keely said. "Grab the large corner booth. I'll go find Nick and let him know we're here. Looks like the booth still needs to be cleaned off from the lunch crowd."

Fee looked around the mostly empty restaurant. It was too late for a late lunch and too early for an early supper. Through the connecting door, the bar, however, was hopping. College basketball tourney games played on three large flat screens and the locals had gathered and were vocally cheering their favorites on.

"There's a lot of empty…"

"Don't question it," Elana told Fee as Keely moved past them and into the bar in her search for the owner Nick. "Keely—for that matter, all of the SSI operatives—like to sit in that one booth. They can protect their backs while having a view of all the entrances."

Fee recalled she'd sat with Keely in that booth the first time she'd come to Idaho.

"Has there been much need to protect their backs?" Pia leaned around Fee to ask.

"Oh, hell, yeah," Elana said. "The most recent incident was just over a month ago. There was a shoot-out with some hired guns who were after Keely and Riley."

Deja vu. Mercenaries had tried to kill Keely the day Fee had delivered Riley.

"DJ arrived and helped Keely save the day, along with Callie, Risto Smith's wife." Elana patted her tummy. "This pregnant lady, DJ's mom, and some other civilians piled into *Ma*'s safe room with Nick and his gun protecting us."

"Safe room?" Pia turned to her mother. "*Mamá*, we'll need to have such a safe place also. Sounds like we didn't get away from all the violence by coming here."

Carmela nodded. "It is a good thing I brought my gun."

Fee cringed at the thought of Pia's mother shooting anybody, but merely said, "You'll need to make sure you can carry it here."

DJ overheard the end of the conversation. "We'll get Ren to make sure you're legal to carry concealed, Señora. As for your diner's security, he'll most likely put in the same defensive measures he added for Nick and Ma. Ren likes the places his people eat to be defensible since SSI's enemies don't care who they hurt to get to the operatives or their families."

Tweeter's new bride looked over toward the bar. "Looks like Keely found Nick, but they got stopped by some of the locals. Let's just bus the table ourselves."

The group moved to the booth and quickly cleaned off the dishes, utensils, and the glasses. Pia found the bucket with soapy water and a cloth and wiped down the table. By the time, Keely and the burly owner-cook Nick reached them, Elana had even placed rolled up silverware at the table for everyone.

Nick chuckled, taking in the table. "Y'all want jobs? I need some help."

A chorus of "nos" and "no thanks" came from the table's inhabitants.

Nick turned to Carmela and held out his hand. "I hear you'll be opening up a diner between here and Sanctuary.

Welcome to the community. Always room for one more diner for the locals to hang out at."

Carmela smiled and placed her tiny hand in Nick's huge one. "I am sure we can share the business. My place will be Tex-Mex. I won't be competing with your dinner and late night bar crowd. I'll only be open for breakfast and lunch, Monday through Saturday."

Nick grinned. "Sounds good. I may cut back my breakfast hours then and offer a brunch on Sundays. With you taking the early birds, I'll get more rest. I ain't getting any younger and need my beauty sleep."

Fee and the others laughed as Nick rubbed a beefy hand over his balding head. Nick and Carmela shook hands once more. A deal had been struck, and Fee wondered if Ren had anything to do with it. She looked over at Keely who winked and nodded.

Was Ren a silent partner in *Ma's* also? It made sense.

Moving to Idaho had been the right decision for Fee—and for Pia and her mother. The SSI family took care of their own and those special to them. Too bad, the only person in her family who had the same philosophy was Price. Her father had always been a hard ass; he'd figured providing a roof, food, and clothing was all he needed to do. No matter how hard she tried, she could never please him. Her older sisters were a lot older than her and Price, and had gotten the hell out of the house as soon as they could. She and Price had relied on one another for mental and emotional support.

After everyone gave their orders, Pia turned to Fee. "Okay, what happened with the date last night? Why are you with us and not Trey?"

Fee's face burned with embarrassment. "Geez Louise, Pia, just trot my private life out for everyone and their brother to hear."

Pia looked around. "It's just our table," she waved a hand in the general direction of the lunch counter, "and that woman over there, and she doesn't look like she's interested in our discussion."

Everyone looked toward the counter.

"Hey, Tara." Keely waved at the tall, lanky brunette wearing a Park Ranger uniform shirt and well-worn skinny jeans. "Come join us."

The brunette smiled and came over. "Hey, Keely. Are you sure your friends don't mind?" She looked around the table and nodded. "Hello, ladies."

"Gals, this is Tara Nightwalker. She moved to the area not long ago." Keely introduced everyone at the table, ending with Fee. "Fee, are you okay with Tara joining us? I'm getting the sense from Pia's question that you might need some girl talk and maybe some intel about my brother-in-law."

Fee glanced around the table. Each of her shopping companions looked at her with a mixture of curiosity and sympathy. She was comfortable with these women, who hadn't been shy about sharing their own stories about how they hooked up with their SSI men. Some of the stories had been amusing; all of the stories had involved danger. The SSI women were strong and had definite opinions on how to deal with an alpha-male. Fee was more than interested in getting their advice about how to deal with Trey. In fact, after last night and this morning, she was damn sure she needed as much help as she could get.

"Hey, Fee. I can leave," Tara offered with a commiserating smile. "Keely has sort of put you on the spot."

Tara's offer showed a particular sensitivity for Fee's feelings. She immediately sensed that Tara was cut from the same cloth as the other women at this table and would become another good friend.

Fee had never really had a lot of close female friends before Pia, and was discovering she liked the camaraderie she'd found with the SSI women in the short time she'd been in Idaho.

After a few moments of consideration, Fee said, "What the hell … stay. The more, the merrier."

Tara grinned and pulled up another chair to the table.

Pia gestured hurry up with her hand. "So, fess up. Did you take my advice?"

"Yes, I did."

Pia high-fived her. "Way to go, my shy, retiring friend. So? What happened? Why aren't you still with him? God, don't tell me the sex was bad. Was he mean?"

As she pondered which of the many questions she'd address first—

"Whoa, hold the phone." Keely frowned at Pia. "Trey isn't mean. Plus, the sex couldn't be bad. From what I've overheard from the locals he's dated, his reputation is that of a frick-fracking sex god…"

Fee groaned. That was not what she needed to hear, especially since she'd already observed he was hung like a stallion. In that instant, she hated every woman he'd ever fucked … local or not.

Jealous much?

Keely continued talking, "…a lot like his brother. So tell all. I have experience with the Maddox-protect-the-little-woman-from-herself, macho mind-set. That's what happened, right?"

"Maybe." Fee bit her lip.

Not maybe.

She obviously misunderstood the over-protective, dominant breed of male since she'd always kept her distance from men of that ilk. But she didn't want to stay away from Trey. So—"We went back to his place."

"And?" Keely leaned over the table.

"Nothing."

"Nothing?" Keely echoed. The other women looked almost as shocked as Keely sounded. Well except for Pia who knew just what a coward Fee really was.

"Okay," Fee sighed. "See … it's this way. Ever since I first met Trey, he's told me over and over that the next move in our … whatever this is between us …would be up to me."

Keely nodded. "Just what I thought—he's protecting you even from himself."

"Yeah." Fee swallowed. She coughed, her throat and mouth dry from tension. She really needed that Diet Pepsi she'd ordered. The ladies remained silent, allowing her to gather her thoughts. Clearing her throat, she continued, "My past experiences with men have been … well, let's just say, less than stellar."

"And then there was the stalking-rapist son of a bitch," Pia added.

"May he burn in hell," Carmela said, crossing herself.

Keely muttered "frick-fracking Stall." Fee had almost forgotten she'd told Keely about Stall last June, in fact, in this very booth.

Elana, DJ, and Tara's expressions ran the gamut from sympathy to anger. Tara, in particular, had tensed when Pia had mentioned "stalker-rapist."

"Yeah … and him." A Diet Pepsi appeared in front of Fee. She grabbed it and drank a healthy swallow. "So … for many reasons, I didn't feel I could take the lead or even the next step with Trey. Truth be told, I don't want to take the lead. It's not … me."

Mostly because in the past you've picked losers to have sex with.

Elana patted Fee's hand which she'd fisted on the table. "Not all women want or can take the lead. I know I wasn't able to when I first met Vanko."

"Really?" Fee turned to face Elana.

"I wouldn't lie about that," Elana said. "So what was Pia's suggestion?"

"She said a man like Trey…

"A man's man," Pia put in as if the ladies at the table hadn't already known that. Tara raised an elegant raven-colored brow, her lips twisting into a slight smile.

Fee shot a glare at Pia, then said, "…a man like Trey would get the message I was ready for sex if I took off my clothes as I headed toward his bedroom."

The women laughed.

"So … did it work?" Pia asked, bouncing in her seat.

"I thought it had." Fee frowned. "Well, let me back up. Before I took off my clothes, I sort of improvised."

At Pia's groan and muttered "*mierda*," Fee hurried to add, "He has a hot tub. I commented on it. He asked me if I wanted to sit in the hot tub and look at the stars. I said yes and asked what we'd wear. He said nothing."

The ladies hooted.

Fee waved them off. "But then he immediately backed off and offered me some of his draw-string shorts and a T-shirt."

A chorus of boos went around the table.

"So? Keep going. What happened next?" Keely wiggled her fingers in a gimme-more.

"I stripped down to my underwear." Fee took another sip of her drink. Talking about her sex life was thirsty work.

"Good move, Fee." Keely gave her a thumb's up.

"That's my girl," Pia said.

"What kind of underwear?" Carmela asked. "Sexy or granny panties?"

"*Mamá*!" Pia looked shocked at her mother's question.

"*Mi hija*. Men like sexy underwear." Carmela smiled. "My Manny likes red lace."

"*Mamá*!" Pia blushed. "I don't want to know that—ever."

Fee giggled at the look of horror on Pia's face and found for the first time that day she felt lighter, happier. "Carmela, it was very sexy underwear. Sheer green bra and a matching bikini panty edged in lace. FYI, I don't own granny panties."

Carmela gave her two thumbs up.

"Oooh, I know those undies. Good choice." Pia grinned. "So, come on. What happened next? No red-blooded male could resist you in that underwear."

"He kissed me." Fee sighed. "His kisses are the best sex I've ever had."

"That can't be true." Elana frowned.

"Sadly, it is." Fee took a deep breath and let it out slowly. "After the kisses is when it all went wrong."

The women went quiet once again.

"Don't stop now," DJ broke the moment of silence, "what happened?"

Fee heaved a sigh. "Trey left to get me some wine. I got into the hot tub … totally naked. The hot water eased some of my tenseness. I was so ready for more kissing and whatever … then he brought back the drinks, got into the tub, and cuddled me. He's a great cuddler."

The women all sighed.

"Was he naked?" Carmela asked with a gleam in her dark eyes.

"*Mamá*!" Pia warned.

"No," Fee said. "He kept his boxers on. Not the loose kind, but, you know, the kind that cling."

Every single woman nodded.

"But how big was his sex?" Carmela asked.

Pia gasped. The other ladies laughed as her friend turned even redder with embarrassment over her mother's questions.

"Big." Fee's pussy dampened as she recalled the bulge outlined by the cotton knit fabric.

"Man, I'd give a lot of money to see Trey mostly naked," Keely muttered. When everyone looked at her as if she were crazy, the little blonde shrugged. "Purely scientific interest here. My hubby is a god. So, I'd like to see if the Maddox genes bred true."

DJ snorted. "Scientific interest, my ass. Now, I've trained with both men, and from my casual observations, I'd say they both are hung like bulls."

Keely punched DJ in the arm. "Why are you staring at my

husband's and Trey's junk? You hussy, you're married to my brother."

"I'm married, not dead." DJ grinned. "Oh, and yes, Carmela, my Ace is hung like a bull, too. From what I can gather—again from casual observation—all the SSI male operatives are well-equipped. Must be all that alpha-male testosterone."

"Frick-fracking hell," Keely muttered. "You are evil, DJ. Now, I'll be checking out all the SSI operatives' crotches."

Fee laughed, because she could see Keely doing exactly that. Damn, she was extremely fortunate to have such a fun and sympathetic group of women with whom to discuss personal issues.

"Enough with the men's cocks. Continue, Fee," Elana urged. "I'm getting the idea you didn't get laid last night at all. So what happened?"

Fee's laughter died as quickly as it had come. "I fell asleep in the hot tub."

A chorus of moans met her revelation.

Her breath stuttered and she sniffled as tears of remembrance threatened to spill down her face. "When I woke up this morning, I was in his bed. Naked. Alone. He was gone. No note. Nothing. So I left. And here I am." She looked at her lap. "I'm such a loser."

"No, you're not," Tara said.

"Why not?" Fee turned toward Tara.

"Let's back up a bit," suggested Tara. "In the past you were stalked and raped. Your Trey, I assume, is aware of this?"

"He is," said Fee.

Tara nodded. "You just shared he's been considerate— moving slowly with you, treating you carefully—right?"

"Yeah. He visited me in New Mexico for over nine months," Fee said.

Tara whistled. "Okay, now that's a real man. He knows what he wants. Realizes you needed both time and space. So he patiently sets about getting what he wants while having a care for you. They don't make too many like him."

"They do at SSI," Elana put in. "I think no one gets into the group if they don't have those qualities."

Keely and DJ nodded. Pia sighed and looked as if she were missing Levi, who was still in New Mexico, and had similar attributes.

Carmela muttered, "Just like my Manny."

"Good to know," Tara said, interest flashing in her eyes. "Fee, from what happened or didn't happen last night, my first thought follows along the line of what Keely has said—he's continuing to take care of you. Being the sort of man he is, there's no way he'd take advantage of an unconscious woman. Brownie points for him. And the fact he wasn't there this morning tells me he got called away. Probably hadn't planned on being gone long, or he would've left a note or something.—Does that sound like Trey?"

Tara addressed the last question to the table at large.

"It does," Keely said, "and that was what actually happened. Trey went out on an intruder alert call with my hubby Ren. There was a breach on Sanctuary's eastern border. The investigation took longer than expected, because the intruders killed a bear and then escaped into the national forest lands. Ren and Trey tracked the frick-fracking bear killers, found where the bastards were squatting. They also found drugs, so they called in the park rangers and turned the case over to them."

Tara nodded. "I backed up the rangers who first responded. Didn't hear your men's names, but had heard SSI had called in the incident."

"Okay, so, you think I'm overreacting," Fee concluded.

"Yeah," Tara said. "I bet he was disappointed you weren't still in his bed when he finally got home."

Fee winced. Now she felt bad for leaving. What must he think of her?

Tara cut into Fee's morose thoughts. "But what I don't understand is—why you're so reluctant to ask for what you want from him? Why resort to visual clues and not just use your words? I can see you being hesitant after having been stalked and raped, but Trey doesn't sound like the fucker who hurt you, or you wouldn't have stripped in front of him." She held up a hand before Fee could respond. "And if I'm getting too personal, just tell me to shut up—but I'm not seeing the problem here. You've got a good man who's shown he's patient and cares about you, you should be jumping all over that."

"Exactly what I've been telling her for months." Pia raised her glass of iced tea in a toast to Tara.

So far sharing with the gals had been fairly painless. But could she go even farther and share what she perceived as her sexual inadequacies?

Gut it up. This is a friendly, non-judgmental audience. Tell them.

Fee picked up her glass and took another couple of bracing sips. Everyone stared at her. Patience and sympathy hung heavy in the atmosphere.

Yeah, she'd share. Maybe they could help.

Fee put the glass down with a definitive thunk. "The problem isn't Trey. It's me. My past sexual experiences have been pathetic."

"How?" Tara asked.

Hesitating, Fee bit her lip.

"God, Fee, just tell them," Pia said, exasperation in her voice. "I'm betting all of these gals have had crappy lovers."

Energetic nods bobbed around the booth.

Fee huffed out a breath. "When I asked for certain … things … sexual things … to help me get aroused … some of my previous lovers got mad." She took a deep breath and let it out. "They fucked me and left, leaving me hanging."

"Frick-fracking pecker-headed douches," muttered Keely.

Fee snickered at Keely's colorful epithets. "There were others who got off and tried to get me off, but I couldn't respond quickly enough ... so they gave up and found reasons to leave."

"Selfish assholes," Elana said.

The other women murmured their agreement.

Heartened by the support, Fee continued, "Later, I heard rumors." Her breath hitched and tears welled in her eyes. "They ran the gamut from me being a ball-buster to a frigid bitch."

"Fuckers," DJ muttered. "You do know the problems were theirs, right?"

"That's what I told her," muttered Pia.

Fee shrugged. "At first, I told myself that. But the disappointing sexual encounters continued to occur. I began to think I lacked something. Eventually, I just stopped dating. Then I was raped."

Somber silence settled over the table. Nothing like spoiling what had been a fun day of shopping. Fee sighed. "Hey..."

Tara held up a hand, halting Fee's words. "Okay. Let's put this in perspective ... your previous lovers were self-centered, stupid, little boys. Now, you've found a real man, an alpha-male from what I'm gathering from the previous conversation. And you're afraid if you tell him what you need from him to get aroused and reach your pleasure, he'll get mad at you and call you a bitch?"

"Basically," Fee said.

"That's bullshit." Tara smiled, taking the edge off her blunt statement. "In my experience, strong men want their women to tell them what they desire sexually. It fulfills their primal instincts to provide and care for all their woman's needs."

"What she said," DJ pointed to Tara. "If you don't get off, it's on your man for not listening to you and paying attention to your body's cues. I didn't think I could have a normal sex life either until Ace became my lover. He's so into me and what I need that, oh lordy, he makes my panties melt and gives me good loving each and every day."

Keely punched DJ's arm. "What didn't you understand about me not wanting to hear about my brother and his sex life?"

DJ grinned at Keely. "This reticence from the woman who walked through the Lodge's great room and asked Scotty about locating a zucchini squash—as he tells it—which would approximate the size of Ren's erect dick." DJ turned to Fee. "This was so she could bait Ren into taking her virginity. You have no shame, Keely Walsh-Maddox, so shut it."

Keely giggled. "God, the look on Ren's face when he ran into the Lodge, half-dressed and his jeans not all the way zipped. But my plan worked. I lost my cherry to Ren and not a cold veggie … oh, wait, squash has seeds inside, so it's a fruit." She looked at Fee. "Whatever it is, Scotty has a nice selection of zucchinis in the fridge. We could probably find one Trey's size. I'll help you pick it out."

Fee shook her head, a smile on her face. "Um, I'm thinking you just want to compare it to one Ren's size."

"Yup." Keely laughed and turned to see Nick approaching with their food. "Good. Time to eat. All this talk of sex makes me hungry."

Nick turned brick red. "Keely, do I have to tell your husband you're talking about his cock again in my diner?"

"Nope." Keely snagged a sweet potato fry. "I'll tell him." She winked. "The story should be good for a fun spanking and then maybe three to four orgasms. A total win for me."

The ladies laughed as Nick swore under his breath and turned even redder, if it were possible. Fee snickered.

After Nick left, they all concentrated on eating.

While Fee ate, she ruminated on all that had been said. "So, bottom line, I should try again."

"Yeah," Keely said. "This time start off by talking about your fears. Give him a short, sanitized version of the past dating fiascos. He already knows about Adam-frick-fracking-Stall, and that's one of the main reasons he's been so patient. If you need him to take the lead until you are more comfortable with him and can ask for sex when you need it, then tell him that also. But I'll bet you anything that you two will find that level of sexual communication from the beginning, because even while laboring in a cave to give birth to Riley and then afterwards, I sensed the chemistry between the two of you."

"Laboring in a cave?" Tara asked and looked between Fee and Keely.

Fee would've explained, but her phone rang. "Hold that question. Got to take this. I'm not on call, but there could be a big emergency and the ER might need me."

She looked at the unknown number. A pang of fear tore through her, then she got mad. She'd ditched her other phone and had gotten a new number with a new phone provider when she'd moved to Idaho. How had the asshole found her number?

"Shit, shit, shit." Fee swore. "Unknown number ... again."

"Give it to me." Keely wiggled her fingers.

Tara frowned and reached for Fee's phone just as Fee answered it.

Fee didn't hold back. She put every ounce of rage, frustration, and, yeah, fear into her voice. "Dr. Teague. Who is this?"

"Fee?" Keely reached for the phone. "Gimme the frick-fracking phone."

Fee shook her head.

There was no answer. Just harsh breathing.

"Fuck this." Fee put it on speaker. "Hello, you mother-fucker. Why do you keep calling me?"

The heavy breathing sped up. Then a snarl like that of a wild animal split the air.

The stunned silence at the table was only broken by the

sounds of harsh breathing mixed with crazed growls coming over the phone.

God, he'd gone over the edge from sociopath to a raving psychopath.

"Answer me, you coward," Fee shouted into the phone.

"I'm coming for you, bitch." Then Adam-fucking-Stall disconnected and the dial tone sounded.

"Frick-fracking hell." Keely leaned over the table. "Gimme that phone. I can try to track the call. How long has this been frick-fracking happening? And don't lie."

Whoa, this was the bad-ass Keely who'd outmaneuvered the mercenaries all those months ago.

Fee handed over her cell with a shaky hand. "Off and on since right after I moved to New Mexico. He started by calling and hanging up or leaving a voice mail with only silence and a hang-up. He used a lot of different numbers. I reported them to my cell phone provider. They said the calls came from throw-away phones bought all over the U.S. I changed my number and the calls stopped for a while. They started again a few months before I left New Mexico. I got rid of that phone and signed up with a new phone provider and number when I came to Idaho."

"So, the calls aren't connected to that cartel business," DJ said.

"Cartel business?" Tara asked.

"Another story for another time," DJ said. "So this is someone stalking you."

"Her rapist-stalker, Adam-frick-fracking-Stall," Keely said as she tap-typed on her phone's screen, doing something Fee probably wouldn't understand.

"Yeah, I always figured it was Stall, and his voice just now proved it," Fee said. "But why? He won. No one believed me. I left. And how is he getting my numbers? Each time I change it, he has it within a few days or so. Thank God, he doesn't know where I live."

"Sorry to be the bearer of bad news, but he probably does have your address since he is getting your numbers from somewhere that either had your billing address or," Keely paused and then swore, "frick-fracking hell. He's probably getting your info off your medical student loan repayment service. It's a Federal program. They have databases and shitty security. Even if he couldn't hack it himself, he could pay the worst hacker in the world to get into the one that has your data. The loan site is not the Pentagon or NSA."

Keely held up another phone. "I'll give you my satphone to use until we can get you your own secure satphone that works over the NSA satellite SSI uses. Stall won't get that number. You can use SSI's corporate phone number and PO Box for your loan site. I want to keep your phone so when the frick-fracking douche calls again, Tweetie and I can more easily track his ass. Why have NSA-clearance and not use it for the family of SSI operatives, right?"

"But…"

"No, buts." Keely got a steely look in her eye. "You're Price's sister, and I'm betting my brother-in-law has plans to keep you, so you're part of the SSI family. We protect our own."

Keely's actions only proved what Fee had suspected—SSI women were as alpha and over-protective as their men.

Tara nodded. "Fee, I think you should let Keely do her thing. Psychopaths once they get on target tend to stay there. At least you live on Sanctuary and from what I've seen that place is a fortress."

"I don't … live on Sanctuary, that is." Fee shook her head. "I live over my clinic, just outside Elk City."

"Jesus, Fee," Tara said. "I know that building. It isn't safe. We've got survivalists and meth cookers hiding in the forests around Elk City. A single woman needs a more secure place to sleep at night."

"She turned down a guest suite at the Lodge on Sanctuary," Pia tattled.

Fee frowned at her friend. "I needed to be near the clinic while I got it up and running."

"It's up. It's running. I'm living in the Lodge," Pia said. "We can ride to the clinic and back together. In fact, the hour drive each way will be more fun with company."

Fee took in all the concerned glances. "Okay, I'll take Keely and Ren up on their offer for a suite of rooms in the Lodge … if the offer is still open."

"It is." Keely laughed. "Plus you'll be closer and can get to know Trey better."

"I'd like to get to know him better," Fee said. Lots better.

"Yeah, I figured. Just a warning … Trey wants you to move into his place," Keely said. "Trust me on that. I sort of overheard Trey tell Ren that when he yelled at my hubby for dragging him out of bed and away from you." She paused. "Why don't you pack up and move into the Lodge this evening? Then we'll see how long you stay there."

DJ grinned. "I bet she'll be moving in with Trey as soon as she hits Sanctuary with her stuff."

Elana sniffed. "I'm not taking that bet since I know you're probably correct." She turned to Tara. "SSI men don't mess around when their women's safety is concerned."

"I gathered that," Tara said. "I look forward to meeting some SSI men." She winked. "I am totally single and available. Just saying."

As the ladies laughed and chatted with Tara about the SSI operatives who were eligible and looking, Fee realized she wasn't freaked about the idea of moving in with Trey. If he insisted, she wouldn't fight him on it.

Because it feels right.

Yeah, it did. More right than anything in a long time.

CHAPTER 17

Fee's Elk City apartment

"You don't need to help me load my car," Fee told Tara who followed her up the outside staircase and into her apartment.

Keely and the other gals had argued about the most efficient way to get Fee back to Elk City so she could pack her things and move into the suite at the Lodge today. Fee had argued she could spend the rest of the weekend at the Lodge as planned and then ride into work on Monday with Pia. After the end of her Monday clinic hours was soon enough to pack and make the more permanent move to Sanctuary.

Keely at that point had pointed her finger at Fee and said, "By Monday, you'll have found a frick-fracking lame excuse not to move here at all. So we're striking while the iron is hot."

Tara had then said, "Your girl is right. I can take you back to Elk City today. It's on my way home."

After being out-argued and out-maneuvered, Fee had given in—because Keely had been on target, Fee would've manufactured an excuse not to make the move—still might.

"No problem. I'm here so use me." The taller woman looked around the one-room studio that had served as Fee's home for the last three weeks and grimaced. "What a dump. How could you even stand it?" She turned and stared at Fee. "Are you so scared of a personal relationship with Trey Maddox that you'd rather live here and punish yourself instead of living in comfort on Sanctuary?"

"Well, I never…" Fee huffed. Tara was outspoken and blunt, that was for sure. "You don't know me. You don't know Trey. You know n-n-nothing…" She sputtered to a stop, gasping and trying not to break down and scream or cry or both.

The emotions she'd buried since her kidnapping and the recent long-distance move were bubbling just under the surface and could explode at any time. She hated feeling out of control; it made her look like a weak, emotional woman.

"Not true." Tara lightly touched Fee's arm as if in apology for being so harsh. "I *know* you. I've *been* you."

Fee gasped. "You?"

"Yeah, me," Tara said. "I've been stalked … and raped … worse even."

God, what could be worse? Fee squeezed Tara's hand. "I'm sorry."

Tara nodded. "Fee … you're a smart, independent professional woman who feels she should've been able to avoid all the violence, all the drama. I felt the same way … but shit happens. You can't avoid some things. You have to stop beating yourself up and trotting out the 'if I had only done this' arguments, and move past it."

"How?" asked Fee in a plaintive tone.

Tara hugged her. "Hey, you've already started. You have a great group of gals as a sounding board. Plus you've found a man like Trey Maddox. From what I've heard so far, he's the kind of man who'll be in it for the long haul and will help you work through this. Wish I'd had a man like him after my traumatic experience."

Fee backed out of Tara's hug and observed the strain on the woman's face. She clutched Tara's hand and squeezed it. "Thanks … look … if you ever need to talk … I'm willing."

Tara grimaced. "Oh, babe, I've talked … and talked until I ran out of words. To domestic abuse counselors. To shrinks. I've examined what happened to me to death. I've even managed a few boyfriends and intimate relations since my ordeal."

Well, that was more than Fee had accomplished. Instead of seeking help, Fee had run from Detroit and then from Trey.

"For the most part, I'm doing good. The aftermath of what happened to me only rears its ugly head now and then." Tara paused and gave Fee a look filled with empathy. "But for you, your trauma still seems as if it happened yesterday, because your rapist got away with it and is still stalking you. You need justice. Until you get it, you'll have a hard time getting past the pain and burying the memories. So, tit for tat, I'm here for you. But you also need to share with Trey what you told me and the other gals at lunch. He can't help you overcome your insecurities and fears if he doesn't understand all the underlying causes."

"Do you have a counseling degree or something?"

Tara snorted out a laugh. "Or something. It's called life experience. We might be close in age, but I think I've had a lot more experience than you've had."

Fee nodded. "That wouldn't be hard. Thanks, for the offer … and, well, everything."

Tara was correct Fee needed to work through shit and not just Adam-fucking-Stall, but also the other men who'd made her feel as if she were less than adequate—and that included her father.

Fee frowned and could hear her father even now yelling at her because she'd run home crying after she'd been bullied at school. *"You're a weak, sniveling coward. Teagues never back down from a fight."* She'd been eight-years-old at the time. The scene had been repeated over the years; no matter how much she accomplished, her father had always belittled her.

"What caused that look on your face just now?" Tara asked.

"Daddy issues." Fee frowned. "He always told me I was a wimp."

"Fuck him," Tara said. "I see a woman who has the inner strength to be a survivor. I bet you're calm and cool in a crisis, too."

"Maybe." Fee smiled. "Thanks." She pulled out her big suitcase, put it on the lumpy bed and then started piling her few clothes into it.

Tara continued to stare at her, a look of concern on her face. "You okay?"

"Getting there." Still a bit overwhelmed by Tara and the other gals' support and manipulations in her personal life, Fee changed the subject. "So-o-o, since you're here and are willing, could you use one of those boxes over there and pack my toiletries?"

Fee angled her head toward the pile of boxes she'd used in the move from New Mexico and had never found the time to break down. "I didn't bring much more than the few clothes I had in New Mexico and a few personal items since this dump was supposedly fully furnished."

"Do you think anyone from the hospital has ever set foot in this place?" Tara accepted the change of topic and snorted. Hands on her hips, she looked around the apartment once more. "Furnished apartment? More like Goodwill rejects."

Fee laughed. "Pia called it early hovel. If any of the female doctors had seen it, I expect things would've been nicer."

Or not. After all it was a clinic in the back of the beyond and the medical center didn't have the kind of money to upgrade the place. She figured they counted on the resident doctor to find and rent his or her own place. The administration had probably been shocked when she'd moved in.

"Hell, Keely had it cleaned up for me," Fee added. "I can't imagine how bad it was before that."

"Yeah, clean is always good. Though, torching it would've been better." Tara picked up a box and headed into the bathroom. "Jesus, woman, you travel light. I have a thirteen-year-old cousin who has more stuff than this."

"Ha, funny. I'm not much for cosmetics. Don't really need it for the clinic since many patients are allergic to anything that has scent." Fee eyed her suitcase which now contained all her clothing. "Most of my clothing and household goods are in storage in Detroit. That's why I had to buy all those things at the outlet mall."

Fee should ask one of her sisters to arrange to ship at least her winter clothing to Idaho. Or maybe she and Price could go to Michigan for a short visit and arrange a long-distance mover to bring all her things to Idaho.

And visit dear old dad?

Or maybe not.

Fee zipped up her suitcase and rolled it to the door. "I'll take this down to my car and then come back and pack my books and electronics. With what you're packing, that'll be the whole of it."

"Okay," Tara shouted from the small bathroom. "I can help with the other stuff once I finish packing this box. Then I'll help you carry the boxes down."

"Thanks," Fee called over her shoulder, then bumped her rolling suitcase down the rickety outdoor staircase. Thank God, she wouldn't have to make this trip too many more times. This staircase was an accident-waiting-to-happen.

When she reached the ground, she tugged at the suitcase as it got stuck on the last step. Swearing under her breath, she turned and dislodged the loose board that had caught on the wheels and made a note to tell Tara to watch it when they came down later with the boxes. Then still looking at the ground for any other obstacles, she turned and walked into a wall of bad-smelling flesh, muscle, and bone.

Fee inhaled sharply and instantly regretted it. The smell was worse the second time around. She'd autopsied corpses

216 | Monette Michaels

during medical school that smelled better than this. Whoever this was had needed a bath days, no, weeks ago.

Still she had run into him. So—"Excuse me, I'm so…" She looked up, saw the gun in the man's hand, and stuttered, "…s-sor-r-y." Her primitive brain told her to scream and run, but her body wasn't cooperating.

Staring down at her, a nasty grin on his dirty, stringy-bearded face, the man she'd run into said, "You the doc?"

Fee nodded as she finally moved, only to back into her suitcase and almost fall over it. He really did smell. He was also scary. His grin was definitely not of the relieved-to-find-medical-assistance kind, but more of the I'm-a-bad-ass-mother-fucker kind. The gun he'd pointed at her chest underlined the latter interpretation.

The mountain man—because he was huge and dressed for roughing it in the wild—caught her arm and kept her from falling on her butt.

Her "thanks" was automatic. So was tugging at her arm to get him to let go.

"Teeny little thing, ain't ya?" He didn't release her as his smile grew wider to display a mouth full of stained, rotten teeth and diseased, bleeding gums. He either had really poor dental hygiene or was a crystal meth user. Or possibly both.

Fee disregarded his comment on her size. Maybe she was overreacting and he was only here to seek medical help. She eyed him and found no obvious injuries, just a lot of dirt.

And a big gun? Aimed at you.

"A-r-re you injured? S-s-sick?" Fee couldn't keep her fear out of her voice. She forced herself to focus on his face and not the big black gun. She forced herself to ignore his blatant leer. His eyes were dilated, so much so she was hard-pressed to say what color his eyes were. He blinked a lot, and his body moved constantly.

Shit, shit, shit. If he wasn't a meth addict, she'd turn in her brand-spanking-new Idaho medical license and take up knitting.

A bad situation had just gotten dangerous. Meth users tended toward paranoia and wild mood swings, depending on when they'd had their last hit.

Fee tugged at the arm he still held, but he didn't release her. Her heart rate went into overdrive and she struggled to breathe past the tightness in her throat.

Her captor laughed at her puny efforts to escape his touch as he dragged her toward the front of the clinic. The door stood wide open. The broken door jamb was evidence that the man had pried the door open. So much for clinic security.

"I ain't the one needin' doctorin'. Need ya to look at my brother," her dirty captor said. "He's been shot. You fix him."

Gunshot wound? Her captor's suspected meth use? She recalled something Tara had mentioned earlier about meth cookers living in the wilds of the national forest. And what were the odds these guys would find their way to her clinic?

Somewhere, in her past, her karma had gotten extremely fucked up.

Swallowing hard, Fee prayed her voice wouldn't tremble as much as her knees. "Yes, of course, I'll help your brother." She used the soothing voice she used on all injured patients—and their concerned friends and relatives.

She didn't want to startle this guy in any way. So far he'd seemed to be dealing with reality and merely wanted medical help for his brother. She could do that. Then maybe he'd take his gun and brother and go away.

But first, she needed him to let go of her arm.

And point the gun elsewhere. And lose the leering looks.

Fee refused to carry that last thought any further until the man actually became a clear and present danger.

Head in the sand much? Well, what about Tara—in her uniform shirt with a gun on her hip? Think he'll ignore her when she comes to find you?

Fee's blood ran cold. If this guy saw a uniform and a gun, he could easily turn violent and harm them both. She'd seen it happen too many times in the ER. Cops plus drug users equaled chaos and usually more patients for her to fix.

"Um, could you shut the door, please?" she asked after they entered the reception area. "We don't want any wild animals attracted to the smell of blood coming inside. I heard there are bears in the area."

"Yeah, that's why Zeke got shot." After dragging her farther into the small reception room, the man kicked at the door until it closed part way. "We kilt us a bear for some meat, then some assholes chased us away from our kill. Then the fuckers found and tromped all over our camp and called the rangers on us. Had us a shoot out when we circled back to camp."

Holy shit. He just confessed to at least two crimes, three if they were cooking meth in that camp. Not good. Then it hit her, these were the guys that Trey had left this morning to investigate. Did she have an ill wind following her around?

"Well, that's none of my business." With her pulse pounding like an air hammer, Fee forced herself to focus on the task at hand. Once again she tried to tug her arm away from his grimy grip. "I can't help your brother," she rasped out the words, her mouth as dry as a desert, "um—help Zeke— with you holding onto me."

As if he'd heard his name, a man groaned piteously from her only exam room which was immediately off the reception area. The door was partially open. "I may need you to assist me in helping with Zeke. My name's Dr. Teague. What's yours?"

Asking for his help had a two-fold purpose. First, it gave his drug-fogged mind something to concentrate on other than fixating on her or his need for a fix. He seemed genuinely concerned about his brother. Second, she wanted to give Tara time to get away and call for help. The ranger had to have heard the man's painful groans through the floor. There was no insulation in the clinic ceiling at all.

"I'm Bo. Get moving. That-aways, Abe can check out the other broad upstairs." The man cackled as if he'd told a joke.

Fee wasn't laughing. They knew about Tara. Her gut clenched. She prayed Tara had heard and was away from here and calling for help by now.

Gun now pointing at her head, Bo shoved her toward the exam room just as a man cried out, "Bo, where the fuck are ya? Get the fuckin' doc in here. I'm hurtin', man."

"Hold onto your dick, Zeke. The doc's comin' in now." Bo followed on her heels as she entered the small room.

Another tall man just as dirty, smelly, and unkempt as Bo stood over the examination table where Bo's brother lay.

"Abe, you go on and get that other woman," Bo ordered. "Bring her down here where we can keep an eye on her."

"Hell, yeah." Abe stripped Fee with a single, encompassing glance as he brushed past her to leave the room. "Hope, she's as good-lookin' as the doc. I ain't had me a piece of choice ass in some time."

"The doc's off-limits," Bo said. "For now."

Immediate, stomach-churning fear twisted her insides into a frigid knot. Then just as quickly, the knot was seared away by a rage so strong, she was amazed smoke hadn't risen from her skin.

Adrenaline poured into her bloodstream. No way. No how. She refused to be a victim. Not a-fucking-gain. She'd fight the bastards to death and into hell if she had to. They were on her turf now and she'd defend herself.

Scalpels are sharp.

Yeah, they were. Plus, she knew exactly where to cut or stab to do the most damage. She'd do what she had to do in order to survive and deal with the aftermath later. Survival trumped the Hippocratic Oath.

Trey will be around to support you this time.

Yeah, he would. That thought made her feel even stronger.

"For now. Gotcha." Abe smirked and pointed a shaky finger at Bo—and tried to wink, but failed. His eyes were almost all-pupil. He also displayed visible signs of being a meth addict, but for a longer time than Bo or Zeke. Abe's skin was covered in open sores which complemented his missing teeth and raw, bleeding gums.

While Bo was nominally the leader, Abe was the most dangerous of the three.

"I looked around a bit." Abe's feral stare made her feel unclean. "The doc's got a drug safe. One of the old-style ones with no timer. Bettin' there's some good shit inside it. Once she fixes Zeke, maybe we can get her to open it for us."

"Fine idea. Now get a move on, Abe. Don't let the other bitch get away."

Abe threw Bo a deathly glare as he stomped out of the exam room, leaving the door wide open, and then exited the clinic with a slammed door.

Tara had to have heard Abe's exit.

Fee feared for her new friend's life. If the ranger hadn't heard what was going on, Fee needed to warn her in some other way, without getting killed herself.

Bo shoved Fee toward the examination table. "Get to work, doc."

"Of course." She looked around to find a way to make some extra noise to alert Tara. "Bo?"

"Yeah?" He stared at her chest and smiled before moving his wild-eyed gaze to her hair. "Like me a red-haired woman. You a true red-head, doc?" He zeroed in on the juncture of her thighs and snickered. "I'm bettin' you are."

Fee clenched her jaw against a whimper. She'd love to have the guts to kick the bastard in the balls, but Bo still had a gun and Zeke was watching her like a cat watched a mouse. His wound was in a shoulder, so while in pain, he was still mobile and dangerous. She'd never get away with it.

Patience.

"Bo … could you push that cart closer to the table?" She indicated the one she wanted and then moved to wash her cold, shaking hands and put on gloves.

"Sure." The man ambled to the cart whose wheels she and Pia hadn't gotten around to oiling. The racket it made when moved was enough to wake the dead, let alone alert Tara.

While the cart clanked and screeched its way across the room, Fee positioned herself on the side of the exam table which allowed her to see into the reception area. This served to keep Bo's back to the doorway.

"Damn, woman. Ain't you got any oil?" Bo kicked at the cart, making even more noise.

"No." She bit her lip, holding back the insane urge to giggle at his incredulous look, and focused, instead, on the dirty white towel someone had secured on Zeke's shoulder wound. She unwrapped the towel which had been soiled with God only knew what before being pressed against the bloody wound.

"Shit." The wound was crusted with dried blood, dirt, and fibers from his filthy shirt and the equally filthy, cheap towel. Infection couldn't be far behind. She slipped her fingers under his shoulder and found no exit wound. *Deja vu.* But this time the wound wasn't as deep as Aznar's lung wound had been and she should be able to get this bullet out.

Picking up a large square of sterile gauze, she soaked it with an antiseptic soap and sterile water and then began cleaning the wound.

Zeke, who'd lapsed into a sort of pained semi-consciousness after glaring at her mere seconds before, jerked and howled as she manipulated the wound. He struck her with a flailing fist, catching the side of her jaw. He screamed again, since he'd hit her with the arm on his wounded side.

Stepping away from the table, Fee rubbed her jaw with the back of her forearm. She was lucky the wounded man hadn't been at full strength, or she would've been on the floor.

Bad news was she'd have another nasty bruise on the side of her face to match the last one that had only recently fully healed.

More good news—there was no way Tara hadn't heard Zeke's scream of pain.

Bo reached across his brother's body, grabbed her arm, then shook her. "Why'd you hurt Zeke?"

She shrugged off his hand. "I was cleaning the wound," she said. "You don't want the wound to get putrefied, do you?"

Bo looked at her as if he didn't know what she was talking about.

Use your nickel words, Fee.

Fee heaved a sigh. "The wound is at risk of becoming infected." She pointed to the remnants of Zeke's shirt around the wound. "His shirt is dirty. The towel used to stop the bleeding was dirty. I need to clean the wound and the area around it thoroughly before I remove the bullet." She pulled some scissors from the cart and began to cut away more of Zeke's shirt.

"That's why we came here." Bo's wild-eyed gaze fixed on her every move. "Me and Abe don't know how to dig out bullets."

Pulling off her dirty, bloody gloves, Fee threw them into the red bag where she'd tossed the towel and Zeke's shirt. Bo's suspicious gaze followed her every move as she went to the sink, cleaned her hands, and then pulled on clean gloves. Returning to her patient, she ignored Bo's narrowed eyes and began to clean the area beyond the wound.

Abe stomped back into the room. "The other bitch is gone." He moved to Bo's side and glared at her. "Where is she?"

Fee didn't look up from her task. She tsked under her breath. Her patient was a pig. His skin was as dirty as his clothing. She had to toss the gauze in the red bag and use another to get the layers of grime off. All sorts of dirt and bacteria would be in the wound track along with the dirty bullet and whatever else these two had introduced into the wound while applying pressure.

Zeke, like Aznar had, needed a hospital for infection control. Her patient would soon be coming down off whatever combination of drugs already in his system. There was no way the man hadn't self-medicated after being shot. Her little clinic was set up for everyday illnesses, well-baby and pregnancy care, and basic triage on trauma cases—and not equipped for drug addicts in withdrawal with a gunshot wound and the potential of septic shock.

She must've said some of her thoughts out loud, because Bo snarled, "He ain't goin' to a hospital. Now answer Abe. Where'd the other bitch go?"

"Don't know. Now shut up and let me concentrate." She stared down Bo as he moved to strike her. "You hit me, who's going to help your brother?"

"Just watch your mouth, woman," snarled Bo as he drew back his hand and used it to fondle the barrel of his gun.

Fee ignored his threat, even though her heart had leapt into her throat at the anger in his tone. "Wash your hands and your forearms—use the soap by the sink—and put on some gloves. You're gonna have to help me by holding your brother down while I remove the bullet."

"You ain't giving the orders around here, bitch." Before she could back away, Bo reached across his brother's now fully unconscious body and tugged on her shirt pulling her almost on top of her patient. "I am."

Fee took a breath and let it out. Staring into his crazed eyes, she enunciated, "Let. Go. Of. Me. You're shedding dirt and skin cells all over his wound. Do you want him to get sepsis? He could die."

Yes, sepsis would take a while to take hold. But she wouldn't allow her patient's condition to worsen that far. She'd fight to save Zeke despite him being an asshole drug cooker and addict. But Bo didn't need to know that.

Bo stared, a frown on his face. "What-sis?"

Fee sighed. "Blood poisoning."

Bo grunted and lessened his grip.

Fee pushed his hand off her shirt, tore off the now-soiled gloves, and moved to the sink to don another pair of gloves.

"He'll need antibiotic IV therapy for a while even if—and that's a big if—I can clean all the dirt, the bullet, and any other foreign matter out of the wound track. Do you understand?"

"No. You fix him. Just you." Bo continued to stand sentinel as she resumed cleaning the area around the wound.

"I'll do my best. But infection is a high probability and he could require a hospital." She turned her back on Bo and opened the drug safe Abe had noticed. She took stock of her anesthetics.

"We'll just come back then," Bo said. "You can fix him again."

"No. I don't have a lab." Fee sighed and shook her head. Why was she wasting her breath arguing with a meth-head? She looked over her shoulder. "What's Zeke on?"

"What do ya mean?" Bo muttered, his gaze bouncing around the room.

"What drugs are in your brother's system? I need to use a local anesthetic and give him a pain killer. I'm concerned about drug interactions."

"He took some meth earlier," Abe called from the doorway where he'd retreated when Bo had gotten aggressive with her. "We all did. Quality control, ya know?"

"Great," she muttered under her breath as the man verified what she'd already guessed. She was lucky they hadn't gotten more violent with her.

To be safe, she'd use a local only and not risk a pain killer. She had no clue how much meth was in his system—or if he'd mixed it with anything.

"Oh, and if you're thinking of taking me with you, don't. It would be one of the worst mistakes you'll ever make." She injected the local around the entrance wound with multiple pricks. "My man is a former Marine, Spec Ops Marine, and the last time someone took me he blew shit up to get me back."

"I'll do what I want," Bo said. "Look at me when I'm talkin' to you, bitch."

Fee ignored Bo's posturing. The man thought he was an alpha-male, but Fee had met the real thing. Bo was a poor excuse for a man, hopped up on drugs and his own sense of self-worth. He was a pathetic waste of oxygen and testosterone. Still, he was dangerous, a time bomb with a faulty fuse due to his coming off a drug high. He could easily rape or kill her.

Judging the local had taken some effect, she injected small amounts of anesthetic into the exposed subdermal layers to help deaden as many nerve endings as possible. Probing for the bullet wasn't going to be fun for the patient or her. She hated causing people pain, even criminal assholes like Zeke.

"Did ya hear what I said?" Bo shouted.

Pulling on every bit of grit she could muster, Fee turned an icy gaze on him. "Yeah. You obviously didn't hear what I said. So I'll spell it out. I'll help your brother the best I can. Then you'll leave. If you're stupid enough to take me, you'll be dead … sooner or later. Believe it. Now, since you didn't clean up as I asked, stay the hell away from my patient. You'll contaminate my sterile field."

Obviously more concerned about his brother than angered by her backtalk, Bo stepped away from the table. His posture read as pissed-off. She figured she'd pay for her words later, but right now, he needed her, so he'd leave her be.

"Lordy, lordy, she's a feisty one, ain't she, *boss*?" Abe stressed the word boss.

"Shut the fuck up, Abe." Bo turned and glowered at his partner in crime. "Or I'll shut your mouth for you."

As Fee worked, she noted the stare down which Bo eventually won. Defeated for the moment, Abe snorted and then moved to the reception area where he paced back and forth like a caged creature. He was getting more and more agitated. God, he was a bomb with a shorter and shorter fuse.

226 | MONETTE MICHAELS

Abe's savage, dark-eyed gaze never left her, even as he retraced his steps time and time again. Then he stopped, lifting his head as if listening. "Bo, I heard something outside."

Fee stopped probing and stifled a gasp. She spotted movement past one of the reception area windows visible from her position in the exam room. Luckily, Bo and Abe's backs were to that particular window.

"Go check it out," Bo ordered. "Take care of whatever it is."

Abe ran from the reception area like a hound on the scent of a fox.

Bo eyed her closely. "Why'd you stop. What's wrong?"

It had to be Tara outside. Had she already called for help? Though help in this neck of the woods could be over an hour away. Elk City wasn't big enough to have a police force or even a town constable. The Idaho County Sheriff's office covered the area and it was a huge area to cover.

And why in the hell was Tara luring Abe out?

Ever hear of divide and conquer?

Was that even a good idea? Could Tara even take Abe down without alerting Bo?

Fee faked a cough to the side and then refocused on what she'd been doing. "Zeke's wound track is more irregular than I'd expected."

Which was true.

"Dammit, what I wouldn't give for a portable digital X-ray machine right about now." Fee kicked the cart in a not-so-make-believe fit of pique. The noise was loud and jarring, keeping Bo's attention on her and what was going on in this room. The noise even startled the unconscious Zeke.

Tara popped up at the reception room window and gave Fee a thumb's up sign. She must've gotten the drop on Abe. The thought relieved Fee's tension immensely. However, eventually, Bo would realize his friend wasn't coming back.

Deal with that hurdle when you come to it.

Right. Fee tossed the bloody probe on the cart. "I'm out of clean probes. I need to sterilize the ones I've used."

"Do it." Bo leaned over his brother, totally ignoring her warning about contaminating her sterile field. "Why's he still asleep?"

"Not asleep, but unconscious." Fee rinsed off the probes with alcohol and distilled water and then placed them in the autoclave. "He's in shock. The wound was traumatic to his system. The pain added to the stress. Stress causes production of adrenaline and cortisol which eventually results in post-adrenaline drop. He's fighting a fever also. The human body tends to shut down under any one of those circumstances. The combination, even more so."

Bo grunted. "Will he be okay?"

"With care. He needs a hospital. I can only do so much." And that was the truth.

Thank God, Bo was fully focused on his brother, since Fee could see Tara carrying a very limp Abe in a fireman's carry past the reception area window toward the back of the clinic.

Tara turned her head just before she passed out of view and mouthed, "Stall," then winked and was gone.

Stall? That meant even now SSI, local law enforcement, and Tara's fellow rangers could be on their way. The situation would end soon—one way or another. There wasn't one thing she could do about any of it except keep moving forward.

Once again Fate had taken control out of her hands. Obviously control was an illusory concept. Humans could only do what they could do to stave off disaster from one moment to the next.

Right now, she'd focus on the disaster lying on her exam table.

Main Lodge, Sanctuary

TREY SAT ON ONE OF two leather sofas that flanked the fireplace of the Lodge's great room. He held an untouched beer.

"What do you mean Fee went to the clinic?" Trey glared at his brother's wife and the ladies who'd accompanied her on the shopping trip. All the ladies, but Fee.

"Just what I said." Keely sat on the arm of the other sofa, next to her husband who glared at Trey.

"Why?" Trey spat out. "She was supposed to spend the weekend here."

"Well, you'll be thrilled to know, she went to get her car, pack her stuff, and move into a suite in the Lodge. So you can frick-fracking thank me and the others for talking her into it. She was sort of freaked out that she woke up in your bed—alone—this morning."

"I had to go out on a fucking intruder call with your husband."

"I know. Ren left *me* a note. We explained the situation to Fee." Keely grinned. "Tara confirmed the intruder alert was real since she'd heard about the asshats killing a bear and y'all chasing them into the national forest. Tara even drove Fee to the clinic since it was on her way home, saving us all an extra round trip."

"Who in the fuck is Tara?" Price asked, from one of the club chairs that made up this particular seating area. "I would've helped my baby sis get her car and shit."

"Tara Nightwalker. She's a park ranger. Keely knows her," DJ said, sitting on the sofa between Trey and Tweeter.

Keely nodded. Ren grinned and said, "Tara's a great addition to the local ranger contingent. She's also a hot shot. Missoula, Montana trained. You'll meet her, Price, when you take your wild lands fire training. She's one of the instructors."

Price grimaced and took a healthy gulp of his beer.

DJ added, "If you want to help, Price, you can take Fee's packages up to her room. She bought a shit ton of stuff since she needed warmer clothing and some other girl-type things."

Price set his beer down, then got up and walked to the piles of bags the girls had dumped in the entryway. "Tell me which are hers and I'll lug them up the stairs."

Trey cut him off. "Leave them. They might be going to my place."

Price turned and frowned. "Does my baby sis know this?"

"Not yet." Trey's lips firmed. "But I'm hoping to convince her." He turned to Keely and then sought out each woman in the shopping party. "Thanks, ladies, for smoothing my way with Fee."

"You're welcome." Keely started giggling and looked at DJ. "Did we call it or what?"

DJ laughed. "Yeah, good thing Elana didn't take the bet."

"As if I would." Elana snorted. "I know Trey and the type of man he is too well—plus, I got the impression Fee really wants to be persuaded."

Trey grinned. "I take it Fee won't be surprised when I ask her to live with me?"

"Nope." Pia sat on the sofa with Keely and Ren while her mother was in the other club chair. "The gals pretty much told her you wanted her to move into your place."

Trey would've asked how the topic had come up when Ren's phone rang. His brother answered it, a laugh in his voice. "Ren Maddox."

Ren listened to whoever was on the other end and as he did so, his face grew grim. "How long since you got away, Ranger?" The amusement in his voice was gone, replaced by a tone that matched the grim look on his face. He grunted and nodded. "We'll be there as soon as we can. Call me if there's any change in the situation. No, you did the right thing. Out."

"Well, the lack of safety and security on Fee's clinic is now a proven fact." Ren headed toward the Lodge's side exit off the back hallway.

"What the fuck is going on? Is Fee hurt?" Trey and the others ran to catch up.

"Not yet. But she does need a rescue." Ren exited the Lodge. "Let's get the Hawk out and ready to go."

Price ran ahead to the helicopter hanger next to the garage area. DJ and Tweeter joined him. The three of them would get the chopper operational as quickly as possible.

Trey stuck with his brother. When they entered the hanger, the other three were already pushing the chopper out of the building.

Ren keyed in the code and used the palm plate to open up the armory which was located in the back of the hanger.

"Who has Fee?" Trey asked as he pulled weapons out for himself, DJ, Tweeter, and Price.

"Some fucker is holding her at gun point inside her clinic." Ren checked over his weapon of choice. "Tara said the men who invaded the clinic are the same ones who killed the bear this morning and who we ran off our land. The rangers we called in after we found the fuckers' camp had a gun battle. One of the asshats is hurt, Tara reported."

"Fucking cocksuckers. If they hurt Fee…" Trey trailed off as he handed off some weapons to DJ, who'd joined them.

"If they hurt her, we'll deal with them," Ren assured his brother as they moved to the chopper. "Tara got away and called the sheriff, her fellow rangers, and us. Now she's going to try to reduce numbers by luring one of the three men outside."

Price had run toward them to help with the weapons and extra ammo and overheard the last part. He cursed. "Crazy fool woman. What's she thinking?"

DJ eyed him. "She's thinking of reducing the size of the clusterfuck by one armed and dangerous douchebag. She's doing her damn job." She checked over the rifle Trey had picked out for her. "I talked with her a bit at *Ma's*. Her training is every bit as good as mine, but she got hers in the Air Force. So she'll do the job."

"Good," grunted Trey, happy that Fee had someone taking her back. But it should've been him. "Goddamn-fucking-son-of-a-bitch, if I hadn't left her this morning, we'd still be in my bed and she'd be safe."

Trey leapt into chopper's cabin, strapped in, and put on a headset. Ren and Price joined him, while DJ took the pilot's seat and Tweeter, the co-pilot's.

"Forget regrets. Let's just bring her home, brother." Ren gripped Trey's arm and squeezed as DJ took the Hawk up and headed for Elk City at top speed.

Trey nodded at his brother. Through the cabin window, he spotted Keely, Elana, Pia, and Carmela huddled together to the side of the landing pad. The women held onto each other, fear on their faces. Fear for his Fee.

Damn straight, he'd bring her home, and he might never let her out of his sight again.

CHAPTER 18

April 16th, just outside Elk City

After a short flight from Sanctuary, DJ put the chopper down in a field one mile out of Elk City. Trey, followed by the others, evacuated the helicopter and jogged to the small back road which led into Elk City and ran behind the property on which the clinic was located.

Ren was on his satphone with Dan Adams, the Idaho County Sheriff, who was bringing his SWAT team. Trey figured they'd beat the SWAT team by precious minutes, and any one of the SSI team could snipe with the best of the people on the sheriff's team. Dan and his men could do mop up.

"Trey." Ren caught up with him. "Slow the fuck down, brother. You can't go rushing in there like a Viking marauder."

"Fuck off." Trey kept moving at a land-eating jog.

"Goddammit, Trey." Ren grabbed his arm and pulled him to a stop.

Trey turned. His fists up and lips twisted in snarl. "If that were Keely in there…"

"I'd grow some ice balls and formulate a plan to take the fucker out who's holding my woman," Ren said. "And I wouldn't do anything without backup from my team."

The others caught up with them.

"Ren's right," DJ said. "You'd be the first one to tackle your brother to the ground for doing what you're doing."

Fuck, they were right. He couldn't rush in there like some goddamn rookie.

"Talk and move." Trey set off once more. "God, I can't stand this. After all Fee has been through ... how much more can she take?"

"What she has to." A woman's voice floated on the brisk spring breeze.

"Tara?" DJ called out.

A tall woman with long dark hair, the cheekbones of a Native American, and wearing a Park Ranger shirt uniform and jeans, slid out of the thicket of trees lining the road. She stood, still as a statue and waited on them to approach.

"Hey, DJ. Heard the chopper. Figured it was you." Tara nodded at Tweeter's wife and holstered the gun she'd held at her side. "Guess I won't need this right now." She eyed the group and nodded with satisfaction. "Seems like you brought more than enough firepower to take out the asshole holding Fee hostage."

"Sit rep," Trey barked out as he strode toward her.

For a split-second, Tara stiffened as if she were coming to attention. Trey concluded she hadn't been out of the military for too long since she still responded to the authority in his tone.

Her penetrating, dark-amber gaze roamed over each of the men's faces before settling on his. "You'd be Trey ... Fee's man."

It wasn't a question. Something primal in him stretched and preened at her instant recognition of that fact.

"How is she?" Trey hesitated and then asked, "Have they hurt her?"

"Fee's fine. She's stringing the lead asshole along while tending to the one who's wounded. She's a strong woman." Tara tilted her head to the side as if contemplating his reaction to her words. "But you know that, right?"

"Hell, yeah, she's a strong woman and she'll hold, but..."
He shook his head. "Everyone has a breaking point."

"This isn't hers." Tara's lips twisted slightly. "She has more
brains than the one holding her. The other guy is wounded
and not dangerous at the moment. Plus, she knows I called for
help and that you'll come for her."

Tara turned and walked toward the stand of trees from
which she'd appeared. "Follow me. We can sneak up on the
clinic this way. It's a much shorter route than the road." She
walked confidently through the thick undergrowth. "All that
is needed to end this is one well-placed sniper shot. Who's the
best shot?"

Ren laughed. "My wife, but she's back at Sanctuary. Any of
the rest of us could do it, though."

Tara looked over her shoulder as she continued to maneuver
around trees as if she were on auto-pilot, or maybe the forest
talked to her. She looked at home in the wild, a forest deity
communing on some psi level with the trees. "You're Keely's
husband?"

"Yeah," Ren replied.

Tara chuckled. "God, I can just visualize the great Maddox
zucchini debate now."

"What?" Ren asked.

"Later," DJ said. "You had to have been there."

The smile on DJ's face told Trey that Keely had shared one
of his brother's most embarrassing, bone-headed moments.
Despite the seriousness of the situation, Trey snickered.

Ren slapped him on the back of the head.

Tara walked quickly and quietly, leading the group
efficiently through the rugged terrain. When they'd reached
the edge of the denser part of the forest, she held up a fist. The
group moved in closer to Tara and stopped. The ranger's gaze
wasn't on the clearing ahead where Trey could see the back
of the clinic, but on the ground to her right where a man lay
trussed up like a hog for roasting.

"Fuck me," Price breathed out in a voice that carried no farther than the group. "How did you lure him all the way over here?"

"I didn't." Tara's gaze was now on the clinic. Her stance alert as if she were listening for clues on the wind. "Took him out at the clinic and carried him here."

Fee's brother eyed the distance from the clinic to their current location. "That has to be a quarter mile, all up hill."

And over uneven ground.

Price sounded skeptical, but had good reason to be. The bound-and-gagged man was an ugly customer, big and scarred and filthy. Trey could smell the remnants of rancid bear-kill and the man's own body odor from six feet away. The guy wasn't a light-weight either, all big-bones and lots of stringy muscle; he had to weigh at least 180 plus pounds. Tara was tall, just shy of six feet, and looked to be in shape, but probably topped out the scales at 140 at the most.

Carrying her captive all that way, plus tolerating his odor, made her a fucking warrior in his book.

Tara shrugged a shoulder. "Trained with my brothers who are Missoula smoke jumpers. The National Forest Service wouldn't let me jump fires, even though I passed the physical. But I can hold my own in strength and endurance." She turned to eye them all. "With me taking out Stinky, the good news is, there's only one guy between us and Fee. Bad news is, he's on meth—and maybe something else mixed in—and is coming down, if old Stinky's condition is any indication."

Stinky? Trey really liked Tara Nightwalker. She reminded him of Keely, DJ, and even Fee. Though his little doc would never admit it. All of them were spirited and courageous in the face of danger.

"So, Fee's captor will be agitated and paranoid," Trey concluded. "Which means we need to take him down with the first shot, or he could do a lot of damage to Fee before we got inside."

"Yeah." Tara turned back and eyed the clinic. "As I said, a sniper shot is the best bet. There's a potential shot through the north window. Fee's in a small room off the reception area. The door to the exam room was open the last time I looked. The window gives an unobstructed view into the room. Fee was on the far side of the exam table and saw me. The dude holding her hostage had his back to the window."

"There are some issues here," Trey said. He wanted to move, but knew that they needed to iron out the plan and have backups in case shit happened. "If the exam room door's closed, no shot. Or if the asshole blocks out Fee, then—

"We can't use any ammo that will go through the bastard … we could hit Fee," Price said.

"Yeah." Tara eyed Price's sniper rifle. "That baby could take out a HumVee a mile away. If you don't have a shot, Dead-Eye, I can always lure the SOB out just as I did old Stinky, and we could take him outside."

"But he could take Fee with him, use her as a shield," Price pointed out, a scowl on his face.

"Which we want to avoid at all costs," Trey added.

Tara nodded. "The bastard's taller than Fee, by about a foot or more. An upper chest or head shot would be doable."

"Price," Ren called out, "you focused enough to take the head shot?"

Trey wasn't pissed Ren had singled out Price to take the shot. A former SEAL like Ren, Price had been his team's sniper and he still trained every day.

"Fuck, yeah. No one holds my baby sister hostage." Price stroked his Remington sniper rifle, the same model he'd used as a SEAL.

"You that good?" Tara asked Price.

"Yeah, I'm that good." Price stared at her until she nodded, one small abrupt movement.

"Fee might not like Price blowing the asshat's brains all over her," DJ pointed out. "Doctors have this thing about doing no harm."

"She'll deal," Tara said. "If her captor wasn't high on drugs, he'd notice how pissed off Fee is."

"Okay, so," Ren summed up the plan, "we'll surround the clinic. Price will get in place and take his shot.—And, please, try not to kill him. Dan hates the paperwork SSI causes him. Then we'll move in."

"Let's do it." Price looked toward Tara. "You lead. Show me where you want me to set up."

Tara nodded. "Follow me."

The two of them moved off to circle round to the north window Tara had mentioned.

"I'm first in," Trey said.

No one argued with him.

Trey led the rest of the group out of the woods and straight toward the back of the building. DJ and Tweeter took up a post by the back door and would take the guy down if he tried to escape that way. He and Ren moved around to the south side where they'd be in position to move in after Price took his shot.

Ren was on his satphone, advising Dan to keep his people and the park rangers back, that the situation was under control. They didn't need anyone stumbling onto the scene and fucking things up.

FEE HAD DONE ALL SHE could for Zeke. He was still unconscious, but his vitals were as good as could be expected considering he was coming off meth and whatever else the idiots had mixed with it. She'd seen a lot of speedballing in Detroit and New Mexico. Depending on what was available, the extra drug was probably heroin or fentanyl. She'd place her bet on fentanyl.

Fussing over Zeke's wound, she stalled for as long as she could. Where was the rescue team? How long had it been since Tara had signaled help was on the way?

Fee glanced at the clock. A half hour at least, but it seemed longer.

"Why is Zeke still sleeping?" Bo asked for what had to be the tenth time. He sounded like a seven-year-old demanding if they'd reached their destination yet.

"He's not sleeping. He's in shock. I explained that." Fee tried to keep her exasperation out of her voice, but must not have done a good enough job since Bo back-handed her for the second time since the ordeal had begun. At least, he hadn't used the hand with the gun.

Holding a hand over her abused cheek, she licked her bleeding lip where she'd bit it and blinked away the tears caused by the blow. Damn, the pain still reverberated over her face and down onto her neck.

"Listen … Bo…" Her voice wobbled a bit. "H-hitting m-me isn't going to change my answer or bring Zeke around any faster. It is what it is. He'll rouse when his body's ready. That could be in two minutes or two hours or two days."

Bo snarled. "Or you could give him something. We need to get moving. We'll take your car." He looked over his shoulder toward the reception area. "I need to find Abe."

Abe was out of the picture, thanks to Tara who was scarily effective.

"You go then." She firmed her mouth and winced at the pain. "I can't give your brother anything to bring him around. I don't know all the drugs that could be in his bloodstream. Any amphetamine I might give him could push him into cardiac arrest." She eyed Bo. "You do understand—with the drugs you guys use you're flirting with a heart attack each time you shoot or sniff that shit into your body?"

"You don't know nothing. Been taking the shit for years and I ain't dead yet," Bo sneered. "I ain't leaving my brother."

"My medical degree says I do know," she said, quietly. "I've seen more DOAs in my ER because of drugs than any other causes. Leave him with me. I'll make sure he gets to Grangeville and to the hospital."

Zeke needed a hospital. Unfortunately, Zeke was in no mental state to understand that proposition. Bo's response was another snort of derision.

Bo wasn't in good shape, either. His body moved constantly. When he wasn't jiggling, he was tapping his feet or snapping the fingers on his free hand or swaying from side to side. His dilated gaze bounced wildly around the room, alighting on everything, but seeing nothing.

What worried her the most as Bo was coming down was the evil, sadistic light in his eyes. The combo of drugs she suspected he used often increased the user's libido. If he attacked her, she'd be forced to stab him with the scalpel she'd secreted under Zeke's shoulder. The thought of fighting him, stabbing him, turned her stomach, but she couldn't let him rape her. She'd kill him to protect herself.

Bo began to pace the short width of the exam room. As he did so, he mumbled under his breath. Foul things. Crazy things. He was decompensating quickly now. But if she gave him something to make him high again, to even him out, he could be even more dangerous to her.

Movement at the window in the reception area caught her eye. Tara popped up and signaled "okay" with her fingers and thumb.

Relieved, Fee tilted her head in acknowledgment. Something would happen soon. But what? They wouldn't rush the clinic since Tara would've told the rescuers Bo was armed. A sniper. They would take him down through the window.

She found she was okay with that. But she sure didn't want to be a secondary casualty. She could almost feel the cross-hairs on her and Bo at that very moment.

Bo still paced, a moving target with no rhyme nor reason to his movement. There was no way to anticipate which way he'd move next, or if he'd stop directly in line with her.

You have to make him stop. Line him up with the window, dummy. And you need to be somewhere else.

How?

Then Zeke moaned, and Bo came to point like a hound on a scent. He fixed his berserk gaze on his brother.

"Bo, talk to him," Fee urged. "Reassure him he's okay and that you're here. A familiar voice helps rouse patients."

Bo moved to lean over his brother. "Zeke. Wake up, brother. We gotta go."

Fee moved away, toward the sink at the side of the room, putting a wall of cabinets between her and danger.

The shot came so fast, she'd barely taken a breath after she'd stepped away.

Shot in the upper back, Bo toppled onto his brother. He screamed and raised his arm, the one holding the gun. "Bitch!" His gaze darted about, wild with fear and pain.

"Down, Fee!" Trey's roar echoed off the walls of the empty reception area.

Fee dropped to the floor and rolled under the exam table, figuring Bo wouldn't shoot through his brother's body.

But she didn't have to worry.

Trey pounded into the room, grabbed Bo's wrist on the hand holding the gun, and twisted. She winced as she heard Bo's bones break and the man roared his anguish. The gun fell inches from her face.

She'd have one more patient—maybe two, if Tara hadn't killed Abe.

More feet pounded into the clinic, vibrating the floor like a mini-earthquake. Then Trey was there, pulling her out from under the table. He picked her up and cradled her against his chest.

"Fuck, fuck, fucking hell … I was so fucking scared, baby." He interspersed his cursing with kisses over her face and against her throat as he held her as if he'd never let her go.

Tears of relief and joy slipped from Fee's eyes as she buried her nose against his throat. He smelled like pine trees and healthy male sweat. He smelled like home and safety.

"I wasn't worried," she whispered against his skin. He shuddered and held her even more tightly. "Because I knew you'd come for me."

Trey looked down at her and frowned. "I could kill him for hurting you." He brushed a feather-light kiss over her bruised cheek and cut lip. He rubbed his jaw over the top of her head. "I am so sorry he got to you, baby. You had to be so scared."

Fee wouldn't deny being scared, because he'd know it was a lie. She was shaking like an aspen in his arms even now, but the ordeal was over and she refused to dwell. If she had nightmares later, she wouldn't be alone, because Trey would be there to hold her.

So she petted his chest, soothing him since he seemed to be even more upset than she was. "I'm fine now. I'm okay."

"Fee!" Price ran into the room, a rifle in one hand. Tara followed on his heels.

Her brother had taken the shot.

"I'm fine, Price. Damn good shot, big brother." Fee smiled at him and then looked at Tara. "Thanks, Tara. For everything." She looked up at Trey, whose loving gaze seared away any lingering fear in her and warmed her heart and other parts of her body. "I think you can put me down now. I have patients to treat."

"See?" Tara said. "Guts and brains. Makes me proud to be a woman. However, you don't need to treat these assholes. Sheriff Adams called in Life Line out of Grangeville."

"I know I don't." Fee sent Tara a smile. "But I'm going to take care of them until my relief gets here."

"I'm so damn proud of you, little doc." Trey set her down. "I'll be right here as you patch them up. I'm not letting you out of my sight for a long while."

Fee rubbed her cheek over his chest. "I can live with that."

"You can live *with me*," he muttered against her hair. She heard tension in his voice.

"Okay." Trey wanted her with him, and dammit, she wanted to be there. Yeah, she still had qualms about being woman enough for him, but she didn't doubt he cared for her and would be patient with her.

Trey exhaled and the tension in his body lessened. He brushed a tender kiss over her forehead. "Thank you, sweetheart."

"You're welcome." Fee angled her face up and touched her lips to his. What she'd meant to be a light kiss quickly turned deep and hot as Trey groaned into her mouth and took over.

Fee lost track of time and place. She didn't even care that her cheek throbbed and her cut lip twinged as Trey made love to her with his mouth. Only the hoots from the others halted the kiss from going any further.

"To be continued," Trey whispered with one last light brush of his lips. He groaned and touched a tip of a finger to her bruise and cut lip. "Oh, baby. I'm so sorry. I could kick my own ass. Did I hurt you?"

Breathless from the kiss and the look of adoration in his eyes, Fee could only shake her head. Then she moved out of his arms and got to work on the wounded as the sheriff's deputies and Tara's fellow park rangers descended on her clinic. The sooner she took care of medical business, the sooner she could move in with Trey.

And then what?

She'd figure that out as she went along.

CHAPTER 19

April 16th, evening
Trey's house

J ust as he had the night before, Trey watched as Fee moved around his great room, touching first the back of the sofa, then fluffing a pillow. Her movements were tentative ... bordering on unsteady. Her gaze, vague. This wasn't the in-charge doctor who'd gone straight from being held hostage to caring for the wound of the man who'd held her at gunpoint.

Fee stopped and stared out the wall of glass doors leading onto his deck. She muttered something under her breath as if she were arguing with herself.

Christ, what was she thinking about? Was she reconsidering moving in with him?

Earlier, she'd agreed so readily. He'd helped her move her few possessions into his house. They'd both taken showers—separate ones because such an intimate step was always hers to make—and then shared a meal with the rest of the SSI gang at the Lodge. She'd seemed fine during all that, but now—"Fee?"

In response, she turned her head. Her expression was hard to read.

Gut-wrenching dread swamped him. Had he lost her before he ever had her?

"I love your house."

What the fuck did that mean? She loved his house, but not him?

"Thank you?" Trey hesitated, the most unsure he'd been since he met her. Until he figured out where in the hell her head was, he'd follow along with her conversational gambit. "You can change anything you don't like. I want you to be comfortable here."

Hell, she could raze the whole house and start over as long as she stayed with him. All he wanted was her.

Fee looked around. "I like it the way it is. Well…" She scrunched her nose. "…maybe a few more personal items to make it ours. It's comfortable while still being minimalist." She bit her lip and focused on a pillow she'd picked up earlier and still held in her hands. "I don't know what to do. What to say. How to…" She shrugged.

"How to what, Fee?" He moved toward her.

"Damn, shit, damn. Grow a pair," she muttered under her breath.

"Fee?" When she looked up, there was fear in her eyes.

He stopped, still several feet away. She was afraid of him? He swore his heart stuttered. His stomach heaved. He was sure he was going to be sick.

Talk to her. Tell her what you feel.

"Sweetheart, don't be afraid of me. Moving in with me doesn't mean I'm gonna attack you," he crooned in a low and, he hoped, calming tone. "The next moves are all yours, little doc, just as I promised. I love you, Fee."

Fee's eyes shone briefly with so much joy that his heart rate steadied and the nausea melted away. He moved to take her in his arms.

But she stepped back, holding up one trembling hand. "Stop, please stop." Her voice shook and the happiness in her eyes was gone as if it had never been.

Bad move, shit for brains. She's probably had enough of overly aggressive males looming over her for the day.

"Fee?" He opened his arms, silently urging her to come to him.

"I love you, too," she said.

Joy swept through him like a healing wind. The truth was in her words and voice, but still she didn't come to him.

Fee's breath jerked and tears welled in her glorious turquoise blue eyes. "Trey, I love you so very much, but … but you don't understand." She blinked away a couple of tears and sniffed.

Why was she crying? God, now his heart hurt. Loving him made her cry? "Fee … sweetheart … talk to me. Whatever is making you unhappy, we can work it out."

"Dammit. I'm such a wimp." Fee threw the pillow down and walked the length of the couch and then back. As she paced, she waved her arms wildly. "I think I've loved you from the beginning. You're devastating to a girl's senses, ya know?"

He wasn't sure what the proper response was, so he went with—"You're not a wimp. You are one of the bravest women I know."

"That's just it … you're wrong." Fee kicked the pillow out of her way. "You don't know me as well as you think you do." She paused and eyed him. "You think I'm this smart, got-it-together doctor. But that's so untrue." She began her frenetic pacing once more. "I want you to make love to me more than I've wanted anything in my whole life, but I keep fucking it up."

"Fee"—he took another step or two closer until he was at the end of the sofa—"you aren't fucking up anything. If moving in with me is freaking you out, I can wait until you're ready."

"And *there's* the problem." Fee stopped and looked at him. "I love that you have a care for my past traumas with Stall and Chavez."

Her expression and tone were pleading. Whatever she was trying to tell him was important to her, so it was crucial for him to hear her and understand.

"You want to give me the choice of taking our relationship to the next level, but, Trey, I want…" Her breath and words caught in her throat.

When she didn't finish her thought, he asked, "What do you want?"

"…I want you to make the moves." She swiped at tears running down her cheeks. "I know that's not very progressive of me and I'll probably lose my feminist card, but the truth is … I suck at sex. I need you to lead. Please."

Had he heard her correctly? All her trepidation was because—"You think you suck at sex?"

"Not think … know." Her lips twisted into a facsimile of a smile. "But I'm damn sure you know what you're doing in the bedroom. I want you to show me what I've been missing all these years. I need you so much."

Relief made Trey's knees weak for a split second. Then he closed the distance between them. "God, Fee, I need you, too."

He pulled her into his arms, then bent to take her lips in a searing kiss. A kiss that had his cock hard enough to drill holes in concrete. His heart pounded until his blood roared in his ears.

Never breaking the kiss, he picked Fee up and carried her into his bedroom.

As he lowered her to the bed, she moaned, "No, don't leave me," and held onto him with her arms and legs.

If they hadn't both been fully dressed, he would've taken her right then and there.

"Baby, let go," he muttered against her mouth between licks and nibbles of her full, luscious lips. The taste of her was rich—addicting—and he was darn sure he'd never get enough.

"No, don't want to. Want your weight. Love your kisses. Best I've ever had." She arched and peppered his face with eager kisses. "Make love to me, Trey. I want you so much."

"Oh, that'll happen, sweetheart, but…" He untwined her arms and legs and nudged her toward the middle of the bed. Then he lay down next to her and stroked her trembling body. "…first I need your promise you'll tell me when you like or don't like something. I might be leading, but I'll need directions, little doc."

Tears formed in Fee's eyes yet again and she stiffened under his hand. "I've found men don't like directions in bed."

Trey chased her tears with his lips. "Who told you that bullshit?"

"No one told me. Experience showed me." Then she poured out a litany of her past sexual failures, as she called them.

Trey really didn't want to hear about the guys she'd slept with before him. But in the end, he was glad she'd shared, because he now understood why she lacked confidence in her sexuality.

"Mother-fucking, pecker-headed, loser dirtbags." The last time Trey had wanted to seek out and destroy some guy was when he and Price had gone to Detroit to put the fear of God into the raping fuckwit Stall.

Fee giggled even as tears streamed down her face. "Yeah … they were."

"God, baby, don't cry. You're killing me." He tugged Fee into his arms and was thrilled when she snuggled against him with no hesitation.

Trey brushed a kiss over the top of her head and stroked her back. She let out several tremulous sighs and eventually relaxed into his hold. When her sniffling stopped, he tipped her head up and demanded, "Names, baby. I'll find every blessed one of the sorry SOBs and punch their lights out for hurting you like that."

The smile she gave him was radiant. "You don't know how much your offer means to me … but you don't need to waste your time." She kissed the underside of his jaw. Even that slightest of touches had his cock begging for release from the tight confines of his jeans. "Part of it had to be my fault."

"Fuck that." He cuddled her closer and inhaled the sweet female musk where her neck met her shoulder. "Any man worth the name sees to his woman's pleasure. If she's not finding it, then the asshole should ask what she needs. And, sweetheart, all women need foreplay. Those fucking asshats were too selfish, wanting only to get their rocks off. And, Fee, I'm not them."

"No, you're not." She inhaled sharply as he slid a hand inside her shirt to cup her lace-covered breast. "Definitely not. Just being with you, kissing you, and I'm more aroused than I've ever been in my whole life."

"Good. Now, let's see what I can do to make you ever hotter." Trey closely observed Fee's reactions as he played with her breast. First, he pulled the lace of her bra down so he could fully cup the luscious handful and then squeezed gently as he teased her nipple with light sweeps of his thumb. Her breathy gasps were gratifying, but he wanted more. He wanted her moaning and groaning and … wet.

Trey expected she needed more stimulation than most, maybe a bit of pleasurable pain, but she wasn't asking for it. She was still too gun-shy from what the a-holes had said about her being too demanding.

Hell, Trey liked a woman who let him know what she liked … what she desired. He needed to give his lover pleasure; it fed his dominant nature to care for all of his woman's needs. He needed to keep in mind they were just beginning their sexual journey. Eventually, Fee would get more comfortable with telling him what she wanted. For now, he'd experiment a bit.

And while he did so, he planned to make sure Fee enjoyed every fucking second.

In that vein, Trey squeezed the under curve of her breast and rubbed his thumb more firmly over her nipple. Fee threw her head back, against his shoulder and moaned and writhed in his arms.

There it was. The reaction he wanted.

Moving his hand to the other breast, he layered on another sensation by licking then lightly biting her ear lobe before nuzzling his way down her neck.

"Tr-trey, I really ... really like that." Fee groaned and arched her neck, giving him more access while, at the same time, thrusting her breast more fully into his hand.

"So do I." He teethed the sensitive area where her neck joined her shoulder. Her scent drove him wild.

"More." She twined her arms around his neck, pulling her to him.

Trey pinched her nipple, hard, then soothed it with gentle brushing strokes.

"It feels so much different when you touch my breasts." Fee turned her face into his neck, then licked and nipped his skin.

Trey was thrilled at her uninhibited response. She sucked at sex?—Fuck that. She was a natural.

"Unlike those other asswaffles, you and I have chemistry. Plus, we have trust and love working on our side. With all those things going for us, the sex will be sizzling."

He turned her on her side so her front was plastered against his. Her curves mated with his angles ... a perfect match. His cock twitched and jerked against her abs. His little brain knew what it wanted. It wanted Fee naked and then wanted inside her pussy.

His cock would have to learn patience. He needed to begin Fee's education into the pleasure he, and only he, could give her.

"This is already far better than any sex I've ever had." Fee tilted her head and licked the underside of his chin. She slipped her hands between their bodies and began unbuttoning his flannel shirt. "I'm suffering here. I want more."

Trey groaned as she shoved his shirt open and ran her fingers through the smattering of hair on his chest. "You still sure you want me to lead, baby?"

She nodded eagerly. "Yes."

Thank fuck.

Fee cupped his face and looked him in the eyes. "No condom. I'm on birth control and clean. I know you are." She blushed. "I sort of checked your medical records after Ren contracted with me to be on-call as the SSI private physician."

She wanted him, all of him. His cock jerked at the thought of nothing between him and her. He hadn't had unprotected sex ... ever.

"Then get ready, sweetheart, 'cause I'm gonna give you so much pleasure. I want to hear you moaning and begging for my cock." Trey took her mouth in a tongue-thrusting, tongue-sucking kiss and only broke off when Fee fingered one of his nipples.

He groaned. "Love that, baby. But your pleasure comes first—and second—and third. Then you get to play. Now let's get rid of these clothes." He smoothed his hands down her sides and pulled at the leggings she wore. He got them down over her hips, and with her help and a lot of wriggling, she kicked them off.

Trey rubbed his still-clothed cock over her silky nakedness and thought he'd come right then and there.

Shit, damn, fuck ... he had more control than this.

He gritted his teeth and focused on tightening the reins over his libido. He wanted this night, this first time, to be perfect for her. He refused to be those other guys and leave her hanging while he got his rocks off.

"Yes. Clothes off. Now." She pulled her long-sleeved tee over her head and threw it onto the floor. Her bra followed. Then she returned to finish unbuttoning his shirt, but her hands shook so hard, she was all thumbs.

"Let me." Chuckling, he moved her hands away. At the rate her shaking fingers were moving, it would be morning before she got his clothes off him.

Fee bit her lip. "I've never undressed a man, well, in bed, that is. I usually cut clothes off patients in the ER."

The image of Fee cutting off a man's clothes—no, his clothes—had a spurt of pre-cum wetting his boxers. He tightened his groin muscles, throttling back the urge to come. As the desire to shoot his wad retreated, the sense of what she'd said and what her past experiences with the asswaffles had been like hit him like a ton of bricks.—Basically, she was a "virgin" when it came to making love. His cock stood at eager attention and pulsed.

Fee was his … all his. He was eager to spend the rest of the night making her fully his.

But first, his jeans needed to go. He moved away from Fee.

"No … Trey … come back," she reached for him.

"Shh, I'm not going anywhere. Now, lie back and stay still." He shoved her gently onto her back. "Just getting rid of my clothes."

"Good, that's good." Fee watched with an eager expression on her beautiful face. The look in her eyes was doing a lot for his libido as he stripped down to his skin. "You are so cut. So gorgeous." She sat up and reached for him with both hands, then stopped. Her gaze was questioning, almost pleading.

Fuck, she was unsure again.

"You want me, baby?" he husked.

She nodded.

"Then you'll get me. Now lie back." After she complied, he kissed the palm of each of her hands before placing them back on the bed, one on each side of her head. "Keep them there. Remember? Your pleasure comes first. Always. If you touch me right now, I won't be able to hold back. And, trust me on this, baby, you aren't ready for me to take you as rough as I'd like … yet. Later"—he murmured as he bent over and placed a kiss above the neat little patch of golden-red curls at the top of her cleft—"after I've made you come a few times, then you'll be ready for the strength of my lust for you."

"Please…" Fee shifted restlessly against the sheets.

"Patience. Not gonna rush this. I've waited so long for this first time with you." Trey then proceeded to nibble and kiss every square inch of her soft skin, down one leg, all the way to her toes. She wiggled and mewled under his mouth, tongue, and teeth, but stayed in place.

"That's my girl." He kissed his way up the other leg and ended by nuzzling the curls framing her pussy. He was tempted to dive in and kiss and suckle her clit and her labia, but first, he had breasts to taste, to pleasure, as he fingered her to her first orgasm.

Eating her pussy would be her second orgasm.

Her third would be when he combined the first two methods, brought her to the brink, and then made her completely his.

FEE WAS GOING TO DIE.

If Trey didn't let her come soon, she'd expire in a frustrated puddle of goo in the middle of his bed.

The man had the patience of a cunning predator and the control of a religious martyr.

She eyed Trey's body as he lay next to her kissing and suckling her breasts and teasing her pussy with his finger. She so wanted to trace every muscle, every sculpted angle of his body with her fingers, her tongue, but he'd stopped her every time she'd tried. Then he'd stop touching her and give her a stern look. After which she'd place her hands back where he'd first put them—God, it seemed like hours ago.

And then—damn him—he'd begin all over again, tormenting her, giving her such excruciating pleasure that all she could do was moan and whimper.

"What do you need, baby?" he muttered just before he sucked her tightly beaded nipple into his mouth and plunged two fingers inside her hot channel.

"Trey," she shoved her hips upward and moved a hand to grab his hand to hold it where she needed it, right on her throbbing clit. There. Pressure was what she needed. Yes, that was it.

"So fucking good," she moaned. Then just as she was about to come—

"No, baby." He pulled his hand away. Picking up her hand, he took it to his lips and nipped the ends of her fingers and then firmly put her hand back on the bed by her head.

Trey's gaze, the pupils dilated in arousal until she could barely see the green of his irises, was fierce. His nostrils flared and the red flush of arousal on his high cheekbones was darker than ever. "Keep the hands where I put them, or I'll restrain them."

Her groan and a full body wiggle had him grinning.

"You like that idea, huh?" He petted her body, long smooth strokes from right below her breasts, bypassing her mound, then down her legs. Again and again, he smoothed his hand down one side then up the other.

Her arousal had cooled for what seemed like the hundredth time. It simmered under her skin. Her climax was once again just out of reach.

Well, dummy, stop moving your damn hands. He warned you.

A sharp pinch to her nipple got her attention and made her hiss. Another tweak had her moaning as the zing arrowed straight to her needy clit. "Answer, me, baby. Do you like the idea of me tying your hands to the bedposts?"

She did and she didn't. Why was that?

Suddenly a cold chill shot down her spine. She whimpered as a dark arctic void in her mind opened up and threatened to swallow her and take her back to a place she'd thought she'd finally buried.

Tossing her head from side to side, she attempted to shred the gelid blackness to let the light and warmth of Trey's love to shine through. "I-I d-don't know—"

Well, that was a lie, she did know. Her body definitely wanted his dominance.

But it also wasn't a lie, because she couldn't vocalize her needs—her head wasn't fully on board with all aspects of what that dominance might entail. Her memory held minefields and they'd inadvertently tripped one.

"Talk to me, Fee." Trey covered her mound with the heel of his hand and made small circles over her pussy, maintaining their connection, but keeping it at a low simmer. "What's wrong, baby?"

"Effin' Stall," she choked out. Tears streamed down her cheeks unheeded.

"Aww, fuck. Sweetheart, forgive me." Trey gathered her into his arms and held her against him while she shivered as the half-formed memory fully resurfaced for the first time since she'd been raped. She'd blocked it, buried it under thick layers of inky darkness in a corner of her brain.

"He tied me down." She rubbed her cheek against Trey's hairy chest, inhaled his musky scent now mingled with hers, and let it soothe her.

As quickly as the memory had surfaced, it receded. Fee was safe in Trey's arms.

"Okay, okay. Shhh." Trey rocked her against him. "We'll forget—"

"No." Fee pushed against his chest.

Trey immediately let her go. His expression, a mask of concern for her.

"We'll try it—tying my hands—some day." She pulled his face to hers and murmured against his lips, "When you first mentioned tying my hands, my body was all for it. I even shivered with excitement when you said it, but then the damn memories…"

Trey kissed the rest of her sentence right off her lips. "I understand. For now, put it out of your mind. Let me see if

I can get you back to where you were before I put my foot in my mouth."

"Trey, it's not your—"

He kissed her again. "Shh. It's okay." He cradled her in his arms, then slid a hand down her stomach to her pussy and fingered her until she was wet.

Her man knew exactly how to touch her. He'd learned her body over the last hour.

Fee relaxed into his touch ... his warmth. His kisses sent little ripples of electricity over her skin, even as his fingers slid over her pussy lips and clit, slowly building her need until release became a prime imperative.

"How's that, sweetheart? Have I got your attention back on this sweet little clit? The clit I want to nibble, lick, and suck after I've given you your first climax."

"God, yes." Fee threw her head back as Trey slid one then two fingers into her pussy and pumped them in and out as he thumbed her clit. His fingers excited other nerves inside her. She clenched around them and knew his cock would feel even better.

When he lowered his head to lick her neck and then trailed his lips and tongue down her body to one painfully beaded nipple, every sensation coalesced and the pleasure swamped her senses. She screamed. The orgasm dominated her body and mind. Nothing else existed but pleasure, pleasure so overwhelming it was like an out-of-body experience; except it wasn't, since she could feel Trey's every touch, kiss, and nip. He used his considerable talents to milk her orgasm, prolonging it until all she could do was moan.

"That's it, baby," he muttered against her ear before biting the lobe. "Give me more."

And somehow, she wasn't sure how, the pressure in her core began to build again. She climbed so high, so fast, she was scared. Fee wasn't sure she could handle the perfect storm of sensations again. "No ... I can't."

"Oh, you can. You will," he muttered. "This time, I want to hear you scream my name."

Trey swept down to her breast and suckled the nipple as he curled his fingers into a spot inside her that had her—"Trey … oh God, Trey. Fuck, fuck…"

Once again she lost the ability to speak. She could only moan, mewl, and grunt as he pulled every last paroxysm out of her body.

When it was over, Fee lay quivering, bonelessly, in Trey's arms. Her body covered in sweat, hers and his. Her heart still galloped.

Trey nuzzled her ear, then whispered, "Again … you'll come for me again."

"N-no, no," she mumbled. "Tired." Shivering as her naked sweaty body cooled, she attempted to burrow into Trey's big warm body.

"Trust me, baby." Trey pulled back. "I need to come inside you."

With the loss of the protection of his body, cold air touched every inch of her.

"Come back. Cold. So cold." She reached for him, but he moved even farther away and the mattress shifted as he left it. Warmth in the form of a blanket was pulled up and over her body. "Trey?"

His lusty chuckle had her opening one bleary eye. He stood by the side of the bed, his cock erect and pointing straight out from his groin.

Okay, now she was hot again. Lust seemed to be exothermic.

Fee licked her kiss-swollen lips. Sweet Jesus, she bet the tip of his erect penis could reach his navel. She lifted a limp arm to see if she could test that theory, but—

"Hands on the bed, baby. I'm not done with you yet."

Fee gave him a come-hither smile, or at least what she hoped was one. "Come inside me, Trey."

"I will. But not quite yet." His gaze was ardent as he tucked the blanket up until her lower half was exposed. She swore little flames licked her nakedness. "I'm gonna feast first."

Feast first? "No, Trey ... I don't think I have another orgasm in me."

"Oh hell yeah, you do. In fact, you have lots more in you." He got on the bed and moved her legs apart and crawled between them. "But that's for another time. Tonight, we'll stop with the three I'd planned."

As he lowered his head to place gentle kisses up her inner right thigh, she squeaked, "Three? Do I have any input into these plans?"

"You made me leader, remember?" He nibbled her labia. She cried out. Then he licked around her opening until she moaned. "And I say you need three orgasms. I'm claiming you, little doc. Thoroughly. Breasts, clit, and vaginally. So, lie back. Keep your hands on the bed and feel free to scream and moan all you want."

"God, Trey, I can't. Oh my God," she cried out as he took her clit into his mouth and suckled it.

He teethed the tender bud before releasing it. "Yeah, that sounds good." He kissed her inner thigh. "God, I love how you taste. How you smell."

He returned to her pussy and lapped at her clit, sucked her pussy lips ... with an occasional thrust of his tongue inside her. As the sensations built on one another, all Fee could do was grip the blankets and feel.

What was the saying—oh yeah, *be careful what you wish for, you just might get it.*

"COME FOR ME." TREY SUCKED Fee's swollen clit into his mouth and pumped three fingers in and out of her hot, wet pussy. His other arm lay across her hips, holding her in place as he forced her up to another climax Her third this go-round.

Fee's screams of completion had his balls tightening to the point of pain. All reins on his libido were now gone. He couldn't wait to get inside her one fucking second longer. Her responsiveness and trust had brought them farther tonight than he'd originally planned.

It was time to make her fully his.

"Hold on, sweetheart." He pulled his fingers from her pussy and sat back on his haunches.

Fee still writhed in the twisted sheets as post-orgasmic convulsions shook her. He grabbed her by the hips and pulled her toward him. Her eyes flashed open and her mouth formed an O of shock. She shook her head. "So tired."

"I know, baby. Just one more time. I promise. Then we'll rest," he murmured.

Trey placed her quivering legs around his hips, then lifted and cradled her small shapely ass with one hand. She clutched at the sheets beneath her as the rest of her weight was placed on her shoulders.

Wanting this first time to be good for her, he watched her carefully for any signs of fear as he fisted his cock and guided it into her opening. "You okay, love?"

She looked into his eyes. "Yes. Because it's you. Make me yours."

"All mine," he said and then inched his cock inside the ring of muscles still clenching and unclenching from her last powerful orgasm. God, her pussy felt amazing. He had to focus so he didn't come too soon. He wasn't even a fourth of the way inside her yet.

"Ohmygod, ohmygod," Fee cried out. Her shocked gaze caught his as he held still and let her adjust to his girth. "I feel you throbbing." She shook her head. "Oh God, the pressure. It's building again."

"Come for me." He slid his cock another couple of inches into her slick, tight heat and placed his thumb against her engorged clit. Fee hissed and then moaned. She had to be ultra-sensitive at this point, so he applied a deeper, firmer pressure and made a tiny circular motion over the bundle of nerves. "Come for me, baby."

As he manipulated her clit, he seated his cock fully, his balls lodged against her sweet ass. "Fuck, yeah, that feels so good. So damn good. It feels like heaven and hell."

"Trey?" Her voice wobbled, then she inhaled sharply and began coming. Her screams were soundless now as she arched and writhed in his grip as she fell into pleasure once more.

The pressure in his balls had grown more insistent. He groaned and began thrusting into her with short, powerful movements of his hips. Her vaginal walls alternately strangled and massaged his cock with the strength of her orgasm. It was no surprise that it didn't take long for him to roar, "Fuck, I'm coming."

He held her hips in both hands now and pounded furiously into her. Wanting to wring out every bit of pleasure for both of them, on each downstroke he ground his pelvis over her mound. His balls tightened and then his cum filled her. He arched his back, held her hips tightly to his, and grunted through the most painful pleasure he'd ever experienced.

Pulling out, he groaned as several last spurts of cum coated her mound and clung to her golden-red curls like seed pearls. The sight satisfied the primitive male beneath the civilized veneer.

Mine.

"Fuck, you're wonderful." He leaned over and took Fee's mouth with a tender, loving, but still deeply carnal kiss. "You were made for me."

Fee responded by moaning into his mouth, tangling her tongue with his. Maybe with not as much energy as earlier, but it was still a lusty response.

His little doc looked exhausted. It was now his job to care for her, make sure she rested. He'd hold her all night, surrounding her with his body and keeping her safe from all harm in and out of her dreams.

Trey moved off Fee's body and lay next to her. She didn't move or make a sound. He traced her rosy full lips with a finger tip. She muttered something incomprehensible and kissed his finger.

Fuck, she was sweet, and all his. He pulled her close and pressed her head lightly against his chest. He pulled the covers over them. He'd clean them both up later. Right now, he needed to hold her, savor the calm after the storm—revel as she relaxed in his arms, trusting him with all that she was.

After all the months they'd spent apart, he hadn't realized how much he needed this first claiming until now … after it was over.

Fee was marked now, inside and out. She was his. His to protect. His to pleasure. His to treasure. And if that made him an alpha-male throwback, he didn't give a fuck, because he was Fee's alpha-male throwback.

CHAPTER 20

April 17ᵗʰ, morning

Floating on warm waves of pleasure, Fee moaned. A light breeze cooled her skin even as the sun bathed her body in heat and light. As the sensations ebbed and flowed over and through her, she moaned and arched her hips. "Awww, God. Please."

Awakened by the building ecstasy, Fee gazed with blurred, half-awake eyes at the beamed ceiling of Trey's dawn-lit bedroom. Just as she had the morning before, she lay, naked, amid the soft linens in the huge bed. Unlike yesterday, this time she wasn't alone.

Fee arched into Trey's talented hands and mouth. She now knew exactly what to expect from her lover—and wanted it … craved it. Their long night of love-making had also demonstrated Trey's desire for her seemed to be limitless—and that she didn't suck at sex.

"Trey…" His name was a mewling sigh on her lips. Her orgasm hovered just out of reach.

"Patience, sweetheart." He chuckled. The vibration did amazing things to her clit. "I'm having fun."

He rubbed a bristly cheek against her inner thigh. Her skin was so sensitized the abrasive touch shot an electric tingle straight to her pussy.

"Please … please…" She thrust her mound toward his lips.

"Greedy, aren't you?" He kissed, then lightly bit the tender skin of her thigh, before he resumed eating her out. "Fuck, you smell good … taste good."

"Oh, God-d-d that's so-o-o-o good." She reached for him and held his head to her, stroking shaky fingers through his thick, dark hair, and begged for—"More."

"Hell, yeah, I'll give you more." Trey gave her one last lick, then pulled away from her hands. He knelt between her thighs and placed her legs over his shoulders. "Watch me as I take you."

Trey stroked his erection. His shaft was heavily veined and his dark-plum-colored glans glistened with precum. She still couldn't believe she'd taken that width and length in her several times already, but she had and now couldn't wait to feel his rigid thickness inside her again.

"Baby, my eyes are up here." His tone was both amused and totally immodest. He liked her looking at him, and he was worth looking at.

Fee's hungry gaze traveled up his torso and traced each abdominal muscle, the same muscles she'd mapped with her tongue after their initial round of sex. She continued her visual journey with his marvelous chest which had just the right amount of hair.

Trey was hers now. Last night, she'd claimed him just as much as he'd claimed her.

Finally, she stared into his emerald-colored eyes—eyes which burned for her with so much love and adoration that her heart stuttered at the enormity of his feelings.

"There you are." With his hands on her hips, he stroked a finger into her opening. "So wet and ready for me. Can't be gentle this time, baby. If you're sore, tell…"

"Take me, Trey. Give it to me hard."

"Fuck, I love you. So sweet and generous." He lined up his cock and plunged into her throbbing and hungry pussy.

"Ohmygod!" A powerful orgasm instantly swept her into a maelstrom of sensation as Trey jack-hammered his hips. His long, thick shaft rubbed every nerve going in and coming out. The pace was both rough and exciting, pushing her pleasure even higher.

"Open your eyes. Look at me." Trey's voice was guttural ... animalistic.

Eyes she hadn't even known she'd closed flew open at his demand. The expression on his face was a rictus of pleasure and pain. His eyes had darkened to a stormy green.

"Fuck ... fuck ... so fucking good." He lowered her hips to the bed and leaned over her as he continued to thrust. Bracing himself on his arms, he kissed and nibbled her breasts. "Love you."

"Love you, too. Come for me." She clutched his shoulders and held him as he threw back his head and came, grunting and quaking over her.

"Fee..." Trey brushed a kiss over her sweaty forehead. "... sex has never been this good before."

He rolled off her body, immediately tugged her into his arms, and pulled the comforter over them. He'd never been a cuddler, but he was now. He'd found throughout the night he couldn't handle her being too far from him.

"Really?" She leaned her head back on his supporting arm and gave him an incredulous look.

"Really." He kissed the tip of her nose, then nibbled her lush lower lip. He shuddered as his cock seemed to be trying to find its second wind. His recovery time hadn't been this quick since his teens. "Baby, what are you doing?"

"Petting you." Fee turned her face toward his chest and nuzzled a nipple. "I think we need to document this amazing recovery time ... for the Guinness World Book of Records." She licked then took a delicate bite of the nipple she teased.

"Any ideas about what I should do with this?" She swept a gentle thumb over his very wet and sensitive cockhead.

Trey had a lot of ideas. All of them had to do with never leaving this bed, but they needed to eat, if for no other reason than to keep up their strength for more love-making later in the day.

"Shower-sex … tongues and mouth only since you have to be sore. Shower. Clothes. Then we'll hit the Lodge for breakfast." Trey threw off the comforter and got out of bed. Gathering her into his arms, he headed for the master bathroom. "After breakfast, we'll come back here and sit in the hot tub. It'll be good for any soreness you might have."

"TREY, I'M FINE. I'M ALSO on board with all your suggestions." Fee rubbed her cheek over his shoulder, inhaling the combined musk of their love-making. "I could cook you breakfast, you know?" Mostly because she wasn't sure she wanted to face the interested looks from her and Trey's friends.

"That would be a miracle…" Trey laughed as he held her one-armed against his side as he turned on the shower. He'd shown throughout the night that he didn't like her too far away from him. "…because like Mother Hubbard's cupboards, mine are bare. We'll need to make a trip to Grangeville sometime today to buy food."

Trey looked down at her. "Never feel you have to cook for me, little doc. You have a busy schedule between the clinic and your ER shifts. We can always eat at the Lodge. Scotty always makes more than enough food."

"I want to cook for you." Fee rubbed her hand over his six-pack abs. Her man needed fuel to keep his gorgeously hot body running in tip-top form—and to have the energy to make love to her. "I like cooking … it relaxes me."

"Fuck, baby." Trey's voice was a low sexy growl. His cock nudged the arm she'd positioned across his lower abs. Yep, fully erect, the head of his cock did reach his navel. "I just had an image of you wearing a frilly apron and nothing else."

"Um…" Fee clenched her thighs as her clit twinged. The picture he'd painted and the lust in his voice had her wet and needy again. "I could do that … as long as I wasn't frying anything. Kitchens aren't really safe places for unclothed bodies."

Do not discourage the man, dummy.

Trey grinned. "I'd keep you safe. First, I'd clear off the center island, cover it with a large towel so your skin wouldn't touch the cold granite. Then I'd lay you down gently on top, with your legs hanging over the edge, and eat you for my appetizer. After I ate the meal you cooked me—which you'd serve naked—I'd clear the kitchen table, bend you over it, and have you for dessert."

Fee moaned. God, who knew cooking and eating a meal at home could sound so sexy? She wanted to act out the scenario he'd described … maybe a couple of times a week. "We need to buy an apron. I don't have any."

"For chrissakes, Fee. Don't encourage me." Picking her up, he carried her into the huge shower, then lowered her to sit on the built-in bench. He knelt between her spread thighs. "Fuck. I want you again. But I've already taken you more times than I should've."

Fee cupped his face. "Look at me." When his eyes, dark green with arousal, met hers, she said, "I want you now. I need you inside me. I think I'm addicted to your cock."

Trey had a naughty grin on his face. "Let's make sure you're ready for me. I need another pre-breakfast snack."

Before she could reassure him she was more than ready, he leaned down and began nibbling her pussy. Her orgasm came out of nowhere. She wasn't sure it was his mouth or the lascivious images his words had created, but her climax was stronger and harder than any of the others he'd given her. The pleasure was so devastating she collapsed against the glass brick wall, unable to hold herself upright. Even with the pleasure threatening to drive her out of her mind, there was something missing. "Cock. Inside me. Now."

"Fuck, yeah." Trey stood, then pulled her up and into his arms. "Put your legs around my waist."

"I can't." She tried, but was shaking too hard. Her arms and legs were limp as the debilitating orgasmic waves still shuddered through her.

Trey braced her back against the tiled shower wall, then lifted her hips with one hand and wrapped one leg around his hips. Somehow she managed to get the other one anchored and then crossed her ankles at the top of his ass.

"Put me in." He muttered the words against her breast right before he sucked a nipple into his mouth.

"Aww, gawd." Fee fumbled and felt blindly for his cock. Finally, she fisted his thickness and notched it into her still-spasming opening.

Trey took care of the rest by ramming his penis home. The tempo he set was wicked good and exactly what Fee needed. The pressure in her core built again, like a soda bottle being shaken, and then it exploded. She screamed, a long wail that echoed in the cavernous bathroom.

"God, baby, I'm coming." He wrapped her tightly against him, one arm under her hips and the other around her upper back. "Hold on."

Fee wound her shaky arms around his neck and buried her lips against his throat.

Trey thrust upward in short, hard jabs. His pubic bone ground over her clit with each upthrust and the orgasm she'd thought was over found new life.

"Ohgod, ohgod, ohgod," she whimpered against his neck. "It hurts so good. So fricking good."

"Jesus … fuck me … you're fucking perfect." Trey grunted as his hot cum flooded her depths—and squeezed her so tightly she couldn't catch a full breath.

Light-headed, all strength sapped, Fee lay limply within his hold. She was vaguely aware of him sitting on the shower bench and shifting her so she was cuddled on his lap.

Tears—Of what? Relief? Release? Gratitude?—flowed down her cheeks. She sniffled and tried to hold them back, but it was a brief, losing battle.

"S-s-sorry," she inhaled sharply. "I d-d-don't know why I'm cr-cr-crying."

"Shh. It's okay, baby." Trey's voice soothed even as his soapy hands stroked over her still-trembling body. "I've got you. You're safe."

"I know." She turned her head and kissed his shoulder. "I know." Then she let out a long sigh and relaxed even more into his hold and let him tend to her.

THE LAST TIME FEE HAD eaten breakfast in the Lodge was the morning back in June after she'd delivered Keely's baby. She and Price had eaten early that day, crack of dawn early, with only Scotty for company. Afterward, she and Price had hit the road for Boise for her flight to Santa Fe.

Today, however, the breakfast nook in the kitchen hearth room was filled with laughter, sweet baby noises from Riley, and the rumbling of multiple conversations. This time, she had nowhere else to go. She was home.

The smells coming from the buffet set up on the huge kitchen island were amazing. Her mouth watered and her stomach growled ... loudly. She placed a hand on the offending body part and felt herself flush with embarrassment at the sudden silence in the room as she and Trey entered. They were now the center of attention, and not because her stomach growled.

Trey covered the hand on her tummy and leaned over to whisper against her ear. "Seems you've worked up an appetite, little doc."

Fee turned into his body and patted him on his ass. "Yes, very hungry," she said in a tone only he could hear. "You should be also, with all that work you did." She kissed his jaw. "Fuel up, lover. I have some things I want to do to you."

"Now, why did you have to go and tease me like that just as we're about to sit down and eat?" He brushed a kiss over her cheek.

Price coughed. "Um, could you two hold the public displays of affection for later. There are innocents present."

Fee sent her brother a glare. "You haven't been innocent in years, big brother."

"Good one, sweetheart." Trey hugged her and this time kissed her on the lips until Price buried his face in his hands and shouted, "Have mercy."

The rest of the people sitting in the breakfast nook laughed at Price. Tweeter punched Price in the arm and whispered something against her brother's ear that had him giving Tweeter the finger.

Fee eyed their breakfast companions—Pia, Carmela, Keely, Ren, Price, DJ, Tweeter, and baby Riley. Every single adult had a "I-know-what-you-two-did-all-night" smile on their faces, except for Price who looked painfully embarrassed. Riley merely cooed and held his hands toward them while bouncing in his high chair.

"I think we're outed," she whispered. Trey snorted. "And Riley wants his uncle."

"Riley's a Maddox male and he wants you." Trey urged her toward the table. "Go give him a smooch. He likes all the ladies smooching him."

"Good morning, everybody." Fee made her way to stand by the open seat next to Riley. The baby's attention had totally turned toward her and away from what looked to be the strained peaches Keely was trying to shovel in his mouth.

Fee leaned over and gave Riley a great big noisy kiss on his cheek. She inhaled his clean baby scent and everything in her clenched as her hormones, already elevated by the vigorous reintroduction to sex, went haywire. "Such a big boy you are, Riley."

Riley bounced and held his arms up. Fee picked him up and out of his high chair, then snuggled him against her shoulder. She could care less that he wiped his peach-covered mouth and cheeks on her T-shirt. It would wash. She looked at Keely. "I'll feed him so you can finish your food."

"You sure?" Keely smiled at her child who'd decided Fee's curls were his new favorite toy. "He loves to spit his peaches out and make bubbles with them. Then he laughs like a loon."

"Yeah, I'm sure." Fee sat, and Trey scooted her chair in so she had just enough room to hold Riley on her lap and still reach the table. She scooped up some peaches and aimed them at the little rosebud of a mouth and Riley slurped it down. "I'm new so he'll eat until he gets bored. Then I'll pass him off to his Uncle Trey who might manage to get even more down him."

"And his Uncle Trey will take him." He leaned over and kissed her cheek and then the top of Riley's head. "What do you want from the breakfast bar?"

"Eggs, bacon and"—she looked at DJ's plate—"some of those pancakes that DJ has."

"Whole grain pancakes, Trey," DJ said. "Scotty will make them to order."

"Gotcha. Be right back." Trey rubbed Fee's shoulder before moving away.

"Um, so, things are good?" Keely asked, with a bright smile.

"Yes." Fee slipped another spoonful of peaches in Riley's mouth. "Very good. Stupendously good."

"Aw, geez, Fee," Price groused.

Ren choked on his coffee and said, "Um, I don't think I need to hear anymore about how good my brother is. So, stop poking your nose into Fee and Trey's business, sprite."

"I didn't frick-fracking ask for specifics." Keely turned indignant eyes toward her husband and then toward Price who snorted.

"You would've." Ren leaned over and kissed the tip of his wife's nose. "You wouldn't be able to help yourself."

Tweeter nodded. "Yep, imp, you would. Leave the embarrassing girl talk for when your menfolk aren't around."

"Afraid of what you might hear?" DJ nudged her husband with her shoulder.

"Hell, yeah. You women are brutally lethal." Tweeter toasted them all with his orange juice. "We menfolk have very sensitive psyches."

"Sensitive, my ass." DJ snorted.

"I adore your ass," Tweeter muttered as he turned his attention to the mound of eggs on his plate.

"Tweetie!" Keely flicked a blueberry at her brother, who snagged it out of the air and popped it into his mouth with a wink. Shaking her head at her brother, Keely turned to Fee. "So, Fee—Tweetie and I tracked down the cell towers for those stalker-ish phone calls and…"

"What stalker-ish phone calls?" Trey thunked a plate of food in front of Fee. The loud noise and his tone of voice silenced the other conversations around the table.

"Uh-oh," Keely said, her face red. "You didn't tell him?"

Fee's stomach lurched. "Um…"

"No, she didn't tell me," Trey muttered, a scowl on his face. He sat, moved his chair even closer to Fee, then placed his arm around her shoulders. "What calls, little doc?"

Riley oblivious to the tension, grabbed his uncle's finger and began to gum it.

Fee set Riley's food on the table. Stroking the baby's back, she turned to face Trey and returned his scowl. "I'd planned on telling you on our first date back in New Mexico … but I've been sort of busy. Ya know? Getting kidnapped. Moving across country. Held hostage. Taking care of an injured bad guy at gun point. And then last night … well, last night … hell, Trey … you made me feel happy and beautiful and sexy—so the calls slipped my mind, okay?"

For just a second, Trey's frown disappeared as his expression softened and his green eyes glowed with love.

"Trey, I just got the phone from her yesterday," Keely said. "So…"

Trey's face went stony once more and he shot Keely a pissed off look. "Okay, I understand your part in this, but"—Trey turned back to Fee—"what I want to know is how long *before* Keely learned of these phone calls were you receiving them?"

Well, hell. Fee focused on Riley whose blue-eyed gaze had turned almost as accusatory as his uncle's. Heaving a sigh, she snuggled Riley's head against her shoulder and rubbed his back as the baby resumed gnawing on Trey's finger. "They started almost as soon as I got settled in New Mexico." Fee picked up a napkin and wiped some peachy slobber from Riley's mouth and Trey's finger.

"Fee, for chrissakes why didn't you come to me?" Price asked. "The calls have to be from that douchebag Stall." He looked at Trey as if seeking agreement.

"Watch your tone, Price." Trey glared at him even as he placed a burping pad between Riley's head and Fee's shoulder. A half-asleep Riley searched for and latched onto his uncle's finger again, letting the therapeutic gumming lull him to sleep. Poor baby was cutting teeth.

Ohmygod. Her heart melted. She wanted a child with Trey. They'd need to work as a team—as parents and life partners. Partners didn't lie to one another, directly or by omission. She hated that she'd hurt Trey, and he was hurt, she could feel it, so—

"I'm sorry." She rubbed her cheek over Riley's head and let his baby smell soothe her. "I should've told you, both of you, when the calls first started, but—" She heaved a sigh. God, she couldn't cry—she had to explain.

Trey must've heard the tears in her sigh, because he pulled her, and Riley along with her, onto his lap. She laid her head on his shoulder and let his warmth and scent soothe her.

"Go on, baby. I'm listening." He kissed her forehead.

She nodded. "All the time while growing up, I was told not to be weak. To stand up for myself. To be self-sufficient. That a Teague didn't ask others to solve his problems. A Teague was the one who solved other people's problems."

"Fee, dad was a fucking asshole," Price muttered, then pulled out a quarter and slid it to Keely. "For the effin' f-word jar." Then he looked at Fee. "You aren't weak. You're smart and strong and a freaking survivor to the nth degree. Dad was wrong on every count. It isn't weak to ask for help when you need it."

Fee snuggled into Trey as the past threatened to overwhelm her with images of all the times her father had called her a waste of sperm and a coward. Knowing something wasn't true didn't make the accusations any less traumatic or hurtful. "I know that, Price, but the little girl in me still hears him. Can you understand that?"

Price grimaced. "Yeah. I still hear some of his shit, too."

Fee sent him a grateful smile. "So … when the calls started, I handled things in what I felt was a logical way."

"What did you do?" Trey rubbed her back, soothing away knots she hadn't even realized had formed.

"I called my phone provider, first, and reported the calls. Found out the calls were coming from pre-paid cells which had been purchased all over the eastern seaboard. The phone company changed my number. That stopped the calls for a while, then the calls started again."

"Are they from Stall?" Trey asked. His eyes flashed green fire. A muscle in his jaw clenched and unclenched.

His anger was on her behalf and not aimed at her. Her man liked to be in control. She should never forget that, and would have to find ways to assuage his need to wrap her in cotton wool and to deal with anything which upset or threatened her. In the future, she would have to negotiate a fine line between Trey having too much control versus not enough.

"Yes. They're from Stall. I recognized his voice yesterday, but I suspected him before that. Before yesterday the calls were mostly dead air." She sighed. "Listen … I really felt I was handling the situation, being the responsible adult I was taught to be." She looked at Trey, pleading for understanding with her eyes. "I was being careful. There was no overt threat."

"It's okay, baby. I understand." Trey kissed her on the mouth, a gentle brushing of lips that calmed her, eased the tightness in her throat. "But I'm here now. Forget all that crazy shit your father browbeat into you. I want to know when something bothers you. I'll back up your moves and decisions and only take over when you need me to."

There was the line of compromise. He'd spelled it out without her even having to discuss or negotiate it with him.

"I love you." Fee kissed his jaw. "You've given me much-needed space for months. You've listened to me, learned to know me. I know in my soul you'll never let me down."

"Damn right, because you're mine, and I love you more than anything else in this world."

"God, I'm going to cry," Keely said, her eyes glistening. "That's so beautiful." She turned to Ren. "Wasn't that beautiful, big guy? I'm thinking you Maddox men are very romantic … well, in a macho, alpha-male badass sort of way."

Everyone laughed, even Fee.

Trey shook his head at his sister-in-law who was now on Ren's lap being cuddled. "So, little doc, what changed with the calls?"

"The earliest calls were mostly hang-ups. So for a while I thought they were wrong numbers or maybe pranks. But then they changed to heavy breathing…" Trey stiffened. Price muttered and slipped Keely a quarter even before the blonde had glared his way. "…and on the call yesterday, he made growling noises. When I demanded to know who he was, why he was calling me … he threatened me. The gals all heard it."

"Yeah," DJ said. "Made the hairs on the back of my neck stand up."

"Threatened you?" Trey's voice was calm on the surface, but underneath Fee sensed a volcanic anger ready to explode.

"Frick-fracking asshole said he was coming for her," Keely said. "That's when Fee 'fessed up to us. I asked her for her phone so Tweetie and I could investigate. Gave her my SSI-issued satphone so she wouldn't be without."

"How's he getting her new numbers?" Price asked.

"From the Federal medical student loan program," Tweeter answered. "Keely asked me to check to see if I could hack the site and get participants' identity information. I did and I could. Stall probably hired a hacker, if he couldn't do it himself. The site seems to update as soon as a participant updates their personal info, so it would explain the small lags of time between him getting the new phone numbers."

"Shit," Trey muttered. "So, earlier, I interrupted Keely … she was saying something about…"

"About cell towers," Keely said. "Cell phone companies are required to keep call detail records for six months. Some companies keep them longer. We lucked out, and Fee's carrier keeps them for one year. Tweetie and I split up the unknown calls Fee received, eliminated auto-dialers and solicitation calls, and tracked the ones left to a single prepaid phone carrier's throw-away phones. Yeah, Stall used the same company each time he bought a new throw-away. The call detail records show the location of the cell towers used during the duration of the each call."

"Were the calls all from the Detroit area?" Fee's stomach clenched until she thought she'd throw up.

"In the beginning they were," Tweeter said. "But the last few were from New Mexico, near the Mexican border."

"Fuck," Price said and looked at Keely who told him, "You can have that f-word, *gratis*."

Price grinned and shook his head.

"He'll have discovered she's moved by now. He'll eventually find out where. He'll also keep calling her at the current number." Trey looked at Keely then at Tweeter. "Keep tracking him. I want to know when he heads north."

"That was the plan," Tweeter said.

Trey tipped up Fee's chin. "While he's at large, I don't want you working at the…"

"I'm not giving up my job." Fee's voice was firm. Her stomach, however, was twisting and turning like a Mobius strip. "He's taken so much away from me already. I'm not going to run or hide from the bastard any longer."

Trey massaged her lips with his thumb. "You didn't let me finish, sweetheart. I was going to say I don't want you working at the clinic alone. Also, we'll improve the security at the clinic to add stronger doors, locks, and surveillance cameras in the public areas and around the outside of the building."

"Okay." Fee loved this man more than ever. How she'd lucked out, she didn't know. But she thanked the fates that put her in Trey's path and led him to loving her. "I know you're worried. I'll admit Stall scares me"—Trey growled and she stroked his jaw—"so I won't do anything stupid. I'll do my part. I promise to stay in touch. If anything bothers me at the clinic or on the road to or from the clinic or the ER, I'll shout out immediately."

"Hell, yeah, you will," Ren said. "We'll always be able to find you since you have the Sanctuary identifying tracker."

"What tracker?" Fee asked.

"Oh, shit," muttered Keely as she punched her husband on the arm.

"Trey?" Fee laid her hand along his clean-shaven jaw. "Talk to me."

He grimaced. "That flu shot you got from Lacey?"

"It wasn't a flu shot?" Fee frowned.

"It was, but it also injected a small tracker. We all have them," Trey said. "It's part of the security system for Sanctuary, besides being a way to find our people if they get lost or are taken."

Fee looked around the table and found a lot of nodding heads, including Pia's and Carmela's. "So why didn't you tell me about it?"

"Well, you weren't actually living on Sanctuary," Trey said, "and you were sort of adamant about not living here, and we all were concerned about…"

"Fee, they're all concerned about Chavez and *El Hacha*," Pia said. "The cartel put out a bounty out on you and me, and probably by now everyone who got us out of Mexico. So, I am sure Trey wanted you covered in case the assholes came after us."

Fee touched the spot on her arm where she recalled Lacey had used the pressure injector. "Okay, I'm sort of pissed you didn't tell me. But then again, I'm not, because you did it for all the right reasons." She stroked Trey's jaw and then pinched his chin. "But don't do anything like that again without telling me. Also, don't hide any threats from me, either."

Trey grasped her hand and brought it to his lips and then kissed the back of it. "I won't. I want you to wear an emergency alert necklace, so you can send out an alarm if some dangerous fuckwit invades your clinic again."

"Like senior citizens wear?" Fee wrinkled her nose. "Don't you think that would be too noticeable"—she swallowed past the lump of fear in her throat—"if Stall got a hold of me? He'd probably recognize what it was."

"No, no, you can have a bracelet," Keely interrupted. "See mine?" She held up her wrist and showed off a set of bangle bracelets with all sorts of charms on them. "Tweetie and I made them a fashion statement."

"Fashion statement for you, maybe." DJ snorted and pulled a necklace from under her long-sleeved T-shirt. "Mine's a necklace. It looks nothing like the senior citizen ones."

To Fee, it looked like a Greek medallion necklace.

DJ continued, "It's easier to wear, and I don't fricking jingle all the darn time."

Keely shook her arm, and the tinkling and clinking of all the bracelets and charms had everyone laughing.

"Okay—" Fee looked at Trey. "Get me a necklace like DJ's. I can't wear bracelets when I examine patients. It wouldn't be sanitary."

Trey touched his forehead to hers. "Thank you, baby, for understanding." The expression in his eyes, serious. "Stall won't hurt you again. I promise."

"You can't promise that," she whispered against his lips.

"Hell, yeah, I can." He kissed her once more and cupped Riley's head. The baby still slept, snuggled on her chest. "Now, give the baby to Keely and eat. Then we can go grocery shopping and pick up any other things you might need to get you fully settled into my place."

"Like a couple," she murmured. "I like that."

"So do I." Trey grinned at her. "So do I."

CHAPTER 21

April 23rd, 7:30 a.m.

"Shit." Standing just inside the Grangeville Medical Center's emergency room doors, Fee looked outside. "It's snowing!" She turned to look at one of the ER nurses also coming off the Friday-night-to-Saturday-morning shift.

The nurse laughed. "Welcome to Idaho. It'll melt. We'll be in shirt-sleeves by Monday." She waved and headed out the door into the blustery storm, which while not quite a whiteout was close.

"Okay, dummy," she mumbled. "You've driven in worse than this in Michigan." Hell, she'd survived worse last June when she and Keely had outrun and out-smarted mercenaries. "Clean the car off and hit the road. There's a warm bed with a hot man in it waiting on you to start his day with a bang." She chuckled at her double entendre and followed the nurse into the storm.

Being height-challenged, she had to stretch to scrape and brush snow and ice crystals off the Beast, the name she'd given the humongous SSI Hummer Trey had insisted she drive for work. Good thing she'd started the vehicle first and had the defrosters on high, because there was no way she could reach all of the windshield; her arms were just not long enough.

As she moved around to clear off all the lights, she couldn't help recall how she'd begun each morning over the last week … until today, that is. Wake-up sex was the best thing ever, mostly because Fee got to wake up next to the sexiest, most wonderful man in the world. She'd never been so happy in her life.

Tonight would be their one-week anniversary of moving in together. She didn't have to cover the ER, so she'd planned a fabulous meal and had the perfect set of lingerie to wear for the occasion. She'd let Trey handle the sex portion of their celebration; she still wasn't all that comfortable initiating their lovemaking, and might never want to take on that role—especially since Trey was so good at it. He made sure she came first each and every time—and often more than once—before he sought his own release. Fee had no complaints. The man was a sex god besides being loving and caring and, well, just perfect … though slightly over-protective.

After climbing into the Beast, she sighed as warmth enveloped her. It was damn cold outside, and the light-weight jacket which had been a perfect choice on Friday afternoon when she'd headed out to work, now provided zilcho protection against the wind chill factor and the heavy wet snow.

Fee snuggled into the heated leather seats and groaned. Heated car seats? The best invention ever.

She patted the Beast's control console. "Such a good car." Then she used the blue-tooth phone connection on her steering wheel to place the Trey-required call through the car's audio system. If she didn't call him, he'd call her, and she hated talking on the phone and driving at the same time.

Out of the blue, a strong gust shook the heavy vehicle, underlining the point that phone conversations and driving didn't mix, especially in these kinds of driving conditions.

"Hey, little doc." Trey's voice was full of love, relief, and, uh oh, concern. She mentally geared up for an alpha-male display of fretting. Though if she ever used that word with him, he'd probably spank her. Real men didn't fret. "You on the road yet?"

"No, just cleaned the Beast off and got it warmed up." She checked her mirrors and all the windows—they were clear. The Beast had an excellent defroster system and heated side mirrors. "I can see to drive. I'll be home soon."

Home, and didn't that word make her feel all warm inside.

"Baby, the weather radar indicates the conditions are bad in Grangeville, but they're worse at our elevation. You want me to come pick you up?"

Trey's tone urged her to agree.

Fee thought about it for several seconds, looked at the weather radar on the on-board computer which was connected to the same satellite system SSI used. The weather was dicey, but not life-threatening. The Beast was built for this kind of weather. Besides she really was an excellent driver. She lived here now and it snowed in Idaho a lot. Trey couldn't come pick her up from work each and every time the weather turned bad. So, she'd have to draw a line in the snow and begin the way she meant to go in their relationship.

"Trey"—and she let her exasperation through—"I'm from Michigan. I know ice and snow—and even blizzards. Do the words 'lake effect' register?" She smiled at his snort. "I'm quite capable of driving home in this weather. Fix me something warm to eat, and afterward you can take me to bed and warm me up even more." She paused. "I missed you last night."

His growl of frustration was loud, but his soft "I missed you, too" was full of love.

She smiled. "Good. I promise to be very careful. See you in an hour or so."

The drive from Grangeville to Sanctuary usually took about an hour, but she figured with weather and road conditions, it would be more like an hour and a half. Good thing her ER coverage was only every other Friday; she couldn't imagine doing this drive every day.

"Take your time, Fee." His tone had turned all alpha-male protector. "If you have issues, pull over and call me. I'll come get you. I'm up and dressed."

"Dang it," she said. "I was imagining you buck-naked in our bed, waiting for me."

Trey chuckled, a rumbling sexy sound that gave her goose bumps and had her pressing her thighs together. "That'll happen … after you're home and safe."

"Love you, Trey."

"Love you back. Take care of my little doc."

"Will do." She ended the call and put the vehicle into gear.

The Beast proved to have excellent traction on the snow-covered parking lot. It should— it weighed like a gazillion pounds and had all-wheel drive. The roads this close to town had already been plowed and were down to wet pavement, but were slick in spots. As she passed *Ma's Bar and Grill*, located on the far outskirts of Grangeville, she honked at Nick who shoveled snow off the sidewalk in front of his place. He waved and went back to shoveling.

From *Ma's*, it was all uphill to Sanctuary. Trey's summation of the conditions proved to be correct—the roads got measurably worse. Still, the Beast handled the worsening road conditions like the armor-laden behemoth it was. Only the best and safest vehicles would do for the Maddox brothers, especially where their women were concerned. Fee could still remember hanging onto another Hummer's sissy bar as the pregnant-and-laboring Keely had taken these same mountain curves at speeds she wouldn't have attempted even on dry pavement.

Today's drive was nothing like that dangerous situation. Thank God.

"This is a piece-of-cake drive." Fee patted the Beast's dashboard. "Wish I had you during lake-effect blizzards back in Michigan."

Fee passed Carmela's small diner which was still in the midst of renovations, but not today. Today, the parking lot was a blanket of undisturbed snow. She smiled, remembering Carmela's excitement as she and Pia showed Fee and their new SSI family the designer's drawings and the fabrics and colors to be used in the Tex-Mex-American fusion restaurant.

The Beast slipped toward the railing as she entered a sharp curve.

Head in the game, Fee.

Fee shifted her focus back to the road. There were few vehicles out. The tracks that were on the road were filling in with the snow being blown around by the ferocious mountain winds. Just ahead, lay the first set of S-curves. She'd need all her concentration to get through them without slipping and sliding even with the Beast's excellent traction.

While there were railings, she didn't want to test them. The drop to the valley below was over a thousand feet at points. She planned to hug the mountain-wall side of the curves as much as possible. With no traffic to speak of, she had room for error.

Slowing as she entered the first curve, she caught a glimpse of lights in her driver's side mirror. Someone was coming up behind her at a high rate of speed.

"Asshole," she muttered.

As she exited the first curve, she slowed even more and steered toward what she knew was a generous shoulder on the right-hand side of the road. There was a short straight-away leading into the next curve.

"Go on, pass me, jerkwad," she muttered as the approaching car, also a Hummer with rental plates on the front, was almost upon her.

But the idiot driver didn't pass her, instead, he rode her rear bumper and flashed his lights.

"What the…?" Was he signaling her to pull over and stop? Like hell.

Clenching the steering wheel, Fee sped up and took the next curve at about twenty miles per hour more than she should've under the current conditions, but she wanted to put some space between her and the crazy person behind her.

The asshole remained on her tail. His vehicle's flashers blinking irritatingly in her rearview and side mirrors. She gritted her teeth and drove, pushing her speed. She blessed Trey for giving her the Beast to drive.

When Fee pulled out of the last curve in this particular grouping of S-curves, the bumper-riding jerk pulled up alongside her. She glanced at the driver.

Ice chilled her veins and shock had her gasping. It was Stall.

Fee choked up on the steering wheel, gave the Beast more gas, and pulled away. History seemed to be repeating itself. Here she was in another fox-and-hound chase, but this time she was the fox driving the car and there was only one hound in pursuit.

And all she could think was—"What would Keely do?"

The answer was "change the game, become the hound."

Fee knew the road, knew the terrain—and knew what she had to do. Quickly, she formulated her plans, because if she'd learned nothing else from her experiences with SSI, it was always best to have more than one plan.

Then she hit re-dial on the blue tooth connection on her steering wheel.

"What's up, Fee? You need me to come get you?" The sound of Trey's voice emboldened her … strengthened her. He had her back. She didn't have to face problems alone any longer. They were a team.

"Stall's tailing me. I can't shake him." Her words were breathy. There was no way Trey hadn't heard the tension in her voice.

"Where are you?" His words were spaced out. He was furious, but in control.

"Too far from Sanctuary." She noted the mile-marker. It was one with which she was far too intimate. "I'm coming up on the set of S-curves right before the turn-off to the ranger access road."

And the cave where she'd delivered Riley.

"Has he tried to run you off the road?"

Fee could hear movement in the background. Trey was on the move, getting ready to come get her. She let out a sigh of relief. All she had to do was hang tough, stay alive, and he'd take care of the rest.

"Fee, baby, has he bumped you?" Trey enunciated the words as if he were gritting his teeth at the same time.

"No, not yet. He, um, keeps flashing his lights. He pulled up alongside me. That's when I saw who he was. I pulled away."

She glanced at the rearview mirror. Stall was a mere car length behind her. Too close. She accelerated even more.

"He wants me to pull over. I'm not going to."

"Good. Don't." Trey was running now. She could hear his feet pounding and his respiration elevate slightly. "I'm getting backup. We'll be heading out in the helicopter. I'm also calling the sheriff and the State Police."

"Trey…" She swallowed hard. "…if he rams me…"

"Whatever you do … keep driving. The Hummer can handle a few bumps. We'll be there before you know it. Leave the line open, okay?"

In her gut, she knew they wouldn't get here in time. Her Plan A had been to outrun Stall, lead him toward Sanctuary, and let Trey and the others intercept and take care of him. Fee wasn't sure she could handle Stall ramming her and still manage to keep control of the Beast. The window for her Plan B, going to ground at SSI's cave, was narrowing, but she'd hold onto Plan A as long as possible since that was what Trey so obviously wanted her to do.

"Yes, all right." She focused on the road and listened as Trey alerted Price, Ren, Tweeter, and DJ. The knowledge help was on its way encouraged her.

Then Stall hit her rear bumper. Hard.

Fee couldn't help it … she screamed even as she tightened her hold on the steering wheel and struggled to control her vehicle. The Beast lurched toward the left-hand side railing, and she barely managed to get the vehicle back to the middle of the road on the sharp S-curve.

Under control once more, she pressed the accelerator and took the rest of the curves at sixty miles per hour. The Hummer ate the curve like the beast it was, snow and all. It was as if the Beast knew she needed it to perform at its optimum to keep her safe.

"Fee?" She could barely hear Trey's voice over the sound of the helicopter's engines in the background. "What happened?"

Yes, help was on its way, but she had decisions to make now. The road wouldn't be any easier to navigate farther ahead. The conditions were once again approaching whiteout.

Plan B was looking better all the time.

"Fee, goddammit, baby. Talk to me." Trey's voice was all animal growl now.

"He's ramming me from behind." Fee took a quick glance in the rearview mirror as she entered the next curve. The Beast slid to the left, and she made the correction, careful not to overcorrect. "I've gained some space on him. But with the steep drops … I'm sorry … at these speeds, I'm afraid of going over the side. So, I'm going to take the ranger access road and head for the cave. I remember the pass code for the outer door."

But first she'd have to get up that mountain path without being spotted by Stall. She'd worry about that later.

"God, baby. He could catch up to you on the ground." Trey cursed. "You aren't armed."

Even if she were armed, she couldn't shoot worth spit. Note to self: Frigging learn to shoot better. Trey could teach her.

"I'll be fine." She hoped. "I know where I'm going, he doesn't. I have the advantage." She also knew how to cover her tracks, thanks to Keely.

"Fuck … just fuck." Trey's breaths were harsh and raspy over the connection. She could almost picture him, struggling to regain control and not yell at her … not order her to obey him. Instead, he growled, "Stay alive."

"Planned on it. I have a lot to live for." Fee made a sharp right off the state road and bumped onto the rutted, snow-covered access road which led to the ranger station and to a trail head parking area. She traveled at a speed that would've bottomed out any normal vehicle.

Keeping the Beast at a steady fifty miles per hour, she was jostled from side to side and bounced up and down; she was thankful for the shoulder harness. Still, she'd have bruises where the harness dug into her body. After one huge dip in the road, she bit her tongue, tasted blood, as the vehicle found some air, then landed hard. All too quickly, her arms and fingers cramped as she struggled to keep the Beast on the road and out of the thicket of trees which lined both sides of the narrow road.

Stall could still be on her tail, but she couldn't risk looking. Even if she did look, she wouldn't be able to see with all the snow blowing around and being thrown up by her tires. If she took her eyes off the road, she could easily lose control. Plus, she needed to keep her eyes open for the turnoff to the trail head parking area. The SSI cave overlooked the clearing where hikers left their vehicles for day hikes; in fact, the cave, while on SSI property, was just off one of the more difficult public hiking trails.

There it was. She took a hard left and arrowed her way onto the narrow, snow-filled, gravel-based lane. The trees were much closer on each side of the track. The scraping of the tree branches over the Beast's exterior sounded like fingers on a chalkboard. The screeching noise grated on her already overexposed nerves. She firmed her jaw to keep from screaming. A tension headache throbbed behind her eyes and made her sick to her stomach.

God, please, not now.

She took several breaths and forced her jaw to relax, hoping to stave off the blinding headache.

Just as Fee thought she couldn't handle one more foot of this nightmare of a lane, she was in the parking lot. She drove toward the sign displaying the map of the area trails. She slammed the brakes, threw the car into Park, shut off the engine, and stumbled down and out of the Beast. Her head met the door, and she fell and landed in snow up to the middle of her shins.

Pain and shock blinded her for a split-second. Flashes of white light and floating dots of yellow and blue swarmed her vision. She held onto the Beast's door like a life preserver as the world spun around her. She swallowed the hot, acrid nausea.

Get your ass moving. Be sick later.

Fee closed her eyes for a few seconds and let the world and her stomach settle a bit. But her headache was here to stay, a constant thrumming which threatened to take her down.

Don't let it. Move.

Over the ticking sounds of the Beast's cooling engine and the wind whistling as it whipped the snow around, the sound of a car's laboring engine came closer and closer.

Fee got out the SSI satphone Keely had given her and made sure the line was still connected to Trey. The sound of the helicopter coming over the line told her it was.

"I'm heading to the cave," she panted into the phone.

She didn't wait for a response, wasn't sure she could hear one anyway over the pounding in her head and the helicopter noise. She pushed forward, moving toward the head of the trail that led to the disguised entrance of a side trail which would take her to Cave A-5.

Soon the fear, the altitude, the cold, and, yeah, Fee's own lack of cardio-training began to take their toll on her. *Deja-fricking-vu.* She'd also been out of shape the last time she'd run from danger on this mountain. The good news was this time she only had her ass to cover and only one bad guy trying to take her out. The bad news was she could still die.

"Stay safe. Stay alive. We're not far now." Trey's deep voice reached her, cutting through the white noise. His words became her mantra. Just the sound of his voice gave wings to her feet and put hope in her heart that once again she'd defeat death.

"Hurry, Trey." Her teeth chattered. Her words were slurred. But she knew he'd gotten her message when he yelled at DJ to hurry up and fly the damn bird faster.

Her feet numb and her body convulsively shaking from the wet and cold, Fee stumbled from rocky spot to rocky spot, trying not to slip or disturb the snow so as to leave as little of a trail as possible. When there weren't rocks, she moved to the more heavily treed areas where less snow had accumulated and the piles of pine needles had melted the snow that had fallen.

Stall had no way of knowing about the hidden side path to the SSI cave. She'd parked by the trail head sign for a reason. There were three trails originating at this particular parking area. She could've taken any one of them; two of the trails led to the ranger station farther up the mountain. Stall might assume she was going for shelter and help.

She couldn't think about the possibility of him choosing the one trail she'd taken. If she did, her fear of being caught would paralyze her and he'd catch her. She'd promised Trey to stay safe ... to stay alive. She planned on doing that.

For several long, hard minutes, she huffed and puffed her way uphill on the expert-level hiking trail through dense trees and over uneven ground. Every muscle in her butt and legs protested the torture. Her lungs burned. The altitude she'd cavalierly thought she'd mastered in the month she'd lived in Idaho was proving to kick her ass.

Then she spotted the holly bushes that marked the side trail. She cried out with relief. Her breathing was shallow and inefficient. She wheezed to catch a full breath. Tears streamed down her icy cheeks and froze on her skin. Fee needed to lie down, preferably in a warm dry place and burrow—like the SSI cave or Trey's bed—but neither of those were anywhere close yet.

For now, Fee had to keep moving, had to get behind the bushes, then she had to climb to the lookout where she would allow herself a short breather. From that vantage point, she'd be able to see the parking lot and her back trail—and exactly where Stall was.

Covering the last ten feet or so toward the bushes was a labor worthy of Hercules, but Fee made it and slipped between the bushes and the mountain wall. Once past the holly, it was another five or six minutes up a sharp incline to the overlook where she'd first met Trey last June.

By the time Fee reached the lookout, she was drenched from sweat and snow and ready to collapse. Leaning on the stacked rock wall which bordered the overlook, she worked on catching her breath and focused on her back trail. The dark blue Hummer Stall drove was in the parking area and blocking her Beast from leaving.

She snorted softly. Asshole wouldn't be leaving, either. Trey, Price, and the others would take his vehicle out to ensure that.

Fee searched the area for her nemesis. She found him halfway up the trail she'd taken from the parking area and heading for her position.

Dammit, either he'd seen the trail she'd taken, or he'd guessed correctly. Right now, he stood in the shelter of some trees, tracking his surroundings with the scope on the rifle he held.

God, she wished she had a sniper rifle or any weapon. Yeah, she probably couldn't hit the broad side of a barn, but she sure would give it the old college try.

Stall stood still. He looked to be breathing hard. Good, he was also out of shape, probably more so than her. Yay. If it came down to it, she could probably outrun him.

Energized by that conclusion, she turned to move up … toward the cave's entrance.

The shot took her by surprise. A piece of rock splintered by the bullet sliced her cheek even before she heard the *crack* of the rifle echoing off the mountains.

Fee dropped down, behind the stacked rock wall. Dammit. He'd seen her movement through the rifle's scope.

Trey's voice startled her. "Fee! Was that a shot?"

For a moment, she'd forgotten the phone was connected.

"I'm okay," she muttered into the phone. "He saw me. But he hasn't figured out how to get to me yet."

"Stay put. Don't give him a target. You'll be exposed going up the path to the cave."

Picturing the side trail, she realized Trey was correct. There was a short shot where anyone looking up might see her, but the exposure would only be for maybe a space of six or so feet, then she'd be sheltered behind solid rock.

If she had to, she could run the short distance where she'd be most exposed. She couldn't stay here and let him come upon her. He'd shoot her, disable her, then, well, she didn't want to think of how much damage he could do in the time it would take Trey and the others to get to her.

"Fee…" Trey's voice was insistent and his next words demonstrated he knew how her mind worked. "Don't try it. Even a bad shooter could get lucky."

"I can't sit here and wait … I c-can't." She stuttered to a halt as Stall called out.

"Fiona!" Only Stall and her father ever drawled her name that way. She hated it. "I'm coming to get you, bitch."

Fee whimpered at the back of her throat. "Trey…"

"We're less than five minutes out, baby. Hold on for me. Stay hidden."

Fee would love to hold on and stay hidden, but already she sensed her stalker closing in. Looking around, she searched for anything that could be used as a weapon.

Her gaze passed over the man-made rock wall which bordered the lookout. There were massive cracks in the layers of rocks. She then pictured the angle of the slope below the overlook. The slope was steep and covered in rocks from erosion and past rock slides.

Sharp angle. Leverage. Force. Loose rocks. Rock slide potential.

Fee needed leverage to expand the cracks, weaken the stacked rocks. Then she'd have to apply the right amount of force at the right spot. With luck, she could start a rock slide that would cover the winding trail leading to her. This would block Stall from getting to her, or with luck, hit him if she timed it correctly.

Keeping her head down, Fee knee-walked back to the precarious stacking of rocks that someone at SSI had built as a defensive position. She studied the layers of rocks. If the undergrad physics class she'd taken years ago was right, she needed to apply force—"Here," she muttered as she applied pressure with her shoulder and pushed.

Pain shot up and down her arm and into her neck. "Sweet Jesus, these are heavy." She let up for a second. Another shot, over her head, pinged as more rock chips flew. "Fuck you, Stall."

Fee leaned into her chosen rock and shouted *"Aiyeeahh!"* to focus her energy. It only shifted slightly. She was too weak. Falling on her ass, she huffed out several breaths and felt like crying.

Strongest part of a woman's body for $1,000, Alex.

What were legs and hips?

Fee lay on her back and raised her legs, bent at the knees to resemble the tabletop position in Pilates. She tightened her core and placed the flats of her feet on the spot she'd decided to use. She inhaled, then exhaled, and applied all the force she could, pushing up and through her heels. The rocks moved a bit. Grunting, breathing through the movement, she did it again and a few rocks moved and then rolled down the slope.

Stall's shouted "fuck" made her heart happy. She applied even more force, panting as if she were pushing out a baby, and even more rocks slid down the side.

It was working.

Then more rocks crashed and were answered by a scream and "Fuck you, bitch! Gonna hurt you … hurt you…"

Fee froze at his threats, was thrown back into the memories of him grunting over her and hurting her.

Shit, shit, shit. Snap out of it, Fee.

She gritted her teeth and shoved against another place on the rock wall. Stall was still mobile and heading her way. Fee had to stop him before he got to the holly bushes. He knew where she was. He'd easily find the way up now.

Fee grunted and panted as she shoved harder than before. These rocks were slightly bigger than the earlier ones. When she managed to get two big rocks loosened and sent them tumbling, she could hear even more rocks join them farther down the slope.

Yes!

"Fuck, bitch. Gonna kill you … by inches," shouted Stall. His voice was shaking, breathless. Hell, if nothing else, she was keeping him occupied and off-balance and tiring him out.

Gun? Bang bang. You're dead. Keep pushing.

Yeah, there was that. Fee began putting pressure on other areas. Some places she dislodged a rock or two, but some she could barely budge. By now, her breathing was a series of wheezing inhales and grunting exhales.

"Fee?" Trey's shout caught her attention.

She kept shoving with her feet and placed the phone to her ear. "What?" She panted, trying to catch her breath. Her head, her whole body, screamed with pain and exhaustion. "Sort of busy here."

Spacing out Trey and the noises from the helicopter, she kept working on loosening more and more rocks. But still, in the back of her mind, she heard the fear in Trey's voice and was driven to reassure him she was okay … that she was holding off Stall until Trey and the others got to her.

"I'm rolling rocks down on him." She grunted and then shouted, "*Aiyeeahh.*" Panting, she continued, "If I can move enough of them, I'm hoping to start a rock slide and keep him from coming up the path."

"That's my woman," Trey said.

Trey's pride in her and the affirmation from the others in the helicopter would've made her smile if she'd had the energy, but she needed all her strength for dislodging rocks.

Go for the gold, Fee.

One more giant thrust resulted in the sound of a large amount of rocks grinding and sliding down the slope. Stall's resulting screams and cries of pain followed by silence broken only by the whistling winds made her weak with relief.

"No rush now, guys. I got this," Fee shouted. "I did it. He just screamed. He's down."

Fee let her legs drop, and then she turned onto her side and curled into a ball to try to keep warm now that she wasn't exerting. She really should get up, go to the cave, and get out of the cold and wet … but she had no energy. She'd just lie here until Trey came to get her.

CHAPTER 22

Minutes earlier, SSI helicopter

"Push it, DJ," Trey growled. "He's shooting at her."

"Do you want to fly this bird?" DJ shot a glare at him.

Tweeter shook his head violently and sliced a finger across his throat in warning.

Yeah, what was he thinking? He'd practically accused DJ of not knowing what she was doing. The weather was a bitch, and DJ was pushing the Hawk better than any of the men could. Of all of them, she had the most hours in a Black Hawk and had flown those hours in some of the worst hellholes and climates in the world.

"Sorry, DJ." Trey watched the ground, searching for landmarks through the swirling snow. "Just worried."

"I get that," DJ said. "But Fee is smart. She'll deal until we get there. And when we get there, just how do *you* want to handle this?"

"Fly over the parking area so we can get an idea of where Stall is," Trey said. "If he's well away from Fee, then we'll take him down from the air."

"Damn straight," muttered Price who absentmindedly stroked the barrel of his rifle as if it were a much-favored lover.

"If he has her," Trey gritted out, "we'll cross that bridge when we come to it."

"What's going on with her now? Can you hear anything? Any more shots?" Price's gaze was also fixed on the terrain passing beneath them.

They were flying so close to the treetops, Trey swore he could smell the pine needles.

A gust of wind batted at the helicopter causing it to swerve. DJ easily steadied the chopper as she flew into the teeth of the storm.

Trey couldn't hear much over the open line. Was she okay? What was going on?

"Fee?" Trey shouted into the phone.

"What?" She sounded pissed. "Sort of busy here." She let out an *oomph*.

"What the fuck are you doing?" Trey yelled into the phone which he'd piped into the chopper com system.

"I'm rolling rocks down on him." She made noises culminating in a shouted *aiyeeahh*. Her breathing was extremely erratic, and Trey heard pain in her voice as she continued to explain her plan to tumble rocks on the fucker.

His little doc was damn smart.

"That's my woman." Trey turned to Price and grinned.

"Way to go, baby sis!" Price shouted.

Ren laughed and shook his head. "Sounds like something my sprite would do."

"Told you Fee was ballsy." DJ took the chopper into a wide turn and brought it around the last mountain between them and the trail head parking area. "We're in the valley now. The winds aren't quite as bad. Tell Fee to keep rolling rocks, we're almost there."

"Fee, we're close." As the snow lightened for a split-second, Trey could see the parking area just ahead with Fee's vehicle and another one blocking it in. "Stay down. We've got this."

"No rush now, guys. I got this," Fee shouted. "I did it. He just screamed. He's down."

Trey looked out the cabin window toward the area where Fee had hunkered down. He laughed. "Damn, Price, she did it. Look at all the rocks and snow sliding down from the overlook."

Pride, love, and relief demolished the nagging fear and tension that had jabbed at his subconscious like hot pokers since Fee had called from the road.

Price whooped and high-fived Tweeter. "She did it."

"Shall I land?" Just above tree level, DJ swooped over the rock slide area. There was just enough space between the trees to show a man half buried by the snow and rocks. "Or is he still a potential danger?"

"He's definitely down," Tweeter said. "I see him. He's partially buried. He's not going anywhere soon. We may even have to life-line him out to the hospital in Grangeville."

"Land in the parking area, DJ." Ren looked at the others, finally settling on Trey. "We'll approach with caution ... do this by the numbers, brother. Stall could still have his gun and use it."

Trey's gut vied with his training. He wanted to rush in and go straight to Fee, but his brother was correct—Stall was still a potential threat.

Price and Tweeter nodded as DJ said, "Roger that."

"Fee, stay where you are, baby," Trey ordered. "I'll come get you as soon as we make sure Stall's no longer a danger."

"O-o-okay." Fee's voice sounded shaky, not like the kick-ass woman who'd just taken down her stalker. "D-d-did I k-kill him?"

"Can't tell yet, sweetheart. But if you did, it was justifiable. He stalked and shot at you."

"O-o-kay. Hurry. I'm s-s-o-o-o c-c-cold." Her teeth chattered audibly over the line. "Hypo-hypothermia is s-s-setting in."

Trey cursed as he recalled what she'd worn to work the night before. Jeans, a long-sleeved T-shirt, a light denim jacket, and high-top Keds. The clothing had been fine for the balmy sixty-degree-evening. Overnight a front had come through, dropping the temps and turning the predicted rain into a snowstorm. Not atypical for this time of year, especially at this altitude, but Fee wasn't used to it and didn't think to have an extra-warm coat and boots in her vehicle.

And Trey hadn't thought to tell her.

Fuck him. He wasn't taking very good care of her. He'd have to step up his game. She was too important to him to be so careless of her health and well-being.

"You guys handle Stall," Trey ordered as he pulled out a couple of blankets from the survival supplies kept on the chopper. "I'm going straight for Fee. She's not dressed for this weather."

Price nodded. "If the rest of us can't handle that douchebag piece of shit that my baby sis has already beat up on, then we need to hang up our guns and take up knitting. We'll let Dan handle Stall's medical requirements. You get Fee and head straight back to Sanctuary on the chopper with DJ."

"Sounds like a plan." Trey waited anxiously for DJ to set the chopper down. When the skids kissed the snow, he opened the cabin door, scooted under the rotors, then ran for the trail.

Price, Ren, and Tweeter were on his heels.

As they neared the rock slide, Trey noted movement from the man buried from the lower back down by the rock fall. The man's gun was within reach.

Trey approached swiftly with his weapon aimed at Stall's head. "If you go for that gun, I'm taking you out." For a split-second, he prayed the fuckwit would go for his gun so he could justify shooting the fucker.

Blood burbling from his mouth, Stall groaned and flattened his hands on the snow-covered ground. Lower down where his legs were buried the snow had turned pink from his other injuries. "Help me."

The pain in the bastard's voice was obvious. Trey let out a breath and shook his head. "Price?"

Price moved up next to Trey and said, "I've got him covered. Go get Fee."

Ren approached Stall from the opposite side, reached down, and grabbed the rifle. "If he has any other weapons on him, doesn't look as if he can get to them."

DJ joined them just as Trey turned to head up the trail. "Guys," she said. "Dan is heading up the access road now. He's got an ambulance with him. Trey," she called after him. "I'll be in the chopper and be ready to take off as soon you're on board with Fee."

"Roger that." Trey clambered over the rocks Fee had dislodged, which now covered part of the trail. He picked his way, quickly but carefully, so as not to send any more down on the others. When he hit the clear part of the trail, he practically leapt up it. Before he even made it to the holly bushes marking Cave A-5's path, Fee shimmied around the bush and stumbled toward him.

"I-I-I heard you c-coming." She tried to smile, but it was a puny effort. Weaving slightly, she leaned against a rock as if her legs could no longer held her.

Moving forward, Trey slid his weapon into his back holster. Unfolding one of the blankets, he wrapped it around her and scooped her into his arms just as she began to crumple. He tucked the blankets more snugly around her trembling body and held her tightly against him, rocking her. He took a second before moving out to bury his face in her cold, damp curls.

"God, baby, that was too fucking close." His voice broke, closer to tears than he'd ever been in his life. He could've lost her.

"Uh-huh." Fee buried her cold nose against his throat. "You're s-s-so warm-m-m." Her body shivered convulsively.

"Need to get you home." Trey turned and carried her down the trail.

Going down was easier than going up since Stall and the others were away from the rock fall area and Trey didn't have to worry about loosening any more rocks. When he got past the rock slide, the EMTs were strapping Stall onto a backboard.

DJ and Dan were waiting for them in the parking lot near the chopper.

Dan approached. "I need to—"

"No," Trey growled at his friend. "Later. She'll give her statement later. At my place. After she's been checked over and is warm and rested. Just make sure that fucking douchebag is under lock and key. She's suffered enough at his hands."

Dan frowned and looked at Fee who'd burrowed into Trey. "Go on. Take your woman home. I'll be by tomorrow." He shot a narrow-eyed glance at Stall who was now being loaded into the ambulance with one of Dan's deputies going along for the ride to Grangeville. "The fucker will be in lock-down at the hospital. He's not going anywhere."

Fee turned her face up. "Maybe I should check…"

Trey cut off the rest of her offer by brushing his lips over hers. "Fuck no, baby. I don't want you anywhere near him."

"But Trey…" Fee protested.

"No." He tucked her head back against his shoulder and turned toward the chopper's open cabin door and climbed inside with her still in his arms.

DJ got in, sat in the pilot's seat, and then looked at them over her shoulder. She snickered. "Give it up, Fee. Trey's alpha-protective streak has taken about all it can handle. You didn't even let him take the badass down. So, you need to give in on this one."

"O-o-okay," Fee mumbled against his throat. "I didn't really want to anyway, but just thought I should offer." She licked the pulse throbbing in his neck, then scraped it with her teeth.

Her voice sounded stronger now and she wasn't shaking as much. "You warmer, sweetheart?"

"Yeah. But … I know how to get even warmer." She looked up, a mischievous gleam in her eyes.

"How's that?" He rubbed his cheek over her hair.

"Hot tub. You and me." She patted his chest. "I think we can warm me up faster that way."

"Sounds like a plan." Trey kissed the tip of her nose. "But only after Lacey and Pia check you over."

Fee looked at him for several long seconds, then nodded. "Okay. You need that." She yawned. "So tired."

She snuggled closer to his body, her muscles relaxing and her breathing evening out. And just that fast she'd gone to sleep.

"Yeah," Trey muttered under his breath, "I need that." He secured his harness over both of them and put headphones on them both. "Take us home, DJ."

"Roger that." DJ looked Fee over with affection and concern on her expressive face. "Post-adrenaline drop hit her hard. Not sure she'll have the energy for those hot tub plans."

"Yeah." He rubbed his cheek over the top of Fee's curls. "But there's always later."

There'd be lots of time later. Fee was his to protect. His to love. His to keep.

CHAPTER 23

Hours later, Trey's house

Trey groaned and his cock jerked as Fee twined her tongue around his heavily veined shaft. When she applied suction and just a hint of teeth, he jolted awake.

"Baby?" His voice was husky with sleep and arousal. "Whatcha doing?"

Letting his cock slip out of her mouth, she smiled and looked up his long, muscled torso from her position between his legs and smiled. "What do you think I'm doing?"

She stroked his erection. He was so thick she could barely get her fingers to meet around it. "I'm claiming my man."

His lips curved. "God, I love you." He threaded his fingers through her curls and cupped the back of her head. "Baby"—he tugged on her hair gently—"you should've woken me up."

Fee tucked a stray curl around her ear with one hand while she kept her grip on his cock with the other. She gave him a sultry, slumberous look. "I just did." She rubbed her flushed cheek over his hairy, muscled thigh as she stroked his erection. "You taste all salty and earthy." Turning, she kissed his leg. "I like it."

Trey covered her hand on his erection and gently pulled it off.

"Trey!" Her little pout made him smile.

"Patience, baby. You can have him back in a bit. Just need to check in with you first."

Then he sat up and hooked his hands under her arms, then pulled her onto his lap with an ease that never ceased to amaze her. He was so strong.

Cuddling her, he urged her head to his shoulder. His cock twitched against her naked bottom. She snickered and imagined his hard-on bitching at the loss of her mouth.

"I liked having your cock in my mouth." She nipped his jaw.

"How long have you been awake?" he asked.

"Not long." She grinned. "I woke up, and there was this beautiful hard-on just begging to be sucked. So I did. I bet myself I could make you come before you woke up. I guess I lost."

The fact she'd had the confidence to take what she wanted, what she needed from Trey, proved she'd come a long way in a short time. The only reason she had come so far, so fast was due to Trey. He'd fostered her new-found assurance with his patient, and as she now knew, loving pursuit of her.

He tipped up her chin with one long finger and kissed her lightly on the mouth. "When I come, sweetheart, I want to be inside you." He tapped the tip of his finger on her nose. "But first, I need to know—how are you feeling? After all, it was only hours ago you were fighting for your life."

The man petted her as if he had to touch her. He was also driving her crazy since he was avoiding all the good parts. The big tease.

Fee teethed his lower lip. "I'm fine." She yawned and looked around. "What time is it?"

He looked at his watch. "It's just short of five o'clock."

Running her fingers through his chest hair, she snuggled into his shoulder. "I slept for almost six hours. Man, I never nap that long."

Trey kissed her forehead. "Running from danger and shoving rocks on the bad guy took it out of you. You needed the sleep."

After DJ had flown them back to Sanctuary, Lacey and Pia had checked Fee over. Her injuries had been light, mostly bruises on her shoulder and aches and pains in her lower body from shoving rocks on Stall. Other than those, she'd been diagnosed as slightly hypothermic and exhausted.

After Lacey and Pia had left, Trey had carried her into the shower and helped her clean up. Once he had her all tucked in bed, he'd spoon fed her some hot oatmeal. She was fairly sure she'd been half asleep even then. The fact he'd crawled into bed with her made her heart turn to mush. He was so protective of her.

She could tell he'd been scared for her and was mad at himself that he hadn't been there to take care of Stall for her. He needed to get over it.

"Stop worrying about me." Fee leaned her head back and looked him in the eyes. "I handled it. Nothing that happened today was due to any lack of care on your part. We had all the bases covered and the safety measures put into place worked." She touched his forearm and rubbed it lightly with her fingers. "Stop frowning."

He captured her fingers and kissed them, then took her hand to his chest and held it over his heart. "You being in danger is totally unacceptable. I should've—"

She placed a finger on his lips. "Trey, love, you can't anticipate everything. Shit happens." Her lips quirked into a teasing smile. "But I understand you alpha types get all bent out of shape when your women are in danger."

He captured her fingers and kissed the tips. "We alpha types are supposed to protect our women."

"And you did." She leaned up and nipped his jaw. "Knowing you were on your way gave me the strength to do what I had to do to stay out of his hands."

"You did good, baby. But I plan to take better care of you in the future."

"You already take good care of me, Trey."

"I'll take better care," he repeated, a firm note in his voice. "Hungry?" He smoothed some hair off her forehead and then twined the curls around his fingers as if her hair fascinated him.

"Changing the subject?" she arched a brow.

"Yep." He kissed her firmly, then leaned his forehead against hers. "So, do you want to eat? I can fix us something, and we can eat it in bed."

Okay, yeah, she could eat, but what she really wanted was to make love with Trey and sometime tonight get his dick back in her mouth. She wiggled on his lap. His cock jerked and pulsed against her sensitive bottom. If he admitted it, he wanted that, too.

What had the girls told her? To ask for what she wanted, right?

"Well—" She pulled her hand from his and walked her fingers over to his nipple and traced it with one finger. "What I'd like to do is make love with you. Then I'll fix the one-week anniversary dinner I had planned. Then I want to suck your cock."

"Are you sure?"

She nodded.

Trey stared at her for several long seconds, then nodded. His green eyes glowed with love and desire.

"Okay…" He shifted and got out of bed with Fee still cuddled in his arms. "Considering all your bruises, I want you on top … and in the hot tub."

Holding her against him with one arm, Trey snagged a fur throw and covered her with it. Then he strode out of the bedroom and crossed the great room toward the folding patio doors.

The tub cover was already off, so he must've prepared it earlier for warming her up and she'd fallen asleep as he fed her. God, the jets and hot water would feel good on her sore muscles and joints.

Fee shivered against him. "It's cold outside."

"You'll be hot soon." He pulled open the door. "Would I let you be cold?"

"No." She looked at the grey sky and smiled. She loved snow if she wasn't being chased by bad guys in it. "It's snowing again. Big fluffy flakes."

Fee tipped back her head and caught a flake on her tongue.

"So sweet and sexy." Trey groaned, then kissed her, thrusting his tongue inside as soon as she opened for him. He dropped the fur blanket onto a bench under the protected part of the deck, then moved to lower her into the tub. "Is it too hot?"

"No," she moaned as she leaned back on the seat. "This feels wonderful."

Trey slid into the tub and opened his arms. "Come here and straddle me. I need to catch you up, so you'll be ready to ride me."

"Catch up? I was already there." She floated over to him and straddled his lap. Her hand found his cock immediately and fisted him. "Why do you think I was sucking your cock?"

"Because you wanted to wake me up?" He grinned.

"That … and I was horny. I was dreaming about you making love to me and woke up wet and aching and surrounded by you and your scent."

"I woke up with my cock surrounded by the warm, moist silk of your mouth. And trust me, baby, I am all in favor of that … but, in truth, all I have to do is scent you…" He nuzzled the damp curls lying against her throat. "…and my dick gets hard."

Fee tweaked one of his nipples. "I think I'm addicted to you, too. I'm fairly sure I can't live without you now."

"You won't have to live without me. I'm here and I'm not going anywhere. And I've been addicted to you since the day I met you." Trey caught her chin between his fingers and his thumb. "I adore you. Treasure you. Worship the ground you walk on." He brought her mouth to his and kissed her. "I love you."

"And I love you." Fee leaned in and touched her forehead to his. "Thank you for being so patient and careful with me." She brushed his lips with hers. "Thank you for never giving up. If you had, I'd never have known the wonder of being with you."

"God, sweetheart." Trey stroked her back. "Don't thank me. I'm so fucking grateful you took a chance on me. Are you gonna make me the happiest man in Idaho and marry me?"

Fee startled and leaned back. Tears welled in her eyes. "Really?"

"That's been my goal from the beginning. I want you to be mine in every way."

"Alpha-male throwback." She teased as her heart rate beat double time with joy.

"So, is that a yes?"

Her man needed the words, and she was happy to give them to him.

"Yes. I love you, Trey Maddox, and would be honored and happy to be your wife."

"Thank you … thank you…" He punctuated his words with small kisses.

Fee laughed and returned them in kind as happiness bubbled through her body.

Finally, Trey took her mouth fully, deepening the kiss.

Fee responded by opening to him and twining her arms around his neck. She rubbed her body over his, tempting him, arousing herself.

"God, baby, I'll go mad if I don't get inside you soon." He groaned, resting his forehead on her shoulder, catching water droplets off her skin with his tongue.

Fee moaned and shifted on his lap just enough to get her hand around his cock.

"Un-unh, sweetheart. You come first … always." He moved his head down to take one perked nipple into his mouth. He nibbled and teethed the tip. He slipped a finger in her pussy and thumbed her clit.

"Trey," she sighed and held his head to her breast. "I need you inside me … now."

"Climb on, sweetheart. Take what you need." Trey steadied her with one hand as she straddled his hips. His other hand still teased her clit and pussy.

The orgasm came on quickly and hit her like a tsunami. "Trey-y-y," she screamed.

Trey kissed her, swallowing her screams, as he petted her pussy until she whimpered and went lax. She pressed her face to the side of his throat. She swore her heart might just pound out of her chest.

Fee turned her head and began to place biting kisses over his shoulders and then onto his chest. Finding her second wind, she straightened on his lap and undulated, rubbing her swollen, very sensitized pussy over his rock-hard cock.

"Fuck, that feels good." Trey fondled her breasts. "Hold onto me."

"Always." Fee gripped his shoulders.

Trey lifted her up. "Guide me home, baby."

Fee held his cock steady against her opening as Trey lowered her slowly onto his erection. When he was fully seated, they both shuddered. Her skin tingled as if a gentle electrical current ran over her whole body. Her clit pulsed in time with the rhythmic throbbing of Trey's cock inside her vagina.

Trey fondled her breasts as he kissed her forehead, the tip of her nose, and then her chin. "I want you to come while I'm inside you. But if I move now, I'm gonna blow in seconds."

"Move." Fee squeezed his cock with her inner muscles. "You feel so good." She moaned and arched her back. "Take me now, Trey. I'm close. I need you hard and fast."

Her words, her need, acted like a match to gasoline.

Trey set a fierce pace, shoving her hips down even as he thrust upward to meet her. Each stroke hit a spot inside her that had stars crossing her field of vision. All Fee could do was hold on as the race to her second orgasm was at supersonic speed.

Within seconds, she screamed as she came and Trey joined her a nano-second later. "Fee." He roared his completion to the cloud-filled sky.

Trey held her close as she continued to move on his cock and lowly moaned with each downstroke.

"Fee." Trey kissed her with a deep-rooted reverence. "You are my soul, my heart, my eternal love. Let's get married as soon as we can."

"Yes," Fee muttered into his shoulder as she finally relaxed and snuggled into his body.

"Yes?" He leaned back to look down at her. "Really? If you want a wedding with…"

Fee placed her fingers on his lips. "I want to be yours as soon as Idaho will let us. I don't need a fancy wedding. All I need is you … and a ring. And you have to wear a wedding band also."

"I'd wear a ring through my nose if it made you happy."

"Euww." Fee scrunched her nose. "So unsanitary. A ring on your finger will do just fine."

"We can be married next week. It doesn't take long in Idaho." He twirled one of her curls around his finger. "Are you hungry? Cold? Tired?"

"Next week is perfect. Yes. No. Not yet. But first…" Fee sat up and began to ride his amazing cock, which was still inside her and getting harder by the second. She really needed to see if he might make the Guinness Book of World Records for the quickest recovery time in a thirty-something man. "…I need to take care of this…" She squeezed around his cock. "…and then I'll make us some supper so we can keep up our strength since I have plans for you."

She grinned and winked. "I never did get to finish sucking your cock."

"That sounds nice … right after I eat you for dessert." Trey held her hips and began another punishing rhythm. "Now, hold on tight."

"Always."

~THE END ~

"Bad news." Keely kept her eye on the scope and flexed her finger, lightly touching the trigger, and then let up, adjusted the aim of the barrel, and chambered a bullet before fingering the trigger once more.

"What kind of bad news?" Fee watched as Keely took several deep, slow breaths and pulled the trigger. The sound was louder than she would've expected and echoed off the rocks. A split second after the first shot, Keely ejected the casing, chambered another round, and fired again.

Keely looked away from the scope. "Six bad asses instead of three. Two are now down—injured but not dead 'cause I rushed the shots—and the rest scrambled to hide like the frick-fracking rats they are. I just bought us some respect and time. Let's go." She pocketed the bean bag and stood up, cradling her rifle.

"Shit … shit…" Keely gasped and panted as she moved to lean against the rock behind her. "The contractions are coming closer together. Pain is stronger too. Doesn't that mean the birth canal is widening?"

"Yes." Fee frowned and timed the contraction. And yes, it still lasted approximately forty-five seconds, but this one had been far closer to the last one. "Tell me about the pain," she demanded as Keely struggled to take a full breath after the contraction ended.

"Like I'm splitting in two. My back hurts as much or more than my pelvis." She hitched a breath. "I can barely concentrate on breathing. I feel as if I'm hyperventilating. Even now, the pain is there, just bubbling and ready to explode."

"Shit, sounds like they're overlapping." Fee braced Keely as the woman dropped her rifle on the rock and bent over, both arms holding her stomach, as another contraction piled right on top of the previous one. "Damn, I hate it when I'm right."

Keely moaned and gasped. "Fee … help…"

"Shit, shit, shit. Fuck. Just fuck." Fee placed an arm around Keely's waist in an attempt to keep her from falling to the ground. Because if that happened, Fee would never get her up and they'd be delivering the baby here, in the open.

"Is that any kind of language for a doctor to use?" A deep male voice came from behind her. "What's wrong? Is Keely ready to have the baby?"

Fee slipped the machine gun from Keely's shoulder and managed to keep an arm around the woman's waist as she turned to point the weapon at the man. He was tall with dark hair and piercing pale eyes. He had an ugly-looking gun, but it was aimed at the ground. The look on his face was a mixture of affection and concern for Keely.

"Who are you?" She was pretty sure this was Keely's brother-in-law, but it didn't hurt to ask. If he gave the wrong answer, she'd figure out how to use the damn machine gun if it killed her.

"Trey Maddox. We heard Keely's shots. Tweeter's moving down the path to provide some interference so I can get you ladies to the cave. Here," he held out the gun in his hand, "hold this for a second so I can pick up the little warrior. Do you know if she hit any of the fuckers?"

"Um, two, she said. Not dead, just injured. There's six total." Fee found herself holding yet another gun as she relinquished her hold on Keely.

"Yeah, I saw that from above." Trey pulled Keely into his arms and held her against his chest as if she weighed nothing. "Stay close. I might need that gun. Leave her rifle here. Bring the field kit. The assholes won't make it this far to steal the Lapua. I'll be lucky if Tweeter leaves me any bad guys to tromp on."

Normally, Fee would've refused being bossed around on principle. Trey Maddox reminded her too much of her brother and father, but oddly enough not of Adam or any of the other losers she'd dated. Plus, she was out of her element, and not being stupid or suicidal, she'd follow his instructions and take whatever help she could get.

She and Mother Nature would be in charge once the baby started coming. Although, she had a sneaking suspicion this man could deliver the baby if she weren't around. He looked immensely competent and confident. It was in the way he carried his large body and in his calm demeanor. And, yes, in the gentle way he spoke to Keely, soothing her as he carried her laboring body up the mountain.

Want to read Stormy Weather Baby?
It's a FREE download.
Go to my Extras page on my website,

HTTP://MONETTEMICHAELS.COM

and find the link to get your free copy.

About the Author

A Hoosier born and raised, Monette still lives in the heartland near Indianapolis, Indiana. Married to her college sweetheart and soul mate, she has one son.

After many years of practicing law, Monette found that all the clients, opposing counsel, and the problems she handled ignited the need to write fiction. So she started writing — first, romantic suspense/thrillers, then adding a touch of paranormal and scifi and, eventually, a sexier side (as Rae Morgan).

Monette (and Rae) loves to hear from her fans.
E-mail her at MONETTEMICHAELS@GMAIL.COM.

Visit her at:

Website: WWW.MONETTEMICHAELS.COM

FaceBook: HTTPS://WWW.FACEBOOK.COM/AUTHOR-MONETTEMICHAELS

Twitter: HTTPS://TWITTER.COM/MONETTEMICHAELS

Pinterest: HTTPS://WWW.PINTEREST.COM/MONETTEMICHAELS/

OTHER BOOKS BY THIS AUTHOR

Writing as Monette Michaels:

FATAL VISION

DEATH BENEFITS

GREEN FIRE

VESTED INTERESTS

BLIND-SIDED (WITH JANET FERRAN)

THE VIRTUOUS VAMPIRE,
A GOODEN AND KNIGHT MYSTERY, CASE FILE #1

THE DEADLY SÉANCE,
A GOODEN AND KNIGHT MYSTERY, CASE FILE #2

EYE OF THE STORM,
BOOK 1, SECURITY SPECIALISTS INTERNATIONAL

STORMY WEATHER BABY,
BOOK 1.5, SECURITY SPECIALISTS INTERNATIONAL

COLD DAY IN HELL,
BOOK 2, SECURITY SPECIALISTS INTERNATIONAL

STORM FRONT,
BOOK 2.5, SECURITY SPECIALISTS INTERNATIONAL

WEATHER THE STORM,
BOOK 3, SECURITY SPECIALISTS INTERNATIONAL

STORM WARNING,
BOOK 4, SECURITY SPECIALISTS INTERNATIONAL

HOT AS HELL,
BOOK 4.5, SECURITY SPECIALISTS INTERNATIONAL

PRIME OBSESSION,
BOOK 1, THE PRIME CHRONICLES TRILOGY

PRIME SELECTION,
BOOK 2, THE PRIME CHRONICLES TRILOGY

PRIME IMPERATIVE,
BOOK 3, THE PRIME CHRONICLES TRILOGY

PRIME CLAIMING,
A PRIME CHRONICLES SHORT STORY

Writing as Rae Morgan:

DESTINY'S MAGICK,
BOOK 1, COVEN OF THE WOLF SERIES

MOON MAGICK,
BOOK 2, COVEN OF THE WOLF SERIES

TREADING THE LABYRINTH,
BOOK 3, COVEN OF THE WOLF SERIES

"NO SECRETS,"
BOOK 4, COVEN OF THE WOLF,
IN THE ZODIAC: PISCES ANTHOLOGY

EARTH AWAKENED,
A TERRAN REALM BOOK

ENCHANTRESS

"EVANESCENCE,"
IN THE EDGE OF NIGHT ANTHOLOGY

"ONCE UPON A PRINCESS,"
IN AIN'T YOUR MAMA'S BEDTIME STORIES

CPSIA information can be obtained
at www.ICGtesting.com
Printed in the USA
LVOW03s1517090218
565962LV00001B/16/P